GHERE'S INFERNO

PAUL E COOLEY

SHADOW
PUBLICATIONS

Published in the United States of America
By Shadowpublications.com

Copyright © 2017 by Paul E Cooley

Cover design, cover art, by Scott Pond
Scott E. Pond Designs, LLC (www.scottpond.com)

Edited by Sue Baiman

Library of Congress Cataloging-in-Publication Data
Cooley, Paul Elard
Ghere's Inferno//Paul E Cooley. -1st ed.

ISBN: 978-1-942137-07-8

PRINTED IN THE UNITED STATES OF AMERICA
FIRST EDITION: DECEMBER 2017

ALSO BY PAUL E COOLEY

For information about upcoming projects, publishing news, and podcast series, please visit Shadowpublications.com.

The Derelict Saga

Derelict: Marines (Book 1)

Derelict: Tomb (Book 2)

Derelict: Destruction (Book 3)

The Black Series

The Black

The Black: Arrival

The Black: Outbreak

The Black: Evolution (Fall 2018)

Children Of Garaaga Series

Legends of Garaaga

Daemons of Garaaga

Other Novels

Closet Treats

The Rider (with Scott Sigler)

For Carolyn Cooley:
Who taught me how to smile.
Who taught me to have faith in humanity.
Who taught me what family means.
Who always loves.
For being Mom.

Chapter 1

P sat naked on the black asphalt. After days of steamy weather, the blacktop was still warm enough to burn against his balls. He barely noticed; he was too focused on the line of warped and rotting shotgun shacks. Their foundations were falling apart and they listed toward one another like a mouthful of crooked teeth.

A soft breeze kept the mosquitos away, but did little to alleviate the sticky humidity. A thick layer of moisture-swollen clouds filled the early morning sky, but there would be no rain. The city lights reflected back down, cutting through most of the gloom with a wan glow.

He lowered a long paintbrush into the red can, twirled his fingers, and slowly pulled it from the liquid. The smell of gasoline stung his nostrils and he grinned.

He drew the sign on the asphalt, pausing to freshen the brush's tip with more fuel. When he was finished, he rose and bowed to the sigil. He stepped carefully around it, made his way to the nearest shack, and bowed to it. The swollen wood smiled a crooked smile. His palm itched. He opened it and picked out the wooden match.

Reaching forward, he struck the match against the side of the shack. His grin widened as it burst into flame. He took a step back, and dropped the match in the slick grass.

Eager hungry flames licked upward against the soaked wood. He reached down with his left hand and stroked the length of his shaft. When the fire had taken hold and the wood steamed with heat, he quickened the pace.

Thank you, God whispered.

His face burned. He felt his chest hair curl. Every cell of his body burned with excitement and the heat. When the roof caught fire, he sprayed his semen into the flames, swooning with the long orgasm.

Must not linger, God said.

He nodded, wiped the last drop of cum from the tip of his penis, and headed back to the soft shoulder. He pulled another match from the small box next to the can of fuel. With another quick strike on the ground, he lit the symbol. He smiled as God sighed.

He stared back at the shotgun shacks. Fluttering teardrops of red, yellow, and blue flicked out from the broken and rotted shingles. A shudder ripped through him and he felt the need to cum again.

Watch. Remember.

He sighed as he gathered up his tools and walked quickly to the car. He placed the can and box in the trunk, slid on a pair of shorts and a wife beater, and turned to get into the driver seat. His eyes slid over the burning symbol on the road. The fire was already guttering— God's eye was closing. No matter. It would open again for him. Anytime he asked. And, anytime It called.

He shuffled into the car, turned on the ignition, and sped away down the old, broken asphalt. He didn't need to check the rearview to know the fire was still going. Far away, he could hear the sounds of sirens. But they wouldn't be for this fire. Not yet. Not here. Soon, though. Soon.

A few quick turns and he was on the feeder. He joined the traffic on I-45 and kept to the speed limit. In no time, he'd be home. His penis twitched. The fire would make the evening news. His fire. For his God. He and God could commune with the memory. He absently rubbed himself through the gym shorts, grinning as he made his way through the city.

Chapter 2

Dawn had kissed the horizon with pink and purple. Emy wiped sweat from her brow, the back of her hand brushing against the scars on her forehead. She'd only been at the site for two hours and already her long, black braid was wet enough to wring.

She hooded her eyes against the flashing firetruck lights and the powerful mobile halogens. Her eyes felt like the sandman had rubbed diamond dust on her corneas. She walked past her boss to the other end of the site. A path had been set up with plastic sheets so the techs could travel around without destroying evidence. The material was a little slippery, but at least it kept the flat-foots, and her, from contaminating the site.

When she'd first arrived at the scene, the Houston Fire Department (HFD) had already staunched what was left of the blaze. The air, thick with smoke and the stench of burning wood and plastic, singed her nostrils. The fire hoses had filled the drainage ditches with water, adding to the already punishing humidity.

Before she'd left the house, she'd checked the temperature—92° with 72% humidity. The heatwave made the nights ridiculously warm and the days dangerously hot. In the poorer neighborhoods, like this one, the elderly had been dropping dead from heat exhaustion in droves. Without A/C, the houses from the 1930s would easily get into the upper 90s during the night, let alone during the day.

Blackened, dripping wood lay in heaps. The row of shotgun shacks had abutted one another. When the first one caught fire, the flames spread until they engulfed the entire row, causing the walls of the shacks to fall against one another like dominoes.

Half-buried wire and spring skeletons of old furniture jutted out from beneath the collapsed roofs and walls. Emy knelt and stared at the nearest jumble of torched and broken wood. "Here," she said aloud. "This is where it started."

She pulled a flashlight from her belt and turned it on. As the light swung across the scorched grass, she saw it—a footprint. Emy reached into the pocket of her Arson jacket and dragged out a collapsible flag. She unfolded it and shoved its end into the ground next to the print.

Emy swiped at the beads of sweat dripping down her nose. Although the jacket was made for warm conditions, it was stifling. The residual heat of the fire coupled with the ridiculously hot summer morning made it impossible to keep cool.

She removed a digital camera from her pocket and snapped multiple shots of the footprint. The camera's bright LED flashed with each button push and wiped away the last of her night vision. She replaced the camera in the pocket and waited for her eyes to clear.

Blades of once green grass had turned brown and yellow. The heat from the fire had scorched them. Either that or the drought had. She sighed as she scanned the ground near the footprint. There was nothing. No fibers or threads that she could find.

Emy turned in a slow circle and tried to make out the path leading to the print. Another divot in the dirt was inches away. Her lips turned up in a grim smile.

By the time she'd followed the path to the street, she'd planted eight separate flags and taken nearly fifty photos. The footprints were of bare feet. They wouldn't give the forensics team much to work with, but at least they would be able to get a size match and maybe even height/weight. As always, that was a crapshoot.

Emy stepped out onto the asphalt a few feet away from where the prints began. The sun was over the horizon now and the street was filled with shadows. Using her flashlight, she scanned the asphalt looking for evidence. The blacktop had pebbles, dirt, and the occasional glimmer of glass shards, but no remaining signs of human interaction.

"Find something?" a lilting voice asked.

She jumped. "Dammit, Brett." She rose from her knees and turned to face her boss. "Why do you always do that to me?"

Brett was smiling. Sweat streamed down from his short, sandy-blonde hair. The lithe man, a shade under six feet tall, looked dapper in his Arson jacket. Unlike Emy, he still had it zipped. "Sorry."

"Right," Emy rolled her eyes. She pointed to the flags she'd planted in the grass. "We have footprints."

Brett followed her gaze. "So we do," he said. "I'll get the forensics team over here. I'm sure they'll appreciate the help."

"Uh-huh."

He turned back around to face her. "That wall back there? Is that the ignition point?"

She nodded. "More than likely. I think we have a firebug, boss."

"Yeah," he said and crossed his arms. "Glad I called you in. This doesn't look...well, accidental." He walked past her and knelt next to the nearest footprint. "Our bug walked barefoot. Smart."

"Or stupid. I think forensics needs to scan the asphalt for blood. He might have cut his feet walking to the grass or on his way back."

Brett pulled a small pad from his pocket, slid a pen out from the spiral wires, and jotted down notes. "Right."

"How long before the HFD showed up?"

He finished writing and then clicked the pen to retract its point. "I called you when I got the page. By then, the fire had been going maybe ten minutes?"

She shook her head as she stared at the row of destroyed structures. "Burned fast."

"You know what these were?"

"Yeah. Some of the original housing for indigent folks back in the thirties."

"More than that," Brett said. "Goddamned historical site."

She raised an eyebrow. "Crap. Anyone living here?"

"We'll have to check into that, wait for the cops to tell us. But," he said and pointed down the block to the large crowd gathered behind crime scene tape, "I would say they were black, Hispanic, or Vietnamese. But I haven't heard tell of any bodies."

The crowd was dressed in pajamas, wife-beaters, robes, anything but jeans and collared shirts. The fire trucks and ambulances had woken everyone within a several block radius. Emy wondered how long it would be before they started crowding in to get a better look at the devastation.

"Third ward," she said. "Can't wait to read the police reports."

Brett grunted. "It'll be the same old song and dance, Emy. 'I saw nothing. I saw no one.' If anyone knows who did it, we'll be the last to find out." He pulled a partially soaked handkerchief from his pocket and wiped sweat from his forehead. "Any ideas on accelerant?"

She shrugged. "We need to get out the chemistry set. I took some photos of the wall, but we'll have to wait and get our hands on the official CSU photos and video." She nodded toward the other side of the street. A woman dressed in khakis and a dark blue jacket panned an HD camera around the site. "I can model the fire when we get those. But as far as ignition?" She shook her head. "Chromatograph time."

Brett nodded. "Okay. I'll tell CSU it's definitely arson and make sure they preserve the wood from that wall. We'll get the evidence later this morning and we can play with molecules."

Emy smiled. "My favorite."

"Yeah, I know." Brett returned his stare to the footprint. "What is it with heat waves and bugs?"

"Dunno, boss. Ask the shrinks."

"Right. Because they're always helpful."

She chuckled. "I'm going to take some more pics and walk the other side of the perimeter. I want to make sure the flatfoots don't destroy anything else."

He raised a brow. "Else?"

"Yeah. I think they already contaminated the area near the street."

"Why do you say that?"

She pointed at a chubby man in an HPD uniform. "That ole boy there spilled his coffee in the grass."

Brett growled. "Okay. Good work, Emy. I'm going to chew some ass and make an initial report. Tick off anything useful."

"I didn't think you were into fat-guys?"

"Not my preference," he admitted. "But I'm going to take a piece of that one." Brett smiled, but his eyes didn't. "Let's get to it."

Her boss swung on his heel and made a bee-line for the cop. Emy watched his angry steps and felt a pang of sympathy for the poor flatfoot. Brett was a kind, caring man. But, if you pissed him off, he'd let you know in the most polite, yet savage way possible.

She clicked off her flashlight. The sun was fully over the horizon now and the shadows had all but disappeared. She turned to head to the other side of the perimeter and then stopped. Emy looked back at the asphalt near the last footprint. There was a mark.

She walked to it and knelt down. The asphalt was discolored. There was a shape there. She lowered herself further and stared at the spot until the rest of the world went out of focus. It was an arc. She duckwalked around its edge. There was more to the shape than a simple arc—it was a circle. The lines were very faint, but there also seemed to be something inside the circle. Emy grinned. "Bug with a signature," she said aloud. "Your ass is mine."

***

S he peeled off the jacket and tossed it atop the washer. It hit the metal with a wet fwap. Emy sighed and pulled her t-shirt over her head. The fabric clung to her skin and she had to wrestle it off. As she placed it beside the jacket, something bumped her in the ass.

"Dammit, Luna." She turned and faced a grinning, white dog. The pit bull mix wagged its tail in a propeller motion, pink polka-dotted ears twitching. Emy pursed her lips. "Look, you," she scratched behind the dog's ears, "I have to clean up. Go behave yourself."

The dog snorted at her, turned, and left the small laundry room. Emy unhooked the belt of her jeans and they fell to the hardwood. The denim was moist from sweat. She was suddenly very glad Brett had encouraged her to go home and get a shower before heading to the office.

Once she had placed her panties and bra alongside the other wet clothes, she stepped out of the laundry room and headed toward the master bath. Luna appeared from the kitchen and followed her, a squeaky ball in her mouth.

Emy ignored the animal and approached the counter. She didn't look in the mirror as she unhooked her necklace and placed it on the white faux marble. Emy had worn the necklace, a family heirloom given to her when she was four, since she was old enough to take care of it. Three chains, each progressively longer than the last, joined together to form a loop. Polished, brilliant lapis lazuli stones adorned the smaller chains. Well, most of them were blue. Two of the stones had drained of their color, turning a milky white as though sucked by a gem vampire.

Her neck still had a red ringed scar from the jewelry. The house fire that had nearly killed her, had raised the temperature enough for the metal to become white hot against her skin, branding her. Emy glanced up at the mirror and frowned. The reddish ring was just another scar to go along with all the others she had on her face, neck, and shoulder.

Luna sighed and Emy shot her a reproachful look before stepping into the shower. She slid the clear, glass door in its tracks until it thumped closed. The dog lay down on the bath mat. Emy undid her braid, and turned the faucet.

The cool water pattered against her skin leaving her shivering, but she didn't mind. She'd been at the site for more than four hours and the Houston heat had been extreme. She and Brett had downed bottle after bottle of water, but it hadn't put a dent in the near heat exhaustion. For weeks, the Houston weather had been stuck in a rut. The humidity was high, the clouds dark and gloomy; but they refused to rain. The heat index was off the scales. Some were calling it the hottest summer on record.

Asphalt roads buckled under the incredible heat. Water mains were constantly bursting. Cars frequently overheated. People were dying. And fires were everywhere.

Northwest of Houston, a large brush fire had broken out. The smoke could be seen from thirty miles to the south. I-45 and 2920 were grey with smoke and ash. Residents of the northern areas had been advised to limit their exposure to the outside and always use recycled air in their cars. If the Gulf winds shifted, all that smoke and ash would hit Houston. If that happened, the damage to the indigent would be extreme.

Emy turned in the shower and smoothed her hair beneath the stream of water. She closed her eyes as her long black hair soaked. Once she was covered with goose pimples, she found the knob with her fingers, and bumped it toward hot. The water warmed at once and she groaned with pleasure.

Warm water splashed across her upturned face, washing away the grime of soot and ash. Emy opened her eyes, soaped up the loofa, and scrubbed at her face and arms. The soft petals rubbed against the pink, puckered scars running the length of her left arm. She followed their tracks up to her neck and face.

The smell of the lavender soap finally dispelled the stench of ash and smoke that had been stuck in her sinuses. The two things she hated the most about her job were the smells of a fire site and the blackened, twisted flesh of dead bodies. Luckily, she hadn't had to deal with the latter today.

When she'd left the smoldering row of shotgun shacks, a single firetruck and two HPD cars remained along with the CSU van. The CSU van was still parked on the side street and the techs roamed the area looking for evidence. They'd taken casts of the footprints and gathered samples of ash and wood from the suspected ignition site. Before they'd hand off the evidence to the Arson division, CSU would check for DNA, hair, and fiber. Emy was certain they'd find nothing.

Although CSU might determine the bug's shoe-size, height, and weight from the footprints, they'd find little else. If the bug had been wearing shoes, they would have been able to narrow down the type of shoe and make guesses about the bug's job, habits, and possible social circle. By walking barefoot, the bug had removed those from the equation.

The techs had scraped the asphalt where she saw the remnants of a symbol. They'd also taken dozens of photographs with high def cameras. With any luck, CSU would have all that back to her by tomorrow at the latest. Until then, she could only write a summary report.

Emy finished washing her body, turned off the shower, and wrung out her hair. Streams of water rushed from the thick, dark mane. She slid open the stall door. Luna still lay on the bath mat. The dog was snoring.

Mischievous grin on her face, Emy knelt down and shook her hair. Droplets showered the dog. Luna yelped and ran from the bathroom. Emy laughed, toweled off, and dressed for the day.

E my yawned into her coffee mug. After five cups, her brain should have been sizzling with activity. Instead, she was fighting to stay awake. The words on the screen kept blurring into one another. She tabbed away from the text editor and the pictures of the burned out shacks jumped into view.

She stared at the blackened wood and scorched foundations. It was hard to believe anyone had once lived in the small structures. It was even more difficult to believe they had been considered an historical site, given the fact they were used to house "negroes" long before the Civil Rights Act of the 60s. The shacks had been so much like the sharecropper structures in the old south before slavery was ended. She didn't understand why the NAACP hadn't insisted the damned things be destroyed. Why anyone would want to remember that time was beyond her.

As she sipped her coffee, she flipped over to the bug's "signature." CSU had placed the high-res digital photos on the encrypted shared drive. The raw photos were incredibly detailed shots of gravel, cracked asphalt, and the dim outline of a shape.

Emy tapped her fingers on the edge of the keyboard tray. She sorted through the photos and finally found one that seemed to have the best contrast between the shape and the asphalt. Smiling, Emy opened the photo in her editing software. The image appeared in the middle of the screen at negative magnification. She selected the shape and cropped the image. After zooming in, she set the parameters for a filter and clicked "apply."

The asphalt and gravel disappeared leaving ghostly lines. Emy applied another filter and the shape popped. She sipped the last dregs of the coffee as she studied the symbol. The circle was thin and black. A large misshapen

'V,' looking more like a forked tree branch than the letter, spread from the bottom with its arms reaching to the top of the circle. A smaller, thinner branch lay inside the large one. Knobs, or maybe they were meant to be budding leaves, stuck out from the branches toward the outer circle.

Emy frowned. She'd never seen anything like the symbol. When she'd first noticed it at the site, it had appeared like something a heavy metal band would have on their cover. Or, for their sigil.

But this was something else. It didn't look Nordic or "satanic"; it wasn't the kind of thing you'd see from amateurs trying to piss off parents and stoke the imaginations of their fans. This was something she'd have to run through the image databases.

It would have been much easier if the sigil was easily recognizable. Hell, even a stupid peace sign would have been better than this. She knew from her classes that profiling bugs was easier when they showed a lack of imagination or education. But this might be something from ancient history. Or just the scribblings from a damaged mind.

Emy saved the filtered image to the case folder on the shared drive. Her photos and those of CSU were carefully titled and marked with metadata. She added her own keywords to the filtered image so she could easily find it. With any luck, one of the Homeland agencies had seen it before. If not, she'd have to go digging through database after database or even, god forbid, the internet.

"Feel like I've been kicked in the head."

Emy jumped in her chair and turned. Brett was leaning against the cube wall, looking crumpled with fatigue. "One of these days you're going to get coffee thrown at you."

Brett smiled sheepishly. "Sorry."

"Uh-huh. What's up, Boss?"

He shook his head. "Not much. Just waiting on your report before I put mine together."

"I'm still working on it," she said.

Brett pointed to where the photos were still splayed across the screen. "I can see that. Although that doesn't look much like writing."

He stepped forward, pulled his glasses from the small chain he wore, and stared at the screen. This close to him, she could smell his cologne. Say what you want about him, but Brett always looked like he'd stepped out of a salon—fresh, crisp, clean.

"Where did you get that?" he asked.

She shrugged. "I told you I noticed something at the site. Could be the bug's signature."

"That doesn't look like anything. Just, well, lines. In a circle."

Emy double-clicked the filtered photo and brought it up on the screen. Brett sucked his teeth.

"Okay," he said, "I stand corrected. Contrast?"

"Yeah. I just applied some plugins to the image. And that's what our bug drew on the asphalt."

He nodded. "That looks a lot less random." He dropped the glasses from his nose and they bounced on his chest. He ran a hand through his thinning blond hair. "You really think that's the sig?"

She shrugged. "Looks like it. I mean, I hate to say this, but unless our bug sets another fire and includes the same mark, it's impossible to tell."

"Right," he agreed. "So all we can do is hope this isn't the beginning of something."

"Could be the bug's already been in business and we're just now catching on." She turned to him. "Since we have access to Homeland, I think we should probably run it through their systems and see what they say."

Brett nodded and then groaned. "Novak is going to *love* that."

She grinned. "That's why you get paid the big bucks, right?"

His frown flipped into a wide smile, but his eyes had turned hard. He leaned in close to her. "Dealing with him isn't worth the money."

Emy laughed. "He'll retire soon, don't you think?"

Brett slapped the grey cube wall. The metal clinked. "Don't you believe it."

"Right."

"We have pictures of the crowd," he said.

She raised her eyebrows. "I take it CSU is running them through the standard routine?"

Bugs were known to hang out in the crowds that gathered around a fire. Just as serial killers were bound to follow police investigations and watch their handiwork being carried out of murder sites, fire-bugs wanted to see the destruction their flames caused. Standard procedure was to photograph or use video cameras, as subtly as possible, to document those in the crowd.

"They're running it through now," Brett said. "Maybe we'll get lucky."

"Or maybe we're just going to catch a few bad guys with outstanding warrants."

Brett smiled. "Or that. Just more noise for the cops to deal with."

"Unless we get a fire-bug hit."

He nodded. "I know it's not PC and it's against everything I believe in, but sometimes I really wish juvenile records were unsealed. Would make catching these bastards so much easier."

Emy found herself nodding. "People make mistakes. Especially young people."

"Unless they're strangling animals, peeing the bed into their teens, and starting fires." Brett slapped the cube wall again. "Okay, I'll leave you to it. You think you'll have the report ready before quitting time?"

"Yeah," she said. "Shouldn't be a problem."

"Good. Then get it done. You have anything else on your plate?"

She shrugged. "Just looking through the cold cases."

"That would be for tomorrow," Brett said. "Your boss commands you to get some sleep. You look like a woman in desperate need of a spa day."

She harrumphed. "Isn't that every day?"

"Whatever," Brett said. "Lee and I are going out for drinks later. You're welcome to join us."

She squinted at him. "That's not going to help me sleep."

"No," he agreed. "But it will make staying awake so much more fun." He pointed to the screen. "Get it done and go home. And call me later."

She saluted. "Aye aye, sir."

Brett laughed and left the cube. She watched him go, her lips turned up in a subtle smile. She didn't have many close friends, but she'd bonded pretty well with Brett and his husband. If Novak, the head of the Arson Department and their boss, knew Brett was drinking with his subordinates on a regular basis, he'd have a conniption fit. But it was good for morale and Emy liked having the company. Brett and Lee seemed like the only people on earth that didn't look at her scars twice. To them, the scars were just another part of her. And for the first time in her life, she'd finally felt, well, normal. As long as Brett and Lee kept inviting her, she'd keep going out with them. But not tonight. Tonight, she was going to sleep like the dead.

She turned in her chair, sighed, and brought up the report. Her eyes tried to swim, but she forced them to focus. She was exhausted and definitely needed a nap. But until she finished the report, she couldn't go home. Luna's excited face drifted across her mind and she smiled. A little doggy cuddling was definitely in order.

"First, work. Then, snuggles," she said to the screen. Her fingers began clicking the keys and the words flowed. It only took her another 45 minutes to finish the report. By that time, she felt like she could sleep for a week.

Chapter 3

The warehouse district was less than vacant. Workers of all color were walking toward the METRO station or into town to catch the light rail. He looked across the alley and saw the empty hulk of Minute Maid Field. They could be playing baseball in it, but the Astros and their victorious opposition would likely be the only ones in attendance.

He sighed into the air conditioned breeze and luxuriated in the shadows. The sun was behind the baseball stadium and the convention center. He drove past the line of expensive condos and townhouses and deeper into the district.

Metal buildings, small run-down strip malls, and Vietnamese businesses lined the road. He passed by them before turning east onto a ragged street. The concrete had buckled years ago. Rather than ripping up all the concrete and properly resurfacing the road, the city of Houston had applied blacktop patches that shimmered in the heat. As he drove over one of them, he was surprised the tires didn't stick in the soft surface.

He passed by a group of kids jumping through the water of a broken fire hydrant. Their black bodies seemed to smile with relief. Dewhurst wished he was out there with them.

The car bucked and shimmied as it rattled down the cracked pavement. He slowed as he tried to read the graffiti on the walls. The taggers had spread their gang symbols across the sides of the warehouses. Tiny crosses had been painted over several of the letters. Dewhurst knew what that meant—the tagger had been killed.

He passed the next alley and glanced toward the left warehouse. Its wall was completely barren save for a single symbol. A large, lazy, crimson spiral that ended in a hook seemed to glow from the grubby white wall. Dewhurst gritted his teeth and tried to ignore the shiver that ran down his spine.

When he reached the last section of warehouses before the bayou, he braked and put the car into park. The sound of the engine was barely audible over the rush of the air conditioning. He turned his head to the right and stared at the warehouse complex.

Not so long ago, he'd been here in the winter. The warehouse street had been crammed with police cars and ambulances. Trey Leger had made it out of the warehouse alive. His friend, Dick Dickerson, had died a day later. As bad as that had been, it was nothing compared to what they'd found inside the warehouse.

Dewhurst sighed. He knew coming back to this section of the district just to stare into the open sore of his guilt wasn't healthy.

Tony had told him more than once that he needed to let it go. Jackson had said the same. But they weren't cops—they didn't understand. Dewhurst put the car in drive, performed a tight U-turn, and headed back down the road.

Even as the sun was setting, the outside temperature gauge read 102°. Dewhurst punched the gas and hurried through the long line of warehouses. When he made it out and onto Travis, he traveled beneath the overpass and into the remains of rush hour traffic.

He'd been killing time and he knew it. Jackson was no doubt waiting for him at Mongoose Versus Cobra with a drink in hand and a question on his lips. If he was lucky, Tony would stop by and distract the journalist. He considered Jackson a friend, but the man didn't know when to quit being a reporter.

The week's case load had been light. Relatively, that is. There had been several assaults and two murders. All easily solved, easily filed, easily forgotten. When the heat was this bad, people inevitably lost their shit. Tempers flared more easily even in the air conditioned bars. Without football, basketball, or a decent baseball team, there was little to entertain anyone that didn't like soccer. So the drinking was to stave off boredom. The fights were another way to relieve that boredom. And the murders were just people unable to control their tempers.

He drove through the green lights and headed into midtown. As he drove past the Mercedes dealership, he turned left and into the pay-for parking lot. The attendant shook a flag at him. Dewhurst rolled down his window and stared at the young Latino.

"Five bucks," the man said in perfect English.

Dew smiled and reached into his coat pocket. He produced his badge.

The man stared at it and then at Dewhurst. "Thought I recognized you. Cops park for free," he said with a grin. The attendant pointed his flag toward the back of the parking lot. Dewhurst mumbled thanks, closed the window, and drove toward the back. He parked next to Jackson's BMW and sighed.

The heat hammered him as he walked the hundred feet to the bar. A large sign covered the building's facade with a furry looking mongoose swiping at a coiled cobra. Dewhurst liked the place, but damn it was pretentious.

He walked through the doors and into cacophony. The bar was cluttered with couples and groups of friends ordering their drinks. Dewhurst loosened his tie and got into line.

The hipsters wore their designer jeans and shirts, drank their microbrews, and argued about bands. After a few moments, he managed to get a bartender and ordered a Buried Hatchet. When the pint of pitch black beer arrived, he headed toward the back.

Jackson sat at a large table with his laptop. The reporter typed in staccato bursts, oblivious to everything. Dewhurst made his way to the table, carefully placed his beer on a coaster, and sat in the tall chair. Jackson looked up from the laptop and held a single finger in the air.

Dewhurst sipped his beer and peered at the entrance, willing Tony to appear. Any second now, Jackson was going to flip the laptop closed and—

"So, Dew," Jackson smiled. He closed the laptop, sipped at his pint, and then splayed his fingers atop the computer. "What's happening?"

Dew sighed. "Same old, same old."

Jackson nodded. "Crime rate's up, bodies in the streets, and you're not busy?"

"Bodies in the streets," Dew echoed. He glared at the reporter. "You're so full of shit."

Jackson laughed. "Little birdie told me you already cleared those two homicides."

Dew shrugged. "Didn't take much to figure it out. We practically had confessions in both cases."

"Just rage?"

The detective nodded. "Yeah. You could say that."

"You got any news on that homeless thing?"

Dewhurst gulped from his pint. "Nothing new."

"Liar," Jackson smiled. "You're just not going to tell me."

"How's Jenny?"

Jackson nodded. "She's fine, Dew. Thanks for asking. Hopefully she'll get out of work early enough to join us."

"Heard from Tony?"

"Not today," Jackson said. "I know he had a few things to do this week."

"You mean he went to see the kid."

Jackson shrugged. "Once a week. Just like you and that fucking warehouse."

Dew glared. "Careful, Jackson."

"Sorry." Jackson finished the rest of his beer in a single gulp. He tapped the pint on the wooden table-top. "You two need to get over it." They stared at one another for a moment and then Jackson looked past him. He raised a hand. "You ready for another stout?"

Dew nodded.

A young woman dressed in a black mini-skirt and black halter top stopped at the table. She made eye contact with Jackson and then cocked her head at Dewhurst. "Thirsty?"

"Need another blond and another—"

"Stout," she finished.

Jackson grinned. "Yes."

She smiled and headed back to the crowded bar.

Dewhurst picked up a paper coaster and tore at it. "I read your column," he said.

"And?"

"I think you need to be careful about what you print. The Gomez case isn't a slam dunk yet."

Jackson rolled his eyes. "I didn't give anything away."

Dew crossed his arms and said nothing.

"Okay, so I let slip there was some audio evidence."

"Let slip?" Dew asked in a raised voice. "That's not a slip. That's arming the fucking defense!"

"Whatever, Dew. Word is the cartel's not going to risk their necks to save this asshole."

"And if the Feds want him to flip?"

Jackson shrugged. "Hate to say it, Dew, but when this trial's over, win or lose, that Mexi is probably going to end up with his throat slit."

The waitress returned with their beers. She placed the blonde in front of Jackson and carefully placed the pint of pitch black beer in front of Dew. "Mr. Jackson? On your tab?"

"Yes, ma'am. And it's just Jackson." She nodded and weaved her way through the crowd. Jackson shook his head. "I never thought I'd be the creepy old guy."

Dew grunted. "Keep hanging out at places like this and you're always going to be the creepy old guy."

Jackson lifted his beer and sipped. "Well, they have good beer." He placed the pint back on the table and tented his hands. "You're a surly bastard today, Dew. What's up?"

The detective tapped the side of his glass. "Just waiting for the other shoe to drop."

"Cartel?"

Dew nodded. "Yeah. You say he's not going to make it in prison? I'm worried about him even making it to trial."

Jackson raised his hands. "So what? Doesn't he deserve a good shiv after that chainsaw enema?"

"And then some," Dewhurst said. He sipped his stout and then wiped the foam from his upper lip. "He's still got guys around, Jackson. Gomez was hands on, but he still had soldiers."

"Ah," Jackson said. "Think they'll come gunning for you?"

Dew shrugged. "I can handle that. More worried about the prosecutor. Boss says not my job."

Jackson laughed. "Then you're not supposed to worry about it, are you?"

"Guess not," Dew said. He tapped the table. "You writing a column this week?"

Jackson's smile turned into a leer. "When don't I?"

"And what's the spectacle this week?"

"Ah," the reporter said and took a gulp from his beer. "Taking a look into the shotgun shack thing."

Dew raised an eyebrow. "What shotgun shack thing?"

Jackson rolled his eyes and then laughed. "You know, for a cop you don't know shit about what's going on in this city."

Dew growled. "Some of us work for a living. I don't stay glued to the AP."

"Okay, so those shacks down there? By UH?"

"Yeah," Dew said.

"They're gone. Someone used 'em for kindling early this morning."

"Christ." Dew took another sip of stout. "Historical landmark wasn't it?"

"Exactly," Jackson nodded. "So I'm going to do some history on the thing. See if I can find a race angle."

"'A race angle.'" Dew shook his head. "You're going to lay this off on some skinheads?"

"No," Jackson said. "I'm not going to lay this off on anyone. I want to get to the bottom of it."

"I'm sure Arson will greatly appreciate that."

"Oh, come on, Dew. I'm an investigative reporter. I investigate."

"Yeah, yeah," Dew laughed. "Okay, fine."

"Besides," Jackson said, "there's a lot of history there. Went through some searches today and those shacks had been around a long damned time." He sipped his beer. "And you know how much I love history."

"I know," Dew said. "So where are you going to start?"

Jackson shrugged. "Like a certain detective I know, I'd start with the site. See who was living there. Check out grudges. Stuff like that."

Dew smiled. "You know Arson will do the same thing, if it was intentionally set."

"Yeah, they will." Jackson's face turned into a grin. "And if they do, I have my sources over there."

"Sources everywhere," Dew said.

The reporter nodded. "And maybe, just maybe, you'll be one of 'em."

Dew shook his head. "I'm not a source, Jackson. I just occasionally share information when I'm not telling you to quit being an asshole."

"I'm always an asshole," Jackson said in a deadpan voice.

"Right, but I like you anyway." Dew raised his glass and clinked it against Jackson's. "Now, where's that pretty lady of yours?"

Chapter 4

Emy's father was snapping his fingers. She opened her eyes and stared up at him. His short-cropped, black hair was tipped with white. His smile showed off the missing front tooth in his lower jaw.

"Emilyza?" he asked in a hoarse whisper. "It's time to wake up," her father said in his native Tagalog.

She smiled up at him. Her brown-skinned father wore a black t-shirt and a pair of tattered shorts. His thin mustache twitched. The blank expression he wore faded into a frown.

"Why are you smiling?" he asked. "Don't you feel It?" Her father turned aside in the doorway. A hungry, yellow and red light flickered behind him. "Don't you feel It?" he asked again.

As Emy watched, a long, sharpened rod of flame slipped past the door-frame and curled around to touch the wall. Smoke rose as the plaster blackened. Three more fiery fingers appeared. A thick, black cloud belched from the wall as the paint ran and melted.

Her father turned and watched as the hand of fire knocked against the wall. "See, Emy? You have to get up. It's very hungry."

The house shook as something roared. The fist opened and a finger beckoned to her. Emy opened her mouth to speak and breathed in scorching air. Her eyes watered as she coughed and coughed. "Can't breathe," she said between ragged breaths.

Joseph Aninzo shook his head. "You have to breathe in the blessing, girl. You have to take it in." He took a deep breath and scraps of flame flowed off the beckoning hand and into his nose. Her father's eyes went black and then he sneezed fire. "Breathe the blessing." His voice had become the sound of stones clicking together.

Emy shook as she tried to hold her breath. Her lungs screamed in agony and her vision darkened. The room was a furnace and she felt her skin beginning to burn and blister. Finally, her body revolted and she took in a breath of painful, scorching air.

Her father smiled. "It blesses," he said. "It blesses all of us. Wipes away the past." He turned to the unseen creature beyond the door and beckoned it inside the room.

As Emy watched, a tall, wide burning figure entered, its face a moving visage of the oranges and reds at the heart of a campfire. The thing's white-hot eyes glowered at her. It opened its mouth and sharpened teeth of coal-black clicked together. With each click, the world roared with the sound of hissing steam and burning wood. Black smoke rose from the thing's misshapen legs and arms. Its horned feet crushed the floor as it walked, carpet catching fire with each step.

"It wants you," her father said from behind the beast.

The thing turned its head toward him. A pair of impossibly white, smoking eyes blinked at her. The thing sneered and raised a hand above her father's head. It looked back at Emy and grinned before slamming a first downward.

He didn't scream or make a sound as flames devoured him from head to toe. He smiled at his daughter as smoke billowed from his mouth and his eyes popped like wet pine knots.

Emy tried to scream for him, but the raging heat stole her voice. There was a crash from the hall and a wall of flame entered the room. The creature turned, its fingers spread wide as it crept toward her. A rushing wind of fire and smoke filled the room. The thing reached out its hand and stroked the side of her face.

Pain wracked her. The stench of burning hair and flesh added to that of plastic, wood, and paper. She felt her jaw sag as the muscles caught fire. The creature looked into her eyes, a finger sliding toward her mouth.

The scream tore from her throat as she opened her eyes. The world wasn't smoking. There were no reds or yellows against her vision. Something licked her face and she flinched. The dog whimpered.

Emy turned her head. Luna was laying next to her. Even in the mostly dark room, she could see the dog's worried look. Emy loosed a shuddering breath and touched the dog's short snout.

"Sorry, baby," she said. The dog licked her face again and Emy giggled. "Didn't mean to wake you."

Luna placed a paw on Emy's chest and whined as she yawned. Emy scritched behind the dog's ear and Luna groaned in doggy bliss. She hugged the dog closer and stared at the ceiling. In a moment, the dog was snoring.

It's hungry, dream-dad had said.

She fought the urge to touch the scars on her face, and clutched the necklace instead. The panic and adrenaline from the dream faded a little. For some reason, the necklace and its brilliant stones had always managed to calm her. She took a deep breath and slowly exhaled, willing her heart to slow. The necklace, with its river rock like stones, felt cool in her hand.

Closing her eyes, she kept one hand over the chain, the other beneath her head. Just float, she told herself. Just float and find your center.

The darkness took her for a moment, cradling her in peace. But the black edges of night slowly eroded into rips of orange and red. The flame monster from her nightmare stepped through the colors, its infernal visage grinning at her. She pushed it away with some effort, replacing it with her father's face. That didn't help either. The image kept morphing into the creature she'd seen in her dream. That father, consumed in fire and smoke, had been smiling as he disintegrated into ash.

"That wasn't the way it happened," she said aloud.

Yes it was, her father's voice said in her mind.

Emy shivered and cuddled against the dog. A few moments later, she fell into a dreamless sleep.

Chapter 5

Dewhurst opened the apartment door after fumbling with his keys and stepped inside. Dew placed his valise on the floor and then shrugged out of his suit coat. Even in the dark, his hands knew where the hanger was. He pulled it from the peg and hung the coat on the hard plastic. He then placed the hanger and managed to find the peg on the first try.

A pair of yellow eyes blinked at him in the darkness. The lights from the city illuminated the living room enough to make them glow. He smiled. "Good evening, Frankie," he said.

The eyes blinked and then a bell jingled as the cat walked toward him. The torty rubbed against his calf, her purr a welcome sound.

"Bet you're hungry."

The cat chirped and then walked back toward the living room. Dew reached out a hand and flicked on the light. His eyes burned as the hallway overheads lit up. As his vision cleared, he saw a swishing black and caramel tail near the kitchen.

Dew sighed and followed on unsteady feet. The patchwork cat sat by the kitchen pantry. Although she appeared patient, he knew the swishing tail meant she was angry he hadn't been home hours ago.

He cleared his throat and drawled. "You're more and more like a wife, Frankie." The cat meowed at him and continued staring at the pantry door. He moved her away with his foot, grabbed the food container, and walked to her bowls at the other end of the kitchen.

The hard plastic food dish had kibble on the edges, but a divot lay in the middle. Dew turned and glared at the cat. "There's food in here, girl." The cat meowed in response. Shaking his head, he poured food into the bowl, the kibble rattling as it hit the plastic. Frankie trotted to the bowl, collar jingling, and stuck her head in the dish. She snarfed the food as if she'd been starved.

Dewhurst turned from the cat and opened the stainless steel fridge. He moved aside the cans of stout and pulled out a large bottle of water. He'd had too much to drink. His brain buzzed and an acidic burp lay beneath the aftertaste of heavy beer.

Jackson's girlfriend had driven him back to the apartment. It was hardly a long drive, but he wasn't looking forward to hoofing it to the car in the morning in the thousand degree heat. "Have to wake up even earlier," he said aloud.

The cat turned from the dish and blinked at him as he took a long pull from the bottle. Frankie seemed to shrug and went back to eating. Dew put the cap back on the bottle and placed it on the kitchen island. The blue speckled formica countertop was spotless, as always. The sink was empty save for a single plate and a clear pint mug.

He loosened his tie as he headed to the bedroom, slid off his pants, hung them carefully in the closet, and did the same with the tie. He kicked off the black oxfords and placed them on the cedar shoe tree. Dew stared at the other suits hanging from the racks. Two more days and he'd have to visit the dry cleaners; he knew two of those suits were too smelly to wear. The horrendous heat had left the fabric coated in sweat even through his undershirts and dress shirts.

Dew walked to the bed in his underwear, still wearing his black socks. Frankie sat on the comforter, staring at him. He reached over and scratched the cat beneath the chin. The torty raised her head in return. Dew smiled as the cat loosed a rumbling purr.

He stared out into the living room and cursed. He'd left the lights on. You really are drunk, he said to himself with a smile. The cat followed him into the kitchen as he grabbed the bottled water and killed the lights.

Dew weaved through the darkness and back into the bedroom. As he reached the bed, he heard the thump and jingle of Frankie jumping up. She always liked to be on the bed first. "Do I have your permission?" he asked the darkness. There was no response. Grinning, he pulled back a corner of the comforter and lay upon the crisp, cool sheets.

He stared up into the darkness as the cat crawled on top of him. Frankie kneaded his bare chest, claws in, and then lay down. The ceiling fan swooshed the air and it felt wonderful against his hot face.

He should have showered before getting into bed, but that was for tomorrow. Jackson had kept buying him round after round. Jenny had only had a couple, not bothering to try and keep up with the macho drinking contest. Both he and the reporter had been hammered when they finally left the bar.

"You're going to slam dunk the Gomez case." Jackson's words had been slurred and he'd slammed his glass on the table hard enough to draw stares. "That sick fuck is going to burn."

"I'll drink to that," Dew had said as he downed another mouthful.

"Who's the audio guy you worked with?" Jenny asked. She'd sat next to Jackson, a gimlet rolling between her fingers.

"Henrichs."

"Christ," Jackson said. "The rap producer?"

Dew shrugged. "Best I have access to for audio forensics. And as I understand it, he'd rather be producing other music, but hip-hop pays the bills."

"He pulled audio off a damned cell phone?" Jenny asked.

"Yeah," Dew nodded. "He's good." Dew thumped his fingers. "You know this scumbag," he said pointing a finger at the reporter, "is going to start researching that fire."

Jenny nodded. "That scumbag is my boyfriend, but yeah, he is a scumbag."

"Hey," Jackson said, "I'm sitting right here!"

She looked at him and smiled. "We know."

"Doesn't matter," Dew said. "He's going to run into brick walls when he starts asking around."

"Really?" Jackson grinned. "Wanna bet?"

"Sure," Dew had said. "I'll buy the tab next time if you get anything important." They'd clinked glasses, finished their drinks, and then Jenny had announced the night was over.

The fan continued to turn. Dew closed his eyes and concentrated on the sound. The whirring push of air was soothing and he started to drift. Frankie's purr lessened in volume. She would be asleep soon. With any luck, so would he.

Chapter 6

Heat radiated off the pavement in waves. Her Arson jacket felt wet and heavy and she'd only been wearing it for a few minutes. Another twenty minutes of standing on the concrete parking lot and she'd be able to wring sweat from the garment.

She stared up at the still smoking west wing of the dingy motel's second floor. The roof had collapsed once the fire ate into the beams and joists. Considering how old the building was, it was a miracle the whole damned thing hadn't burned.

The "Palms Motel" had hourly room rates as well as extended stay pricing. In other words, it was a roach and rat infested sty. Working girls made their Johns pay for the rooms. Dealers often rented the rooms by the month so they had a more or less permanent base.

Her phone had gone off just after six am. She'd looked at the message and leaped into her clothes. Luna had had only a few minutes to potty before Emy had to leave the house and drive like a bat out of hell to the scene.

Average HFD response time in this part of town was around eight minutes. But in eight minutes, a lot could happen. In this case, the three most western rooms on the second floor had been utterly destroyed. The fire department had managed to quickly control the blaze, but it was a miracle the flames hadn't spread through the flimsy walls to the other units.

The air smelled of burned plastic, insulation, and wood. The thousands of gallons of water that had been sprayed onto the burning hulk merely added a subtle sewer stench. Emy hated it.

She watched water drip from the saturated second floor balcony on to the parking lot. The fire department had no doubt flooded the first floor in trying to save the building. Emy wondered how much the insurance bill for that was going to be. Assuming the place had insurance.

"Fancy meeting you here," Brett said.

Emy turned. Her boss wore a pair of clean khakis and a black polo. His hair was swept back but random corkscrews stuck up at odd angles.

"You got here late," Emy smiled.

Brett shrugged. "Well, can't always be early. Besides," he said as he pointed up to the burned out rooms, "looks like we can't even go in yet."

"Marshall said ten minutes or so. I imagine that means real soon," Emy said.

The lithe man pulled off his arson jacket and wrapped it around his waist. "How the hell are you wearing that thing? It's hot enough to roast a chicken out here."

Emy wiped a sheen of sweat from her forehead. "Good question," she said and pulled off her jacket. She tied it around her waist the same way Brett had. The word "Arson" would be visible as it draped off her waist. "I started sweating before I climbed into the car."

"Not surprised," Brett said. "You check the weather this morning?"

"No," Emy said. "Another day over a hundred?"

Brett nodded. "106° by 3 pm."

"Great." Emy turned and pointed to the distant freeway. Even from half a mile away, it was easy to see the motionless line of cars. "How many car fires will there be today?"

"Not our problem," Brett grinned. "Just be glad you're not stuck in that crap."

"Side street commutes are best," she agreed. "Living in the city does have its privileges."

Brett turned back to the building and frowned. "What do you think?"

Emy followed his gaze to the blackened, burned out rooms. "Have to get in there. But I doubt it's arson."

He nodded. "Probably some asshole overcooked his meth."

"Wouldn't surprise me," she said. "You guys go out last night?"

"No," he said and wiped at the runners of sweat rolling down his cheek. "Decided to stay home and get some sleep. But since I stayed home, I did read your report."

Emy felt a stab of insecurity. For the first few months she'd worked in

Arson, every report had been a trial of nerves. She could write a first class analysis, model the hell out of a crime scene, come up with reasonable deductions, and make very educated guesses. And most of the time? They were dead on. But even now, several years later, her stomach fluttered before she sent a report to her boss. The fear of being wrong, of making a ridiculous case, haunted her as much as her scars. And after she hit send? She'd spend the rest of the work day, or even after work, fretting about it, second-guessing herself, and more or less being miserable. Yesterday's report on the shotgun shack fires had been no different. Actually, it was worse. After the press conference the Mayor had held, she knew the entire city was watching their every move.

She cleared her throat. "And?"

"It's good," he said. "Actually, it's very good."

"Thank you," she sighed with relief.

He pursed his lips. "Just be prepared for Novak to question it."

Emy rolled her eyes. "Why?"

"Because we don't have any other sites with that symbol. So he's probably going to take issue with your hypothesis about this being a potential serial case. Until we have more evidence, he's not going to back it."

She felt a shudder of fear in her stomach. "But it could be the first. Or maybe we just haven't noticed other sites."

"True," Brett said. "But this is Novak we're talking about." He pointed at the burned out second floor. "He might even look at this fire and ask whether or not you think it's the same bug. Although that would be assholeish even for him."

"Sounds like him," Emy muttered.

Brett laughed. "I'm not saying he'll take issue with it for sure. I'm just saying you need to prepare yourself. He wants a meeting later today, assuming we get this sorted out."

"Hey, Cullum!" a man dressed in HFD blues called. He walked toward them, his badge glowing in the sunlight. "We're ready for you."

Brett and Emy looked at the second floor. Two firemen stood outside the burned out rooms, still dressed in their bunker gear. Their coats were unzipped and the two men were talking.

"Let's go," Brett said. "Time to do the investigation. Bet you $20 it was caused by a meth smoker."

Emy smiled. "No bet."

T he smell of burned plastic, furniture, and wood was still with her. She picked up a fresh cup of coffee and sniffed. The pungent odor cleared her nose. At least for the moment. She knew after she put the cup back down, the stench of the fire site would return. Emy touched her tongue to the steaming liquid. The taste was heaven.

Emy took a long sip and put the coffee back on the desk. Her computer was lit up with yet another report document. The second screen was filled with CSU photographs of the room where the fire started.

The small motel room had been rented for the month by a Jacob Marsters. HPD had put out a BOLO on the man, and an officer was waiting for him at the motel. Marsters wasn't an arsonist—he was an idiot.

Emy and Brett had found the source of the fire almost instantly. Although the plastic had melted, the hotplate's switch was in the "on" position and it was clear the cord had been connected to the outlet. In simple terms, Marsters had cooked his breakfast and left the device on. With nothing to draw off the heat, the hotplate, sitting next to the bed, had set fire to the bed spread. Once the bed caught fire, the room was doomed.

As if Marsters wasn't a big enough idiot, the motel management was in bigger trouble. Although the motel had passed the last three fire inspections, the sprinklers in the room had "failed." Based on what she'd seen in the other two rooms that burned, it appeared the entire floor was without working sprinklers. If the motel was lucky, it would get away with a large fine. If not, the entire building would undergo a massive inspection that would no doubt result in it being shut down.

She had written up the situation report, explaining how the fire was anything but arson. Emy had managed to keep from making snide remarks about how she and Brett were getting called to investigate "common" fires. Then again, the shacks would have been considered a "common" fire if not for the way it spread. At least HFD had some investigative abilities—they'd spotted the shack fire for being out of the ordinary and made the call.

The only reason Arson had been called to the motel fire was...well, it was a shady place. A fire set by the owner would no doubt bring in some much needed insurance money. The Mayor loved to crack down on insurance fraud, unless of course, it was one of her cronies.

Emy put the final summary together with the manufacturer and model number of the hotplate. If Marsters was half-way bright, he'd try and make a claim against the maker of the device, or the motel ownership would. This was the third fire she'd investigated that involved a common "household" device, and each time it was obvious the fire had started due to negligence. In each case, the homeowners tried to sue the manufacturer of the coffee pot, toaster, or electric kettle. And each time, they'd lost. But that didn't keep idiots from trying to make it a "your fault, not mine" kind of case.

She saved the document, digitally signed it, and emailed it to Brett. Her boss would probably rubber stamp it and send it on to Novak, especially since Brett had five other investigators to deal with. This summer's fire rate was 200% higher than last year. That meant the six arson investigators, plus Brett, were on the scene more often than not. Each incident required its own investigation, its own report, and its own supervisory assessment. In other words—they were damned busy.

She closed the document and brought up her original report on the shack fire. Novak wanted a meeting to discuss it. Emy's stomach churned with acid, although she wasn't sure if that was from the endless cups of coffee or from anxiety. Who was she kidding. Of course it was anxiety.

Every meeting with Novak required her to defend her assumptions, her findings, and her conclusions. Regardless of how many times she'd faced the portly, pompous bastard, she never got used to his condescending manner. The only saving grace was the fact he never used racial slurs, homophobic remarks, or engaged in sexual harassment. But from the way he looked at her, at Brett, and at the other non-white forensics personnel, she knew damned well those thoughts ran through his mind. He was a pig.

An alert popped up on her screen. Shit. Fifteen minutes until the meeting. The fire in her stomach raised in intensity another notch. Emy leaned back in her chair, closed her eyes, and tried to focus. Her left hand slowly rose to her neck, fingers playing with the stones on the necklace. Think about nothing, she told herself. Think about nothing.

Instead of nothing, the firebug's signature appeared in her mind. The lines glowed crimson, minuscule flames flaring from them. The sigil. What the hell did it mean? What was the bug trying to say?

So far, her trips through the image databases had come up with nothing. Absolutely nothing. It was as though the design simply hadn't existed before. The chances of that were next to nil, though. There had to be some connection. A bug's signature was always something personal. Well, not always. The smart ones, the ones that hadn't gone truly insane, tried to leave false trails. In the process, however, they revealed more than they realized.

If a sig was a word, it said something about their personality. If a sig was a string of numbers, it said something about their education level. And if it was a symbol? Well, it could mean anything.

But symbols had origins. Symbols had history. Symbols were the best clues a forensics investigator could find. The truly crazy bugs, like some serial killers, sent letters to the cops or the news stations that justified their actions, or threatened more destruction. In today's society, any communication left trails and investigators loved to backtrack them.

The days of Jack the Ripper, the anonymity of a single killer in a huge city, were gone. Nearly everyone used the internet or the post office. And if you used the internet, someone could find you. Eventually. Unless you knew how to cover your tracks just enough to make it take time.

Time. That was the problem. Time and frequency. Bugs could disappear for months at a time, especially if they were contractors working their hobby as an actual vocation. But in those cases, the building in question left motives behind. Who gained from the fire, who lost from the fire, and was there an economic or political reason behind them, left plenty of open doors for investigation.

The low hanging fruit for the shack fires, of course, was good old fashioned racism. Someone could have had a beef with how the shacks had been marked as historical. Or they could have lit the fire to intimidate the mostly black and Hispanic neighborhood.

If she hadn't found the signature, those were the most likely motives. The signature, however, was something else. There was a reason the bug left it. She just had to figure out why.

Her computer beeped and she opened her eyes. A message from Brett stared at her from the screen.

"Ready? He's already in the conference room."

Emy sighed, put her hands on the keyboard, and responded. She was ready. Or at least as ready as she could get. She grabbed her laptop, drank the last of her coffee, and headed into the lion's den.

Novak tapped his pen on the table. The head of the arson department sat at the head of the table facing the large projection screen. "I think the fire improved the Palms Motel," he said with a grin.

Emy tried not to roll her eyes. Brett, sitting two seats down from Novak, didn't even bother to try. Luckily for him, Novak didn't bother making eye contact with either of them. The way he grinned made her think Novak may have actually been there. Probably with the cheapest prostitute he could find.

When no one laughed, Novak's eyes narrowed and his half-jovial smile, it was only ever half-jovial, disappeared into an angry frown. "Your report, Ms. Aninzo, looks accurate to me. I don't see any cause for us to continue the investigation." Brett nodded and typed into his computer. Novak slowly swung his head and nodded at Brett. "Good job," he said.

Emy ground her teeth, but said nothing. If it was a "good job," Brett got the praise. If it was a shit report or something Novak didn't immediately agree with, he called out the investigator by name. She didn't mind the boss getting the applause from Novak, that was all part of being a team. A win was a win for everyone. But the double standard Novak employed, calling out Brett's subordinates as though they reported directly to the head of Arson, sickened her. She couldn't wait for him to retire. If they were ever that lucky.

"Now, to more important matters," Novak said. He leaned back in his chair, his round belly touching the edge of the conference table. "I assume you both listened to the Mayor's press conference."

Brett nodded. "Read the transcript," he said. "We were a little busy when she made it."

"Right," Novak said. "So you know that she's promising fast results on the shack fire. The NAACP is on her ass, as well as the historical societies. They want to know if this was racially motivated and they want to know damned soon."

Emy frowned. How the hell were they supposed to figure that out? They didn't have a clue about the perp yet.

"So I have authorization for you to work overtime, make whatever calls you need, and make use of any resources available to speed the investigation," he said.

Brett cleared his throat. "Although the Mayor didn't give us a deadline—"

"The deadline," Novak interrupted, "is as soon as possible."

"Right," Brett said. "But you have to realize that could take a week. Or a month."

"Not acceptable," Novak said. "You have five days to find the culprit."

Emy's mouth opened in a wide O of surprise. "That's not going to happen," she muttered.

Novak turned his head to glare at her. "You have something to add, Ms. Aninzo?"

A blush rose on her cheeks. She really hadn't meant him to hear that. "I — I said I don't think that's realistic."

"And why not?" Novak asked. "You'll have all the resources. Although I don't believe that shape you mentioned in your report has anything to do with this."

The blush of embarrassment turned to one of frustrated rage. It was so easy for bureaucrats to second-guess, question, and demand. On the other hand, it was goddamned difficult to get the idiots to listen to reason.

"I'm not sure that's the case," Brett said. His eyes had narrowed and locked with Novak's. "Sure, we need a little more investigation, but it's the best lead—"

"If that's the best lead you have, Brett, then you better work to find a better one."

Brett sighed. Emy could almost see the thoughts in his mind. She was sure Brett was going to ask Novak how many cases he'd cleared in less than a week when he was an investigator all those years ago. From the files, he'd never solved one in less than a month.

"We'll do our best," Brett said in a low growl. "But you shouldn't expect anything immediate."

Novak leaned forward, hands flat upon the table. "If that's the case, then I'll make sure you explain to the Mayor why that is."

Brett nodded, his expression giving nothing away but grim determination. "We'll do our best," he repeated in that same tone.

The large man sighed and flattened his tie against his belly. "I expect daily status reports. Work with HPD on the race angle. I'll be sending the report, such as it is," he said, glaring at Emy, "to HPD this afternoon. The captain of detectives has promised to put his best man on the job. So you'll be coordinating with them. Hopefully tomorrow."

The room went silent as the three traded stares, the whooshing of the air conditioner and the projector's fan the only sounds. Emy dropped her eyes, unable to stand the look on Novak's face, not to mention the vitriol hiding behind his eyes.

Finally, he pushed back his chair and stood. "Get to work," he said and left the room without another word.

Brett hissed air between his teeth. "Close the door," he said. Emy rose from her chair and followed orders. "Take a seat," he said. "We need to talk in private for a moment." Emy nodded and returned to her laptop. He tapped a finger on the table while staring at the projected image. "Switch that to the shacks," he said.

With a few mouse movements, she brought up the case file for the shack fire along with the pictures she and Brett had deemed the most relevant. He pointed at the sigil. "Bring that up again." Another click and the picture of the shape took over the screen. "What do you think?"

She shrugged. "I still have to perform an exhaustive search through the FBI databases, but I haven't found anything." She pursed her lips in disgust. "I compared it to the well known racist and white supremacy symbols. Nothing. Not even close. It doesn't bear resemblance to anything on record. Unless it's hiding somewhere in the archives."

He shook his head. "Keep looking, but I don't think you're going to find anything."

"Me neither," she said. "But I'll keep at it."

Brett ran a hand through his thinning hair. "I know Novak doesn't realize this, and it's awful to say, but I don't think we're going to have any answers unless this asshole burns another building."

She felt a shiver. It's exactly what she'd been thinking all day. The easiest way to catch the perp was for him to commit another atrocity. Each new fire would provide more clues to the past ones. And if he was a real firebug, he'd have to keep going. It was an illness, a disease, a compulsion to start new fires, to watch, to revel in the destruction. Racial motivation was immaterial unless it provided clues. What would he burn next was the real question.

"Do you think it would be helpful," Emy said, "to find other sites he might target? If he's a racist shitbag, that is?"

Brett thought for a moment, his eyes still glaring at the sigil on the screen. He shrugged. "Not a bad idea, but I don't think it's going to net us much. I'm sure HPD is doing the same thing. Besides," he said with a glance, "I want you on this. No distractions."

"No distractions," she echoed.

A smile crossed his face. "Unless, that is, you're joining Lee and I tonight. He wants to make sure you're not falling back into being a hermit."

She rolled her eyes. "Okay, okay. I had some sleep. I can handle the club for a few hours. Assuming they're having drink specials."

He laughed. "Of course they are. Plus," he said with a grin, "it's 80s night."

"Great," she said. "Erasure, New Order, and Soft Cell. Sounds like hell to me."

"Whatever," Brett said. "Now. Go do research and let's hope Novak doesn't completely destroy your shack report."

She saluted and closed the laptop. "Time for another coffee."

"Amen to that," Brett said.

Chapter 7

Dewhurst felt like monkeys were flinging poo at his brain. Four cups of coffee hadn't managed to dispel the haze. When he'd awakened, he'd donned a pair of shorts, sneakers, a muscle shirt, and headed to get his car. At seven in the morning, the heat and humidity had filled the air like a furnace. Just stepping outside was enough to clothe his body in sweat.

Traffic had already been building on the feeders, side streets, and freeways. Overheated cars seemed to block passage every day. Dewhurst sincerely hoped the heatwave would break soon, else the city would just shut down.

When he'd reached the parking lot, Jackson's car had still been there. Since Jenny had driven them both home, he'd expected that. Jackson was a late riser, and after last night's drunk-a-thon, the reporter probably wouldn't awaken for a few more hours.

Dewhurst drove his car back home, fed the cat, showered, dressed, and headed to work. The station had been bustling. Apparently more arrests had been made at the bars the night before. In addition, road-rage was starting to becoming epidemic on the freeways. People were coming unglued. And as if he hadn't felt bad enough, emails awaited him when he sparked up the computer.

While most were the standard communiques from the Chief, a few updates from the DA on the Gomez case, one stood out. Captain Spillane, his direct boss, had sent him a wonderfully pithy email mentioning yesterday's shotgun shack fire. Dewhurst narrowed his eyes as he stared at it.

Apparently Spillane had promised Arson his best detective. Dew grunted at the ego stroke. When Spillane wanted to motivate him, he always kissed Dew's ass. Even after several years of working together, Spillane hadn't figured out that Dew didn't need motivation—he just needed an interesting case. Regardless, Spillane made it clear both the Chief and the Mayor were on his ass for a quick resolution. "Good luck with that," he mumbled.

He worked his way through the standard morning notices while he sipped his first cup of coffee. By 1100, he'd filled his cup five more times. Dew let out an acidic burp, his queasy stomach on the verge of revolt. Water. He needed water and a lot of it.

As he rose from his chair, his right hand hovering over the mouse to lock the computer, a new message appeared on the screen. Spillane had sent him a link to the new case file on the shared drive. Without sitting down, he clicked on the report and read the three sentence summary. Dew raised an eyebrow and slowly settled back into his chair, both his need for water and his queasy stomach suddenly forgotten.

Arson had determined the fire was, in fact, an act of arson. An investigator named "Emilyza Aninzo" had put together a very tightly written report explaining how it was set and the results. As Jackson had said the night before, there were no casualties of a human nature, only historical.

Gasoline poured on the wall. A simple match. Fire. Whomever did it wasn't exactly going out of their way to be original.

CSU had also put their initial findings in the file. The perp had walked in the soft ground with bare feet. Without mud, there were no signs of skin texture or identifying marks. Dew frowned. Would have been so much better if the perp had worn shoes. At least then they'd have something.

Based on the indention of the prints, CSU guessed the perp was male and somewhere around 170lbs. Height was between 5'8 and 6 six feet. CSU found no scraps of fabric, no threads, and no other chemicals. The perp had been careful. Dew both loved and hated careful criminals. They provided a challenge, sure, but that also meant they were likely to repeat offenses. Sometimes that meant more innocent people died.

He flipped back to Aninzo's report and frowned. The last paragraph wasn't in the same voice as the rest of the document. It was as though someone else had written the final summation or a portion had been excised. He opened the report's header page and hissed through his teeth. The report had been written by Investigator Aninzo, edited by Senior Investigator Brett Cullum, and then reviewed by Arson Director Thomas Novak.

"Well, that explains it," Dew muttered. Novak was a prick of the highest order. Dew had worked with the man before and had no doubt the report's sloppy ending was his. Probably Aninzo or Cullum had written a summation he didn't like and he'd replaced it with his own shitty writing. "Probably Aninzo," he said aloud. Would certainly track with Novak's view of women.

He opened a black notebook on his desk and started writing. As the pen scratched against the pad, he looked up at the report. Gasoline. Match or some other incendiary ignition device. Bare feet. Fire before dawn.

Dew tapped his pen against the notebook and closed his eyes. The crime scene photos and CSU photos showed the fire's aftermath. The shotgun shacks had collapsed like dominos once the flames had weakened the structures. The report had also contained some historical pictures and a brief history of the shacks. He doubted Aninzo wrote that portion so much as ripped it from one of the internet sites.

He opened his eyes and flipped through the photos again. CSU had taken dozens of hi-res, digital photos. They'd photographed every angle of the burned out hulks. He zoomed in on areas of the images, trying to find any details CSU might have missed in their reports. When he flipped past the pictures of the houses, he came across a darkened image. The metadata description said it was a photo of a symbol left on the blacktop. There were four such pictures, but he wasn't able to tell what they were pictures of.

Dew flipped back to the Arson Division's report and read it again. There was no mention of a symbol, or anything left on the blacktop. He went back to the report's header page and clicked on Aninzo's email address. He added Cullum to the CC field and referenced the case number in the title.

Investigator Aninzo:
CSU included photos of a "symbol" found near the site. However, I find no evidence of it in your report. Can you please elaborate as to why?

He signed the email and sent it. His computer let out a ding as the email left the server. Dew stood from the desk and shrugged into his neat, blue suit jacket. He needed to visit the site. This time of day it was going to be hotter than hell, but the photos weren't enough to give him a feel for the area. Time to do a little investigating of his own.

Chapter 8

The small, bustling cafe felt like home. Dew's nose twitched at the smell of fresh coffee, grilling meat, and spices. As usual, the crowd was a mix of races and dress. The counter was stacked with customers waiting to order and or carry away their food. Dew walked past the line and toward a table near the back of the restaurant.

A husky man sat in front of a cup of coffee reading a book. A salt and pepper shoulder-length pony-tail lay flat against his back. Dew pulled an empty chair out from the table. The man didn't look up. Dew shrugged out of his suit coat, hung it on the back of the chair, and sat.

"Señor?" a female voice said.

"Isabel," Dew said and turned to face the middle-aged Cuban woman. "Coma estas?"

"Bien," she said. "Un café?"

"Yes, please," Dew said.

"Señor Downs? More coffee?"

The man across the table looked up and smiled. "Por favor," he said.

The waitress nodded. "We eating lunch?" she asked with a knowing smile.

"Yes," Dew said. "We most definitely are."

She nodded again and scurried away from the table and into the back.

Dew turned and faced Downs. "Tony? I thought you were just going to keep reading your book."

Tony shrugged and placed the book on the table. "Sorry. Latest Lansdale." He sipped his coffee. "Kind of got caught up in it."

"Right," Dew said. "How you doing? Long time no see."

Tony blushed. "Yeah, sorry about that. Wasn't able to get away from the hospital last week." He shook his head. "We've had an outbreak of psychotic episodes. Between Molly and bath salts, I'm beginning to pine for the crack epidemic."

Dew laughed. "Please tell me these folks aren't taking both?"

Tony smiled. "Man, I hope not. How the hell are you, Dew?"

The cop shrugged. "Doing okay. The heat is bringing out the worst in people. As usual. Other than that, nothing too big going on."

"Besides the Gomez case," Tony said, eyes gleaming.

Now it was Dew's turn to blush. "Besides that, yeah."

"You think the cartel's going to come after you?" Tony asked.

"Um, no," Dew said. "They have better things to do. Like figure out how they're going to shiv him."

"If only. I'm sure they'll make a statement sooner or later," Tony said. He leaned back as Isabel appeared and placed a cup in front of Dew. She poured fresh coffee from a battered, steel pot into the cup and refilled Tony's. "Gracias," Tony said. Isabel smiled at him and disappeared. "Don't they usually make their statements with a body count?"

Dew lifted the coffee, inhaled the strong scent, and sipped. The hot fluid burned his tongue, but it tasted too good for him to care. He growled in satisfaction and placed the cup back on the table. "I needed that," he said.

Tony giggled. "It's 103° outside, your shirt is covered in sweat, and instead of a cold drink, you're going to snarf down volcanic coffee?" He shook his head. "I think we need to have a session."

The detective smiled. "Didn't realize my shirt was soaked." He stared down at the dark sleeve of his white shirt. "Besides, you're drinking coffee."

Tony shrugged. "I've also been sitting in frigid air conditioning."

"Point," Dew said. "I imagine I reek."

"Only of diesel fumes," Tony said. "Where the hell have you been?"

Dew sighed. "On a case. You hear about the shacks?"

Tony nodded. "Historical site, sure. You went there?"

"Yeah," Dew said and blew on his coffee before taking another experimental sip. "Was looking for anything out of the ordinary."

"Did you find it?" Tony asked.

"Not really," Dew said.

He'd driven to the site through crowded traffic and the hellish temperature. With the police scanner squawking in the background, Dew had tried to listen to music, but every two songs, the DJ had broken in with the heat alerts. Ozone was off the charts and the heat index was expected to reach 108°. Basically, any outside activity was discouraged.

Which is why when he stepped out of the car and into the heat, he had to smile. Construction workers, EMS, and stupid cops like him were the only people out in the inclement weather.

The trip was mostly a waste of time. The burned out shacks looked just as they had in the CSU photographs. The few scraps of wood that hadn't burned were already covered with graffiti, despite the yellow crime scene tape. Dew sighed as he stepped over the tape line and walked the site.

As Aninzo's report had pointed out, the fire definitely started at the eastern edge and moved west to the end of the block. The uniforms had questioned the folks in the crowd after the fire and received no cooperation at all. The blacks were convinced it was the Klan. The latinos? White supremacists. Dew thought gang payback was more likely, but that was a long-shot too.

The arson investigator had postulated the fire was set by an individual. Dew's experience told him she was right. On more than one occasion, crooked real estate developers had hired freelance firebugs to clear areas. The perps were almost always caught. The mob occasionally firebombed rival gangs, as did the cartels. But it was never done this carefully; there was almost always a history of the site that pointed to some kind of violence between crews. This, an historic site, was something completely different.

The site was far away from the gentrification trend sweeping through the Heights and Memorial area. This was the ghetto. A developer would have to be insane to attempt to move in. Plus, any incursion into the neighborhood would be met with serious opposition from advocates for housing equality. In other words, there were better places to build new housing. No, this wasn't a rogue real-estate developer or organized crime situation. It just didn't add up.

But that left the question—why would someone target the shacks? The white supremacy angle sort of fit, but there had been no incidents involving them in a long time. Between the cartels and the Latino and black gangs, there was little room for skinheads to maneuver without incurring complete and total war. And with that much firepower after them, they'd be wiped out in no time.

Dew made a mental note to check with the gang task force. Another long-shot, but it had to be done.

"Yo."

Dew turned from the site to face the street. A large black woman, a sheen of sweat covering her forehead, stared at him. Rolls of fat jutted out over her bright, red shorts. The detective waved and smiled. "Yes, ma'am?"

"What you doing here? Can't you see that's off-limits?" she asked.

Dew reached in his shirt and pulled out his shield. "Detective Dewhurst, HPD."

"Oh," she said. "You trying to figure out who's burning us out?"

He raised an eyebrow. "Yes, ma'am. Although I wasn't aware there had been more fires."

"There ain't been," she said. "But somebody crazy enough to burn them shacks gonna come after the rest of the hood eventually."

He stepped over the crime scene tape, pulled out a notebook, and approached the woman. "Can I get your name, miss?"

"Jenkins. Latisha."

Dew scribbled her name in the book. "May I ask your address?" She told him and he wrote more notes. "Did the officers interview you yesterday?"

She shook her head. "By the time I woke up, they was all gone. Didn't no one talk to me."

"All right. So let me ask you, Miss Jenkins—you see anyone around here that didn't belong?"

She narrowed her eyes. "You mean like a white boy?"

"Perhaps," Dew smiled. "Race doesn't matter so much, ma'am. Have you seen anyone you didn't recognize?"

She shrugged. "I don't pay much attention to all that. But the hood ain't talking 'bout no one."

"Right," he said. He placed the notebook back in his suit coat. Rivulets of sweat poured down his face. He pulled out a handkerchief and wiped them away, the white cloth square instantly soaked. "Can you do me a favor?" he asked.

Latisha put her hands on her hips. "Is it gonna help you catch the man that did this?"

"I hope so," he said. "And why do you think it was a man?"

"Only a white boy be stupid enough to do something like this," she said. Her voice had become jagged and hateful.

"I'll keep that in mind," Dew said. "Can you ask your neighbors if they've seen anyone suspicious?" He produced a card and offered it to her. "I promise any calls will be anonymous."

She harrumphed. "We heard that before."

"Not from me, you haven't," Dew said.

The woman took the card, read it, and looked up at him. "Okay, Detective. I'll ask 'round."

"Thank you, ma'am," he said. Latisha nodded to him and headed back down the street.

Dewhurst had suffered the heat and walked the site, comparing the wreck to his memory of the CSU photos. The footprints the investigators had found were marked with stakes. Dewhurst knelt down and stared at the indentations. Size 11, maybe. Wide feet. Dew pulled out his notebook and jotted down some notes.

Drops of sweat marked the paper and the black ink had smudged in places. Dew had closed the notebook, returned it to his jacket, and taken one last look at the site. Fire investigations were always hit and miss, but usually on the miss side. Arson division could use chemical analysis and other forensic tools. Cops could only look for blatant evidence.

Feeling defeated, he'd returned to the car and sat in the air conditioning for five minutes before putting it in gear. He'd driven through the neighborhood scanning the dilapidated houses and seeing who was out and about. With the heat wave in full swing, Dewhurst saw no one on the streets. The start of the school year was only a week away, but the heat was keeping the kids inside.

Ghetto or not, the houses weren't tagged. Their lawns were half-dead, but that was the same with most of the city. August in Houston was always bad, but this was the worst Dew could remember.

When he'd realized it was time to meet Tony, he'd quit roaming the neighborhood and headed back downtown. Unless Tony had had another emergency at the hospital, he'd be there. Dew had hoped he would be.

"Dew?" Tony asked.

The detective blinked. "What did you say?"

"Yeah," Tony said, "you were off in cop land."

"Guess I was," Dew said with a blush.

Tony waved his hand. "No worries. So you didn't find anything?"

"Not really," Dew said. "I'm sure Arson will have some more for me soon. I think I'm going to have to visit them tomorrow."

Downs took a sip of coffee. "That should be fun. Seen Jackson lately?"

Dew smiled. "Let's say we tied one on last night."

Tony laughed. "A shame I wasn't there."

"Uh-huh." Dew tested his coffee, found it had cooled, and took a long draught. He purred. "I really wish these Cubans would come make coffee at the office."

"Don't we all," Tony agreed. "So how is Jackson? Haven't talked to him in a while."

Dew laughed. "Jackson is Jackson, Tony. You know that. He keeps diving into the work, into the booze, and into his girlfriend."

"That was classy," Tony grinned.

The detective shrugged. "I have my moments. He's doing fine, Tony."

"Okay," Tony said and sighed. "I worry about him."

"I won't tell him you said that. It'll just continue his absurd ideas that you have a crush on him."

Tony rolled his eyes. "Because he's such a sexy man," Tony lisped. "Seriously, he's not my type."

Dew stared into his cup of coffee.

"Dew?"

He looked up at Tony. "What?"

"You've got that look. What's going on with you?" Tony asked.

"Drove by the warehouse district last night," Dew said.

Tony's brows scrunched together. "I'll bet that was fun."

Dew nodded as a plate appeared in front of him. A steaming Cuban sandwich, dill pickle spear, and thinly cut fries. He looked up at the waitress. "Thank you, Isabel."

She smiled at him and put a plate in front of Tony. "I'll bring you both some water," she said and disappeared.

"How does that woman move so fast?" Dew asked.

Tony grinned. "She does move fast." He picked up his sandwich in his hands. "You okay, man?"

Dew nodded. "Sorry. Just had a melancholy moment."

"You're allowed," Tony said. He bit into the sandwich and his face lit up with pleasure. "I love this place."

Dew stared down at the sandwich. He wasn't sure he was hungry anymore. He lifted it to his mouth and took a bite. His stomach didn't care about his mood—it wanted the food. Dew munched on the spiced ham, pickles, and cheese.

Chapter 9

Sweat stains had already flowered beneath his armpits. He could feel the moisture, but didn't mind—he felt cool. With the heatwave frying the blacktop and concrete jungles, you were supposed to stay inside. P no longer noticed. The heat felt good, reassuring. It made his God happy and that's what mattered.

The neighborhood was quiet. Kids weren't playing outside. Most folks were at work and that left little for him to worry about. Without the incredibly hot weather, people might be walking their dogs or biking along the heated roads.

He stopped at an intersection, carefully looked both ways, and then traveled through to the next street of houses. The wards were full of old homes, many of them over sixty years old. For Houston, a city constantly rebuilding itself, houses that old were considered ancient. They might have been renovated by new occupants, but most were in their original state with some new boards or plank, and "fresh" paint jobs. He'd driven this same route at night, looking for cars in driveways and lights in the homes.

Once God had spoken to him, he'd purchased a used car for cash, affixed magnetic decals, and stolen a uniform. Pretending to be an employee with a "home security" company afforded him invisibility in the neighborhood and allowed him to survey possible targets with anonymity.

The "McMansions," homes where the owners had bought a property and razed the existing building in favor of crushingly huge new abodes, were out of place. This particular subdivision, buried in the heart of Houston, showed a great discrepancy in wealth. Some of the new houses were even for sale, or had foreclosure signs on them. More fallout from the housing crisis where owners went too far into debt to build their dreams. P hoped God would find them wanting the lick of flame.

God had been silent today. That didn't stop him from speaking to Him, asking Him questions. But the deity was being cagey today. He felt It looking through his eyes, scanning the same houses and streets. It flicked his eyes back and forth, searching, deciding, choosing. When He made a decision, He would let P know. Until then, he had to keep driving the streets.

The fire had drawn attention and lots of it. The neighborhood of mostly black and Latinos had all come out to watch the fire and the resulting cleanup. He'd watched it through his networked cameras placed on the surrounding houses. P had also seen the woman that found His sigil.

God had told him it might be a problem. God wasn't afraid of them seeing the sigil, and God wasn't afraid of the attention it might bring. But it was too soon. Too soon.

P had run her image through the databases and found her. Emilyza Aninzo. Filipino by birth, naturalized American citizen. Arson tech. It hadn't taken P long to dig through her past. Degrees in chemistry and history. Plenty of dissertations on the molecular changes involved in energetic expression. In other words—fire.

The man she'd spoken with was Brett Cullum, her boss. Another person with an extensive chemistry background, but he was more a bureaucrat than anything else. He would get any information from Aninzo, not ferret it out himself. God had told him to mark the man, but not to be concerned. But the woman...

Here, God said.

P flinched and slowed the car. He'd been so lost in thought, he wasn't even sure what street he was on. He pulled over to the side and looked left and then right. Cookie cutter houses interspersed with McMansions lined the street. He frowned. Jude Street. Near Howard. P closed his eyes and relaxed. They flicked open as if on their own and then slid sideways.

His eyes settled on a brown ranch house. The building was old and in need of a fresh paint job, but it was clean and well maintained. His eyes moved upward to the canopy of oak and pine trees sprouting up from the backyard. P read the address.

Will you remember? God asked.

P nodded. "I will," he said aloud.

Then remember. And begin.

He looked in the rearview mirror to ensure cars weren't creeping up on him. Someone walked out of the house across from the target. A man in his 60s limped down the walk and to the mailbox. The man waved to him. P waved back and stepped on the gas. He'd made a note of that address too.

The old man had seen him, but showed no sign of recognition. That was good, but not necessary. His route had taken him through these streets and neighborhoods for months. No one would even think about his presence, especially not some old fart just running to the mailbox.

But he could, the voice said.

"Yes," P agreed, "he could."

You'll look up the house. You'll find what I want.

"I will."

P stopped at the next intersection, checked for cars and drove through. He wasn't going back through this way again today—that *would* cause suspicion. Instead, he took the road to the freeway and headed toward the next section of his daily patrol.

"I will," he said again to no one. God said nothing. P smiled to himself as he drove. It would be time soon. It would be time to loose God Flame.

Chapter 10

A thick blanket of clouds clothed the moon. P stared up at the wan moon-light that made its way through the veil. He could barely make out the thin crescent shape. He wanted to stay and watch it fall below the horizon as the sun came up, but there was no time. He had to leave. Now.

He secured the last camera and stared down at his phone to confirm it was correctly positioned. The camera showed a faraway house set at a diagonal. He slid his thumb to the left and the camera zoomed in. P smiled. *Perfect.*

He slipped the phone into his pocket and made his way down from the rooftop. The under construction McMansion three doors down from his target was both taller and further back from the street. P was sure they'd knocked down at least two houses to make the monstrosity. The oaks in the large lot were tall and full of leaves, both brown and green. P had made short work of climbing up the largest trunk. The climbing spikes had proved difficult at first, but he'd managed. A few internet searches, how-to videos, and he'd been ready to use them.

Once in the canopy, P had spent more than half an hour finding the perfect angle. He'd been forced to pull the clippers from his belt and saw through some smaller limbs to thin the crown of leaves. When he finished, the camera showed a long view of the target's roof and one bay window. The single-story house had seemed to glow with Ghere's blessing.

With the cameras placed in the unfinished house's second floor window as well as the trees in the backyard, his job was done. This part anyway.

Once he had a chance to review the video, he'd know exactly how to approach his target. And then he would perform the ritual and make God stronger.

P slid the rest of his tools into his belt and started his walk down the mostly finished stairs. The McMansion's construction had stopped altogether due to the financial crunch. Some of its walls were up and much of the house had been paneled, but Tyvek still wrapped the majority of the outside.

The wooden steps creaked beneath his weight, but he didn't flinch or worry. Frog, cricket, gecko, and birdsong filled the night with enough noise to block out any sounds he might make. Being seen was the bigger risk.

He'd parked his car three blocks south. Dressed all in black and carrying a backpack of tools, he'd made a circuitous route through the neighborhood to get to the McMansion. That trek had taken nearly an hour. He'd had to skirt around teenagers, midnight joggers, and even a cop car. Hiding behind hedges, bushes, and gardens had left his black pants and shirt filthy with dirt. His mask was wet with sweat, but he hadn't even noticed.

Retreating from the house was going to be more difficult. The moon was lower in the sky and people were beginning to stir. The crazies that tried to jog in the "cool" of the day would be getting up soon to pound the pavement. The temperature? A balmy 91°.

P figured he had 45 minutes to make it back to the car before it became impossible to move without arousing suspicion. He took one last look at the phone and ran through the cameras to make sure they were right. Satisfied, he placed it back in his pocket and began his slow prowl back through the blocks.

Do you know when?

He smiled beneath his mask. The deity had been silent as he went about his work, but he could hear It sigh in his mind when he had the cameras sighted in. *Tomorrow,* he told It.

Yes, It said. Its voice was a purr in his mind. *New world. New life.*

Yes, P agreed. He hid behind a tall hedge as a car made its way down the street. A single, dim headlight cut the remaining night, illuminating driveways and burnt lawns. P wondered if the driver had even realized all the street lights were out. He hoped the early morning joggers would notice and head back inside. He checked his watch and hissed—he was an hour behind schedule.

He flitted through the hedge and rounded the house's corner. A row of bushes had been allowed to coalesce into a single bushy line. He duck-walked behind them, barely able to hear his own feet on the hard ground.

The shade from the bushes coupled with the torturous drought had long ago removed any grass. He stopped when the bushes ended and peeked around the corner.

The way was clear on both sides. Grinning beneath the mask, he stepped out from behind the last bush and ran across the street. His gloved fingers grabbed the top of a wooden fence and he vaulted over it. Panting from the exertion, and the incredible heat, P ran through a back-yard, jumped another fence, and made his away around a pool. He started for the next fence when he heard a door close.

He immediately squatted next to the fence and waited. The house had a front-porch light that was on. Through the cracks in the fence, he made out the silhouette of a tall man jogging in place. P held his breath and waited. The man's arms reached up to his ears and the man was gone. P heard the sound of running shoes on concrete and he smiled.

P waited until his breath calmed. If the jogger was coming back for something, it would happen now. He felt It grin inside his mind. P rose from his spot, leaped up, and swung over the wooden boards. When he hit the ground, he was in the jogger's back yard.

He pulled the tool belt off and headed toward the blind side of the house. His backpack waited for him. The clothes in the backpack were sweaty, but not drenched like the ones he wore. He pulled on a pair of running shorts, a muscle shirt, socks, and running shoes. It took a moment for him to fold his castoffs so they fit in the pack without making a lump. The tools took even more time, but he wasn't worried now. He checked his watch again and smiled. It had only taken him fifteen minutes to make it back here. He thanked the falling moon, zipped up the pack, and shrugged into it.

"Final touch," he said aloud. He pulled a pair of ear buds from his shorts pocket and placed them in his ears. He tethered the other end to his phone and dropped it back in the pocket. After a deep breath, he swung open the gate and stepped into the easement between the two houses.

He stuck his head around the corner to make sure no one was looking. Satisfied he was alone, P jogged out onto the street and headed down the block. When he reached the car, he made a big scene of stretching, pulling a plastic tube from the pack's top, and pretending to drink. When he was certain anyone who might be watching would just see a midnight jogger returning to his car, he typed in the combination to the door, opened the car, and stepped in.

The backpack lay on the passenger seat. He pulled the keys from the console, started the car, and cranked the A/C. Rock music whispered from the speakers. He changed all the vents to point toward his sweaty face and breathed deeply.

We must leave now, Its voice said in his mind.

"I know," he answered It. He put on his seatbelt and put the car in gear. P checked both ways before pulling out into the deserted street. In no time at all, he was at the freeway and on his way home.

Chapter 11

E my sipped her coffee. It was her fourth and it had finally cleared away the morning fog. When she awoke that morning, the sun was already above the horizon and burning the city with 95° heat. The only saving grace was the layer of puffy white clouds obscuring the sun. As usual, no rain in sight, and none expected.

More car fires on the freeways, more brush fires in the Big Pine forest. HFD wasn't the only fire department on high alert and responding to blazes. The Forestry Service was already calling for help from municipalities near Nacogdoches. Emy was starting to wonder if Texas was going to have any forest left before the summer was over. At this point even the weather forecasters were praying for a storm.

The high pressure system that had been sitting over the state simply would not move. Other states were getting pounded with rain and severe weather, but East Texas was a dead-zone for moisture.

Her phone rang. Emy glanced at the LED display, smiled, and picked it up. "Emy."

"It's Brett. But you knew that," her boss' lilting voice said. "We have a visitor. Meet us in con 4."

"Um, okay," she said.

Brett laughed through the phone. "See you in a minute."

She hung up the phone and stared at it, her stomach tightening as the butterflies returned. The detective had arrived. Someone new to embarrass herself in front of.

Emy rose on unsteady feet, coffee cup and notebook in hand, and headed out of her cube. Novak stood near conference room 4, his rumpled blue suit adding to his sour expression. She stopped in mid-step, stared down at her coffee cup, and shuffled toward the break room. It was one thing to face off against Novak in his office with Brett present. It was something else to be alone with the man in a conference room. Emy wasn't afraid of Novak and he wasn't particularly menacing. It was really down to the fact that he made her uncomfortable, partly because he was the big boss, and partly because she tended to stutter around him. If he was already unhappy the cop was coming to visit, the last thing she needed was for him to prep-talk her into what not to say.

She placed her cup in the machine, selected the darkest grind available, and hit the buttons. The machine whirred as it ground the beans. Emy watched as shards bounced against the transparent plastic shield, and tried to control her breathing.

Brett could have called her earlier. He could have warned her. He could have left Dewhurst in the conference room and then grabbed her. She smirked. That would have been better and she bet Brett knew it. The man was constantly trying to get her out of her shell. Forcing an encounter like this was exactly the kind of shit he liked to do.

Last week when they were at a bar, Brett had intentionally chatted up a stranger so he'd join them at the table. Amidst the drinking college students and gen-Xers, she, Brett, and Lee had gone to the bar to enjoy a little people-watching and drinks. Brett had insisted they go to the swank "Malone's" rather than their usual haunts. Emy had wondered about that until they arrived.

Instead of one of the bars in midtown that had a large gay presence, "Malone's" was downtown, historical, and all about Irish Whiskey, Scotch, and Micro-brews. In other words, it was the kind of place to meet single men. Single hetero men.

The heavily lacquered table they sat at wasn't in the corner—it was right smack in the middle of the bar. Lee and Brett talked with her, laughed with her, but their eyes were always shifting around her. And then Brett had left the two of them alone.

Lee had continued telling her stories about Fire Island in the 70s and the Stonewall Rebellion, sipping his drink in-between anecdotes. Emy had tried to ignore what she knew was coming, but even Lee's tales failed to remove the butterflies in her stomach and the sudden desire to crawl under the table.

Brett had returned with a relatively good-looking man in his thirties. The newcomer slid a rum and coke in front of Emy and took a seat next to her. Brett touched her shoulder. "Emy? This is Bryan."

The man's face was lit in a shy grin. His black goatee and mustache were well-trimmed, but his cheeks were covered in stubble. Bryan's red polo shirt had a Texans logo. He offered his hand. Emy shook it and made sure her grip was firm.

"Hi, Bryan. Nice to meet you," she said, and fought the urge to try and cover her facial scars with her other hand.

Bryan nodded. "Nice to meet you too, Emy." He dropped her hand and cradled his pint. He gestured toward Brett. "Your friend tells me you're a cop?"

She glared at Brett who sheepishly smiled. Emy cleared her throat, brushed a lock of hair down over her scars, and turned to face Bryan. "Not a cop, exactly. Investigator."

"Oh," Bryan said. His deep-brown eyes looked black in the dim bar. "What kind of investigator?"

"Fire," Emy said and took a sip of her drink. "Brett and I are in the arson business."

"Really?" Bryan raised his eyebrows.

She nodded. "Really." Brett and Lee sat close together and holding hands. "And Brett is my boss."

He giggled. "Your boss takes you out for drinks?"

She rolled her eyes. "If he wasn't with Lee, I'd sue for sexual harassment."

Brett and his husband laughed. Bryan shook his head.

"So what do you do, Bryan?"

The man paused with his drink halfway to his mouth. He looked down at the table, a frown across his face. "I set fires," he said in a halting voice. The table went silent for a moment and he started laughing.

"Good one," Emy said and downed the rest of her drink.

Brett and Lee looked at one another. "I think," Lee said as he shook his empty glass, ice rattling like dice, "it's time to get another." He stood up.

"I'll go with you. I think I owe Emy one." He nodded at Bryan. "You need another."

"Please," Bryan said. Brett smiled and he and Lee headed to the bar. Bryan turned to Emy. "I don't set fires. I, um, I'm a curator at the Museum."

Emy's mouth opened and slowly closed. She giggled at the embarrassed expression on his face. "Which one?"

"The Menil," he said.

"One of my favorites!" Emy smiled. "I love to walk the surrealist gallery. All the Magritte paintings. I could just stare at them for hours."

Bryan nodded. "I love to walk those too. But I'm really more of an ancient art guy."

"Ah. Is that the gallery you curate?" Emy asked.

"Sadly, no," Bryan said and finished his beer. "They've stuck me with the Americana."

"You don't sound enthused." Emy ran a hand through her hair. "Don't like the Americans?"

Bryan shrugged. "Not really into the 60s art. And that's mostly what I do."

"So you wander the surrealist exhibit, pine for the ancient art exhibit while showing off and acquiring soup cans?"

He smiled. "Pretty much. The woman who runs ancient art is about as ancient *as* the art. When she retires, I'm next in line. Or," he said as he rolled the empty pint glass between his hands, "I'll move on to the HMNS."

"Another of my faves," she said. The Houston Museum of Natural Science had the dinosaurs, the gems, and quite a few galleries of ancient artifacts. "Did you want to be an archeologist?"

"Yeah," he said. "But afraid my asthma keeps me from being a digger."

She nodded. "I could see that."

"So instead of being out there in the world," Bryan said, "I hide in the darkened buildings and take care of history."

"'Take care of history.' I like that," Emy said. "Someone needs to."

Bryan hoisted his empty glass. "I'd drink to that...but..."

A fresh beer appeared at his elbow. A hand placed a vodka tonic in front of Emy. Brett and Lee stood behind her with fresh drinks in their hands.

"Sorry," Lee said. "Took a while to get the bartender's attention."

"Uh-huh," Emy said. She turned to Bryan. The man was blushing.

They'd talked through the evening until nearly midnight. Brett and Lee had left the bar shortly after 11. Since they had driven her to the bar, Bryan took her home.

When they reached her house, Bryan stopped the car at the curb.

"Thank you for a great night," Emy said and leaned over to kiss him on the cheek. Bryan had tried to turn his face aside to meet her lips. She pulled back and smiled. "Another time?" she said.

Bryan sighed, his face flushed. "Sorry."

Emy smiled. "Another time?" she repeated.

"Yes. I hope so," Bryan said.

Emy squeezed his knee and stepped out of the car. Bryan's car lingered for a moment until she turned to look back. He was staring at her, an embarrassed smile on his face. Emy waved. He saluted, put the car in gear, and drove away.

As she'd cuddled with her dog and tried to sleep, she'd played the night over and over again in her head. Intimacy was her enemy. She wondered if she'd ever manage to make it her friend.

Emy pulled the full coffee mug from the machine and let out a deep breath. She walked out of the break room and into the hallway. Novak was no longer skulking by the door, but the conference room was open. Emy walked to the room on rubbery legs. This was the first time she'd interacted with a detective. Brett usually took these kinds of meetings, but the cop had insisted on discussing the case with her.

Prepared for mental combat, she entered the conference room. The lights filled the windowed conference room in a glare. Brett sat next to Detective Dewhurst while Novak sat across the table from them. He raised his eyes as she walked to the middle of the table. Dewhurst broke contact with Brett and stood. Brett clumsily followed his example. Emy placed her coffee and notebook on the table.

"I'm Detective Dewhurst, Ms. Aninzo." The tall man extended a hand. Emy stared at it a moment before shaking. "Pleased to meet you."

Emy simply nodded—her voice wasn't working. She let go of his hand and sat. Dewhurst and Brett followed suit. When she glanced at Novak, his face was more sour than ever. She ignored him and looked at the detective. The man's face was set in a gentle smile.

"No offense to anyone in the room," Dewhurst said, "but I'd have to say that was the best report I've ever read from this office."

Emy blushed. "Thank you, Detective."

"Call me Dew," he said.

Emy couldn't help but smile. "Dew then. I'm Emy."

"Emy then." Dew folded his hands on the table. "As I said, the report was extremely well written. Except, of course, for the summary." The man's eyes bored holes in Novak. "Which I feel didn't come to any cogent conclusions."

Novak cleared his throat and glared back at the cop.

Dew turned to Emy. "And that's why I'm here. The photos included in the files showed a dark smudge against asphalt. But there were no notes regarding what it was, or what it meant."

Brett waved a hand to Emy as if to say "your turn."

Emy pulled the laptop sitting in the middle of the desk toward her. She typed in her name and password and the screen came to life. After tapping a few buttons, the projector whirred and a blazing rectangle of light appeared on the wall. Emy tapped through a number of folders and finally found what she was looking for. She dragged the images over to the shared screen. It went black as the first unfiltered image of the sigil appeared.

She tapped a button on the desk and the conference room light dimmed. "This is one of the original photographs. It's actually the best of them," she said. With her face staring at the projected screen, she dragged the mouse cursor, and outlined the nearly invisible shape. "If you look long enough at it, you'll notice some slight discoloration. It's still difficult to make out. But," she said and dragged her filtered image to the projector.

Dewhurst growled in his throat. "That's more like it," he said. The man's eyes studied the picture.

The only sound in the room besides the projector's fan was Novak's breathing. The silence seemed suffocating to her. She glanced at Brett. He looked as uncomfortable as she felt.

When Dew finally spoke, she nearly jumped. "You think that's a signature," he said.

Emy stuttered. "Y-yes I think it is."

He nodded, eyes still fixed on the screen. "Never seen anything like that." He broke his stare and his eyes found hers. "Outside of a metal album cover."

She loosed a nervous laugh. Dew smiled.

"It does bear some resemblance," she admitted. "But see how it's incongruous? I've looked across some symbols in the database and most are, shall we say, more regular?"

"Right," he nodded. "Looks more like something a kid doodled. Except for the circle, that is. The lines are kind of—"

"Jittery," Emy finished for him. She turned back to the screen. "Yet it looks like that was done purposefully and carefully."

Dew nodded. "So what does this mean?" he asked.

Emy glanced at Brett. His normally easy smile had disappeared and his eyes flicked toward Novak. Finally, he nodded to her.

"It means to me it's a signature. In fact, it may be something we missed before," she said in shaky voice.

Dew nodded again. "You think this is the beginning or a continuation of a serial."

Emy glanced at Brett again. His eyes smiled.

"Yes," Emy said. "I think it is."

The detective took out a notepad from inside his suit jacket. He scribbled something with a gold Montblanc pen. "Ms. Aninzo, can you send me that file, please?"

"Yes, Detective," Emy said. Her breath was a little ragged. She didn't dare stare back at Novak; she could feel the man's eyes burning holes into the back of her head. "I'll have that for you as soon as I return to my desk."

He put the pen and notebook back in his jacket, his face lit with an amused smile. "Thank you, Emy." He turned to Brett. "I'll need to be informed of any other evidence related to the case. Should your department find anything else, I assume you'll make sure I'm in the loop."

Brett nodded. "We're pretty much in a holding pattern until CSU finishes going over the evidence, but I'm confident they won't find anything else. Our bug seems pretty careful. He was barefoot when he lit the fire. That means to me this was planned with precision in mind."

Dewhurst nodded. "I agree. Which is why I found the report's 'conclusion' incomplete."

Novak cleared his throat again. "My people have shared everything with you, Detective."

"Now they have," Dew agreed. His bemused smile had disappeared. "I expect that will continue."

"Of course," Novak said between clenched teeth.

Dewhurst stood. The others did as well. He offered his hand again to Emy. "Thank you, Emy."

She shook his hand. "Very welcome, Dew."

He did the same with Brett and then turned to Novak. "Mr. Novak, may I have a word? In private?"

Novak's face darkened and the butterflies returned to her stomach. Emy turned off the laptop, grabbed her notebook and coffee, and headed out of the conference room with Brett in tow.

She heard the door close behind her. Emy sipped her coffee and headed back to her cube. She heard her boss's footsteps behind her. When they reached her desk, she sat down heavily in her chair. She loosed a deep sigh. "Well that was tense," she said.

Brett giggled as he leaned against the cube wall. "No shit. I think Dewhurst is bloodying Novak's nose."

Emy shook her head. "He doesn't have authority here," she said.

Her boss shrugged. "No. But that doesn't mean he can't bitch Novak out." He tapped the cube wall. "Make sure you send the detective that file."

Emy logged into her computer. "I'll do that right now," she said and turned to the screen.

"Oh, and Emy?" She turned back to him. He was grinning. "You did great."

"Thanks, Brett."

He clapped the side of the cube and left her alone. Emy took a deep breath, logged into her mail client, and attached the file to an email. She made sure to copy Brett and Novak on it and sent it off into the ether.

She wanted a drink. Either Dewhurst and Novak had crossed swords before, or the detective was aware of Novak's incredible incompetence. If that was the case, then Novak was going to be a serious pain in the ass should there be another incident. And Emy was certain there would be.

Chapter 12

The glass of sweetened iced tea sweated on a paper coaster. Dew sat in the mostly empty restaurant with his laptop on the table. He'd finished his meal more than twenty minutes ago. The waitress had come by several times, refilling his tea, and walking off without a word. She knew the drill. Dew often went there to eat and think.

He stared at the sigil on the screen. Emy's filters had managed to capture every single line and dot. He'd zoomed in several times and followed the pattern. She'd said the bug had marked it using gasoline. The fact she'd spotted a nearly evaporated signature against the blacktop was a miracle. Something Novak should have noticed.

Dew hid a sour belch behind his hand. Just thinking about Novak was enough to fill his belly with acid. The man was a complete and total asshole.

Once Emy and Brett had left the conference room, Dew had tented his hands and stared across the table at Novak. He let the silence of the room become oppressive before he spoke. "Hello, Tom. Nice to see you again."

Novak frowned. "Detective."

"You know," Dew said, "if you'd gotten a different dick on this case, you might have gotten away with it."

Novak rolled his eyes. "Gotten away with what? I simply didn't want to make some unsubstantiated theory known to the public."

"The public," Dew repeated. "You mean the Mayor. Or perhaps your cronies on the city council."

"That's bullshit," Novak bared his teeth.

"No," Dew smiled, "it's not. Do you remember the last time I called you on your political antics?"

Novak looked uncomfortable. "Detective, you have no authority over this office. And if you'll remember, I'm good friends with your Captain."

The cop smiled. "Yes, you are. Good friends with him. But there's something you might not realize, Mr. Novak." Dew leaned forward, his eyes predatory. "I don't give a shit. And in case *you* have forgotten, I'm on the Commissioner's short list to replace him."

Novak opened his mouth and then shut it. The man looked like he needed to take a shit. He squirmed in his chair and tried to smile. "Detective, let's put aside the old and focus on this case."

"Fine by me," Dew said, eyes glittering with menace.

"I'll make sure Mr. Cullum and Ms. Aninzo are at your disposal."

"Good," Dew said.

"But," Novak frowned, "I'm going to make sure Mr. Cullum knows I'm still in charge. I want to know everything that's going on."

Dew nodded. "Fair enough. I'm not here to fuck with your job, Novak, unless you fuck with mine."

Novak scowled. "I'll remember that, Dewhurst."

A grin slowly spread across the detective's face. "Then I think we're done here." Dew stood and offered his hand to the still seated Novak. "Good to see you, Tom."

The heavy man stood and shook Dew's hand. "Right," he said and gestured to the door.

The two men had exited the conference room as if they'd never seen one another before. Dew had stifled the urge to find Ms. Aninzo and Mr. Cullum. As much as he would have liked to talk to them in private, it wasn't the time. He'd have to wait until something else happened. Dew sipped his tea. And something would happen. He was convinced of that.

Serial offenders didn't have an easily discernible time-table. Their motivations were difficult to decipher, sometimes even after their capture. But while they were in the midst of their sprees, calendars meant nothing. The annals of abnormal psych were filled with murderers whose schedules were erratic. Some would go for years keeping to some strange annual date before their monstrous need finally made them slip-up. And it always did. Eventually.

Dew traced the sigil on the screen. What was this person trying to tell them? A signature meant more was to come. That much he knew. But this? This didn't look like something you'd find in a tattoo shop or on wikipedia. But if the symbol existed in any of the databases, Dew would find it. And then maybe he'd have some idea of what they were in for.

The detective slipped some sugar into his tea glass and used the straw to stir. He took a long draught and placed it back on the table. He wondered if Tony might have some thoughts about this bug and smirked. Tony would definitely have some ideas, but they wouldn't be helpful. Not until the bug struck again. He was certain Tony would tell him that too.

He leaned back, the old wood creaking. The meeting this morning had been tense. Anytime he shared a room with a pompous asshole like Novak, he had great difficulty keeping his vitriol in check. The worst part of the meeting, however, was watching how Ms. Aninzo's body language crumpled every time Novak looked at her.

"Emy," Dew said to himself. The woman was obviously intelligent and very good at her job. He'd noticed the way she'd sat with the scarred side of her face away from him. He'd seen the road of ruined flesh that stretched from her scalp down to her chin. The burned flesh looked old and as though some work had been done to repair it. The efforts had obviously failed.

Didn't matter. The woman was certainly self-conscious about them. What she didn't realize though, was they didn't ruin her beauty. Her dark almond eyes, skin, and figure made her a looker regardless of the blemish.

She'd found the sigil, managed to recognize it as a symbol rather than just a smudge on the street.

This, however, had no name to go with it. Even with the extensive image databases compiled by the FBI, there was no guarantee this symbol would show up. They might end up chasing their tails for months over this before finding something. And by then, the bug might have torched dozens of buildings.

Dew took another sip of tea. Could be a one time thing, he thought. But if someone left a signature, it was almost a guarantee there would be more incidents.

He flipped the laptop closed and stared at the wall of televisions. The sports channels were filled with images of past football games, current Astros losses, and noise about the upcoming NFL season. One screen had local news on it. Even without the sound or closed captioning, the car fires on the freeways crackled and burned in his mind. Video from a news chopper displayed fire after fire after fire.

Dew pulled a $20 from his wallet and placed it on the table. The waitress waved at him. Dew smiled at her, put the laptop back in his bag, and stood. He shrugged into his suit jacket and headed back out into the hellish heat, bad memories rattling in his mind.

Chapter 13

In the complete darkness, something stared at him. He could feel its unseen eyes examining his every cell. Waves of hate made his skin crawl. He could hear it breathing in the darkness. It sounded like a dragon.

The darkness was growing warm. His skin prickled against the growing heat. His scalp itched. The hairs on his naked arms and chest began to curl.

A pair of yellow eyes opened in the darkness. The pupils raged with crimson and orange flames, their baleful glow illuminating a misshapen face of ruined flesh and jagged teeth. The thing took in a deep breath. Nathaniel screamed as it exhaled blue flame.

Nathaniel opened his eyes and coughed. His normally dark room glowed with flickering light. The world smelled like burning plastic and wood. He coughed again and sat up, his eyes staring out the open bedroom door. His room wasn't glowing—the living room was on fire.

He leaped out of bed, his naked feet hitting the hot hardwood floor, and he started running. Once he made it to the hallway, he turned left, hand over his mouth to try and staunch the scorching air from burning his lungs. Each pump of his legs down the hallway was an exploration of pain.

The air was filled with smoke and incredible heat. Nathaniel ignored the pain and entered his daughter's bedroom. In the glow from the living room, he saw her lying flat on the bed. She was coughing and a line of drool slid down the corner of her lips. Nathaniel picked up his daughter. Her eyes flitted open in surprise.

He turned to the living room, hoping to make his escape, but the flames had reached the ceiling. Gutters of orange and red ran along the walls. A torrent of black smoke approached from the other side of the house.

His daughter was shrieking in terror, but he could barely hear her over the thumping of his heart and the crackling of the burning house. Nathaniel lifted a hand to the window and smashed it. A wave of pain wracked his arm as the glass punctured his skin and severed a tendon. Blood ran off the end of his hand. He punched the glass again to go through it, but a sound stopped him.

Nathaniel, daughter in his arms, turned toward the doorway. The wall of smoke approached. A pair of eyes stared out from it. A face smiled at him. Nathaniel screamed as the wall turned to fire and rushed toward him.

Chapter 14

The meat-truck had already arrived. Emy watched as the sheet-covered stretcher was wheeled to the waiting ambulance. She looked away and walked back into the site.

Smoke still curled from the hulk's west wall. The house had collapsed in the center. The metal outline of a couch still sat in the living room. The wood and fabric had burned away leaving little but warped steel and blackened springs.

They'd found the bodies in the eastern most room. She'd already taken dozens of pictures, including the bodies in situ. The fire hadn't just burned the bodies—it had turned their skin to charcoal. There wasn't much left in the room apart from the small bed-frame's metal supports.

The room had obviously belonged to a child or tween. The metal toy-box was scorched black, and stuffed animals inside had caught fire from the heat, but they'd still been recognizable. Dark marble eyes had stared up at her from its bottom.

She stared at the broken window. The glass had been pushed out, dried bloody smears marring its surface. Despite the collapsed roof, there were no dangling beams or supports that could have shattered the glass. It had either broken from the heat, which was unlikely, or one of the victims had knocked it out. Based on the sizes of the bodies, she imagined it was the father. The autopsy might reveal glass shards in the skin, or it might tell them nothing; bodies burned that badly didn't really hold a lot of forensic evidence.

But that was the thing. The fire made no sense. Instead of spreading through the entire house, it had snaked its way from the living room to the bedrooms. The other side of the house was burned, but it hadn't experienced the same amount of damage. The bedroom looked like it had taken a direct strike from a fireball.

The heat had been intense in the room, but it hadn't lasted. The fact some of the plaster was still intact spoke to that. She raised her eyes to the ceiling. It was charred, but it hadn't burned. That made no sense.

Emy stood by the window and slowly turned to face the door. The bowed-in roof was within her eye line. The two victims' mouths had been locked in terrified screams. *What were you looking at?*

They hadn't been looking at the roof. Or out the window. Instead, their bodies were turned to stare out the bedroom door. Emy tapped her foot. The monstrous creature from her dreams flicked into her mind. She shook it away and walked from the bedroom and into the living room.

As hot as the fire had been, it hadn't managed to burn all the way to the foundation. Even some of the floor was still intact. She stepped carefully across the path the firefighters had marked and into the backyard.

Brett was talking with one of the firefighters. Streams of sweat poured from his short dark hair, his smoke-stained coat lying on the concrete. As if the fire hadn't made things warm enough, the sun was pounding down with excruciating heat. It was only 9 in the morning and already it was in the high 90s.

Emy wiped a sheen of sweat from her brow and walked to the two men. Brett nodded to her and the firefighter smiled. A flush of embarrassment lit her face and she instinctively brushed a bang down to cover her scar.

Brett gestured to her. "This is Investigator Aninzo."

The firefighter's grin was boyish and flirty as he offered his hand. "I'm Jennings."

Emy took his hand and squeezed. "Nice to meet you, Mr. Jennings."

"Sergeant Jennings," Brett said, "was just telling me about the site when they arrived."

Jennings nodded. "Yeah. Call came in a little after half-past three. We got here in ten minutes."

Emy nodded. "Still on fire?"

The sergeant sucked his teeth. "Like you wouldn't believe. The middle of the house looked like one of those oil fires in Kuwait. Damned thing was just a geyser of flame."

Brett tapped his foot. "How long to get it under control?"

Jennings shrugged. "Too damned long," he said. "I guess we had it contained in about twenty minutes. But damn, it was hot."

Emy raised an eyebrow. "What do you mean?"

The firefighter sighed. "I mean when you put out a fire, you expect steam. You expect the water to evaporate from the heat, but for the flames to go out." He pointed to the middle of the house where the roof had caved in. "But that just didn't want to go out. The water just, well, this sounds crazy, but it just seemed to catch fire. We weren't spraying gasoline on it, but it acted like it."

Brett chuckled and Jennings glared at him. "Sorry, Sergeant." He tapped the man on the shoulder. "Was just trying to wrap my head around it."

A sigh escaped the firefighter's lips. "Man, I know how it sounds, Mr. Cullum. But," the man raised his hands, "it's the only way I can describe it."

Emy stared at the ground. "How long did that last?" she asked in a small voice.

"I don't know, ten minutes or so?" Jennings said. "Once the water started, um, behaving like water, the fire went out fast." He pointed toward the west wall. "There's still a hotspot over there, but it's heat, not fire. We'll walk the site again, see if we can find it and make sure it's out." He pulled a water bottle from his waist and took a long drink. "Christ, it's hot."

"No kidding," Brett said. "Thank you, Sergeant. We'll be in touch."

Brett and Emy were walking away when Jennings said "Hey, what was with the bodies?"

The two investigators stopped and turned toward him. "What about the bodies?" Brett asked.

Jennings licked his lips. "I've seen burned corpses before. But not like that. It's like—" He paused as he searched for the right words. "Like they were in a damned crematorium. Those were more than third degree."

Brett nodded. "I guess we'll have to wait for the pathologist reports." He nodded to Jennings. "Thank you for your help, Sergeant." The well-built man waved and headed back to the seven men by the bright red firetruck.

Emy and Brett headed to the front of the house. Despite the incredible heat of the fire, the grass looked as withered and burned as every other lawn on the block.

Brett pointed to the window next to the door. "The father's bedroom was right there. He could've grabbed the kid and made it out through that window."

She shook her head. "No way. By the time he reached her bedroom, the living room would have been a furnace." Emy stretched her back. "Didn't you see the way the hallway snaked? They'd have been burned to a crisp."

Her boss tapped his foot and the grass crunched beneath his heavy boots. "Guess you're right. We're going to have to run simulations." He looked at her expectantly.

Emy grinned. "You never could model worth a damn."

"Right," he said. "That's your job."

The front of the house was nearly untouched. Except for the buckled roof, it looked as though nothing had happened. "This is a strange fire, boss."

He nodded. "So was the first one." Brett pulled a notebook from his pocket and scribbled something. "We're going to need a full simulation and I want you to personally go over the CSU reports. I want to know if they find anything else."

"You know," she said, "Detective Dewhurst is going to want that too."

"Yes," Brett said. He turned and faced the row of houses across the street. Emy watched as his gentle smile disappeared into a frown. "No one saw anything," he said.

Emy cocked a brow. "Why do you say that?"

He shrugged. "That early in the morning, I seriously doubt anyone was awake. Unless we get lucky and a drunk came home late." Brett thought for a moment. "No. If this was our bug, no one saw anything."

"But we don't know it's our perp yet," Emy said. "I looked around the house. I didn't see anything resembling the symbol."

"I know," Brett said. "Just have a feeling."

Emy turned back to the house. If the bug started the fire, then he would have done so in the backyard. She hissed through her teeth and started walking up the driveway.

"Where you going?" Brett called.

She turned her head. "To see if you're right."

As she walked up the blazing hot concrete, she felt the eyes of the emergency responders. They were clumped together and talking in quiet voices. They're not looking at you, she thought to herself. Don't be so damned narcissistic.

She stopped beneath the burned out awning that used to connect the house to the exterior garage and scanned the backyard. Tall oak trees rose into the sky, their leaves browned from the drought. At least one of the skinny pines had died, probably from bark beetles. Its naked branches seemed out of place beside the giant oaks.

Chewing the inside of her cheek, she let her eyes look at nothing specific. They blurred in and out of focus as she tried to take in the entire yard. The scorched grass had many footprints. The firefighters had had to come through the back in order to get to the fire. Clumps of dirt and grass were spread over the ruined landscape. Her eyes spotted something near a dead pine.

She started walking, careful to try and place her feet in the heavy boot-prints. When the firefighters' boot marks stopped, she halted her advance. There were more prints near the pine. They were shallow and light, mere depressions compared to the large divots the responders had left in their wake.

Emy dug into the pocket of the jacket wrapped around her waist and pulled out a tiny red flag on a stick. She planted it at the end of the firefighter marks. Paying close attention to the grass around the shallow indentations, she walked beside them and planted a flag next to each one.

As she stuck the last flag into the hard earth, Brett's voice startled her.

"Found something?" he asked.

Emy flinched and stared up at him from her crouch. She spread her arms to encompass the route of the flags. "I think our bug was back here. Well," she said with a frown, "someone was."

He nodded and crouched down beside her, studying the prints. "Barefoot again."

"Yup," she agreed from beneath the canopy of one of the large oaks. Her eyes stared at the low part of the trunk and then slowly rose. She hissed through her teeth and brushed hair out of her face. "He climbed the tree."

"How?" Brett asked. "There are no low branches."

She pointed to the trunk. "See those indentations? Pretty sure he used spikes like tree-trimmers use."

"Fuck," Brett said. He tilted his head back to follow the line. The marks on the tree stopped at a large branch halfway up the canopy. "We'll need to get someone out here to take a peek."

She nodded. "If he left his calling card, I'm willing to bet it's up there."

"Yeah," he agreed and clapped her on the back. "Good job. Now let's get out of this heat before we melt."

Emy smiled as slick hair slid forward across her face. She squeezed the bangs and drops of water hit the parched ground. "Good thing I don't wear make up," she said.

The model danced on the screen as she twisted and turned it with delicate flicks on the touchpad. Unlike the shotgun shacks, the records department actually had blueprints on file for the Hartman house.

Creating a 3-D facsimile was fairly straightforward. As always, it was the interior of the house and the ignition points that had been difficult.

She leaned back in her chair, one hand fingering the necklace beneath her blouse. The virtual interior was coming together, but she still wasn't happy with it. Not as though she was ever happy with her models.

Brett knew she would get it finished by the end of the day. He set a deadline for next week, but Emy had created the thing after her shower. It hadn't taken more than 2 hours once she had the blueprints in hand. Now it was late afternoon and her nerves sizzled with too much coffee and not enough food.

The Shpongle soundtrack from her phone pounded into her ears. She hummed along with the wordless music as she hit the "play" button on the modeling interface. The model spun back to the original view of the backyard. A disembodied point of view slowly moved from the trees and through the sliding glass door.

Once inside, the playback paused. A rather unrealistic looking couch filled the screen. A small tendril of smoke rose from the center cushion. Virtual flames spread quickly across its surface. In a few seconds, the couch became a bright collection of rippling flames that reached the ceiling. The floor caught next. A rolling flood of fire spread toward the bedrooms.

The ceiling started to droop and caved in seconds later. The POV moved backward and followed the path of the fire to the little girls' bedroom. At that point, the simulation stopped.

Emy stared at the interior of the room from the doorway. She shook her head. It still made no sense.

The arsonist had obviously used an accelerant. The chemistry folks were still working to determine what it might have been, but nothing she knew of acted like this. Why did the flames only spread toward the occupied areas? Why was the other half of the home only singed in places rather than torched like the rest? And why the hell hadn't the flames consumed everything in their path?

She had worked out the probable temperature ranges for the fires in different parts of the house. While the living room had been nearly 700°, the bedroom where Mr. Hartman and his daughter had died was at well over 1000°. At that temperature, the room should have been completely destroyed. The wood should have disintegrated into ash, metal should have buckled and warped into lumps. In other words, there should have been nothing remaining.

The driveway outside the girl's bedroom would have scorch marks on it from that kind of heat. A wave of heat that powerful would have set the neighbor's house on fire or at least peeled off the paint.

Instead? Nothing. No scorched concrete. Warped metal, yes. But melted? No. The wood was burned, but had hardly turned to ash, especially where the ceiling buckled. It was like someone dropped a napalm canister in the room that only incinerated the human beings inside before immediately dissipating.

She stared at the model and stretched her back. Her hand scrabbled for her coffee cup. It was empty. Emy sighed, locked the computer, and headed for the break room. She was halfway down the hall when her phone buzzed. Fumbling to drag it out of her pocket, she nearly dropped the coffee cup. Emy let out a curse and raised the screen to her eyes. *Bryan*, she mouthed.

"Hello?"

"Hi, Emy," Bryan said. "I, um, should have called earlier in the week."

A smile spread across her face. "That's okay. How are you, Bryan?"

"Doing fine," he said. "From what I've heard on the radio, sounds like you've had a busy week."

She stopped in the break room and put her cup in the machine. "Yeah, you could say that. So what's up with you?"

There was a long pause. For a moment, Emy thought she'd lost the call. And then he cleared his throat. "I—I was wondering if you'd like to have dinner this evening."

She tapped her foot as her mind raced. Dinner. With Bryan. Dinner. With—

"You still there?" his voice asked.

Emy mumbled. "Um, yeah. Still here."

"If you don't want—"

She clenched her fists. "Yes. Yes, Bryan. I'd like that."

He chuckled on the other end of the line. "Okay. What are you in the mood for?"

"I—" She swallowed hard. "I don't know. I pretty much eat anything." Her cheeks flushed in the following silence.

"Um, okay," Bryan said. "What time should I pick you up?"

"Seven?" she said.

"All right. I'll see you then."

She gulped. "Looking forward to it."

"So am I," he said. The line went dead.

Emy stared at the phone as if it was going to bite her. She'd made a date. The first one in a long time. She punched the button on the coffee machine. The grinder whirred as it crunched the beans. Emy slid her phone back into her pocket. The machine burbled as boiling water poured through the grounds.

You going to let him find more scars? a voice asked in her mind. You remember how that worked last time?

Emy shook the voice away. Black liquid sprayed into her cup. She tapped her foot with nervous energy as she watched the stream sputter into drips. The machine let out a burst of steam as it finished its cycle and beeped. Emy pulled the cup away and walked back to her cube.

Work. That's what she needed. If she could focus on the model, on the house, she could forget about the date. She smiled. Of course, he'll have to pass the Luna test.

She imagined the white dog with pink markings sniffing her suitor, checking him for any sign of threat. Her four-legged companion had made her opinions known before. Emy had learned to trust the mutt with vetting visitors. Bryan would just have to take the test, although Luna would probably leave white strands of hair on whatever he wore.

Her fingers typed in her password and the screen lit up with the model in the same position she'd left it. She pulled up the photos of the bedroom where father and daughter had died and placed them on the other screen. She studied the buckling of the roof and compared it to the model. As far as she could tell, they were the same.

"Fuel-air bomb," she said aloud. "Only explanation."

A fuel-air bomb aerosolized an accelerant in the air and provided an ignition source. The resulting fireball pulled in all the oxygen from a wide area and spread. Any possible contaminate in the air was immediately snuffed into non-existence. When the fire exhausted its oxygen supply, it simply disappeared without additional damage to surrounding areas. Whatever had happened in that room was similar; a short-lived intense heat had fried the bodies and the air, but not the rest of the room. Still, it didn't make much sense.

A new mail notification slid across the screen. With a sigh, she tabbed over. Brett was asking for a walkthrough of what she had by 1600. She breathed a sigh, accepted the meeting request, and stared back at the model. Brett wouldn't like her conclusions; Emy didn't like them either.

She looked at the clock on the computer display. She had less than two hours to try and refine that argument. If Novak joined the meeting, he'd be more than a little pissed about fantastical conclusions. Emy clicked on her research tabs and started searching.

Fireball. Fuel-air bomb. Aerosol. She was typing in search terms as they came to her. The database was filled with cases and reports from all over the

United States and some from Europe. Her screen filled with terrorist attacks and nonsense. She tried to think of ways to winnow down the search results, but came up empty.

In desperation, she typed in "house." The computer thought for a moment and returned a shorter search result. Emy stared at the screen and frowned. The database had returned results related to a report from Germany. The translation was clumsy to say the least.

Emy clicked it and read through the text. The awkwardly worded report mentioned a flat whose interior had been completely incinerated without damage to the walls or the building structure. The case was unsolved.

She clicked through the attached photos. Her fingers shook with adrenaline. The bodies were burned beyond recognition. A corpse with its mouth frozen in a scream, was twisted into a semi-fetal position. Emy nodded. When a human body was exposed to intense enough heat, the muscles and tissue contracted. The skeleton would bend and bunch leaving remains in that position.

Emy grabbed the pictures from the report, added them to hers as well as the translated transcript. The date of the report caught her eye—July 12, 2003. No wonder the pictures had a grain to them.

Her fingers hit the touchpad and dragged the cursor back to the search results. She clicked the next one down and stared at it. Marseille, France, March 2nd, 1976. She opened the grainy, low res scans of the crime-scene photos. The translation software had once again done a poor job on the text, but the photos told all. Two adults, one child. All three dead from intense heat, yet the structural integrity of the room in which they were found was intact. She shook her head as she stared at the three bodies. They were nearly melted together, their arms holding one another.

Without a proper translation, she couldn't be sure, but the reports seemed to indicate the cases had gone unsolved. The chemical composition of gasoline stood out on the French report. The German one? Butane. The accelerants had no doubt been used to start the fires, but they didn't account for the incredible wave of heat that fried the bodies.

She tapped her fingers on the desk and stared at the model. Computerized records prior to 1970 were nearly non-existent. She was lucky to have even gotten a hit off the French report. There could be others prior to the Marseille case, but she'd have a hell of a time tracking them down.

Emy opened a browser window and searched for references to the year 1976 in France. The window immediately populated with accounts of terrible drought and unseasonably high temperatures from early spring through early fall. Her heart quickened. She typed in a similar search for Germany and the year of the Munich case. Her mouth opened in a surprised O and then slowly turned into a grim smile.

Germany had suffered a crushing drought the year of the Munich fire. Very abnormally high temperatures. Across Texas? Record high temperatures with Houston at the epicenter. She shook her head and her fingers flew over the keyboard. Now that she knew what she was looking for, mining the database would be much easier.

Chapter 15

The summer sun glared down from the sky. Waves of heat shimmered off the dirty, pock-marked concrete. Dewhurst breathed in the scent of freon and luxuriated in the frigid air before killing the engine.

He sighed and clutched the door handle. Gritting his teeth, he opened the door. The cool air evaporated in an instant and a heavy cloak of scorched humid air surrounded him. He stepped out with his tan blazer on his arm, and closed the door. His skin prickled as the first beads of sweat popped up beneath his undershirt. Dewhurst brushed back a stray lock of brown hair, shrugged into the coat, and cinched his tie.

The grubby, cracked concrete stared back at him. Dewhurst sighed and walked through the maze of pickup trucks, SUVs, and the occasional sedan. Cigarette butts, scraps of fast-food bags, and broken glass were brushed up against the sidewalk. He left the parking lot and walked up the ramp to the three-story stone building.

A single lab-coat wearing smoker stood in the sun, puffing away as fast as she could. Her short hair was damp with sweat. Dew smiled as he walked toward her.

"Well, Millie."

She turned to him, a grim grin on her face. "And when I saw you were on today's list, I just had to smile."

"Uh-huh," he said. "Pass one of those over."

The heavyset woman reached into her lab coat and pulled a black pack of cigarettes. She flipped open the top with nimble fingers and offered them.

Dew pulled one of the smokes from the pack and put it between his lips. "Guess you need a lighter?"

He shook his head. "No, ma'am. Always got one of those." He produced a polished silver Zippo from his pocket and lit the cigarette. The smell of butane mixed with the burning tobacco. He took a deep pull, and let the smoke stream through his nostrils.

"These really suck, Millie."

She cackled. "That's the point, Dew. Get used to the worst possible flavor and no one will bum off you."

"Right." He blew a cloud of smoke into the scorching hot air. "And how's that working out for you?"

"Well enough." She peered down at her watch and grimaced. "We're late."

He nodded. "I *was* early. I'll blame you."

Millie ran her free hand through her hair. "Don't you always?" She stubbed out the cigarette on the bottom of her flat black shoe. "Ready?"

The cigarette glowed even in the sunny heat as he took another pull. He held it before exhaling the smoke out in a rush. He gripped the cigarette between his thumb and middle finger and snapped with his index. The cigarette cherry went flying and hit the ground, smoke still curling upwards amidst bits of tobacco.

Millie was already at the revolving doors. "Move it, flatfoot. I'm melting out here."

"Right," Dew drawled.

He slid the butt into the smoker pole and walked through the revolving door. Air conditioning blasted against his hot, moist skin and a welcome shiver crawled up his spine. He walked to the front desk and flashed his badge.

"Ah, Detective," the desk clerk said. "Thought we'd see you today."

"Carter," Dew said with a nod. He picked up the pen, carefully printed his name, marked the time, and filled in the case number. He slid the clipboard across to Carter. The lithe ginger-haired man initialed the line and tapped keys on his computer. "Not sure why you don't give me a permanent badge."

The clerk shrugged as he tapped more keys. "Millie doesn't even have a permanent badge. And she's here a lot more than you are."

Dew grunted and tapped his fingers on the desk. The printer whirred and spat out a badge. Carter handed it to Dew with a smile. "Dr. Monroig is ready for you in room four."

Dew shook his head. "Not sure I'm ready for him."

Millie put her hand on his shoulder. "Oh, come on, Dew. It's just a couple of human french fries. You've seen worse."

He stifled a nauseous burp, looked at the woman and then back to Carter. "Please don't think all of us are as crude as she is."

Carter waved a hand. "I know better. The Ghoul is one of a kind. Now don't keep Dr. Monroig waiting." He pressed a button on the desk and the heavy steel door in the foyer buzzed. "Have fun."

He followed Millie through the door and into the hall beyond. Their steps echoed off the white walls and the bright lights left him squinting. "How bad is it?"

Millie laughed. "I don't want to spoil it for you."

Dew shook his head. "Great."

She cackled as she opened the steel door with the black number 4. "They teach you to be squeamish in Louisiana?"

"Only of tee-totalers."

She glanced at him. "How did we get the body so fast? We have three others to look into already."

Dewhurst smirked. "I guess the arson fires have the Mayor spooked."

"About fucking time," she said.

The air conditioning in the hall was cold, but the actual autopsy room was frigid. The remaining sweat from the summer heat disappeared in an instant. Dewhurst rubbed his hands together.

"You're late, Detective," a high pitched voice said.

Dew drew in a deep breath and smiled at the large lab-coat clothed black man. "Dr. Monroig."

The pathologist blinked at Dew and looked back down at the steel table. "Dr. Cady has already done the preliminaries."

Millie walked from behind Dew and stood at the foot of the table. "Take a look Dew."

He followed her finger and stared. Two bodies were melted into one. The remnants of flesh looked like hot dogs that had fallen into crimson coals. Curls of charred skin covered the man's scalp. The eyes and eyelids were gone. Dew shivered as he moved his gaze further down. A small bundle of melted skin and bone was cradled in the dead man's arms.

Monroig took a probe from the tray and pointed at the man's charred skull. "There's a hole here. It's definitely post-mortem. Probably from when the roof caved in."

Dew cleared his throat. "So you don't think the arsonist placed them like this."

"No," Monroig shook his head. "See how damaged the dermis is? The shriveled bone? This man probably weighed in at 240 before the fire."

Millie snorted. "Now they weigh a total of 120lbs put together."

Monroig glared at her. "Yes, Dr. Cady."

"Water loss?" Dew asked.

Monroig nodded. "The fire was intense enough to evaporate all the water from the bodies. When that kind of heat hits the bone matter, more fluid escapes. It's the same in cremation, Detective. Get the fire hot enough, and a large human being turns into six pounds of ash."

Millie pointed at the male corpse's arms. "Heat also causes flexion. The only way to separate these two would be with a bone saw."

The detective walked forward and stared down into the faces. The victim's face was anything but peaceful. It was the howling, screaming visage of a man in hell. The ocular cavities were stretched wide, as if the man had seen something terrible in the last instant before he turned into charcoal. The girl, six-years old by the records, had been transformed into a fetal bundle in her father's arms. Her face, what was visible of it, was as distressed as her father's.

Monroig touched the probe to the girl's forehead. "You saw it, didn't you."

Dew nodded. "She looks...different. What accounts for that?"

He shrugged. "Fire and human flesh don't mix well, Detective. There's no way to predict how the facial muscles in particular will react as they're burned."

"Electrocution is easy to determine." Dew looked up at Monroig. "The corpses always have that grin."

Millie smiled wide. "That's because of what electricity does to the muscles, Dew. Fire is totally different."

Dewhurst swallowed another bit of bile as he scanned the rest of the bodies. The man's penis was a charred lump and his testicles weren't even visible. He pointed to the man's crotch. "Is that condition normal?"

"Mucous membranes," Monroig said, "are are the most sensitive to extreme temperatures. Yes, Detective, it's normal."

Dew turned to Millie. "Are we satisfied there was no post-mortem or pre-mortem human interaction?"

"Yup," the Ghoul grinned. "But the flames licked them so lovingly."

Monroig rolled his eyes. "You're sick, Dr. Cady."

The detective shivered in the cold air. "Then there's nothing of forensic importance?"

The huge black man grimaced. "There always is, Detective. But I'd say the Arson Division will have better clues for you than we will. Unless, of course, we find something else. We'll keep looking."

Dew nodded. "Thank you, Dr. Monroig." Dew took one last look. A divorced man, custody of his daughter, working a blue-collar job to support them both. Nice house amidst a crumbling neighborhood. A good, if hard, life. And now? Nothing but overcooked human steaks.

Monroig cleared his throat. "Since this is a rush job, Dr. Cady will get my report this afternoon. I'm certain," he said as he glanced at her, "she'll add her observations as well. So perhaps tomorrow you'll have more answers than questions."

"Doubt that," Dew said. "Thank you both." He turned and walked out of room number four and into the hallway. He still felt cold, but it was better than the freezing autopsy room.

Dew checked his watch as he walked into the foyer. Shortest morgue meeting ever. In and out in fifteen minutes. Of course it wasn't as though Cady or Monroig had any information. He had expected more, but in hindsight, Cady was right—two human charcoal briquettes weren't going to tell them very much.

He handed his badge to Carter. "Until next time."

Carter put the badge into a bin beneath the desk and then smiled. "Next time," he replied.

Dew tipped an imaginary hat and walked through the revolving door into the blistering heat. Perspiration popped out on his brow in an instant. He wove back through the vehicles until he reached his own. He carefully took off his jacket, opened the door, and lay it across the seat.

He'd been out of the car for a total of twenty minutes, yet the car cabin was already an oven. The engine roared to life and he shut the door. Cold air hit his face and he sighed with pleasure.

The station would only be a ten minute drive through scant traffic.

Chapter 16

The conference room was quiet. Emy had already hooked up her laptop to the projector and its fan was the only sound. She stared at the computer's clock. Five minutes early. Her nerves sizzled with caffeinated energy and she tapped her foot.

She was still nervous about Novak. Brett would at least hear her out, although he'd probably think she was crazy. Novak, on the other hand, would more than likely laugh her out of the room. The laughter wasn't what worried her—it was the inevitable snide comments.

If Novak didn't understand something, or felt it didn't jibe with his particular understanding of fire investigation, he tended to bray like a mule and make everyone in the room feel like an asshole. She suddenly wished Brett had invited Dewhurst to the meeting.

When the conference room door opened, she looked up from her screen. Novak waddled through and sat across from her. Brett closed the door behind them and sat two seats away from his boss, a yellow notebook in his hands.

Novak looked bored, and that was bad. If Brett had invited him to the meeting, the director more than likely forced the issue. The expression on his face meant he was waiting for a chance to pounce on a mistake. Anything that came close to violating procedure or an oversight would be brought up. Emy swallowed hard.

Brett smiled at her. "Well, Emy, what've you got?"

Fighting the nervous energy threatening to make her hands shake, she put her eyes to the laptop and dragged the model window to the projector screen.

She cleared her throat. "I modeled the scene using the house's blue-prints. I then matched up the final position of various structural anomalies that occurred in the room where the victims were found."

Novak's face slid into a thin grin. "Anomalies?" he asked.

Brett tapped his fingers on the table. "Emy? Can you bring up the photos of the room?"

She nodded. A grisly image appeared on the projector. CSU had taken the picture from the bedroom door so it showed the entire room. By the window, the two blackened bodies were clearly visible against the sunlight streaming through the broken glass.

Brett pointed to the screen. "See how the ceiling buckled? But the walls are relatively untouched?"

Novak didn't reply, but his jowls shook with his nod.

"That," Brett said, "doesn't make sense. The fire should have consumed the rest of the room. Instead, it's like it just—" He paused and stared at Emy.

Her throat tickled, but she fought the urge to clear it. "It's like the fire blew itself out," she said.

Novak stared at her, eyes dull and uninterested. "Blew itself out," he repeated. "Like an oil well fire?"

Brett nodded. "Yeah," he agreed. Unlike his boss, Brett's face was excited. "Boots and Coots would use dynamite or Semtex to burn off all the oxygen at a well site and snuff a fire. Like they did in Kuwait. But this was, well, more localized."

The Director nodded and pointed to the screen. "Ms. Aninzo? May we see your simulation?"

She swallowed hard. "Of course." She maximized the animation window so it filled the screen and hit play.

The three of them watched in silence as the first person POV moved from a digital backyard and into the model of the house. It paused before the couch. A bright yellow flame rose from the furniture and slowly grew to envelope it. Black smoke rose to the ceiling before the flames licked upwards to touch the plaster.

The ceiling began to buckle. Cinders of plaster fell around the wooden floor as the fire gained strength and spread toward one wall. The camera panned toward the hall leading to the bedrooms. The POV flowed into the hallway and just outside the bedroom door. Two figures were up against the back wall, holding one another. The screen turned a mixture of blue and red as a wave of digital flame filled the room. After a moment, the blaze went out leaving blackened walls and the charred bodies.

Novak shook his head. He glared at Brett and then at Emy. "That's pure fantasy," he said.

She nodded, feeling the creak of the tendons in her neck. "I agree. But the flash points match a sudden intense heat. And then," she paused to tap her pen on the table, "nothing."

"Mr. Cullum?" Novak asked. "You have anything to add?"

Brett flashed a cautious smile. "I haven't had a chance to dig into all the numbers yet, but I trust Emy's assessment. It explains the burns to the, uh, victims as well as the site's relative structural integrity."

"Hmm," Novak said. He stared at the screen. "Can you show me the photographs again?"

Emy slid her fingers across the trackpad and the photos filled the screen.

"Ignition point?" he asked.

After she tabbed through the pictures, the photo taken from the back-yard sliding door popped up above the rest. The metal and spring remains of the couch were in the foreground. She turned back and watched Novak's eyes as he took it all in. The only sounds were his congested breathing and the whir of the projector fan.

Finally, he nodded. "Okay. I don't— Well, I don't have another explanation." His eyes flicked from the screen to Emy. "Anything else?"

She fought the blush trying to color her cheeks. "Yes, but it's, um, not exactly a sure thing."

Brett chuckled. "Right. Because the fireball theory is so easy to believe." He tapped the table. "Let's hear it, Emy."

She brushed back her bangs. Beneath the fluorescent lights, the scar seemed to glow. "I searched through the database looking for similar cases."

Novak shook his head. "Needle in a haystack," he said.

"Agreed," Emy said. "But I found two cases that are of interest."

Novak's eyebrows raised. "Two?"

She nodded and brought the Marseille case photographs up on the screen. "I'll need some help with translation for the case file, but from what I gathered, a very similar fire took place in a small house there."

"What year?" Brett asked.

"1976." Emy tiled the photographs across the screen. Novak sucked in a hiss of air as she zoomed in on the burned corpses. "See how the family members look? It's—"

"—Damned near a match for the Hartman case," Brett finished.

Emy stared at him and smiled. "Right."

"Jesus," Novak said. "That means our perp is French. Also, probably in his 60s."

She shook her head. "I'd say that's possible, sir, but I doubt it." She switched to the German case and brought those pictures forward. "This fire occurred in Munich in 2003. The victims are in almost the same poses and the arson damage is very similar."

Brett stood from his chair and walked to the projection screen. He stared at it, his eyes flicking across the details. "My god, Emy." He turned to her, eyes glittering with excitement. "Are there any other cases?"

She shrugged. "I found half a dozen others in the database, but they're less than perfect matches. Most of those occurred in the USA."

"Meaning what?" Novak asked. "They either match all the way or they don't."

"Well," Emy said as she fought the nervous jitter in her belly, "in four cases, the entire house was destroyed. The investigators suggested the intense heat was caused by chemical explosions. Possibly due to specialty hobbies like photography or home chemistry sets."

Brett sat down in his chair, hands tented on the table. "What about the rest?" His smile had disappeared into a frown.

She quivered with nervous tension as she brought up a spreadsheet. "As with the incidents in Germany, France, and the fires here in Houston, similar fires occurred in Los Angeles and Minneapolis. I've tried to pattern match the dates, but there doesn't seem to be a pattern at all."

"Except," Brett said, "they all happened during the hottest months of the year."

"Right," Emy smiled. "And one more little fact."

Novak crossed his legs. "And what is that?"

"They all occurred during heat-waves coupled with a drought," Emy said.

Brett glanced at Novak. The older man rubbed at his chin. "Heatwaves," he said in a low voice. "Emy? Have you matched all those dates to record temperatures?"

She nodded. "Yes. Drought. Heatwaves. Record temperatures. Summer." Her fingers tapped against the table. "Those are the only common features, besides, the victims."

"Victims?" Novak asked. "What do you mean?"

"Most of the fires that resulted in death had at least one child and one parent. Many had at least three victims."

Brett pointed at the screen. "I assume we can't cross-reference those with other arsons that occurred around the same time?"

"We can," she said. "But I wanted to get through this part of the research before I started digging." She glanced at Novak. "Wanted to make sure you didn't think I was jumping down the rabbit-hole."

Novak nodded. "Appreciated," he said. His eyes seemed to drink in the numbers and dates on the screen. "The model is pure fantasy, Ms. Aninzo. Pure. Fantasy." He pointed at the screen. "But that's good investigative work." He nodded to her. "Good job."

The tingling nervousness departed and a warm flush spread over her skin. Did Novak just give her a compliment? That was a first. "Uh, thank you, sir."

"Brett?" Novak said. "You agree with the conclusions and the track of the investigation?"

He grinned. "Absolutely."

"Then you two should work together on this," the boss said. "Unless there's another case you need to work, Brett, I want you full time on this."

"Happily," Brett said. He winked at Emy.

Novak cleared his throat. "Now, I do have something we need to discuss."

Emy's elation evaporated. Novak was about to say something bad. Bad for everyone involved. She waited for the shoe to drop.

"Rumors," he said, "are already spreading through the Mayor's office. This is the second arson fire in a week. It's bad PR for the city, and bad PR for the health and safety departments." He licked his lips. "We need to close this case and damned soon."

Novak's eyes stared into hers and then switched over to Brett's. Her boss shifted uncomfortably in his chair. "What do you suggest?" he asked.

The head of the department tapped an idle finger on the table. "You are to give Detective Dewhurst your full cooperation. You are to help him day or night with any inquiries. And you need to coordinate with CSU in order to make sure the reports are in order and as detailed as possible."

Emy blinked. After the first arson, Novak had made it clear he didn't like the cop. In fact, he had tried as much as possible to interfere. Now he was insisting they help him?

"Yes, sir," Brett said and glanced at Emy. "We need to set up a meeting with Detective Dewhurst. Whenever he's available that is."

She nodded. "I'll put together what I have and send it to him."

Novak shook his head. "No, Ms. Aninzo. Not until you've had a chance to, well, get the report in some order."

She cocked an eyebrow. "What do you mean?"

His lips upturned in a bemused smile. "Your conclusions, while fantastical, need to be carefully explained. Detailed. I want to make sure HPD has as much to go on as possible. And this needs to be in the official records."

Emy didn't know why, but Brett looked as though someone had farted. Novak blinked at him. "Is there a problem, Mr. Cullum?"

"No, sir," he said. "I'll help Emy with the report."

"Good man," Novak said and stood from the table. "Any questions?" Brett and Emy exchanged glances before shaking their heads. "Excellent. Please forward me a copy of the report when you have it ready." The large man walked to the door and left the room.

Brett rubbed his hands together and sneered. "'Official record?'"

"What are you talking about?" Emy asked.

Her boss leaned back in his chair. "You don't understand politics, Emy. You never really have."

She smiled. "You got that right."

"So let me fill you in," Brett said. "He's hanging us out to dry."

"Guess I'm stupid," Emy said with a frown. "Explain, please."

"It's very simple," he said. "You've calculated the heat. You're going on record saying it was a fireball. You're also going on record that these fires have occurred over decades. You've also made conclusions based on circumstantial evidence."

"So?"

Brett ran a hand through his hair. "This is CYA time, Emy. He's got the Mayor breathing down his neck and no amount of pull is going to save his ass if this doesn't get solved. So he needs a scape-goat if we don't close the case before a third fire happens. Let alone a fourth."

She sighed. "Goddammit. You're serious, aren't you?"

"As serious as I can be," he said with a nod.

She closed the laptop, unplugged it from the projector interface and stood. "Then I guess I better get to work on putting together my 'fantastical' suppositions."

"I think," Brett said, "I need a drink. You coming out tonight?"

Emy's face flushed. "I, um, I have a date."

The sour expression on Brett's face disappeared into a wide grin. "Really? That's awesome."

She nodded. "I guess."

"Is it the gentleman from the club?"

"Yup," Emy said. "And I don't even know what to wear."

Brett shrugged. "Sorry. I do queer eye for the straight guy. Not sure about queer eye for the straight woman."

She giggled. "Yeah, last thing I need is a gay man choosing my wardrobe."

"Could be worse," he said. "Novak could be choosing your clothes."

Chapter 17

He put the travel mug of hot tea back on the coaster, cleared his throat, and stared at the monitor. The dead-drop twitter accounts had finished burping their messages before self-destructing. The cameras he'd placed in the vacant McMansion hadn't warned of any problems. That was good. The camera in the backyard hadn't yet been spotted, but it wouldn't stay hidden for long. Someone would eventually find it. He'd have to remove it later tonight.

The camera feeds had streamed encrypted video to a server on the internet. When they finished, the bot he'd installed sent urls for the videos to the twitter accounts. The bot had self-destructed at 0700 this morning, wiping itself from the infected computer.

P had spent months getting the system working, perfecting the bot on a spare computer. Between assistance from script kiddies and some less than savory characters from the Pirate Bay, it'd been simple to find a vulnerable server on AWS. Unpatched software was laughably easy to infect and covering his tracks was just as easy.

Unless, of course, they found the systems and were able to dig through the encryption. But since the twitter accounts were dead-drops with temporary email addresses and the urls had been encrypted piece-meal between the various messages, he wasn't worried. Ghere had told him he would be safe. And when God spoke, he believed.

He typed a few keys, downloaded the messages, and ran his utility script to decrypt them. Once decrypted, the program spliced together the urls for the videos. BU, Inc, the web company whose server he'd infected, also had an unprotected storage account. Storing the videos there amidst all the clutter and noise had been easy as well. The chances of a system admin finding them were highly improbable.

Still, he wasn't a complete idiot. He logged in through a hole in another server for a different company, downloaded the videos from the URL to their storage array, and then transmitted them to a third server via TOR. If the Feds ever figured out what to look for in the traffic patterns, they could find most of the destination points, but he was willing to bet it would take them quite some time.

The third server, this one in Romania, held the files for him. He licked his chapped lips, started his TOR client, logged in, and transferred the files. The TOR network was less secure than it used to be since Snowden dropped the dime on the NSA, but it was good enough for this. With all the movies, television shows, and other pirated media being tossed around, the chances of anyone tracking these videos was minimal. Plus, it would take a major INTERPOL search warrant to scour the servers there. Ghere had told him he would succeed. Looked like Ghere was right again.

As the videos downloaded, he leaned back in the chair and popped his back. Each camera had recorded several hours of video both before and after his strike times. A house across the street from the sacrifice had had an unprotected wi-fi router; connecting the cameras to it had been all too simple. He'd at first considered using a cell-relay, but decided it was too dangerous. Cellular traffic was fairly easy to trace. Preying upon people's ignorance or apathy was much safer.

He watched as the file transfer numbers increased in bytes downloaded. P opened a browser and scanned the Chronicle's headlines. Sure enough, the Hartman fire was on the top list of links. It hadn't made the front page. Yet. He was sure once HPD and Arson decided it was a suspicious fire, it was destined to be at the top of the newscasts. That might happen as early as tonight.

The early morning trip to the Hartman's house had been tricky. Without much sleep, P had again donned his black jogger uniform and traveled five blocks through the alleys and yards to the McMansion. Once he'd checked the computer equipment, he'd stripped naked and made his way into the Hartman's backyard.

Getting in through the sliding glass door was easy. The locks were old, but he hadn't even had to use them; either Nathaniel Hartman or his daughter had left it unlocked.

The house had been quiet except for the whoosh of the air conditioning and the gravelly whir of the cooling unit outside. The moment Ghere had seen the couch, the voice told him what he had to do.

He'd sat cross-legged on one of the cushions. The fabric had made his balls itch, but his erect penis never touched it. Eyes closed, he drew the symbol with the small can of lighter fluid and said the prayer. The world had gone silent except for his own breathing and the sound of God's growl. The matchbook taped to the lighter fluid can felt damp between his fingers. He ripped it off the side, opened it, and struck the match.

When he opened his eyes, the normal yellow teardrop flame wasn't present. Instead, it burned an angry crimson. His fingers started to burn as the match flame slowly consumed the cardboard. He said the prayer once more and dropped the match.

The far cushion immediately burst into flame. Ghere screamed with ecstasy in his mind. P's body vibrated with energy. He felt his remaining body hair crisping in the heat. He touched himself and immediately sprayed semen across the fabric. The orgasm nearly knocked him from the couch.

Drooling and still shuddering from the sexual release, P watched as the symbol danced in the fire. Woozy, he sat up from the couch and bowed to the flames. A pair of eyes stared at him through the black smoke. P dropped to one knee and felt a wave of heat as God breathed on him. His skin tingled as the searing heat tickled his cells. Ghere wouldn't allow him to die. Ghere would protect him. P wasn't afraid as the symbol burned through the fabric and seared into the wooden floor.

You are done here, a voice growled in his mind. *You may leave.*

P walked into the backyard, his naked skin steaming with heat. The humidity felt cool and refreshing. He'd worked his way back into the McMansion and dressed. He didn't dare watch God's work. Ghere had told him that was what the cameras were for. For Ghere to thrive, P had to stay alive and stay out of jail.

He was blocks away from the house when he finally saw the real flames rise in the sky. From the same backyard he'd used the previous night, P had tossed his sneaking clothes into the backpack and changed into his jogging uniform. The sound of sirens approaching made him move as fast as he could.

When he left the neighborhood, he kept the windows rolled down. He smiled as he made it to the freeway and headed north to his home. The sirens were still in his ears when he'd finally managed to fall asleep.

And now, all these hours later, it was time to witness the sacrifice. He took another long gulp of tea and closed his eyes. He could feel Ghere in his mind. The deity was anxious to see Its own work. P felt the same way.

The computer dinged and he opened his eyes. The progress bars all read 100%. Smiling, he rose from the chair, slid off his shorts and his shirt, and sat back down again. P opened a window and dragged three files to the video player.

The screen filled with one large rectangle with two boxes below. While the camera in the tree was HD, the other two had only been standard definition. But their quality would be good enough for his needs.

He clicked "play all" and leaned back in the chair with the keyboard. The three frames filled with green-tinted black and white images. A timestamp ran in each of the windows. The clocks showed 0230. He held down a key to fast forward and watched as the different vantage points slid by.

A stray cat scampered through the yard at incredible speed. A skunk skulked from beneath a fence and ran behind the garage in just a few frames. The trees shook and jittered. A naked man sprinted through the backyard and into the house. P stopped the fast forward and clicked play.

A wan glow appeared through the glass door. He could see his silhouette crouched on the cushion through the tall glass panes. The fire rose from the couch and flashed in the symbol. P's left hand stroked his cock and he shuddered from the touch.

The single-story ranch house was aglow with unnatural light. He watched himself rise from the couch and head out into the backyard. Within seconds, the camera showed only the house and the flicker of flames within. P's fingers danced over his erection and he moaned. Ghere breathed heavily in his mind.

The video player at the top of the screen grew brighter as flames appeared in the house's windows. Through the sliding glass door, he watched a wall of dark smoke turn and stare into the backyard. A pair of flashing almond eyes looked up at the camera. A shock of pleasure rattled his spine.

Flames licked the ceiling as it turned and headed beyond the living room and toward the bedrooms. The camera picked up a blur of movement as someone ran down the hall. The wall of fire and smoke followed.

Flaming cloven hoof prints burned the wooden floor in its wake. P stroked himself faster. The feel of his calloused hands over his penis left him drooling. The scenes on the screen flashed as Ghere took his sacrifice. P heard the crackle of flames in his mind, and the fiery whoosh as the deity graced their flesh with Its blessing.

The wall of fire and smoke returned to the living room. Its dead eyes stared at the camera before disintegrating into random flames. The house continued to burn as P's orgasm rattled and shook his body. He groaned in shuddering breaths, the deity's mirthless laugh echoing between his ears.

As soon as he regained control of his breathing, P pressed the fast forward button again. Flames licked up from the buckled roof in a rapid dance. And then he saw the tell-tale off-and-on lights of the fire trucks.

Firefighters sprinted into the back yard. With the 3x frame-rate, they appeared to jump and hop. Streams of water blasted through the sliding glass door and into the smoke filled living room. Black and grey plumes escaped through the broken windows. The flames on the roof quickly disappeared as the cascading water hit them.

The firefighters used their axes to clear away more glass and enter the house. P already knew what they would find—Ghere had told him. He hit the space bar and the video players resumed their normal speed. One of the firemen walked out of the house, pulled off his mask, and puked beside the glass door. Shaking his head, he rose from his bent-over position as another firefighter put an arm on his shoulder. P could imagine the words said—no one was left alive.

The men continued spraying down the living room, slowly entering the house to douse the rest of the hot spots. He grew bored as he watched the men go about their tasks and hit the fast forward button again. The black and white scenes slowly grew lighter as dawn came. The sunlight quickly dispelled the shadows surrounding the yard.

The video counters slid past 0600 and kept moving. He was about to shut it off when something caught his eye. A woman walked into the back-yard and entered the house. As she turned, the back of her jacket was visible: Arson. P clicked the rewind button, waited a few seconds, and let the video roll at normal speed.

The woman carried a small satchel and had already donned latex gloves. Her shoes were covered in booties to keep her footprints from covering up any evidence. Long, dark hair flowed down her back. But it was her face that struck him. Even in the black and white images, he could see the scars on one side of her face. Ghere growled in his mind.

"You know her?" P asked the empty room.

Yes, Ghere said. *And we will have to deal with her before the becoming.*

"Why? What does she—"

Ghere silenced him with an angry hiss. *It doesn't matter. To you. It's enough for you to know that we must take her. Soon.*

P nodded to himself. As the video rolled, she disappeared into the house. A man wearing an identical jacket followed her in. P's lips upturned in a grim smile.

When the two investigators didn't immediately return to the outside, he fast forwarded again. He watched as the man came out of the house and talked to the firefighters. When she walked out, she joined them, but only for a moment. Then she made her way into the backyard, eyes scanning the ground.

P felt a shiver of fear. What did she see? The woman pulled flags from the satchel and placed them in the grass.

"Fuck," he said aloud. She crept closer to the tree and then was out of view. "Did I leave footprints?"

Of course you did, Ghere said. *They are meaningless.*

He nodded to himself, and kept the videos rolling, expecting to see the camera jitter and shake as someone found it. That didn't happen. He watched for a few more minutes until he saw her reemerge to speak with the other investigator. The two raised their eyes to the tree, but weren't looking at the camera. He smiled. They hadn't found it. A few minutes later, the feeds stopped.

P wiped his hands on a towel and mopped up his leavings. The deity inside his mind seemed to be thinking. He tried to ignore Its uneasy silence.

He cast a longing glance at the darkened monitor and rolled the video back until the female investigator's face was in its best focus. He printed the HD frame to his desktop and another of her partner. With the two images saved, he needed to clean. Ghere protected him, but that didn't leave room for incompetence.

A few taps of the mouse and he brought up the shredding program. He dumped the video files, his code, and associated documents into the bin. With a sigh, he clicked "shred."

The computer displayed a progress bar as the system wrote over the information, one-hundred times per bit. The NSA and FBI had programs that could recover deleted information, even info that had been shredded, but he'd been assured this was the same program they used to cleanse information. It would take a long time for the computer to crunch and annihilate the files, but when it was done, he could let that worry slip.

He opened the two video captures. Licking his lips, P zoomed in on the woman's face. The scar ran from her left temple all the way down past her neck. That side of her face was a pitted, puffy landscape of pain. Ghere had met this woman. She had escaped. P nodded to himself. He wouldn't allow her to escape again.

Chapter 18

The meeting with Novak had left her with mixed feelings. Brett's words about Novak using the two of them as political scapegoats hadn't exactly warmed her heart. And her boss was probably right. Novak was just the kind of chickenshit to set someone up for failure. And if they succeeded? He'd take all the credit. Perfect. Fucking politicians.

On the other hand, he'd given them carte blanche to take the investigation wherever it went. And, although he hadn't said as much, wherever she wanted to take it. That was the important bit.

Emy had sent out a slew of emails. Trolling through the crime databases had given her the names of the officers or departments involved in the three U.S. cases she could find: Seattle, Minneapolis, and Los Angeles. And the digital case files also told her who to call.

The Seattle case was the oldest and had the least chance of bearing fruit, but she wanted to take the cases in order of occurrence. In July 2009, the city of Seattle suffered through both record setting highs and lows. The high temps were over 100 and the lows broke into the 70s. The city had practically collapsed beneath the stall of heated air.

In that same month, an historic building off Lake Washington burned to the ground. The old warehouse went up in an epic conflagration, yet the fire didn't spread to the other buildings. It was isolated and contained. According to the reports Emy read, the arson investigators were unable to determine what caused it. The case was still open.

Two days later, a house boat caught fire. A family of three burned to death. When Emy found the pictures of the scene, her heart stopped in her chest. Just as with the photos from the other sites, the bodies looked as though they'd been exposed to a nuclear detonation—the bones curled and twisted, the flesh burned into a melted mass, and the faces stuck in the same rictus of tortured horror.

The lead arson investigator, John Pratt, managed to write several case reports before his unsolved murder. The reports included a description of the accelerant (regular old gasoline), and damage done to the dock where the house boat was moored. The damage included what he called "suspect whittling on the wooden bannisters." Pratt concluded there was no evidence the marks in the wood were done by the perpetrator. There were no photos of the markings. Emy jotted down more questions to ask Seattle FD if she ever managed to track someone down. It was a long shot, but maybe someone had taken a photo of the vandalism, and it simply wasn't included in the report.

Pratt also postulated the crime was committed by an adult, probably a repeat offender, because of how "clean" the scene was. But what he couldn't explain was the heat bloom that occurred in the cabins, not to mention why the boat didn't simply sink. It was as if the fire consumed what it wanted and then dissipated enough to keep the hull from collapsing. That made no sense. Pratt, apparently a self-effacing man, noted that particular hypothesis being "a bit out of left field."

Emy shook her head as she read the case notes, wondering what Pratt would have made of both Houston fires. The more she read of the report, the more certain she was that Pratt, if not killed two days later, would have solved the case. He'd asked himself all the right questions, the same questions she and Brett were asking themselves.

She finished reading his reports and then moved on to those filed by his juniors. They weren't nearly as solid. Perhaps after Pratt died, the department lost interest in the case. Or maybe it was because those under his command were in too much shock. Regardless, the case seemed to have become mired in bureaucratic insanity after his death. And Emy knew from experience that that was how cases died and ended up marked as "unsolved" in perpetuity.

She looked through the list of names on the post-Pratt reports. If those folks were still in the department, they might be able to answer some questions. If not, then this would definitely be a dead end.

Emy looked up the number for the Seattle Fire Department and dialed. She put on her headset and waited for the call to go through.

A gruff voice answered the call and, after passing on her badge number and credentials, she was put on hold. She traced the bug's strange design on the desktop. The image was burned into her brain now. It was impossible to take a beat to herself without it entering her thoughts. The only way to purge it was to catch this asshole.

"David Brown," a raspy voice said. A beat passed and she could hear the man's snuffling breath.

Emy swallowed hard, her throat clicking with the effort. "Mr. Brown. This is Arson Investigator Emy Aninzo with the Houston Police Department."

The snuffles stopped. "Yes, Ma'am. What can I do for you, Ms. Aninzo?"

Emy fought against the butterflies in her stomach. Goddammit, why was it so hard to talk to people? "I'm investigating some fires in my area and came across the waterfront and houseboat fires of 2009? John Pratt was the lead investigator."

The man sighed. "Yeah. I was on the team."

Pause. When she was certain he was done speaking, she took a deep breath to try and calm her nerves. "Do you have time to answer a few questions about those cases?"

Pause. "Sure."

"Officer Pratt—"

"You can call him John, Ms. Aninzo. And you can call me David."

"Okay, David. And please call me Emy."

"Emy it is."

She looked at the notes on her screen. "The notes for the houseboat fire mention vandalism on a bannister."

Pause. "Oh, right. Yeah. That was strange, to say the least."

"Can you describe it?"

"I'll try. Might be better if I doodle it and send it to you."

Emy grinned. "That would be great. But what can you tell me about it?"

Brown took a deep breath before his words shot out in a stream. "When we got there, the boat was still on fire and so was the dock. But the bannister nearest the boat was only charred. Lots of things had been carved in it. Band names, youngsters putting their names on there, stuff like that. And then there was that design or whatever you want to call it."

"What did it look like?" she asked.

"It was a circle with jagged branches inside it. Something like that. The circle was crudely drawn. Guess whoever did it didn't have time for perfection." He snickered. "We tried to get a photo of it, but it just didn't really come out. John traced it with graphite and paper." Brown paused. "Not sure what happened to that."

Emy's heart raced. The sigil danced in her mind. She closed her eyes and pictured the wooden bannister, the splintered, untended wood charred and chipped. A crude circle with the lines. It fit. It completely fit.

"David? Were you involved in the Lake Washington fire as well?"

There was a snuffling pause. "Oh. You mean that old building?"

"Yes," Emy said. "Burned a few days before the house boat."

She could practically hear him nodding on the other end of the line. "That was a strange one too. Made no goddamned sense." Pause. "Sorry, Emy. No language to use around a lady."

"What was strange about it?"

"Name something," David said. "The ignition source, the lack of detectable accelerants. Not to mention the fireball. You've read the report?"

She wanted to race past his question and ask a million of her own. Emy closed her eyes. "Yes, David. I read the report."

"What did you think?"

Emy frowned. "Seemed like it was incomplete."

"Incomplete, yeah," David said, his voice trailing off. "No motive. No signs of ingress or egress. The ignition point, near as we could tell, was the direct center of the floor. That's where the concrete was scorched the most. But no accelerants. No sign of what started the burn. And worst of all? No means to start a fire."

Emy opened her eyes and blinked. "What?" What do you mean?"

"I'm guessing you've no idea what that building looked like."

She shook her head. "No. I didn't—"

"It was a warehouse, Emy." She could hear the smile in his voice. "It was tall, it was large, and it was empty."

"Empty?"

"Empty. As in nothing there. The property was sold a few months before the fire. The new owners hadn't yet done anything with the place."

Emy's brows furrowed. "So what burned?"

"Great question," David said. "The only answer I have is 'the building.' Whatever started there on the floor rose forty feet in the air, blew out a portion of the roof, and sent flames cascading over the sides. Whole damned thing was gone in forty-five minutes."

Now it was Emy's turn to pause. A flame that could reach that high without a significant ignition source? Impossible. "You said the flame started at the floor and blew out a portion of the roof?"

"Right. Not just a small area either. It was like someone fired a bazooka at the damned thing. We found wood and steel debris over a hundred feet away from the site. The explosion knocked out windows in some of the other nearby buildings."

The sigil appeared in her mind's eye. "Was there any shape to it?"

Pause. "Excuse me?"

"The roof." Emy clenched her fists. "Was there any kind of shape to the hole in the roof?"

"Hmm." She heard his creaking chair and imagined a faceless, husky man swiveling to face a wall. "Never really thought about that. I'd have to go through the old pictures. I don't remember there being anything spectacularly strange about it. And Lord knows we didn't exactly get much of a look until after it collapsed."

"You have photos?"

"Yeah," David said. "We took a bunch once it was safe."

"Why weren't they in the report?"

David growled. "SNAFU. We hadn't finished the damned report before the house fire. And then—" His voice trailed off, but Emy thought she heard a click in the man's throat as if he were trying to hold back a sob. "And then John died. We kind of didn't get our shit together for a few months. By then, no one wanted to look at anything related to the two cases. Instead, we were all busy trying to find John's murderer."

"Can you find those pictures for me?" The sentence rushed out of her mouth in a rapid fire stream of syllables. Emy blushed when she realized how fast she was talking.

"Yeah," David said, his voice a little tight. "I'll dig them up for you. They should be in the case box. If not, then I'm not sure what to tell you."

"But you'll look?"

David sighed. "Yes, ma'am, I'll look."

Emy swallowed hard. "I'm sorry to be insistent, David. This could help us crack some cases that are going on down here. We already have two dead."

She could practically hear him nodding on the other end of the line. "I understand, Emy. No need to apologize." The tightness in his voice had only increased, his words a dead monotone. "You found that symbol, didn't you?"

Emy said nothing.

"Yeah," David said. "You did." She heard something hit wood on the other end of the line. When David spoke again, the tightness in his voice had disappeared, barely concealed rage replacing it. "I'll get you all the files I have. Every picture, every note. I'll see if I can scour John's private notebook too. But you need to do me a favor."

"What's that?" Emy asked.

"You find this son of a bitch and you fucking execute him."

True to his word, David emailed a slew of photos and copies of notes less than an hour later. When the email notification occurred, she barely noticed it because she was busy scouring the Hartman photos.

After her conversation with David, she wanted to know if there was something they'd missed in looking at the collapsed roof. She assembled the pictures in a gallery and slowly dragged each of them into her photo editor. It took her nearly half an hour to arrange them properly, rotating, cropping, layering, to create a single image. When she finished, she leaned back in her chair. Her skin broke out in gooseflesh.

The roof, right above where Hartman and his daughter had been found, had not only collapsed; something had blown a hole straight through it. The intense heat from the inexplicable fireball that roared out of the child's bedroom smashed through the roof while it immolated Hartman and his daughter.

She wasn't surprised no one had noticed it. It was very subtle. But it was there.

A mouth. A jagged, tearing, screaming mouth. Another shiver rose up her spine. She tried to imagine what could cause the wood to warp and burn that way. It made no sense.

She'd been staring at the photo in silence when the computer dinged. The sound broke her concentration. She exhaled a jittery stream of air and tabbed over to the mail client.

The text above the included photos was succinct and to the point.

Ms. Aninzo:

Please let me know if I can be further help. I'm still working through John's old notebook and I'll have more for you as soon as I can. Find the bastard.

Emy blinked at the message and clicked on the attachment icon. Even with the fast network, it was going to take a few minutes to download that many megs. She locked the computer, stood from her chair, and stretched.

She'd barely moved for the past few hours and her back certainly wasn't happy about it. She grabbed her coffee cup and headed out of the cubicle. One last shot of black liquid before the day ended was exactly what she needed. Hell, maybe the walk to the coffee maker would help clear her mind.

A few people in the hallways smiled at her. Emy responded by making sure her long bangs covered the scars. The break room was empty. It was getting late in the afternoon and most of the staff was trying to get the hell out and start their weekends. Emy checked her watch.

In another two hours, the freeways would be slammed with cars, if they weren't already. People would fight their way home through the traffic, weaving through wrecks, overheated cars, and maybe a car fire or two. All of that while they prayed their own cars didn't overheat.

She put her mug beneath the coffee maker, slotted a pod, and hit brew. Hot water and steam gurgled in the machine. She rubbed her eyes and loosed a yawn. While she'd been sitting in her chair, fatigue was far away and incomprehensible. Too many images, too many possibilities, and too many clues to consider. Her mind had been on fire trying to assimilate them, order them, make sense of them. But now?

She yawned again. The break room filled with the powerful scent of dark coffee. When the machine sputtered a final gout of steam, she pulled out the mug and held it to her lips, but didn't drink. Instead, she exhaled deeply into the cup. Steam rose back at her face and into her eyes.

The weariness departed immediately. The scent was music to her senses. She breathed deeply again. Her eyes had felt like they were covered in sandpaper a few minutes ago, but the steam had cleared them. She turned and made her way back to her cube.

Her desk phone blinked a rapid red. Frowning, she set down her coffee and scrolled through the caller id list. "UNKNOWN CALLER." Emy frowned at the blinking message light. She picked up the receiver, punched the "VoiceMail" button, and waited.

Her ears hummed with the sound of an open line. Barely audible over the hum was the sound of breathing. She watched the seconds tick off on the LED display. After ten seconds, the message ended.

Emy placed the receiver back in the cradle, but didn't delete the message. A cold chill ran up her spine, but she couldn't say why.

Chapter 19

The restaurant had been crowded, but she expected that. Bryan had taken her to a small Italian place near the museum district. They'd shared a bottle of wine before the entrees and joked about Luna.

When he'd arrived to pick her up, Emy had invited him inside. Anyone she dated had to pass the Luna test. And it was time.

Bryan wore khakis and a pressed black silk shirt, his shoes reflecting the light with a fresh shine.

"Well, I feel underdressed," she said.

He smiled as he looked her up and down. His eyes didn't hover over her scar or her small breasts. Her clean blue jeans and white blouse contrasted with her dark skin.

"Nope," he said. "You look wonderful."

The apartment shook with a low growl. Bryan's eyes went wide and his mouth opened as the large American Bully walked around the corner. Her dark brown eyes stared at him and her tail stood straight up. Emy glanced behind her.

"Are you afraid of dogs?" she asked.

Bryan gulped. "Only ones that want to eat me."

Luna growled again, her black snout bobbing up and down as she sniffed the air.

"Luna. Come," Emy said.

The dog stalked forward, eyes glaring at the man in the doorway. She sat next to Emy and sniffed the air. "Say hello, girl."

Luna raised her head in the air and loosed a low, short bark.

Bryan, smiling at the dog, lowered his hand in front of her snout. Luna sniffed again. Her tail began to swish against the wooden floor and her jaws opened. A large, wide pink tongue slid out between the exposed white canines. She panted and then licked his hand.

The dog looked up at Emy and whined. Emy smiled down at her and patted her head. "Good girl."

Bryan looked confused. "What just happened?"

Emy grinned as she pet the dog. "Luna gave you the okay."

He laughed. "The okay? The dog has to meet all your suitors?"

"Something like that," she said. "Luna has great taste in men."

"I firmly hope," Bryan said, "you don't mean she eats them."

Emy patted the dog's wide, muscled flank. "Only the ones that deserve it." Luna looked up at her and Emy smiled. "Lay down, girl."

The dog barked once and ran to the couch. She leaped up into it and curled into a ball, her head pointed toward the door, eyes still fixed on Bryan.

Emy turned and gestured him inside. "Come on in. I promise she won't bite." She grinned and fought back a blush. "I won't either."

Shaking his head, Bryan entered the apartment, and glanced at the walls. "Wow. You like landscapes," he said.

Emy followed his gaze to the framed pictures of mountains and jungle. She shrugged. "They remind me of when I was little."

He walked to one and stared at the waterfall spaying down white and blue waves of water into a green lagoon. "That is beautiful," he said.

She nodded. "Maria Christina."

He turned to her. "Where's that?"

"Near Iligana in the Philippines," she said. "My father used to take me there when I was little."

"Ah," Bryan said. "Is that where you're from?"

"Originally," she said. "But I haven't been back since I left. No idea what it looks like now except for pictures on the internet. You ready to go?"

He nodded. "Sure."

Emy looked at the couch. The dog looked back at her, tail thumping against the cushions. "Sleepy time, Luna," Emy called.

The dog uncurled herself, stretched, and slowly crawled off the couch. She walked to the crate near the kitchen and turned in a circle three times before entering the large metal container. The dog made a show of lying down on her bed and snorted.

Emy rolled her eyes. "You just have to show off, don't you?" she asked. The dog woofed. She gave Luna a jerky treat and closed the crate door.

Bryan laughed. "Man, she's something."

"Yup. She's my girl. Aren't you?" she asked the dog. Luna's tail thumped against the metal. "Let's get some food before she decides we're teasing her." Emy grabbed her small, red purse from the table and put it over her shoulder. "Ready?"

Once they'd reached the restaurant, it was clear Bryan had been there many times before. Each of the fourteen tables had a red crystal urn with a burning candle inside. The flickering flame cast strange shadows in the dim light. The waitress, a tall blonde dressed in a stainless, white shirt with black pants, smiled at them as she led them to their table.

Emy's eyes wandered and took in the small cafe. Photos of Italy, as well as various olive oil company posters, wines, and Italian beers covered the walls. Chianti bottles hung from the ceiling like ornaments.

The waitress led them to a table at the corner. All the other tables were full, but Emy was glad they'd managed this one. It was darker than the rest, away from the door, and across from the kitchen. The only bad part? She'd be expected to have a conversation.

Bryan glanced at her. "Would you like some wine?"

"Sure," she said.

He ordered a bottle and the waitress left them alone with their menus. Bryan didn't bother picking his up.

"Um, you already know what you want?" she asked.

An embarrassed smile lit his face. "You could say that. I haven't looked at the menu in years."

She narrowed her eyes, the corners of her mouth lifting in a sly grin. "And what if they change the menu?"

"Doesn't matter," he said with a shrug. "I've never ordered off the menu. And, um," he said as his fingers dragged it from her reach, "you shouldn't either."

"I don't understand," she said.

The waitress appeared and put a thatch woven basket of steaming garlic bread in front of them. She placed a dish on the table, poured olive oil into it and spooned in pesto. The spoon danced as she stirred the concoction.

"I take it, Mr. James," she said to him, "that you want your regular?"

"As usuall, you're right on the money."

Her eyes turned to Emy. "And for you?"

Emy opened her mouth to speak, but realized she had no idea what to say. After an awkward beat, she shrugged.

The waitress frowned and looked back at Bryan. "You took her menu."

He grinned. "I think she'll have what I'm having."

She turned back to Emy. "You sure you like octopus? I mean, raw octopus?"

Emy gagged.

"Hey!" Bryan yelled in mock horror. "Stop that. This is our first date."

Smiling, the waitress stepped back from the table. "Don't worry, ma'am, he knows how to order."

Emy glanced from the waitress to her date. "I certainly hope so, or this is going to be a very short meal."

"I'll be right back with your wine," the waitress said and left them to themselves.

Bryan pushed the dish of oil and pesto toward her as well as the basket of bread. "You have to try this," he said. "They make the best in town."

She reached into the basket and took two pieces of garlic bread. Her fingers immediately warmed to the touch. "Jesus. They just take this out of the oven?"

His fingers darted into the basket and took a few of the carved squares. "It's always right out of the oven. You could say the chef is a bit obsessive about that."

She swirled a piece of the bread into the dish, waited for it to stop dripping, and popped it into her mouth. Her taste buds screamed in delight and she moaned around it. Bryan's eyes lit up in satisfaction as he watched her chew.

"That is amazing," she said.

Bryan quickly chewed his own, swallowed, and smiled. "Told you. And trust me, the rest will be just as good."

He hadn't been exaggerating. Bryan always ordered the chef's special. Three courses. Spicy, zesty calamari prepared so well that it melted in your mouth. An Italian seasoned steak with onions, mushrooms, shallots, and basted with a garlic crust. And for dessert? The best tiramisu she'd ever had.

The bottle of wine they'd shared was exquisite, but left her feeling drowsy. Bryan ordered them espresso as a digestif.

While they ate, she told him about the Philippines, or what she remembered of it. She didn't mention her mother or her father, except in passing, and Bryan didn't probe. Emy didn't feel like going into detail about her immigration to the states or what had brought it about, so she asked about him instead.

"What got you into the museum game?" she asked as she sipped the dark coffee.

He shrugged. "I love art. Always have. I suck at creating it, but I very much appreciate it. Also, ancient civilizations fascinate me."

"How so?" she asked.

"You ever read about Mesopotamia?"

She shook her head.

He smiled. "Iraq. Iran. Syria. Afghanistan. All those countries you know about from the news were once the cradle of civilization. While the rest of the world was still learning how to farm or living as hunter/gatherer tribes, they invented math, writing, and built temples to their gods. They constructed cities the likes of which had never been seen before."

"Babylon?"

Bryan's smile grew. "Yes. And that was one of the later city states. One of the last, actually. You've read your Bible?"

Emy rolled her eyes. "Catholic. It goes with being Filipino."

"Well, Abraham came from Ur. That was once a city state too. That entire area eventually gave birth to Judaism, Christianity, and Islam. All three share a common origin. All three are rooted in Mesopotamian legend and history."

She nodded. "I guess you love this stuff."

His cheeks flushed. He cleared his throat and sipped his espresso. "Sorry. I tend to get carried away."

"I don't mind," she said. "You study all that in college?"

"Of course," he grinned. "But I always had an interest. Long before then."

"You said the other night you wished you were at the Museum of Natural History rather than the Menil. But you love art." He tented his hands, chin sitting atop them. Emy lifted the white porcelain espresso cup. "So why would you want to change?"

"Good question," he said. "I guess because the Menil is mainly private collections. There's less variety. We miss out on the big stuff. Although, that's no sleight. The HMNS gets more of the touring exhibits. We rarely get those."

"So it's about the exhibits?"

He shook his head. "Not exactly. You know what a curator does, right?"

"Um," Emy paused. Actually, she had no idea what a curator did. "No. I guess not."

"Okay," he said. "Stop me when I start boring you." He finished his espresso and gently laid the cup down. "A curator is responsible for acquisition of cultural items. We're also the folks that study those items or particular periods of history. It's a little different in art than it is with say archaeological artifacts, but the concept is the same. You become a subject matter expert, write papers, examine, and, of course, do your damnedest to protect those items."

"Ah," she said. "So what great finds can I blame you for?"

He shrugged. "I managed to swing us some Peter Max originals from his Patriotic series."

She grinned. "Those the ones with the psychedelic colors?"

"Yes!"

She couldn't help but feel his happiness. The man was crazy for his art, just as she was for her chemistry and physics. It'd been a long time since she'd been on a date with someone who was passionate about anything other than drinking and getting laid.

"Always felt like I was tripping when I wandered that part of the Menil."

Bryan laughed. "That was the point. It's why I put the gallery together that way. Lead you in, let you soak in it, and slowly lead you back out. Just like a good trip should."

"Hmm," Emy said. "Mushrooms or LSD?"

Bryan's face froze for a moment. "Aren't I talking to a cop?"

"I'm off duty," she said. "Also, we're talking past crimes here. Not future ones."

He relaxed. "Never cared for LSD. Only tripped on shrooms a couple of times. You ever had peyote?" he asked.

She shook her head.

"I was invited to a ceremony in Arizona." His eyes bored into hers. "It was...transcendent."

"In what way?" she said and pulled her eyes from his, dropping them to gaze down into the dregs of her espresso cup.

"Well—" His voice trailed off and she looked up at him. His eyes were looking up at the ceiling as he searched for words. "Well, I guess you could say I saw god."

She cocked an eyebrow. "God?"

His eyes flicked to hers. The burning stare was gone, replaced with wistful longing. "Not god like you'd think. Not some deity from any text. But, I guess for a few hours, I felt like I was one with the universe. I understood everything. And my part in things."

"And what part was that?" she asked.

He giggled. "That I'm of no more importance than a grain of sand."

She laughed. "You had to take drugs to figure that out?"

"It meant much more at the time."

The waitress appeared at Bryan's elbow. "Can I get y'all anything else this evening? More wine?"

"God, no," Emy giggled.

"If the lady says no," Bryan said, "then I guess we're done."

The blond pulled a small strip of leather from her cummerbund and placed it on the table. "Whenever you're ready, folks. No rush." She walked away.

Emy started to reach for it, but Bryan slid it away from her. "My idea. My bill," he said.

"Thank you, Bryan. But let me give you some cash. Something."

He shook his head. "If you want to repay me, come to the museum with me tomorrow."

"Which museum?" she asked.

"The good one," he said and then smiled.

"Okay. I'd like that."

"Good," Bryan said. "Now let's get out of here before we order something else."

Chapter 20

The work week was over, or so Jackson had told him over the phone when he invited Dew out to the bar. He'd declined, mentioning only that he had a hot case. Jackson had sighed, called him a workaholic, and hung up the phone. Dew had smiled at that. Jackson could be such a churlish little kid when things didn't go his way.

Hell of it was, a drink among friends sounded like just the right thing. But if he drank with Jackson, it would last until closing time and he'd be useless on Saturday. Worse than that, the reporter would wait until Dew was good and drunk to try and coax out information.

Jackson couldn't help it—he was a reporter and that's what they did. But Dew just couldn't stand the thought of having to put up with it. Especially not when there were a couple of crispy critters in the morgue, courtesy of the firebug. No, he needed to be at the top of his game. Which was why he was only on his fourth beer.

Case file printouts covered the floor in front of the couch. Photographs, CSU reports, and Arson reports littered the area around him. Dew sat cross-legged with a pillow beneath his ass. Frankie camped out on a manilla folder with her legs folded beneath her, purring like a finely tuned engine.

Dew sipped at his stout and placed it back on the table. The photos of the shacks were next to CSU snaps of the house. Emy's rendering of the symbol sat next to them.

Once Emy and Brett had directed CSU to check the large oak tree, they'd found the symbol carved on the trunk. The forensic folks were still deciding what the official report would be, but they'd already told Dew the scarring indicated the mark was made before the fire. How long before was anyone's guess.

Dew picked up the photo taken at the Hartman site and lay it next to Emy's rendering. They were nearly identical. He took another sip of the beer and leaned back against the couch.

Frankie meowed, walked on the papers, and stretched into his lap. She climbed onto his shoulder and then to the cushion behind him. Her head rammed into the back of his. "Okay, girl, okay." He reached up a hand and scratched behind her neck. The cat's purr was a soothing rumble.

Dew wanted a smoke. Something absolutely stuffed with tar and nicotine. The case had only been his for a few days and already it was wearing on him. The fact the bug had murdered a family made the case a priority. Captain Spillane had told him, in no uncertain terms, that the Mayor expected a break in the case damned soon.

The cat lay her head on his shoulder, the purr roaring in his right ear. Dew reached out and moved the papers around. He brought up the CSU report and read through it again.

The casts from the footprints at the Hartman site matched those of the shack fire. CSU was certain they were from the same person. The perp may not know it, but he was beginning to leave more evidence behind. If ever they managed to bring in a suspect, a search warrant to take casts of their feet would at least serve as circumstantial evidence. But Dewhurst wasn't hopeful about that.

For one thing, any lawyer would argue that the scorched grass at both sites made it impossible to tell how long the footprints had been there. And since the Hartman family was in the morgue, they wouldn't be able to testify as to when the footprints might have been made. Basically, they were left with little to go on. There was no pattern and the escalation had happened almost too fast.

Dew tapped a pen on the CSU report and Frankie mewed in protest. He clucked his tongue at her and continued reading. Forensics were still working on the accelerant. Dew couldn't wait to see Arson's latest report, hoping Ms. Aninzo had more answers than questions.

CSU had checked the fences for evidence, but found nothing. No signs of forced entry. No signs of stressed fence pickets. Dew wasn't surprised. The awning that attached the garage to the house hadn't been gated; there was no reason for the perp to vault over a fence when he could have just walked in.

Dew closed his eyes and tried to imagine what the site looked like at night. All he saw in his mind's eye were blurred images. He'd have to visit it. See it the way he'd seen the shacks. Two crimes, one that resulted in a double homicide, and he felt as though he was no closer to the perp. He had to start doing better. It was time to toss the book out the window.

With the Gomez case, he'd hired a consultant, Damon Henrichs, to piece together audio that CSU had said was impossible to use. Henrichs had not only managed to salvage it, but it had been instrumental in putting Gomez in the prosecutor's crosshairs. Until, as Jackson had said, someone from the cartel slipped a shank between his ribs.

Maybe it was time to talk to Tony about the case. The captain probably wouldn't clear it—he hated Tony with a burning passion. Dew sighed and finished his stout. In this day and age, homophobia was supposed to be a thing of the past. But that was a big fat lie; it was alive and well at HPD and nearly every other department across the country. All the HR guidelines and memos in the world weren't going to change it. But perhaps one day, they'd be as accepted as officers who weren't white. One day.

Dew shook his head. The beer was getting on top of him. The four pack was dead, and it was time to switch to water. 9% beer was not something to mess with unless you wanted a hell of a hangover.

"Sorry, girl," he said to the cat and leaned forward. She pulled her head off his shoulder with a protesting cry and crept to the other side of the couch. He stood on wobbly legs, grabbed the empty cans, and headed to the kitchen.

Paper crinkled as Frankie leaped down from the couch to walk upon the case files. Dew couldn't help but smile; she'd no doubt be camped on the paper when he returned.

Once the cans were in the recycle bin, he pulled out a large glass, filled it with water, and drank. The liquid cooled his throat. It was past 11 at night and the temperature outside hovered at 90°. He refilled the glass and looked out into the living room. Sure enough, Frankie was spread out on the paper and flashing her caramel belly.

Smiling, Dew returned to the couch, but sat on the floor next to her. He absently rubbed her belly while he drank water and stared at the photos. The symbol. It was like something you'd see in an ancient text of glyphs. Dew sipped the water. Maybe they were thinking about this the wrong way. Maybe this was a religious thing. A sacrificial thing.

Dew pulled his notebook off the end-table and scrawled a quick set of notes. He loosed a yawn and rubbed at his eyes. The heat. The job. The case. The beer. It was creeping up on him and he needed sleep. He glanced over at Frankie in time to see her glance toward the hallway leading to the bedroom.

"Okay," he said. He placed the glass on a coaster, stood up, and stared down at the papers. The cat rose and walked into the hall. Dew took one final look at the symbol, turned, and followed. By the time he undressed and lay down with the cat in the crook of his arm, he was fast asleep.

Chapter 21

I t wasn't dark enough for P's liking. In fact, it seemed like the moon was lighting the earth in jealousy of the sun. Ghere chuckled in his mind. It was dangerous being near the Hartman house. Hell, it was dangerous being out at night in this neighborhood period. Not because of crime though.

It was the cameras. The damned cameras. What had made him think he could get away with putting them in the tree as well as in the vacant house? The Arson investigator had damned near found the one in the tree. If the cops were smart, they'd find it soon.

On the verge of sleep, the woman's face had jumped into his mind. The scar that marked her was...unique. Only half her face had been damaged by whatever did it. Although Ghere knew what had caused it, the deity wasn't exchanging details.

Do you know her?

Yes, It had said.

The face wouldn't leave his mind. Every time he was close to drifting off, her face would snap him awake. She was coming for him. She was coming for Ghere. She would find the cameras and his oath would be broken.

He'd finally given up on sleep, dressed in his jogger's uniform, emptied his backpack, and headed to the car. It was already getting late, but Friday nights were filled with people coming to and from the bars and shows. He'd have no problem blending in. Except there was one problem he hadn't foreseen—the HPD patrol car parked in front of the Hartman's.

Just to change things up a bit, P had parked his car on a different street. Instead of sneaking behind hedges and bushes, he made his way through the yards he knew had no dogs. It required even more caution than going through the streets. If someone awake saw him moving through their yard, he was more likely to get shot than have to worry about the cops.

P stood behind the fence and stared out at the street. The narrow easement between the McMansion and the house next door was enough for him to see the car. He couldn't tell if there was only a single officer, but considering the city's budget problems, it wouldn't surprise him. The street lamps were out, reducing the car's interior to shadows even beneath the bright moon.

He was in shadow, but so were they. Unless he climbed the fence behind the McMansion and went inside, he'd be easy to spot. With all the construction on the derelict house, he wasn't sure it afforded him much protection either. Cameras. Fucking cameras.

P hadn't been worried about the police or Arson finding them. There would be little they could do to prove they were his, let alone what they had filmed. But the woman. Something about her upset him; Ghere was upset about her as well.

He moved further along the fence-line until he thought he was hidden well enough. As carefully as he could, he raised himself over the fence behind the McMansion. The water-starved grass crunched beneath his feet. He lost his balance and his pack bounced against the fence.

P crouched and tried to see the street through the house's unfinished walls. His heart thudded in his chest while he waited to see if they'd heard him. In the moon-light, the shadows were thicker than the night before. Eyes riveted to the patrol car, he crab-walked to the side of the house.

When he reached the Tyvek covered wall panels, he blew out a sigh, and tried to control his breathing. The backpack slapping against the fence had shaken several of the pickets making him wonder just how rotted the wood was. He'd either have to find a post to climb and return to the neighbor's yard, or find another way out. The idea of waiting for the patrol car to leave left him anxious because there was no way to know if it had been posted there for the night, and impossible to know if the cop would leave the car to patrol the backyard.

The wi-fi enabled cameras weren't very traceable. He'd purchased them via bit-coin months ago when Ghere first started talking in his mind. Trying to trace their point of origin was going to be a nightmare for whomever they tasked with the job.

But the investigator, *her*, might find... What?

You are panicking for no reason. Leave this place. Leave the cameras. They will choke on the evidence.

P shook his head. Maybe Ghere was right. God had been thus far. But if they found the camera in the tree, they'd find the sigil. And if they found that...

Leave, Ghere growled again. *This grows tiresome.*

He lifted a gloved hand and brushed away a sheen of sweat. It wasn't the heat—it was stress.

"I have to get to the tree," he told the deity. Ghere growled in his mind, but said nothing. God didn't need to. He could feel both the disappointment and the anger in the sound echoing in his mind. "If they get it, they'll have more evidence."

You are a fool, God said.

Something banged in the street. P paused in the midst of shrugging off the empty backpack and cocked his head to listen. Was it a car door? No. Couldn't be. He'd been so quiet, so careful.

Fool, Ghere said with a mocking laugh.

"No," P said. "No. Not—"

Escape! God screamed, P's mind recoiling in panic and terror.

Without bothering to re-shoulder both of the pack's straps, he turned and ran through the construction debris. Somewhere beneath the pounding of his heart, a shouting voice erupted from behind. The cop, it had to be the cop, was coming, probably with his pistol in the air and a mag-light shining a bright, wavering cone of light. He was caught. It was over.

Escape, God said again. The fury in the being's voice smashed through his panic spreading a wave of purifying heat across his mind. A new energy flooded through him, something from God Itself, and all thought, all worry disappeared.

He saw the edge of a loose board laying on the concrete slab. P dodged it easily, fitted the loose pack strap without missing a step, and increased his speed.

They won't catch you and you won't leave a trace, the deity promised. *They will never know it was you.*

The words spread across his thoughts like a healing salve and he swung a free hand to push off of a stack of drywall to turn without breaking his stride. The hoarse commands continued, but he could tell the cop had barely entered the construction site. He was going to get away.

P skirted the Tyvek wall separating him from the backyard. There was the fence. P leaped without thinking, his feet striking the boards at the same time his gloved hands gripped the top of the pickets. Nails squealed through the rotted wood as they gave way. The sound of crunching and splintering wood barely touched his consciousness. In a little more than a second, he scrambled over the fence and continued running.

The cop's shouts to stop, to identify himself, quickly faded as he put more and more distance between himself and the threat. A moment later, he was far away from the McMansion and the Hartman ruin. He was free.

Chapter 22

The patio smelled of bacon, eggs, and fresh pastries. Emy stared down at her cool cup of coffee with longing, but she couldn't drink anymore without bursting. Luna's head bounced on her foot in a slow, gentle rhythm. She looked down and the dog looked back at her in expectation, tongue lolling in the heat. Maybe the dog was right; it was hotter than hell and only getting worse. It was time to go home.

Emy stared at the computer screen, finished writing the paragraph, and logged out of her VPN client. She'd done enough for the day anyway. Novak had wanted the report to have as much information in it as possible before she passed it off to Detective Dewhurst. Well, she'd done the best she could.

With a sigh, she closed the laptop lid and put it in her bag. The French cafe was her favorite place to have breakfast and she always took Luna with her. That morning, she'd brought Bryan as well.

When they'd left the restaurant last night, he'd asked if she wanted to see a movie. Emy had thought about it before realizing she didn't want to be around other people. Instead, she'd wanted to spend more time talking with him. It'd been a long time since she'd been on a date, and she wanted to make the most of it.

"How about we just have coffee at my place?" she'd asked.

Bryan paused while he put on his seat belt. "Coffee?" He turned to her with a confused smile. "Like, at your apartment?"

Emy blushed and nodded. "Luna needs some time out of the crate.

Besides, I haven't had any company in forever." She couldn't keep his stare and dropped her eyes. "Neither has Luna."

He laughed. "As long as she doesn't eat me," he said.

Emy opened her mouth to say something suggestive and closed it. This wasn't that moment. Her pulse pounded in her ears. "She won't. Let's go."

Bryan pulled out of the parking lot and within ten minutes, they were back at her apartment. He parked the car on the street and they made their way up the steps into the complex.

It had been over a year since she'd invited a date to her apartment. She'd learned from a long, bitter experience that most men were either horrified at the idea of seeing her scarred face during sex, or simply bailed out when they saw her naked. The scars that ran across her face and shoulder continued down her left side all the way to her thigh. Yet another reason she preferred darkness to light.

But Bryan was different, she had hoped. While they talked on the couch and drank coffee, Bryan's hand petted and scratched Luna's head. The dog was curled up in an adorable comma, eyes half-closed. When Luna started snoring, Emy had stood.

"I think she has the right idea," she said.

Bryan nodded and looked at his watch. It was past midnight. "Wow. Okay. Had no idea it was that late." He held up his coffee cup. "Sink?"

Emy grinned and took it from his hand. She walked into the kitchen and placed the dishes in the sink. When she returned to the living room, Bryan stood by the front door.

"You need to get home?" she asked.

He cocked an eyebrow. "What?"

She rolled her eyes. "Do you need to go home? Wake up early?"

A beat of silence passed before he blushed. "Um, no."

"Then what's the hurry?" she asked and gestured to him to follow her. Emy glanced at Luna and the dog jumped off the couch and headed to her crate. "Good, girl," Emy said.

"That's one well-trained dog," Bryan said in a cracked voice.

"Yes, she is," Emy agreed. "And she knows when she's not wanted in the bedroom." The blush returned to his cheeks. She was at the hallway, standing and waiting for him. Bryan opened his mouth and then closed it. Emy frowned and walked to him.

"I— I'm not used to—"

"Bryan?" Emy said and placed a hand on his shoulder. "I like you. I think you like me. It's been a long time since I've met a man I want to spend time with."

He nodded, a slack-jawed smile on his face. "Just not used to someone being this forward."

She leaned in close and brushed her lips against his. "If you don't want to, no harm, no foul." Emy held her smile, although the butterflies in her stomach cried for her to back out, to let go, to not force the issue. "But I'd like some company tonight."

The blush on his face grew brighter. "Um, I'd like that," he said. "I'd really like that."

She kissed him, her arms reaching around his waist. Her lips parted just as his did. Their tongues touched. She moaned in her throat and pressed her body against him, his erection pushing against her belly.

Bryan's hands moved down from her shoulder and clutched her ass. She moaned again and disengaged from him. He looked at her, confused. She put out her hand and led him to the bedroom.

It was tender. It was passionate. It was fucking followed by lovemaking followed by rampant greed. She touched every part of his body, and he hers. When they were spent, they lay on the bed in a tangle of limbs.

His hand brushed down her left side in a tender caress. The sensation was odd since most of the nerve endings on that side had died when she was burned. She stiffened at his touch. While they enjoyed one another, he'd been very careful to mind where his hands touched her.

Bryan's fingers stopped their journey. "Does that bother you?"

For a moment, she wasn't sure what to say. Past lovers had always cringed at the very idea of touching her left side. Bryan didn't seem to care. "No," she said. "It's just—" Emy didn't know how to explain it and decided to kiss him instead.

His fingers resumed their travels, skirting down her leg before making their way back up to tickle her. A strong chill went down her back and she sighed.

"I don't know you very well," Bryan said. "But I'd like to think we can do this again some time."

She kissed him again. "Anytime," she said.

Around two in the morning, they finally fell asleep in one another's arms. Emy didn't dream about the monster or fire. For once, her mind had other things to think about.

They'd awakened still in each other's arms, sheets wrapping them like a cocoon. Emy had demanded they shower before going out for breakfast. Once the cool water sprayed down, she found herself touching him again. They got dirty. Then they got clean again.

While they were toweling off, Bryan had checked his phone. "Score," he said and looked up at Emy. "Would you like to join me at the museum today?"

She'd been shrugging into a pair of shorts, her black lace bra still wrapping her breasts. The morning after was always awkward for her. Men liked her well enough to have sex with her in the darkness, but in the light, their eyes usually dropped from her body.

Bryan's eyes glittered with a conspiratorial grin.

"Museum? What, you want to show me around the Menil?" she asked.

He shook his head. "No, ma'am. I want to show you some ancient history."

"And how are you going to do that?" she said and pulled on a t-shirt.

He sat on the bed next to her and pulled on his socks. He was already in his khakis and shirt. "There's an exhibit I want to show you before it heads back."

"Heads back where?"

Bryan licked his lips. "The collector. It's a private collection that's been traveling the states for a few years. And if you haven't seen it, this will probably be your last chance."

What about the report? a voice whispered in her head.

"I have some work to do this morning," she said.

He frowned. "What, no breakfast?"

Shaking her head, Emy walked to him and planted a kiss on his lips. "Breakfast is definitely first." She kissed him again. "We'll take Luna with us."

"Luna?" Bryan asked. "A place that allows dogs?"

Emy laughed. "She's always welcome there. Hope you like French coffee."

They had walked to the cafe with Luna leading the way. The dog had been very affectionate with Bryan when they let her out of the crate. Emy was beginning to think maybe this man was what she'd been looking for.

You've been on one date with him, a voice said inside her head. What the hell is wrong with you?

She smiled at the voice. Sometimes you just know.

Bryan had touched her shoulder as they tried to stay out of the sun and in the shadows of the building's awnings. "What are you smiling about?"

"Nothing much," she'd said.

Emy sighed. Bryan had been gone for a little over two hours and she already missed him. She had to remember to thank Brett for that.

Shouldering the pack, she unwound Luna's leash from the chair arm and stood. The dog jumped to her feet, tail smacking against the metal table leg.

Emy smiled and patted her head, eliciting a happy canine growl, and immediately turned in the direction of home.

They left the patio's relatively cool shade and walked into the blazing heat of the sun. Emy held the leash tight as Luna struggled to go faster. If the dog saw something she wanted to chase, or more frequently, someone she wanted to meet, she had a tendency to strain. Emy was barely strong enough to keep hold of her in one hand and Luna knew it. But when they walked home from breakfast, she was usually a good girl.

Emy shaded her eyes against the harsh sunlight. The cornflower blue sky was absent of any clouds. The weather forecast hadn't changed in weeks, with the exception of the heat index. Emy cursed herself for forgetting her sunglasses.

Luna's nose hovered just above the sidewalk, tail swinging in happy circles. Her wide pink tongue hung to one side of her mouth. Emy couldn't help but smile. Usually the best part of breakfast was walking with her dog, but the memory of the night before with Bryan was more than enough to make her grin.

"Two blocks until home," she said to herself and wiped another sheen of sweat from her forehead. Luna pulled on the leash, obviously in a hurry to get out of the heat.

Heat, she thought, it's all about heat.

The VICAP and Interpol research was unable to break her mood, but it did make her anxious. The report was now fully fleshed out. She wasn't sure what more she could possibly stuff into it. The only loose ends were the symbol itself, the firebug, obviously, and the deaths.

When she'd put together the files on the incidents in Munich and Marseilles, the names of the investigators had popped up. She didn't know if either of them would speak English, but she wanted to try and contact them and see if she could glean any more detail.

Since the Marseilles case happened in the 70s, she wasn't all that shocked to discover the officer was dead. If he'd still been alive, he'd have been an octogenarian. But he'd never made it to that age. Not even close. He died within a week of the fire. Stabbed to death.

She wasn't able to read the police report on that one. No one had bothered to digitize the records related to the case. Forty years in the past, it was doubtful anyone on the force would be of much help.

The Munich case, however, was very different. The officer in charge was shot to death six days after the fire. The report had not only been digitized, it had been annotated many times by an officer named Friedrich Van Haufen. The victim's name was Otto Van Haufen. Emy wondered if Friedrich was

Otto's brother or his son. Either way, Friedrich was obviously still looking into the case.

Otto's body had been found in an upscale flat. The resident's name was Til Pfeiffer. Mr. Pfeiffer had gone missing the same day Otto's body was discovered. Van Haufen had been shot five times in the chest with his own H&K P7. The weapon had been wiped clean of fingerprints. Van Haufen's wallet had been stolen as well as his police identification. The notebook with his case notes had also disappeared.

Emy had gone through the crime scene photos and come across one that took her breath away. To the right of the photo, you could see a bloody boot. The center, however, showed a design scrawled in blood. She'd had her cup of coffee halfway to her lips when she'd zoomed in on the design. She'd neared spilled it on the open computer. It was the same sigil their bug had left.

Her mind had raced. She'd tagged the case numbers, as well as made links to the photos, and hurriedly placed them in the report. Once she'd finished putting in the details, she'd flipped over to the American databases. The two incidents that occurred on American soil had very similar ends. Both investigators had been murdered within days of the fires. Neither crime scene, however, had the design. One officer had been found floating in a river while the other had been killed in his home. Both were still marked as unsolved.

A chill had crept up her spine. If you left out the European cases, the murders and fires were mere coincidence and had nothing more than a circumstantial relationship to the Houston cases. But if you allowed for the European incidents, it was beyond obvious—their bug was a killer. And he had been killing people since the 1970s.

And again, that didn't make much sense. Their bug would be what, in his 60s? Plus, the perp would have lived in Germany, France, and several states? None of it made sense.

Her final summary in the report pointed out those facts as well. They weren't looking for some pimply faced youth that was just now getting into the fire game. They were looking for a pro—someone that had been doing this a long time without detection. That was rare, but not unheard of. The fact the bug had been getting away with it so long also pointed to how damned dangerous the arsonist was.

Four murders of police and arson investigators across the world. And those were just the ones she could find. Emy had felt nothing but chills at that thought. If there were more out there, maybe Dewhurst could dig them up. If nothing else, she was sure he'd want to have a conversation with the surviving Van Haufen. She did too.

Emy stumbled into the back of the dog. Luna never stopped on a walk unless forced. Emy looked down at her. The American Bully was staring at the alley across the street. Her fur stood on end, ears and tail pointed straight up, and a low growl had formed in her throat.

"What's wrong, girl?" Emy asked.

The dog didn't respond. The growl in her throat increased as she opened her jaws. The folds of flesh around her mouth were taut in...what? Anger? Fear?

Emy patted the dog's rump. Luna turned to her, still growling. For a moment, she was afraid her companion would bite her, but Luna turned back to the alley and continued to growl.

The alley was dark in the space between the two apartment buildings. Emy followed Luna's gaze into the shadows, but saw nothing. The dog's growl finally decreased and then disappeared. Luna relaxed, whimpered, and turned to face Emy. She sat down on her haunches, tail swishing back and forth.

Emy patted the dog's head and Luna licked her hand. "What the hell was that all about, girl?" Luna yawned and flicked her head in the direction of home. Emy clucked her tongue. Luna turned back and started walking.

She looked behind her, but only saw the regular group of joggers and walkers in the heat. It was time for a nap before the trip to the museum. And maybe some cuddle time with Luna would put them both at ease.

Chapter 23

D ew sat in a lawn chair he'd pulled from the garage. Although he was in the shadow of the giant oak trees, the heat still radiated in waves. His suit coat lay folded on the scorched grass next to the chair. At that moment, he would have killed for a cigarette.

The burned out hulk of the Hartman house was spread open before him. Dead leaves had already swirled in and covered part of the remaining hardwood floor. A dog had left a pile of shit near the sliding glass door. Until the house was knocked down, it would continue to crumble. With the extreme heat of the summer, it might take a while. If Houston ever had rain again, it would fall apart in a hurry.

He glanced at his phone. No messages. He'd called CSU half an hour ago and they still hadn't shown up. Dewhurst hoped they'd arrive soon so he could step into his car for some good old fashioned A/C. It wasn't noon yet and already the temperature was 102°. He considered removing his brightly colored tie, but only loosened it instead.

His blue dress shirt was sopping wet. Even with an undershirt on, he had sweat through both of them. He'd have to get everything dry cleaned. Dewhurst grimaced. This case was going to drive him back to smoking. And back to whiskey.

Walking the site had been a great idea, but for all the wrong reasons. When he'd arrived at the Hartman site, the patrol car was gone. He'd expected that. All the papers published on sociopathic, serial behavior concluded that perpetrators often revisited the scene of the crime. Dewhurst was certain his bug fit this profile too. He'd fought with Captain Spillane over posting a patrol unit to watch the house at night. There was the usual bitching about budget and overtime, but when Dewhurst asked what the Mayor would think, the Captain relented. But only one patrol car. And only during darkness.

After walking the site, he was glad he'd been so adamant. He'd just finished his first cup of coffee for the morning when his phone had dinged. The officer on the night patrol had filed a report about chasing a suspect from the construction site next door. Officer Wilson had sustained minor abrasions from chasing the suspect over several fences as well as a twisted ankle. According to the report, the perp had broken the fence behind the construction site in attempting to slink away. Wilson heard it and came running. As soon as Dewhurst read the report on his computer, he'd showered, jumped in some clothes, and headed to the Hartman's.

When he'd arrived, neighbors mowed their lawns while their kids sprayed one another with water guns as sweat poured off them. A troupe of Mexicans used leaf blowers while others trimmed trees or cut down dead limbs. It was a typical Saturday morning in Houston.

That had at least assuaged his fears the perp would try again when the patrol car wasn't there. Anyone trying to get near the Hartman house was sure to get spotted. Dewhurst was fairly sure someone would have called 911.

The site looked identical to the CSU and Arson photos. The caved-in roof made the house grin with malevolence. The scorched and charred floor had burned down to the concrete slab. The metal remains of a couch still sat in the center of the room. With the exception of the leaves and dog shit, the house could have been in suspended animation.

The yard was the same. The remnants of the plaster casts highlighted the perp's naked footprints. How Ms. Aninzo had spotted them was beyond him, but his respect for her was growing by the day.

Dew walked to the tree where the symbol had been found. CSU had painted an orange circle around it. The marks had definitely been made by a cutting tool, probably a hunting or survival knife. He imagined a naked man stalking through the backyard with a blade, and couldn't do it. It didn't make sense.

If the perp's MO required him to be naked for the act, then carrying around supplies seemed improbable. In fact, he probably used the gas can from the garage and a book of matches to light the fire. Carrying as little as possible sounded more likely.

But when did the perp make the mark? If it had been done before the fire, it meant he had not only been watching the house for some time, but had also managed to climb the damned tree to make the mark. Dew tapped his foot on the crunchy grass and stared up into the canopy.

Despite the punishing heat, the oak's leaves were still verdant green with a few lower limbs of mottled brown. This tree would make it, just like most of the trees in the city. Dew looked at the limbs. They seemed sturdy, but the lower ones with dead leaves made it impossible to know if they'd hold his weight. Sighing, Dew retreated to the detached garage.

It was well-organized. Lawn tools hung from pegs on a wall, save for the old, but well-cared for lawnmower. And the ladder.

The ladder was one of those combo jobs, the kind that you could lock in different positions. Everything in the garage was neat and tidy. Hell, the concrete floor was even free of oil spots.

But the ladder was on the floor. He studied the wall. A faint outline of where it once hung stood out from the unpainted sheetrock. Dewhurst brushed sweat from his brow. CSU hadn't taken fingerprints in the garage, but they'd need to now.

Once he was certain the ladder was the only thing out of place, he headed back into the yard. Dew carefully folded his coat and lay it on the grass. Those low hanging limbs kept drawing his attention.

He pulled the phone from his pocket and called CSU. After wading through a number of transfers and holds, he finally managed to get hold of the shift supervisor. The conversation was heated, but he finally convinced the man to send out a team. Dew knew why CSU didn't want to come back out—it was an admission they'd failed to find everything the first time.

Once the call had been made, he'd stared at those low limbs again. "Fuck it," he said to the empty backyard, and hoisted himself up on the lowest limb. The tree was thick enough not to shake, but the branch quivered beneath his weight. He kept his feet near the base of the limb and climbed to the next one.

It didn't take long before he reached the sigil. His arms burned with exertion and his hands were chafed and scratched. Dew stared at the symbol and then looked up. The perp might have used the ladder to get this high and carve the sigil, but to get higher, he'd have to climb. Dew turned his head. The ruined Hartman house was visible through the leaves, but it wasn't a good enough vantage point to see the roof.

Dew ignored the symbol and continued to climb. Sweat dripped off his face in rivulets as he reached the next branch. And the next. And the next. It took nearly five minutes, but he was finally high enough in the tree to see the camera.

He'd been looking at the squat thing for over a minute and didn't realize it. It was painted to match the ashy color of the oak bark. A black rectangle was taped to it; a pair of cords snaked to the other side of the camera. Mindful of his position on the limbs, he pulled up and looked at the other side. What looked like a mint tin was fastened to the camera with duct tape. The tin's sides had been snipped open to allow access to peripheral ports.

"Fuck me," Dew breathed. CSU had really dropped the ball this time. Shaking his head, Dew began to descend. If he stuck around any longer in the tree, he'd no doubt begin trampling evidence and they needed everything they could get.

It took him several minutes to safely reach the ground, his hands and legs burning with the effort. The heat seemed to have ratcheted up several degrees in the fifteen minutes it'd taken him to inspect the tree. After that, he'd taken the lawn chair off a peg in the garage, placed it in the grass, and rested. All he had to do now was wait for CSU to finally show up.

His mind raced. The perp had placed a camera in the tree. Was it the only one? Was it possible another had been set up somewhere? And what the hell was the crap fastened to the camera? Their perp definitely wasn't some run-of-the-mill nut job. Whoever had placed that camera knew what they were doing and had hidden it fairly well. Under the cover of darkness, that would have been difficult. Doing it in the dead of night without attracting attention? Even more so.

Dew unlocked his phone and started jotting down notes. They were looking for someone with technical expertise. Maybe even someone who installed security systems. It was time to start asking around the neighborhood if anyone had seen strange vehicles, or any vehicles, roaming during the day or night. He was certain the flat-foots had already done that, but they probably only asked about unfamiliar ones. No, they had to see if there was other routine traffic around. The perp knew the neighborhood and might even know the routines of everyone there.

They'd have to dig for the information. Captain Spillane would no doubt be pissed about the overtime. Dew grinned to himself. He imagined the conversation and the fact he'd have to drop the Mayor's name again. This close to election season, he'd no doubt both the City Council and Mayor's office would be screaming for a result at any cost.

He locked the phone and placed it on his knee. His eyes once again studied the Hartman wreckage. He wondered if they'd catch the perp in time to stop another fire.

Chapter 24

E my stood in the large hall. Children yelled, parents told them to hush, and the soft sounds of footfalls echoed beneath it all.

The Houston Museum of Natural Science was a massive building. Spread out from its large concrete walks, the planets were arranged in distance from the sun. Their size was relative to the large sun right outside the main entry doors. You had to walk some distance to encounter Pluto. The first time Emy had been to the building as a child, she'd demanded her aunt let her walk from Pluto to the sun. As hot as it had been that day, it was no wonder her aunt had been grumpy. But she'd humored Emy, just as she did with all things.

Emy had stood outside the large fountain watching a rainbow mirage as the geysers spewed water toward the sky. The light breeze blew a welcome mist across her skin. It was 104° and the hottest part of the day was still ahead.

Now she waited in the hall near the gift shop, her sweat drying in the air-conditioned building. A child, no more than eight or nine, stared at her. The towheaded boy wore an Oscar the Grouch t-shirt and clean blue jeans. He held his mother's hand while she waited in line to get tickets. The child's face slowly turned into a mask of disgusted curiosity.

Emy turned away and brushed locks of hair across the left side of her face. Whenever a child looked at her like that, no, stared, she felt as though she was back in 3rd grade when her classmates made fun of her, called her jerky face, lasagna cheeks, and a ton of other "witty" barbs. The confidence she'd felt this morning had evaporated with a single, surprised gaze.

She stared through the glass of the gift shop. Parents, their children, and a few young adults circled the many different souvenirs for the museum's exhibits. Emy inwardly sighed as her eyes caught sight of a large geode.

A cave of red, white, and grey crystal teeth jutted from the rock's interior. It was beautiful and terrible at the same time. Her father would have loved it.

"See something you like?" Bryan's voice said from behind her.

She turned and smiled. Bryan wore a pair of robin's egg colored blue jeans and a white polo shirt with the Menil logo above his right breast. Unlike that morning, his hair was brushed. He looked even more professional than he had the night before.

"You could say that," she said.

Bryan opened his mouth and blushed. "Um, I meant in the gift shop."

She giggled. "So did I."

"Oh," he said. "Foot? Meet mouth."

Emy grabbed his shoulder. "I'm just joking. You look great."

"Thank you," he said. He shuffled past her and stared in through the glass. "You looking at that geode?"

She turned and followed his gaze. "Yes. It's beautiful, isn't it?"

He shook his head. "Yes, it is. Afraid I'm never going to be able to afford something like that."

Emy nodded. "Me neither. But I can dream." They exchanged a glance and traded grins. "So, um, about this tour?"

"Ah, yes," Bryan said. He pulled a badge from his pocket and handed it to her. It was white with a blue lanyard.

"Museum VIP?" she asked aloud.

"Yup," Bryan said. He put his own badge around his neck. "That means we get to go pretty much anywhere we like." He pointed to the loud crowd of parents and children. "And get away from this rabble."

"You saying they're a horde?"

He laughed. "Aren't they?"

The crowd noise surged for a moment and Emy looked back at the ticket booths. A man dressed in a blue tunic and flowing red robes appeared from a staff entrance. A heavy beard hung from his dark face and oily ringlets of hair protruded from his scalp down past his ears. The man walked through the crowd without making eye contact, arms crossed before him.

Bryan shook his head. "Publicity stunts. Gotta love 'em."

"What is that?" she asked.

He turned to her, eyebrows raised. "What? You've never seen Hammurabi?"

"Hamma-who?"

Bryan put an arm around her shoulder. "Let me educate you."

They'd walked past the hall of dinosaurs and the humongous T-Rex whose bony head was fixed in a silent roar. The model of a giant squid fighting a whale caught her eye as they made their way up the stairs to the special exhibit space.

The gemology hall, nearly vacant, was filled with rocks of all different colors, sizes, and shapes. Emy suddenly remembered she hadn't been in the HMNS in well over a decade. "Everything is beautiful," she'd said.

Bryan had merely grinned, allowing her to stop at each case and look in. She could feel his smile and his patience. Bryan was one of those people who probably visited the place more than once a week, but he seemed happy just to let her drink it all in.

When she felt she'd seen it all, she walked toward the signs that advertised "The Real Sumer." He encircled her waist with an arm and her entire body grinned.

They exited the hall and entered the next. A fatigued purple banner proclaimed it was the last week to see "the wonders of the ancient world." The script was mirrored by pictograms. Emy pointed at the banner. "What are those symbols?"

"Those," Bryan smiled, "are cuneiform. The oldest known written language."

"Oh," she said. "You can't read those can you?"

He shook his head. "Um, no. I mean I can make out the gist, but not actually read. If you put the tablet remains of Gilgamesh in front of me, I'd have no idea what they said without an English contextual analog."

Emy frowned. "I'm not sure what you said was an English contextual analog."

He winced. "Sorry. I mean that the symbols make sense to me only because of what's written above them. I can sound them out, well, some of them, but they're little more than gibberish to me."

"Some curator you are," she said and slapped his shoulder.

"Right," he said. "But I can tell you all about Peter Max."

Arm in arm, they entered the exhibit hall. Emy's eyes widened in wonder. Two large stone tablets stood on either side of the entryway. They were at least nine feet tall and covered in cuneiform. In between them was an informational plaque.

"The Code of Hammurabi," she said aloud. Bryan remained silent as she scanned the plaque text, her lips moving as she read the words. "Oldest known legal document?" she asked in a quiet voice.

Bryan nodded. "Depends on what you call 'legal,' but more or less, yes. Like the plaque says, a lot of our understanding of law comes from this document."

She stared up at the tablets. "They're huge."

"And they stood at the entryway to Babylon. These are facsimiles, obviously. Anyone who entered the city was responsible for knowing the Code and abiding by it. It was posted there so there would be no excuse for a transgression."

She frowned. "But what if you couldn't read?"

His gentle smile disappeared into a thin, serious line. "Then you were fucked."

"That's, um, eloquent," she chuckled.

Bryan grinned. "It's one of the reasons so many folks knew how to read. Illiteracy meant you couldn't enter into contracts and you certainly couldn't know the law."

"Seems a bit unfair," she said.

"Perhaps." He pointed at the symbols. "But these marks are no different than the words on a Supreme Court decree, or a town's charter of rules. It was the law."

"Gotcha," she said. Emy sighed and walked around to the right. Bryan followed.

Maps, relics, statues, and clay tablets filled the exhibit. The more Emy read the plaques, the more questions she had for Bryan. To her delight, he compared everything in "contextual analogs." It was the first time in her life she'd found history to be anything but boring.

They walked toward a display case with a large banner hanging over it that read "The Gods." Gold, copper, and brass amulets lay on black velvet. Each amulet had an image carved into its surface. One had a dog crossed with a snake and read "Marduk." Another was a multi-pointed star inside a circle. The word "Ishtar" printed neatly beneath it.

She continued looking at the symbols, Bryan at her shoulder. They were beautiful, yet somewhat primitive, inscriptions. When she came to the last row, her breath hitched.

"Gibil," she breathed.

Bryan nodded. "Yes. God of fire and light. He's also known by—" He stopped. "Emy? Is something wrong?"

She barely heard him as she stared at a bright gold amulet. Instead of a single inscription on a disc of metal, the amulet's surface contained two 'V' like shapes, one smaller than the other and inside the larger. The branches were clean and devoid of the knobs she'd seen on the arsonist's signature. But apart from those details, they were identical.

Heart thumping in her chest, she read the plaque beneath it. *A rare metal cast of Gibil's sigil.* "Gibil," she breathed.

"Emy? Are you okay?" Bryan asked.

She turned to him, eyes wide. "What's Gibil?"

Bryan put a hand on her shoulder. "You sure you're okay?"

"Yes," she rolled her eyes. "Now tell me, please, who is Gibil?"

He shrugged. "The Sumerian god of fire and light."

"Fire," she said, eyes falling to the floor. The symbol burned in her mind, flames traveling and jumping between the outer ring and the inner lines.

The sound of snapping fingers made her look up. Bryan's face was lined with concern, lips set in a hard line.

"What is it?" he asked.

She cleared her throat. "I need to know everything about Gibil."

"Everything?" he asked, brow furrowed. "Why?"

Emy managed an excited grin. "It's a work thing, Bryan. Can you help?"

He shook his head. "Not a whole lot. Not on this. But I can take you to someone who can."

She put her arm around his waist. "This little trip may have actually saved someone's life."

The museum office was located deep in the basement. Past exhibit posters plastered the stuccoed, brown walls. If she'd thought the exhibit room was cold, this hallway was a freezer. Their steps clicked in time as they walked down the vinyl tile floor.

Bryan didn't ask her what she'd meant about saving lives. In fact, he hadn't said a word since he'd called someone on his cell phone. When he'd finished the call, he'd pointed to one of the stair wells and ushered her down. As they'd descended, the sounds of the loud main exhibit hall had faded into nothing. Now there was only the sounds of their steps, their breathing, and the whoosh of an unseen air conditioner.

They passed closed wooden doors with nameplates. She didn't bother looking at them. Bryan was focused on moving forward, so she followed suit. When they reached a windowless office set with an open door, Bryan stopped and turned to her. "Let me, um, make introductions."

Without waiting for a reply, he stuck his head in the doorway and knocked lightly. "Seamus?"

"Aye," a deep voice laden with an Irish brogue said. "Come on in, Bryan."

He turned to Emy and gestured for her to enter. She cocked an eyebrow and walked across the threshold. A short man stood behind a desk covered in papers, books, and a rubbish field of snack wrappers and soda cans. The man's fingers tugged at the red beard hanging down to his neck. His deep blue eyes blinked at her with owlish laziness. The short man smiled to himself, rose from behind the desk, and offered a rough, pale hand.

"Hello, ma'am. Name's Seamus. Or Doc. Or whatever you want to call me."

She chuckled. The man could have been a Tolkien dwarf. She shook his hand. "Emy. Pleased to meet you."

Seamus took a deep sniff of the air and grinned. He looked past her at Bryan. "I can definitely say, without a doubt, she smells better than you."

Bryan grunted. "Well, at least someone in here smells good." He pointed at the pile of refuse on the desk. "Don't you ever throw anything away?"

The short man shrugged. He walked around Emy and shook hands with Bryan. "You offering to be my maid?"

"I'm most assuredly not," Bryan said.

Seamus turned to Emy and jerked a thumb backwards at Bryan. "You hear how this one speaks? The man hasn't found a sentence he can't slaughter."

"Uh, I'm sure," Emy said. The devilish gleam in the Irishman's eyes made her grin. "Haven't exactly been around him long enough to know."

"That so?" the dwarf said. "Well, if you get tired of him, I'll take you to the Hobbit Hole and we can snort some mead."

"What?" Emy asked.

Bryan laughed. "Pay no mind, Emy. He's a dirty old man. And also one of those vegetarian type people."

Seamus rolled his eyes. "Except for the candy bars, yeah. As far as the phrase 'dirty old man?' I'm no older than you are, Bryan. Well, not much anyway."

"Uh-huh," Bryan said. He pointed at Emy. "She has a couple of questions for you. About the Sumer exhibit."

"Really?" Seamus asked. He seemed a little crestfallen. "You didn't bring her all the way down here just to meet me?"

"You can join us for dinner," Emy said, "if you have some time to answer a question or two."

"Dinner?" the man asked. He slapped his considerable belly. The flesh didn't move. "A free dinner. On Bryan. The richest poor man I know,"

Seamus said. He swept away a pile of cans and sat on his desk. "Sumer, eh? Did you like the exhibit?"

Emy nodded. "Very interesting. I didn't know most of it."

Seamus sighed. "Unfortunately, most of you Americans don't." He wiped at his nose and shook his head. "Nope, that's not very fair," he said to himself, "not many others do either. Still, glad to hear you enjoyed it."

"I did," Emy said. "Who put it together?"

The short man winked at Bryan and locked eyes with her. "Some uncouth Irish bastard helped curate it. But it's more a traveling exhibit. Local curators add a few things here or there, but it's more or less the same wherever it goes."

Emy's brow furrowed. "Where else has it been?"

He shrugged. "Name a place. Most of those pieces have been traveling the planet since the 70s."

"Only since then?" she asked. "Not earlier?"

Seamus grinned. "Most of these artifacts were, um, liberated by Nazi Germany and several other armies in the last two millennia. Although most were returned to their places of origin, the governments of those countries agreed to let them back out into the world. So this exhibit is kind of a traveling circus."

"Not to mention," Bryan said, "certain Mullahs consider them apostasy rather than history."

"Well," Seamus chuckled, "that too. And they're not the only ones, mind you. Certain Christian and Jewish sects aren't big fans either. They feel the history of Mesopotamia somehow undermines the creation myths."

Bryan laughed. "Yeah, if the Earth is only six thousand years old, then the Sumerians were riding the dinosaurs."

Emy rolled her eyes. "Getting back to the exhibit," she said, "I have a question about those amulets."

Seamus blinked. "You'll have to be a bit more specific, lass."

"The symbols of the gods," Bryan said. "The casts."

"Ah," Seamus said. "Those. Yeah, that's a bit of an eclectic assortment. What of them?"

"Gibil," she said. "I guess I'm most interested in Gibil."

"Interesting." The Irishman rubbed his beard. "Not Marduk? Or Ishtar? Why Gibil?"

"Yeah," Bryan said, "why did you, well, react like that?"

The curator's eyes glittered with curiosity. Bryan looked both confused and anxious. Emy sighed. Dewhurst would hang her if he found out she'd said anything, probably Brett too. She cleared her throat.

"That symbol has shown up at some crime scenes."

For a moment, no one said anything. The only sounds were of the air conditioning whooshing through the vents. Seamus scratched at his beard and glanced at Bryan. "Is she serious?"

Bryan shrugged. "Emy? What are you talking about?"

She took a deep breath and tried to ignore Dewhurst's face in her mind's eye. "In the past week, we've had two arsons. One hit the historical shotgun shacks and another at a private residence."

"Ah," Seamus said. "Those crime scenes."

She nodded. "In both cases, a symbol, very much like Gibil's, was left at the scene. Like a calling card."

The Irishman's hands clenched the edge of his desk. "When you say 'very much,' do you mean exactly the same, or sort of the same?"

"I—" She frowned. "I don't know. I'd have to compare the amulet's design to the images we found. I mean, the symbols weren't exactly drawn by a professional, but the overall geometry is the same."

"Gibil," Seamus said to himself. His eyes slid down to the linoleum. "Interesting." He kicked his legs slightly, the heels of his shoes banging off the desk's back. "Gibil," he said and looked up at Emy, "was the god of fire and light. He was responsible for civilization becoming a civilization. The idea he would be involved in an arson spree is...well...would be a profanity to a Sumerian."

Emy nodded. "So anyone with knowledge of history wouldn't use his symbol for a crime?"

Seamus shook his head. "No. It's ridiculous. It'd be like an SS officer wearing the Star of David. It makes no sense."

The nervous excitement in her body fizzled out. She cast her eyes to the floor. "Goddammit. Thought I had a lead."

"Well," Seamus said and pushed himself off the desk and to the floor, "you still may have one." He walked to the wall of bookshelves and peered intently. A single gnarled finger followed the words as he mouthed the title of each book. Emy tried to read the words on the spines, but changed her mind when she realized the small print was impossible to make out.

Bryan smiled at her. She couldn't help but return it and blush. The man had shown her more than a good time today—he'd possibly helped her make a break in the case. For that, she was going to buy him dinner. And possibly invite him back to her place again. *Who are you kidding?* she asked herself. *Of course you're going to invite him back.*

"Ah-hah," Seamus said and pulled a thick tome out from the shelf. A cloud of dust filtered through the strong overhead lights as he wiped his hand across the cover to clean it. Emy and Bryan coughed, but Seamus just smiled. "Sorry," he said. "Guess I'm used to it." He cleared his throat and opened it.

A serpent-headed lion engraving stared out from the soft-leather cover. The ancient, thick paper had obviously been folded by hands that were long dead.

"How old is that?" Bryan asked, finger pointing at the book.

Seamus didn't look up. His fingers rapidly shuffled through the pages, eyes dancing over the words. "1847," he said. "Written by Sir Ellington Wright, a Lieutenant in the 44th Regiment of Foot." He paused and looked up at Emy. "That was, um, during Auckland's Folly. Nasty bit of business in Afghanistan."

"Auckland's Folly?" Emy asked.

"Bloody brits weren't happy enough with India," Seamus said. "They wanted to make sure the Russians didn't get another piece of Asia. So they decided to enter into an alliance with the Afghan Emir." Seamus shook his head. "Bad mistake.

"An entire army was wiped out over the years. Sir Wright, who wrote this book, was one of the few to escape the final battle with his skin." He turned his gaze back to the book. "Just remember, lass, a 'world power' can only go one direction. And that's down."

"So Sir Wright wrote a book about it?" she asked.

"Not exactly," Seamus said. "Sir Wright was more an amateur archaeologist than a soldier." The little Irishman placed the book on the desk and gestured to Emy and Bryan. "The fact he spoke Arabic and Pashto didn't hurt either."

Emy looked down at the open book. Gibil's sigil was hand-drawn on one page. On the facing page was a scrawl of handwriting. "Whoah. Was this his diary?"

Seamus nodded. "For the most part, yes. But there's a little more to it." He pointed to the drawing on the page. "Wright traveled through Syria, Iraq, Iran, and all over what was once ancient Sumer. He didn't really join the military until the 44th moved into Afghanistan."

"Shit time to buy a commission," Bryan said.

The Irishman laughed. "Shit time indeed. Regardless, he used his wealth to hire the right translators, buy the right favors, and was allowed into the royal collections. This," he said, "was housed in Kabul."

Emy stared at the drawing. "It's different," she said.

Seamus glanced at her.

"I mean," she said, "from the amulet upstairs. But it looks more like the one we've seen at the crime scenes."

The curator picked up the book and handed it to her. "You might as well read his notes."

The ancient, soft leather felt cool in her hands. She ran a finger over the page, marveling at the paper's rough texture. The penmanship was incredibly elaborate and small. She imagined Sir Wright must have had excellent eyesight and tiny fingers. The black ink was scratched into the paper like a work of art.

She scanned the page, stumbled over a sentence, and started the paragraph again. "Daemons sometimes hide in the symbols of the greater gods," she read aloud, "and use their glyphs for their own purpose. The symbol of Gibil was sometimes related to catastrophic, but purposeful, fires." She looked up from the page and at Seamus. His dingy toothed smile was alight with amusement. "Daemon?"

He nodded. "You need to forget all the bullshit you might have learned in Bible school. The word 'daemon' pre-dates all the major religions. The Sumerians believed that children of gods and man roamed the earth. Some were good, some were evil, some just lived. All had aspects of their supernatural parents." He pointed at the book. "So while Gibil might be a good guy, the idea that one of his so-called off-spring could go rogue isn't exactly a new one."

Bryan crossed his arms. "But there's no mythology for this?"

Seamus shrugged. "I'm not the expert on Sumer myth, although I'm hardly a student either. I don't remember anything about Gibil having children with men, but it's possible someone might think the god did."

"So then Gibil's symbol would be used simply to signify fiery destruction?" Emy asked.

"I—" Seamus licked his lips. "You deal with arsonists, yes?"

She nodded.

"I assume," he said, "some of them have more than a few screws loose."

"Sure," she said. "Childhood trauma, history of sociopathic or psychotic behavior. Stuff like that."

Seamus took the book from her and placed it on the table. "Throughout history, people have used religion for their own means, yes?"

The fire, she said to herself. *Purification. Daddy deserved it. And so did I.* She shook the thought away and realized both men were looking at her. She blushed. "I'm sorry. What did you say?"

Seamus waved a hand. "Doesn't matter. Basically, it sounds like you've got a right nutter setting fires. And said nutter might believe they're doing the work of 'god.'"

Chapter 25

The broiling air felt good on his skin. He sat on the grass near the outdoor theatre pretending to read a paperback, but he was really watching and waiting.

Tailing Aninzo hadn't been difficult. Once he'd followed her to her apartment, he'd retrieved his car and parked a few spots down from the stairs leading to her home. Aninzo's complex wasn't gated and since it was a Saturday morning, finding parking wasn't a problem.

The dog had growled at him while he skulked in an alley. Ghere hadn't liked the dog. Neither had he. At some point, he might have to deal with the mutt.

Sitting in his car, windows open, he'd had to wait through two hours of NPR news shows before the arson investigator left the house. Without the dog. That at least made him happy.

Ghere talked non-stop in his mind as he followed her to the HMNS. The moment he'd recognized the route, he'd told Ghere where they were going.

She knows something, the deity had said. *You will need to take care of her. She must not be allowed to interfere.*

"She won't," he'd said aloud. "I won't let her. We won't let her."

He'd felt his passenger's grin and it'd made him do the same. When Aninzo turned into the museum parking lot, P had swung the car around the block and headed to the Houston Zoo. The parking there was free and it was a quick walk to the museum. With the heat index approaching 109°, the zoo was bereft of the usual crowds of parents and children. Apparently no one wanted to venture out into the summer oven.

Ghere protected him from the heat, but he'd found a shade tree to sit beneath. The large oak's canopy was unbridled by other trees and had spread into a thick, leafy crown. Shadows played across the well-watered grass as a slight breeze tickled the leaves.

A group of children walked with a few adults across from the parking garage. Sweat stains had already begun to blossom across their t-shirts. P smiled and wiped his brow in sympathy. It came away wet, but he felt as cool as a brisk fall day.

Aninzo had been in the museum for well over an hour. Hundreds of people had traversed the square in that time. The main hall would be echoing with sounds of footsteps and conversation. He closed his eyes and imagined a group of small children staring up at the giant Tyrannosaurus Rex skeleton.

When P had been young and his mother had taken him to the museum, he'd done much the same. The large dinosaur looked as though it was growling at the world, cursing modernity and humanity all at once. He hadn't had the words to describe it then, but he had them now. Ever since he'd seen Ghere's talisman, he'd felt the same way.

Humankind had forgotten its place. It had forgotten the majesty and magic of the old, eschewed the lessons taught by the ancients. Instead, humanity prided itself on the death of the old gods, replacing them with the new idols of technology and materialism. There was no way to turn back the clock. Science had made certain of that.

Without the magic, the mystery, people were doomed. But he'd show them. He and Ghere. When the city burned, they'd understand their modern world could not protect them from the hungry flames of history.

P smiled to himself as he imagined black smoke billowing from the adjacent buildings. The roar of fire engines and their ear-splitting sirens filling the world with plaintive cries and horror filled his mind. Windows exploded outward from the heat and the rock of explosions. The average city-worker caught in a maelstrom of flying projectiles and a wind of toxins. Cars exploded. The tall buildings of downtown burned like torches. The blue sky quickly turned the color of soot.

Ghere's shadow rose from behind the burning city, the burning world. Its oblong face scowled down at the ravaged steel, concrete, and glass. Its diamond eyes opened like shutters in the sky. The black billowing smoke from all over the city rose in a tornado as the deity sucked it in, fed upon it.

You will bring me back, its voice said in his mind.

P nodded. "I will," he said aloud. "Just give me time."

Chapter 26

Saturdays were not good days to be in the Crime Scene Unit. The staff worked hard during the week, splitting up their days and nights so that evidence was constantly being sifted and analyzed. But the weekends were supposed to be light detail for all those involved. Dew hated working a case on a Saturday or Sunday for that very reason.

People wanted to spend time with their kids, watch sports, go to movies, anything but work. Dew had been at the Forensics Institute for nearly two hours, most of that time spent waiting for the techs to study the camera. The CSU team had descended upon the Hartman site with annoyed embarrassment.

When they'd managed to retrieve the camera, they'd bagged it, tagged it, and scanned it. As soon as it was cleared, he'd signed for it and headed to the Institute. CSU had called ahead to let the techs know they had priority homicide evidence coming in.

Once Dew had handed off the camera, he'd eaten a quick and unhealthy lunch, and returned to wait. And wait. And wait. When they finally called him in to look at the camera, it was nearly 3pm.

The tech, Richard Green, had hovered over the camera with a magnifying lens. He'd pushed and pulled the swing arm as he studied the painted metal and plastic surfaces and jotted down notes on a yellow pad.

"For once," he said, "you've given me a good reason to skip the baseball game."

Dew grunted. "Not sure that's a good thing."

The thick-bearded man looked up at the detective. His green eyes glinted with mischief. "It's not. And it is." The tech chuckled as he rolled his chair to the workstation and began typing in search strings. "I need to find the camera model. Looks like our friend filed off the serial number and I'll bet the numbers are gone from the other components as well."

Dew tapped his foot. "So what are those things attached to the camera?"

Green chuckled, but continued typing. "I can tell you exactly what those are. One's a portable power-pack. The other? A Raspberry PI."

"Raspberry whatsit?" Dew asked, brows furrowed.

The tech hit the return key and let the computer start its search. He swiveled around and looked up at the detective. "It's a computer for embedded systems. Hobbyists around the world are making things with it." He pointed to the camera. "I'll have to call someone else in to see if they can pull any programs off of it."

Dew blinked. "A computer? That small?"

Green nodded. "Yup. Pretty damned slow compared to what you can get for $300 in a full sized unit, but it's powerful enough to do all sorts of things. Including video playback."

"The fuck," Dew breathed. "What was he using it for?"

The tech shook his head. "No idea, detective. That's why I have to call in one of the kids." He ran a hand through his shaggy hair. "What I can tell you, however, is that little piece there?" Green pointed to the small, rounded plastic dongle hanging out of the mint tin. "That's a wi-fi connector."

Dew leaned over the table and looked at it. It had been painted just like the rest of the equipment. "You mean that thing was hooked up to the internet?"

Green shrugged. "Probably."

"How? I mean the Hartman house didn't have any equipment like that. Just a hardline."

The tech swiveled in his chair and drank from a water bottle. He wiped his mouth and stared at the computer screen. "I bet if you checked the neighbor's houses, you'd find an unprotected access point. Either that or your perp cracked 'em."

"How hard is that to do?" Dew asked.

"Depends," Green said. "Most folks don't even know to change the default passwords."

Dew hissed between his teeth. "You mean any kid searching the web could figure out how to do it?"

"Yup. That's not all either," Green said. "This setup is fairly elaborate, but it wouldn't be difficult to figure out how to do this either. Anyone with some good tech knowledge could make it happen."

The detective stared at the camera. Its lens had a thin layer of ash on it. This camera had watched the house burn. What else had it seen? "Any idea how long this thing could have been on?"

Green shook his head. "Not until I find the—" His words trailed off and a large smile lit his face. "There we go."

Dew turned to look at the computer. The giant LED monitor showed a picture of a camera identical to the one on the examination table. "You found it."

The tech nodded. "Yup. And now the real fun begins."

"What do you mean?"

"Give me a few minutes and I can tell you about power consumption and how long it could have recorded for. Not to mention how long the PI unit could have remained online." Green had reached for his phone and brought it to his ear. His index finger had stabbed the buttons in a rapid rhythm. "But first, we need to get the code kid." And now the code kid had arrived.

The "kid" was in his 20s, face pockmarked with acne scars, and had a bad attitude. His bleach-blond hair was cut in a flat-top and several tattoos sprawled below the sleeves of his polo. Dewhurst hated him on sight.

When the "kid" walked in, Green pointed at him. "Ah, here is."

"Sup, Dick?" the kid said, emphasis on the D.

Green's face was still smiling, as if he'd already gotten used to this. "This is Detective Dewhurst." The kid glanced at Dew and nodded. "He's brought us something interesting."

"Doubtful," the kid said.

Dew offered his hand. "Dew."

"Mike. Mike Gomersall," he said and shook Dew's hand with a firm grip.

"Well, Mike," Green said and pointed to the examination table, "there's your patient."

Gomersall turned to the table. The bored look on his face turned into an eyebrow scrunch. "What in the hell is that? Is that a PI?"

Green nodded. "Yup. Not sure which model."

Mike's lips upturned in a manic smile. He glanced at Dew. "You found this where?"

"Site of an arson. We think—"

"Man, oh man," Mike said, his words running over Dew's. The code kid's closed-toe sandals squeaked on the floor as he made his way to the table. "Man, oh, man," he said again. "Dick? You check the wi-fi?"

Green glanced at Dew and then back to Mike. The code kid didn't turn around. "No, Mike. I haven't started any of the work. But I got all the specs for you."

The kid harrumphed and headed to his desk in the corner. His monitor lit up as his fingers dragged across the fingerprint scanner. "Logged in" flashed on the screen. Without sitting, he bashed the keys on the small keyboard in a staccato burst.

"You might want to take a seat, Dew," Mike said. "This might take a couple of minutes."

Green pointed to a rolling chair in the corner. Dew sighed, put his coat on the back of the chair and did as he was told.

Mike lifted his head and sniffed the air. "Jesus, Dew. You ever shower, man?"

The older tech's face wrinkled and he snapped his fingers. Mike turned his head to look at his supervisor and instantly cringed. Dew had never seen him look so menacing and was suddenly glad he hadn't been a soldier reporting to the man in Desert Storm. He'd no doubt Green had been a badass sergeant.

"Cut that shit out. Now," Green said. His voice had lost any joviality. "Mr. Dewhurst spent the day in the heat tracking this evidence that CSU missed. You will be courteous and respectful or I'll have your ass. Understood?"

Mike's eyes dropped to the floor. "Sorry, man. I didn't mean any—"

"Whatever you *meant* is beside the point," Green said. "This is a homicide investigation. Get your shit together."

The kid nodded, cheeks flushed with embarrassment. He looked back at Dew. "Sorry, sir. I, um, kind of talk without thinking."

Dew sniffed the air and wrinkled his nose. "You're right. I'm a little ripe."

Mike smiled at Green. "No worries." He pointed down the hall. "Shower down there, if you like. Like I said, Mr. Green and I have some work to do here."

The detective shook his head. "No point. I'm betting I'll be right out there again."

The kid's fingers blurred on the keyboard and his screen lit with up diagrams. He stepped back from the monitor, opened his desk drawer, pulled out a small plastic rectangle, and slotted it into the side of the computer. "I have to load some firmware files here. Just take a sec."

While Mike and Richard worked on their separate computers, Dew closed his eyes and leaned back in the chair. The clicking of the two keyboards combined with the constant whoosh of the air conditioning set him adrift.

The symbol floated in his imagination. It was made of iron and glowed red with heat. He rotated it in his mind, watching how the V shapes joined together. A blue teardrop of flame rose from its center. As he watched, it grew in length. Orange and crimson teardrops rose from the other pieces of steel. The center fire grew and grew as it consumed the other flames and the metal itself.

The burning flame was silent, but he felt its heat. *Is that what you see?* he wondered. *The fire in the ring? The symbol immersed in flames?* The symbol didn't answer.

"Detective?" a voice called.

Dew shook himself and blinked. Mike, the code-kid, smiled at him from the workstation. Dew blushed. "Sorry. Drifted off."

The kid nodded. "Yeah, that happens in here. It's the A/C and the hum of the computer fans. Will do that to you every time." He gestured to his monitor. "Come have a look. You too, Dick."

Green rolled his eyes and then his chair. Dew stood and walked around the table to the workstation. The monitor displayed lines of gibberish.

"And this helps us how?" Green asked.

Mike smiled and tapped a few keys on the keyboard.

The screen flashed. "I decompiled the assembly and compared it to the generic Linux distros. Finally found a match."

Dew clucked his tongue. "You'll have to forgive me. I know computers, but what you just said makes no sense."

Mike clenched his teeth and attempted to hold a smile. It was obviously difficult. "The Raspberry PI unit is supported by several operating systems that use the linux kernel. I found the OS distribution your perp used."

"Okay, is that important?"

"Sort of," Mike said. He turned back to the screen and pointed a finger. "There's no difference in the code bases. Except for one thing."

"Which is?" Green asked.

Mike grinned. "The wi-fi driver. It's a pretty common one, but it does give us something at least."

"Wait," Green said, "how come there are no other differences? I mean there must be something."

"There is, and there isn't," Mike said. "In looking at the SSD, there's evidence certain portions of the memory were written to over and over again."

"Shredder?" Green asked.

Mike nodded.

"Shredder?" Dew asked. "What are you two talking about?"

"Detective," Green said, "I told you the PI didn't have a hard drive, right?

Well, it runs off that SSD he's talking about. Like the kind you have in your camera."

"Okay," Dew said. "So shredding is…what?"

Mike cleared his throat. "If you want to try and make it difficult for people like us to find your data, you delete it, and then you write over that portion of memory over and over again. Basically, it's a way of jumbling up any evidence. Makes it a real bitch to try and recover."

"Try and recover," Dew said. "Does that mean you can?"

The kid cracked his knuckles. "Yeah. And no. Depends on how much is still left. I don't think he had enough power left in the power pack to secure-shred much. Otherwise, he would have nuked the operating system too."

Green nodded. "With an SSD card, it doesn't take much juice to read and write information. But depending on how much information your perp wanted to destroy, he may have been happy just to get rid of his own code and leave the rest."

Dew rubbed his chin. "So now you have to see how good of a job he did."

The kid smiled. "It's a game, Detective. A great one. They see how much they can hide, and I try and find what they've hidden. I am Jesus fucking Christ, man. I resurrect the dead."

Green frowned at him. "Watch your language, Mike."

"Uh, sorry," he blushed. "I get a little excited about things like this. Beats decrypting kiddie porn." A look of disgust crossed his face. "Really hate that shit."

The detective couldn't help but grin. "Mike? Why the hell do you work here? Sounds like you could go make a lot more money with a security firm."

The computer tech shook his head. "Nah, man. You don't get it. I'd get arrested for the kinds of things I like to do. If, that is, I didn't work for the cops."

"Great," Dew said. "Another criminal catching criminals."

"Hey!" Mike said with a grim look. "I've never been prosecuted."

"Right." Dew turned to Green. "So we've got the models and makes of everything here, right? How long before you have something for me?"

Mike and Richard exchanged glances.

Green rubbed his beard. "I can get you a rundown of local sellers of the equipment. But I'm willing to bet you're going to come up empty on that." He pointed to Mike's computer. "If this guy is savvy enough to build and code, he's probably not dumb enough to purchase locally. And even if he did, I'm willing to bet he paid cash."

"Or Bit-coin," Mike said. "He might be that paranoid."

"So," Dew said, "we'd have to go to the Feebs to pull records for online purchases."

"Yeah," Green nodded. "And that's another shot in the dark. But we can put a list together of merchants that take something like Bit-coin."

"Hell, that's the easy part," Mike said. "There can't be that many of those, but those transactions are going to be all but invisible."

"Had to be shipped somehow," Dew said.

Mike shook his head. "Simple re-mailing service could take care of that. We'll look and run it."

Green sighed. "Dew? This might take a couple of weeks to put together. We'll work as fast as we can on it, though."

"Fuck," Dew hissed. "I don't think we have a couple of weeks."

Chapter 27

The air conditioning left the building cold. P fought the urge to rub his arms to improve the blood flow. Goose bumps covered his skin and they itched. He shivered as he stepped through the line and into the exhibit.

The afternoon crowd had thinned. Most of the day's museum visitors were back out in their cars and racing toward dinner or the rest of their evening.

P had watched as Aninzo, her boyfriend, and the curator left the museum together. When he'd seen the curator, Ghere had groaned.

They know, the deity had said.

"How?" P had asked aloud.

As the large oak leaves whispered in the slight breeze, the malevolence in Ghere's voice was unmistakable. *Because the curator knows of me.*

"Knows," P agreed. "What do you want me to do?"

The deity had fallen into silent thought. P had closed the paperback, risen off the slight incline, and headed into the museum. While he waited for the deity to speak, he wanted to see it again. A few minutes in the ticket line, and he'd managed to procure entry into the exhibit.

He quickly walked past Hammurabi's Code, the piece of Ishtar's Gate, and the statues of Marduk and others. The glass case he wanted to see was near the exhibit's exit.

A family of four stood in front of the cabinet. They stank of sweat and fast food. The tall father was stooped downward, his folds of fat brushing against the glass through his oversized shirt. The wife was less round, but just as ugly. The kids? Had to be adopted. No pair that ugly could produce kids that cute.

P smiled to himself as he waited. Ghere wasn't talking, but he could feel the deity's happiness. Whatever concerns It had were in the background—It wanted to see the sigil.

Random thoughts went through P's head. Would Ghere just leap back into the amulet? Would It leave him, abandon him, find someone better?

You are my vassal and vessel, the voice said. *There are no others here.*

"But there have been others?" P asked It.

The deity paused before answering. *Thousands upon thousands of your years have brought me worshippers willing to sacrifice to me. But they are mortal and die. But you,* It said, *are special.*

P's grin widened. The large father smacked his kids' hands away from the glass. The children were obviously bored and ready to go back to the dinosaurs. Mother and father noticed him behind them, apologized, and led their children to the exit.

He watched them go, silently sighing at the room's sudden isolation. He looked around the exhibit. Except for the docents, this part of the installation was empty.

The amulets glowed. Marduk. Ishtar.

"Gibil," he said aloud.

The amulet seemed to flash at the sound of the name.

"Or shall I call you Ghere?"

The hunk of metal gleamed and twitched beneath the glass case. The deity chuckled in his mind.

How you stared at me. And you had no idea I was staring back.

P nodded. "No," he said aloud. "But I felt something."

Just like you felt with the other suitors.

When he'd first visited the exhibit, his head had filled with voices. At first, he'd thought they were the sounds of the crowd. It was the first day the Sumer installation was open and docents had to meter the rabble. After standing in line as long as he did, Donald thought his ears were still echoing with the sounds of the main hall.

Donald had stared at the Code of Hammurabi and stopped. The cuneiform marks seemed to jitter and writhe on the stone. As he stared, the voices in his mind swelled. The alien symbols danced, combined, and spread themselves again. Suddenly, he was able to decipher them.

He read the laws in Sumerian. He sounded them out in their language. The din of the crowd around him faded into silence. The throng of voices in his mind, however, increased in volume. Then he realized he hadn't been able to understand them. Now he could pick out specific words and phrases.

Donald moved past the tablets, shrugged his way through the crowd, and toward the voices. When he reached the glass display cabinet, his eyes were blinded by the halogen light bouncing off the amulets. Copper, bronze, gold, silver... They were all so beautiful.

The voices ceased their incessant babble. He stared down at the amulet labeled as "Marduk." The snake head seemed to lift and stare at him. A blue tongue slithered from its mouth.

He fought the urge to jump back from the cabinet. It was just a hallucination. Then Ishtar's sigil, a star inscribed inside a circle, spun. The points of the star slid out like blades as they sliced the air. Donald rubbed his eyes. When he looked back in the cabinet, the symbol was motionless.

The next amulet was that of Gibil. Two separate lines of gold formed a pair of 'V' shapes on the disc, the smaller one nestled in the crook of the larger. "God of fire and light," he read aloud.

"Yes," a voice agreed.

Donald stiffened as the sound brought him out of his reverie. A short, stout man with shock red hair stood beside him. The man took in a breath. "Gibil," he said in a thick Irish brogue, "was Sumer's Prometheus in that he brought fire to humankind. He was the reason they could cook, fire their metals, and keep the night at bay."

"Who?" Donald started to ask.

The man smiled. "Manners. I'm short on those," the man said and offered a sweaty hand. "Name's Seamus O'Halloran."

Donald shook it, disliking the clammy feel of the man's hand in his. "You work here?"

O'Halloran laughed. "You could say that. I'm the exhibit's curator."

"Ah," Donald said. "I'm Donald."

"Saw you admiring the artifacts."

Donald nodded. "They're very beautiful." He turned back to the case and leaned over Gibil's amulet. A brilliant blue flame spread from the metal design.

The curator was beside him and staring down into the case. "Yes," he said. "That's Gibil's sigil."

The flame winked out of existence as if it had never been there. The curator chuckled. "Gibil," Donald repeated. "God of fire and light."

Seamus blinked at him, seemingly unsure of what to say. "Yes. Gibil."

"Are they still worshipped?"

Seamus laughed. "The people that worshipped Gibil, Marduk, and

Ishtar died out millennia ago." He sighed. "Doesn't matter much, eh? Just another superstitious people, their beliefs no more accurate than today's Christians, Jews, or Muslims."

Donald had barely heard the words. Gibil's amulet continued staring at him, into him, through him. It whispered in his mind, the same thing over and over again. *Flames.*

"Uh, Donald?"

He turned to the curator and blushed. "I— I'm sorry. What?"

"I was, um, just making sure you were okay," Seamus said.

Donald forced a smile. "Yes. I just... Well, I was just thinking, that's all. Superstition."

"Dr O'Halloran?" someone called from the exhibit's exit.

Seamus turned toward the voice and waved. "Sorry, Donald. A curator's work is never done. Enjoy the exhibit."

The Irishman offered his hand again and Donald shook it with numb fingers. The short man quickly moved away and out of sight.

Flames, the voice said in his mind again.

He turned back to the cabinet. The amulet was still burning.

Remember the flames, Donald? *Remember the flames that took your bed? Your house? Your brother?*

He scrunched his eyes as hard as he could. "Won't remember that," he whispered to himself. "Won't remember—"

But you do remember, the voice insisted.

The darkness inside his mind evaporated. He saw himself in the baby's room, the box of matches rattling as he walked toward the crib. His baby brother, only nine months old, was swaddled in a Sesame Street blanket. Cookie Monster, Oscar, Bert, and Ernie dangled from the brightly colored, plastic mobil hanging above the crib.

Donald hated his brother. His brother who got all the attention. His brother who always cried. His brother who stole Mommy and Daddy away. His brother who—

He'd dreamed of this moment. Of striking the match. Of watching his brother burn. And so, he did.

Flames, the voice said in his mind.

Donald opened his eyes and he was back in the museum. The amulet no longer burned. It was no longer melted out of shape. It was just a piece of metal shining beneath the lights.

He shoved the memory of the bedroom from his mind. He hadn't thought about his brother in forever. Or his cat. That had been when he was bad. "When I was bad," he whispered.

When you were you, the voice said. *Before they changed you. Before they took you from me.*

Donald's forehead wrinkled. *Before the home...*

Yes, the voice said. *Before they took away everything.* The voice paused. The filled exhibit room had faded away and he could only hear It breathing in his mind. *Do you want it back? The feeling of power. Of control. Of the fire?*

The baby's bedroom was a torrent of flame. His brother's screams of pain and confusion were barely audible over the sound of fire feasting on dry wood, wall paper, lathing, and carpet. Donald felt arms around his neck. They pulled him away from the growing inferno. The plastic mobil above the fire-filled crib smoked and hissed. Donald's last view of the room was of Cookie Monster dripping blue, molten plastic into the crib of flame.

"I made it," he whispered aloud. "I created it."

The voice sighed in his mind. *I can give it to you again, Donald. You only have to ask.*

"You are Gibil?"

The presence in his mind growled. *I am Ghere. And I am here to save you.*

He didn't know what Ghere had meant then. He did now. He had asked the voice to help him, to bring him life again, and end his meaningless existence. And Ghere had. Donald was dead. P remembered Donald's life, pretended to be Donald, but that man was no more.

The curator and the arson investigator were gone now. He had little doubt Aninzo had asked O'Halloran about the symbols. It wouldn't help her. It wouldn't help any of them.

P had been to the exhibit multiple times to view the amulet, the one he would one day wear around his neck. While the world burned around him, it would be cool against his flesh, and all who saw it would fall before him.

Before us, Ghere whispered in his mind. *But that means you have to take care of things.*

P nodded. "I will," he grinned. "We will."

Chapter 28

The room was dark, just the way she liked it. The laptop's screen painted a surreal panel of light against the curtains behind her, Luna snoring on the couch next to her. Whenever Emy came to a stopping point in her frantic typing, she'd idly scratch the dog's upturned ear. Luna would open her eyes, glance at Emy, and immediately fall back asleep.

It was an old routine. Whenever she worked at home, Luna joined her. If it was after dark, the dog would sleep with her head against Emy's hip. No matter how much noise the keys made as her fingers pounded on them, Luna slept right through it. Or at least pretended to.

Instead of Bryan spending the night again, she'd left him after dinner. Seamus had joined them for the meal, but didn't stick around for drinks. She figured he got the hint they were supposed to be on a date and he was the third wheel.

The Irishman had waded into his meal with reckless abandon, babbling the entire time about Sumer and daemons. While it was interesting, the man didn't leave any pauses for either her or Bryan to talk. Between his ravenous mouthfuls, he stopped talking and pointed a fork at her. "What's that?"

She frowned, thinking he might be looking at her scars. "What's what?"

"Your necklace, lass."

"Oh," she said with a blush. She carefully pulled it out from beneath her blouse so all three chains appeared. "Family heirloom," she said.

"Lapis?"

"Um, yes," Emy said. "They're—"

"Lapis lazuli," Seamus said. He sat back in his chair, idly brushing away crumbs from his beard. "Two of the stones don't look right."

"I know," Emy said. She fingered the two lowest stones on the right side. "I was in a house fire when I was a child. The heat discolored them."

"Doesn't look like that to me," Seamus said. "Almost look like calcite, not lapis."

She exchanged a glance with Bryan. "Well, they used to be the same color as the others."

Seamus smiled. "Lots of legends around lapis lazuli. You know," he said and lifted another forkful of his veggie enchilada from the plate, "the Sumerians traded for those stones. Thought they could repel evil spirits or weaken the unnatural. Kind of like a ward of protection." Bryan chuckled and Seamus glared at him. "What?" He stuffed the food into his face, some of the salsa catching and dribbling down his beard.

"Nothing," Bryan grinned. "You just always have some tidbit of information I've never heard before."

Seamus shrugged. He reached his fat fingers around his pint mug and took a long draught. "I know what I know." He smiled at Emy. "All you have to know in this life is how to know what you don't know."

"Now that," Bryan laughed, "was very profound."

Seamus waved away the remark. "Anyway, Emy, that's a beautiful necklace."

"Thank you," she said.

"Certainly graces you well."

"Christ, you dirty old man. I'm sitting right here!"

"What?" Seamus said. "Can't I flirt with a lady?"

Bryan put a hand on Emy's shoulder. "I'd rather you not with this one."

"My apologies," Seamus said.

They finished their meals while Bryan and Seamus compared notes about museum politics, and the subtleties of exhibit curation and artifact display. Emy listened to the two men, doing her best to follow the conversation. Finally, Seamus sat back and pounded his belly. "Plate clean, pint empty," Seamus stifled a belch and stared at Emy. "Now," he said. "What are you going to do about your nutter?"

"You mean the arsonist?" Seamus nodded. She shrugged. "Well, you gave me another lead. And to be honest, I think we needed it."

"I'll do some more research for you. Now I'm interested." And he let it go at that.

After thanking both her and Bryan, he'd made his leave from the restaurant without looking back.

"Well," Bryan had laughed, "now you know just how much he can talk."

Emy shook her head and chuckled. "He's obviously very good at what he does, but does he have to prove it?"

"You don't get it," Bryan said. "Seamus was one of seven children. I think he learned early on that he has to take the attention when he can get it. I don't believe it's an ego problem. It's a product of socialization."

She moved her seat closer to the table's corner next to Bryan. The plates were gone, as was the flatware, and bread. All that remained of the meal were crumbs and their beers. She took a sip from her bottle of Shiner and placed it next to his.

"'Product of socialization?' Sounds highly technical."

Bryan rolled his eyes. "Sorry. I, um, have a tendency to talk like a textbook."

Emy grinned. "I don't mind. I don't mind at all."

"Well now that you've seen the innards of the HMNS, what do you think?"

"Expected a little more disorganization, to be honest."

"I get that," Bryan said. "Of course you haven't seen the massive storage area that's off-site."

She cocked an eyebrow. "Off-site?"

"Yeah. The collections are far too large to all be kept in the museum itself. That's why they have a huge warehouse." He sipped his beer. "If you're interested, I'm sure I can get a curator to take us through. Maybe even in private."

"That should be interesting. You've been there before?"

"Of course." Bryan tented his hands on the table. "The museums work pretty closely together. And everyone's interested in what everyone else has." He shrugged. "Never know when you'll find that missing piece for a display."

"Good to have cooperation instead of everyone competing."

He laughed. "There's no competition here. We share the same patrons in many cases. You'd be surprised how many wealthy folks are interested in both modern art and ancient antiquities. Or gem stones, for that matter."

"The stone exhibit is pretty impressive." Emy swirled a finger across the top of her beer bottle. "Nothing I'd ever wear, but they're great to look at."

"Most of them are a bit gaudy to put on a ring or wear around your neck." He eyed her bottle. "Besides," he said, "you already have a beautiful necklace. You ready for another beer?"

She thought for a moment and shook her head. "I don't think so. I need to get home and take care of Luna."

Bryan smiled. "That dog. She's not so ferocious once you get to know her."

"No," she laughed. "Luna's really a sweetie. And she has good taste in men."

"Maybe not." He leaned in with a leer. "She liked me."

Emy put her hand across the table and he clasped it. "Thank you for helping me with all this. And for a wonderful evening."

"You're welcome." His lip twitched. "It sounds like you're saying goodbye. Is that just for tonight or—"

She grinned. "No. I want to see you again. Soon. What are you doing tomorrow?"

Emy paid for the meal and drinks. She had to practically arm wrestle Bryan for the check. The moment they stepped outside, the sauna-like summer heat slammed into her. Sweat popped from her pores. Bryan's too. They walked to her car in silence. When she unlocked the door by hitting the keychain button, she turned to him.

"I had a great night, Bryan."

"Me too."

She put her arms around his neck and they kissed. When she finally let go, he was staring at her. "What?"

He grinned. "I wish you'd wear your hair differently."

"Huh?"

He lifted a hand and gently stroked her forehead just to the right of where the scars began. "This," he said, "isn't you. It's just something you wear."

She opened her mouth to speak and stopped. Something hitched in her throat. "I wish I could take it off." Emy dropped her eyes to the pavement. "It'll always be there."

He reached out and hugged her. "I know," he whispered. "But it doesn't matter. You are more beautiful than you believe." He kissed her forehead. "And I'm going to tell you that every day for as long as you let me."

There was nothing she could say. She squeezed him and tore herself away. She wiped away a tear from one eye along with a long runner of sweat, the moisture dripping off her fingers.

"Thank you." She mouthed the words more than spoke them.

An awkward goodbye, a promise to call, and she was in her car. She watched Bryan walk to his vehicle, get in, and start it up. She waited until he left the parking lot. Finally, she felt she could breathe.

She started her car and headed home. *This isn't you,* he'd said. Emy wiped another tear from her eye. The air conditioner was on full blast, frosty air rushing through the vents drying both the sweat on her body and the moisture on her cheeks.

This isn't you.

"This isn't me," she said and glanced in the rearview mirror. Her long hair covered the scar. She focused her eyes back on the road and brushed the hair away.

After she made it home, she'd immediately settled in to work on the report. The profile was getting more complete. Or was it? Who was going to believe there was a lunatic out there who thought he was some Sumerian mythological deity? Certainly not Novak.

She stopped in mid-sentence and stared at the characters on the screen. Luna raised her head and looked at her. Emy scratched the dog's ear and Luna loosed a happy growl in her throat. "You are far too easy, puppy."

The dog responded by laying her head back down and licking Emy's bare leg once. Emy shook her head and returned her eyes to the text.

Gibil. Wright's journal. The collection. Seamus' theories. She was putting it all in the report. If Novak saw it, he'd go apoplectic. Emy sighed and typed the final words.

It took her more than half-an-hour to read through the report and edit. She read it aloud and paused only when she found a typo or an awkward sentence. Dewhurst and Brett were the only two she was sending the report to, but she wanted it to be perfect.

Reading it aloud also calmed her a bit. The words brought the images of the site into her mind, the burned bodies, the symbols, the artifact. It didn't seem so crazy after all, as long as she made sure both men knew she didn't believe their firebug was a Sumerian god or daemon.

The profile was probably little better than the average armchair shrink could do, but it felt right. The racism angle didn't fit. Neither did some sort of fiscal motive. That left mental illness. Either a thrill bug or a lunatic. Those were the only possibilities. Anything else was...

"Crazy," she said aloud.

The dog wiggled and dropped off the couch. Luna headed for her water dish and lapped noisily. Emy watched her. The well-built dog wagged her tail even when she was eating or drinking.

"Treat?"

Luna stopped in mid slurp and turned around. The dog's hopeful eyes glistened in the soft light.

"Treat?" Emy asked again.

The dog sat down, licked her lips, and loosed a low woof.

Emy laughed and headed into the kitchen. She took a biscuit from the container. Luna didn't follow her; the dog knew the drill.

She walked back to the living room and stood in front of Luna. The dog craned her neck. "You ready?"

The dog said nothing.

Emy flipped the treat in the air. Luna watched it fall, moved her head slightly, and snapped her jaws closed on the biscuit. Her teeth crunched it, her tail swishing back and forth across the carpet. The water bowl dinged each time Luna's tail hit it.

Emy walked back to the couch and picked up the laptop. Luna eventually made her way back and curled into a sleepy ball on the cushion next to her.

No. The report didn't sound crazy. Not half bad, actually.

She attached it to an email, and put both Brett and Dew's email addresses in the "To" field. Her mouse cursor hovered over the "CC" field. Her fingers found the home row and she had to stop herself from typing in Novak's email address. Old habits died hard.

Emy stared at the email subject field and the addresses before she finally hit send. A dialog box popped up announcing the email was on its way. She sighed.

"Too late to worry about it now," she said to the room. The dog didn't stir.

It was Saturday night. Instead of drinking wine with Bryan and retiring to the bedroom, she'd spent the last two hours finishing the report. And for what? For both Brett and Dew to laugh at her?

That was stupid. Brett knew her and trusted her. The detective seemed to have his own strange ideas. Maybe she wasn't reaching as far as she feared. But what was more unnerving was the thought she might be right.

Emy closed the computer and set it on the end table. Luna turned around and sat back down on the cushion, her brown eyes staring at her. Emy made a kissy noise and the tail thumped against the cushions.

She stood and stretched. Luna shuffled off the couch again and headed toward the bedroom door. The smell of unwashed sweat hit Emy's nostrils. She lifted her shirt and winced. Blinds down, Emy stripped out of her moist clothes, put them on the washer, and headed to the shower, Luna at her heels.

A shower. Sleep. And then she'd wait to see what Brett and Dew had to say. And maybe she'd be able to get another date with Bryan. She turned on the water and stepped into the stall with a grin, suddenly wishing he was there.

Chapter 29

A complete and total shit day. After spending hours in the CSU while the geeks did their searches, he was ready for a cold shower, a few stouts, and some food. And in that order.

Saturday traffic was light and he was home in no time. The moment he walked in the door, Frankie brought him a toy mouse and cried at him around a mouthful of felt. Dew leaned down, pulled it from her teeth, and threw it down the hall. The cat flipped in the air and sprinted after the toy.

Dew stripped down and headed to the shower. He walked into the stall and turned the tap, wincing as frigid water streamed down from the shower head. The water slowly heated until it was lukewarm. He turned it down a notch and groaned in satisfaction.

Even in the chilly confines of the CSU, the heat had seemed to follow him. While he'd waited for the geeks to make some progress, his skin felt dirty and salty. Just a few minutes outside in the heat had been like standing atop of a steaming kettle.

Dew turned around beneath the water until it sprayed against his neck. He reached backward and nudged the tap, the water cooling at once. This was what he'd needed all day. The cold water didn't just soothe his body, it also cleared his mind.

Richard and Mike had worked through their searches, the two of them quibbling like an old married couple. Dew had found their antics mildly amusing at first, but quickly tired of the jokes and jibes. Gomersall might be a snot-nosed little shit, but he seemed to know what he was doing. Not as though it helped.

They had model numbers, but no serial numbers. That made finding where the electronics were purchased more or less impossible.

The firebug had probably purchased his wares from multiple online vendors. He could have used dollars, a payment service funded with bitcoin, or a direct buy from a dark web vendor.

Dark web. That's what the kid had called it. A place where the average user doesn't have a chance of getting to, and if they do, they're more likely to get cracked and scammed before they even figure out what they're looking for.

But at least now the pieces were coming together. Their firebug was well educated in electronics, computers, network security, and had some skills in the cracking department. That meant the perp was not only intelligent, but skilled. It also meant the bastard was going to be that much more difficult to catch.

According to the research he'd read while Richard and Mike did their work, their perp could have any number of psychological issues. Pair those with an above average intelligence and an in-depth knowledge of computers, and it might take a miracle to apprehend him.

Dew picked up a loofa, spread liquid shower soap on it, and lazily scoured his arms. His skin prickled and he smiled. The shower was exactly what he'd needed. Dew sat on his haunches and scrubbed his legs.

The water flowed down his hair and over his face. He closed his eyes and scrubbed on auto-pilot.

The only question now was how to find the bastard. He knew their best chance of catching him was another fire. And that wasn't a good outcome. There simply had to be another way. The image of the Hartmans in the morgue flashed across his imagination. Their scorched skin, the flexion in their limbs, the looks of horror etched into their faces.

Ms. Aninzo's initial reports on the temperature in the house didn't make much sense either. It was bad enough to find out their perp was recording everything and somehow managing to escape detection during setup, but the extremely localized and focused destruction was inexplicable. If the arson investigators had no clue how that could happen, how did it?

Dew rose and stretched. His back, now relaxed, clicked and cracked. He sighed with pleasure, put the loofa back on the rack, and nudged the tap again until the water turned cold. Shivering, he turned three times beneath the spray before turning off the water.

Skin prickled with goose flesh, he slid open the stall's sliding door, grabbed a towel from the bar, and began drying off. The cool air flowed into the open stall making his teeth chatter. At least he didn't have to worry about sweating as soon as he stepped out of the shower.

Endless drought. Record high temperatures. Fire. He stopped toweling off and stared at the floor. Hottest summer in recorded history. Was there a connection?

That was a line of investigation that could bear fruit. Maybe their perp followed heatwaves around the country. "Thin," he said aloud. "So damned thin."

He finished drying off and walked naked from the bathroom. Frankie sat on the bed glaring with reproach. Dew returned the cat's stare and blinked twice. She readjusted herself on the bed and blinked back.

"Okay, you're hungry. And pissed I'm home late. I get it." The cat said nothing. Dew nodded to her and headed to the wardrobe. He opened the mahogany doors and pulled out one of the shelves. Pairs of perfectly folded black boxer shorts lay on the left side, while crisply ironed undershirts filled the right. He thought about putting on a t-shirt, but there was no point. A pair of undies was fine.

Once his privates were covered, he closed the doors and headed into the living room. He heard the thump of Frankie jumping off the bed to follow. After filling her dish and checking her water, he pulled a bottle of Old Rasputin from the fridge, and poured the jet-black liquid into a pint mug.

His cell phone showed a new email. He grinned at the subject line and the sender. Ms. Aninzo was working late too.

Dew pulled out his laptop and headed to the recliner. He put on some jazz and placed the mug on the end table. As the laptop started up, he took a draught of the beer and growled with pleasure. The shower was great, but this was even better.

By the time he finished his third read-through of the report, he'd cleared the fridge of stout. His brain buzzed a little, but that actually helped. Why? Because the report was insane.

She postulated their bug was not only a technical genius, but also a history buff. Ancient history and mythology, to be precise. The symbols were a perversion of Gibil's sigil. Gibil, the Sumerian god of fire and light, was a helpful god in their pantheon. According to Aninzo's source at the HMNS, a follower of Gibil would never engage in arson.

"But a nephilim would." Dew tapped a finger on the laptop's edge. Frankie leaped up and bumped against his hip. Dew moved his left hand and scratched her behind the ears. The cat's purr was loud enough to add to Miles Davis' scorching trumpet.

Nephilim, the progeny of a god and humans, didn't necessarily follow their parents' virtues. Aninzo suggested the firebug believed he was either a nephilim or possessed by one. Dew shook his head and reached for the pint glass. It was empty.

He closed his eyes and leaned back in the chair. The laptop was getting a little warm to sit on his crotch. Without opening his eyes, he closed the lid and placed the computer on the end table. The aluminum case clinked against the empty mug.

Possession? Reincarnation? That was a special kind of psychosis. The kind Tony might be able to help profile. Might.

Frankie climbed into his lap, her purr louder than ever. He rubbed beneath her chin and the cat responded with a love nip. He smiled despite his mood.

Maybe he should try and see Tony tomorrow. And maybe, just maybe, he should try and get an unofficial meeting with Ms. Aninzo and Mr. Cullum. Perhaps an early dinner tomorrow with the two of them. But first, he'd have to go to the HMNS and see the sigil for himself.

Dew looked down at the cat. She stared back at him. "Ready for bed?" The cat said nothing. He sighed and leaned forward. The cat meowed before leaping off the chair and onto the carpet, tail swishing in an angry arc. "Whatever," he told her.

After a glass of water and cleaning out the mug, he headed to the bedroom. He put his cell phone on the nightstand, pulled off the underwear, and climbed into bed. The cool sheets felt wonderful against his skin as he pulled the comforter over himself. Another thump on the bed and the cat crawled onto his chest. In a few minutes, Dew was snoring lightly.

Chapter 30

It was almost 3 in the morning and his phone said the temperature was 92°. Another hour or two and it might drop down to 91°—the projected low for the day. He had the car windows rolled down, air conditioner off, and he knew he should be broiling in his seat. Instead, the air felt cool and wonderful against his exposed skin. He wanted to be naked and lying on the scorched pavement. He wanted every inch of his skin touching the hot-plate of the parking lot, but that was out of the question. For now.

The row of town houses across the street looked new and inviting. A freshly painted metal fence surrounded the block to keep out the unwanted. Each townhouse had a separate gate and paved path to its front door. Likewise, the houses were separated by more metal fencing.

P's car sat in the parking lot across the street. He stared at the townhouse on the corner. The area was once filled with decaying houses until the gentrification craze started. Now most of the buildings were townhouse blocks like this one. Newer construction, fire-proof roofs, and expensive alarm systems. This was going to be tricky.

The corner house was the home of Brett Cullum, Aninzo's boss. Finding Aninzo hadn't been difficult, but tracking down Cullum had been even easier.

The arson investigator was plastered all over the internet. He and his husband were involved in multiple annual charity events around the city; a simple internet search brought up dozens and dozens of photos, blog posts, and even newspaper clippings. And this was where he lived.

A police car rolled down Roy Street. P ignored it. The cops couldn't see him. Ghere had told him long ago that if he sat still, no one would notice him. And who was going to pay attention to a parked car sitting between several others?

The HPD car increased speed and headed toward the I-10 feeder. P watched his rearview mirror until it disappeared. The patrol car would return in an hour or two, but P would be long gone by then.

He knew the car Cullum drove. He knew the car his partner drove. He knew where they lived. He knew they rescued Papillons. He knew more than he'd ever need to know.

The only question was what to do. And how to do it.

The plan was coming together. A few more targets and Ghere could come to life in this plane. He'd spent more than two months planning the attacks, gathering equipment, programming the hardware and software, and experimenting with different accelerants. He was ready.

Detective Dewhurst, Novak, Cullum, and Aninzo were distractions that had to be dealt with. Ghere demanded Aninzo be consumed. Cullum? That was just icing on the cake and P knew whom he'd burn first.

Ghere's hatred for the woman was palpable. From the moment God had seen her through P's eyes, a pressure had formed at the back of his mind. P didn't understand what it was at first, but now he knew—Ghere's crushing hatred and fury that the woman had somehow escaped Its blessing years ago. But she was here. Now. Days away from Its rebirth, Ghere wanted revenge. But wasn't there something else there? Fear, perhaps?

I. Am. Not. Afraid.

P winced at the growling, slavering voice, loud enough to make his skull tremble. His head throbbed and he closed his eyes.

"I didn't say you were," he spoke aloud, but his words were barely audible even to himself.

You think it. You think you know.

Eyes still closed, he frowned. "I know nothing."

Ghere didn't reply, but P felt God tense. It was ready to pounce on him, hurt him.

For only the second time since he'd seen Ghere's sigil, he felt afraid. After God had first spoken to him in the museum and taken residence in his mind, the strange sensation of It living inside him, looking through his eyes, listening with his ears, and feeling with his skin had been jarring. The fear of losing himself in Its presence, being consumed by the alien personality, had wracked him and left him sleepless. Ghere had finally assured him they would always remain separate, and yet as one. P chose to believe It. What was the alternative?

This, however, was different. Ghere was doing more than talking inside his mind; Ghere was making his heart race, his skin prickle with fear, and his stomach churn with acid. It was part of him now. And if It chose to punish him, It certainly could. He had to choose his thoughts and words carefully.

"How did she escape you?" P asked in a whisper.

He felt Ghere tense in his mind. It didn't want to tell him. It didn't want to say.

"Never mind," P said. "It doesn't matter."

It does, the creature said. *But it's impossible to explain.*

P bit his lip. "Impossible to explain to me?"

It chuckled. P's body relaxed a little. *Impossible to explain to a human.*

P opened his eyes and stared back at the quiet block. A cat moved down the middle of the street, its tail swishing back and forth with nervous energy. The cat stopped suddenly and stared straight at P. Even though the animal was fifty feet away, he saw its fur erupt in a storm of hackles, tail fluffing out. Through the open windows, he heard the feline make an inhuman screech of anger.

Ghere's presence went still. The cat took a few steps and loosed the cry again.

Leave. Now.

P slowly moved his hand to the ignition and turned the key. The car coughed itself awake. The cat was running now. P hit the window buttons and the glass raised with a whirr. He flipped on the headlights, the sudden glare shining on a tabby colored missile of fur. He jumped in the seat as the cat landed full force on the windshield, a streak of blood coating the glass along with a zig-zag of cracks.

Ghere yelled nonsensical syllables in a greasy, sibilant hiss. Just above God's screaming in his mind, the cat's primal shrieks pierced his ears. P put the car in reverse and hit the gas.

The car squealed backward, smoke rising from the tires. The cat slid off the windshield until it dug its front claws into the wipers. Ghere screamed in his head and the cat's impossibly guttural screech added to the din. A film of red descended over his eyes and a jackhammer pounded his skull. P swung the car hard. Tires screeched and the vehicle nearly went up on two wheels. The cat, still hanging from the wiper, lost purchase and slid to the right. P swung the wheel in the opposite direction and the car slammed into something with a metal crunch.

P rocked forward as the airbag deployed. The world became an explosion of hisses, pops, and the smell of burning plastic. His vision disappeared for a moment and came back to him. He lifted his head with a groan and stared out the windshield. Smoke rose from beneath the hood.

Through the ringing in his ears, he heard a car alarm going off. He turned his head to the left, eyes wide in surprise. He'd managed to spin the car right into the side of a large pickup truck.

What is that sound? Ghere asked.

P wiped a smear of blood from his nose. Goddamn that airbag was hard.

What is that sound?

"Alarm."

They will be coming. Leave. Now.

"The car is broken," P said.

Ghere howled in his mind. P put his hands to his skull as if to keep it from exploding.

Run. You must not be caught.

P reached to unbuckle the seat belt, feeling as though he was moving through tacky glue; all his movements were in slow motion. His fingers found the buckle and he clicked the button. The belt released and he tried the driver side door twice before realizing it was embedded in the truck's side. No exit that way. He struggled over the console and into the passenger seat. God, but everything hurt.

Hurry. They are coming.

Ghere sounded...afraid.

P's mind tried to make sense of that, couldn't, and settled for focusing on the passenger door handle. He pulled on it, but nothing happened. He blinked at it and tried again. The latch popped but still the door didn't budge.

THEY ARE COMING! MOVE!

His head rocked with the primal scream. Just as he was about to put his hand through the window, he saw the door was locked. He pushed the button to the unlocked position, nearly broke the door handle, and pulled himself out of the car. He lost his balance and fell to one knee.

RUN!

P pushed off his left foot and stumbled forward. He didn't know where to go. He could run toward one of the apartment blocks, head into the older part of the neighborhood, or rush toward the freeway and hope to catch a cab. Or he could—

That sound. That ear-splitting, cringeworthy screech of a mad animal filled the night. But it was louder now. And it wasn't alone. It was a goddamned chorus.

He didn't dare turn around. He started running as fast as he could, another jolt of adrenaline pumping into his system. His brain vibrated with Ghere's screams and the cacophony of yowling cats. P sprinted for Roy Street. When he reached the intersection with Inker, he took the corner a little too fast and slipped. He rolled onto the concrete, bits of broken glass and gravel ripping through his jeans. P cried out and struggled to his feet.

Claws dug into his pants leg. His face a mask of horror and confusion, P looked down at the screaming thing attached to him. The same cat that had attacked his windshield had dug its claws into the back of his right leg. The creature snarled and bit. P screamed in pain and slapped at the enraged feline.

The howling cat flew to the pavement as P stumbled forward. Over the sound of his pounding heart, the screeching of more cats raised the hackles on his neck. He ignored the pain in his leg and kept running.

You're not fast enough, Ghere's voice whispered in his mind.

P spotted a metal trash can on the sidewalk, its lid canting to one side. He grabbed it as he ran by and turned.

Six cats ran at him, their mouths open, spittle flying from their growling faces, eyes staring with primitive fury. The animals looked rabid and feral. He held the lid up like a shield as the felines leaped.

Screaming, P swung the lid. The first cat's body broke with a snap and tumbled out into the street. The next bounced into someone's yard. The third went under the shield, its claws penetrating the denim and ripping through the skin of his inner thigh. P yowled in pain, raised and dropped the lid on top of its head. The cat dropped to the street like a rag doll.

He looked up and saw that the remaining cats had stopped a few feet in front of him. Their growls lowered in volume, but doubled in ferocity. He heard their claws clicking on the asphalt, the cats practically dancing with fury.

P swung his head and looked behind him. He had a clear path to the main intersection. He could even see the dim lights of the restaurants on the other side. All he had to do was make it down Inker. Another block, and he could hail a cab. If the cats didn't kill him first.

He looked back at the three remaining antagonists. They hissed and spat, but remained out of reach. P took a step toward them. The cats backed off and spread out. They were trying to flank him.

The sound of a squeaking door caught his attention. "What the fuck is going on, asshole?"

P didn't turn to look. The voice was shrill, but definitely male. "The cats! They're attacking me!"

The cats yowled again.

"What the hell are you talking about?" The door closed.

P heard footsteps behind him and then felt a large presence beside him. A grizzled, bearded man in a stained wife-beater and pajamas stood next to him. The man was a full head taller.

The cats took a step back, but continued to spit and hiss.

"Jesus. You're bleeding, dude."

P swallowed hard. "Tell me something I don't know."

The man clapped his hands and walked past P. "Get out of here!" The cats retreated a few more steps and began to close ranks. "I said leave, you little shits!" Mr. Giant ran at them and the cats turned tail, sprinting into the shadows.

P took a deep breath. He was safe. Again.

No you're not, Ghere said.

P looked down at his dented, metal shield and up at the giant.

"Man, I've never seen anything like that." The giant turned around. "You okay, man?"

The lid's edge caught the giant just beneath the chin. The large man stumbled into the street, his hands clutching his throat. P moved in and swung the lid again. After the man fell to the asphalt, P continued hitting him. When he was done, the lid was little more than twisted aluminum.

Chapter 31

She was dead asleep when stinky dog breath woke her. Curled in the crook of her arm, Luna had one paw on Emy's chest, snout flat against her left breast.

Emy opened her eyes and stared at the dog. Luna's tail immediately began to thump against the mattress. The dog's pink tongue flicked out and touched Emy's lips.

"Ugh!" Emy yelled.

Luna jumped up and stood on all fours, tail wagging like a propeller.

"Christ, Luna!"

The dog growled, its tail frantically wagging. Emy sighed and kicked off the covers. Luna shook her head, ears slapping against her head. Emy laughed and reached for her.

Luna leaped and ran to the bedroom door. She turned and stared back at Emy. When Emy didn't move, Luna raised her head and woofed.

"I'm coming, dog. Shut up!"

Emy slid to the side of the bed and put her feet on the floor. She felt hungover, but didn't know why. Then she remembered the drinks from last night. Groaning, she stood up, covered herself in a robe, grabbed her phone off the end-table, and walked from the bedroom and into the kitchen. Luna waited by the food dish, lying on the floor like a rug, paws neatly arranged, looking hopeful.

"Breakfast. For you." Emy yawned. "Sure thing." She went about the morning ritual of filling the dog dish with kibble. Luna's tail swished back and forth across the carpet at the clink of food dropping into the bowl. When Emy finished, the dog lunged forward and buried its head, collar dinging against the bowl's metal side.

Emy yawned again and headed to the coffee maker. A strong cup was exactly what she needed. As she reached for a pod to place in the machine, the sound of her phone warbled over the din of Luna's crunching and slobbering. Brett, an amused smile on his face, stared up at her from the screen. Emy fought back another yawn and picked up the phone.

"Well, good morning, boss."

From Brett's end of the line, she heard the sound of his barking Papillons and his husband telling them to shut up. "And how are we this morning?"

"Fine," she said.

There was pause. "What is that noise?"

Emy raised an eyebrow and looked over at Luna. The dog's snout was buried in the bottom of the bowl, her rabies and name tags clinking loudly against the bowl's edge. "Luna. She's having breakfast."

Brett laughed. "Did you say breakfast? Sounds like a great idea to me."

"Huh?"

"You're not awake yet, are you?"

"No," Emy said. "Not even close. Haven't even had my first cup of coffee."

"Great. Then why don't you head over here? Lee's cooking up omelettes and dusted french toast."

She glanced at the dog. Luna's tail swung in circles. She was the only dog Emy had ever seen that wagged her tail while eating. "I guess I could do that. What's the occasion?"

Brett paused again. "I figure after breakfast we can talk about your report."

"You already read it?"

"Yup," Brett said. "I want to talk to you about it in person before we meet Dewhurst."

"The detective?" Emy licked her lips. "What does he want?"

"You haven't even looked at your email yet, have you?"

She clicked the home button on the phone and brought up the mail application. Sure enough, an email from Dewhurst sat in the inbox. She tapped the screen and read the first few lines. "Oh," she said. "He wants to meet at 2 pm."

"Yes, he does."

"Okay." A sinking feeling hit her stomach. "You think he's, well, angry at me?"

Brett laughed. "No, dear. I think he wants to hear any and all theories.

Besides, I want to see if he knows anything about what happened in my neighborhood last night. Or can at least tell me who to ask."

Emy tapped her fingers on the counter. Her short nails made little noise. "What happened in your neighborhood?"

"We'll talk about it when you get here. Bring your laptop. Okay?"

"Yes, sir," she said. "I'll be there in 20."

"Perfect," Brett said. "Lee should have yumminess waiting for you."

The line went dead and she put the phone back on the counter. Luna had finished eating. The dog looked up at her, tail still wagging. "Okay, you. Let's go potty and then I have to go."

At the word "potty," Luna's normally lazy ears jumped to attention and the wagging went into overdrive. Emy scratched the dog behind the ears and then Luna was running to the front door. "Wait," she said. "I have to get dressed first!"

She didn't make it to Brett's on time. She was ten minutes late after attempting to tame her hair and find something suitable to wear. Walking into Brett and Lee's patio home always made her feel ten years behind in fashion, and somewhat ashamed of her appearance. Despite the heat, she'd chosen a sky blue blouse and a pair of jeans. As usual, she'd brushed her hair to the side to cover her scars. While she did, she'd remembered what Bryan had said the night before and took a good look at herself in the mirror. If not for the scars, she would be pretty. With them? She'd shaken her head and continued brushing her hair.

She parked in the lot several spots away from the smashed up car. Red and yellow police stickers covered its windshield. Whoever owned the car was in a world of shit with HPD. She shook her head as she opened the car door.

With the A/C cranked, the punishing temperature had seemed a bad dream. But the moment she cracked open her car door, a shockwave of heat hit her. Emy sighed and walked out of the parking lot to Brett's. By the time she covered the hundred feet to his home, she was mopping her brow. When the hell was the heatwave going to end?

She opened the wrought iron gate and entered the small yard. Despite the incredible heat, not to mention the water rationing, Brett's lawn looked immaculate as always. The green grass and bushes looked well watered and fed. Perhaps her apartment complex should hire the pair to fix their gardens. Emy smiled.

She stepped to the door and knocked. A pair of dogs loosed a chorus of shrill barks. The sound of little feet running down the stairs, collars jingling, hit her ears. *Oh, yes,* she thought, *the Papillons.*

Brett's voice, muffled by the door, told the dogs to hush. The two animals went quiet at once. A lock clicked and the door swung open on well-oiled hinges.

He stood on the threshold, a freshly pressed white button-up hanging over a pair of creased khakis. "Well, about time you got here." The dogs peered out from between his legs, their tiny bodies shaking from their wagging tails. "Come on in. Breakfast is served."

By the time they walked up the stairs to the second floor, her stomach was howling with hunger. The smell of fresh bacon, eggs, french toast, and french-pressed coffee was more than enough to make her mouth fill with saliva. Fortunately, breakfast tasted even better than it smelled.

After a breakfast of two omelettes, thick sliced bacon, french toast with baked apple topping, and three cups of coffee, Emy thought she'd explode. From the look on Brett's face, he knew how she felt.

Lee cleaned up breakfast while she and Brett retired to the couch in the living room. Emy pulled her laptop from her satchel and put it on the coffee table. Brett put his next to hers, but neither opened the computers.

The dogs ran to the couch. One jumped up beside Emy, the other next to Brett. He scratched the little dog behind its ears.

"So. Please explain to me how you came up with this?"

Emy sighed. She started telling him about the meeting with Seamus and Bryan, how she'd pieced together the similar symbols, and the mythology behind them. When she was finished, Brett looked down into the dog's face.

"It sounds crazy," he said.

"I know."

A smile slowly lit his face. He turned his head and looked at her. "And at the same time, completely believable."

Emy cocked an eyebrow. "You think so?"

"Yes. But you know Novak is never going to go for this."

She shrugged. "Does it matter? Dewhurst is the one we have to convince."

"Oh, so you assume I'm convinced?"

Emy blinked at him. "You aren't?"

"Well..." Brett's voice drifted off. Her boss typically did that when he was trying to find the right words. She'd always admired his ability to say what was on his mind, but he never said it until he could phrase it properly. "I think it's a great profile. I think it's very possible that our bug is just a little more than psychotic. Maybe he's convinced himself he's the second coming of this Gibil nephilim thing."

"I've heard of stranger things."

"Me too. You ever heard of Strickland?"

She shook her head.

Brett laughed. "Didn't think so. Let me enlighten you. Strickland was a firebug that worked Houston twelve years ago. Burned up some places in the warehouse district before it really got gentrified. We did our best to find a pattern or a motive for the arsons, but we were stuck."

"But you caught him?"

He held up a hand. "Finally, someone did some research on the area. Turns out the warehouses were all built by a company named Strickland back in the 60s. Strickland was owned by Alan Strickland and went out of business due to asbestos lawsuits in the late 70s.

"Alan Strickland disappeared off the grid in '82. Just became a non-entity. Turns out he was homeless, in his 70s, and for some reason got it into his mind that the warehouses had been possessed by demons. So he was burning them down to the ground."

"Demons?"

Brett grinned. "The demons were the reason for his bad luck. At least that's what he thought."

"So how'd they catch him?"

"An investigator put together the pieces and started looking for him. Put out an APB and let the unis know who they were looking for. Strickland managed to torch two more warehouses before we caught him."

"What did he say?"

"Just what I told you. He was drunk, crying, and saying he was sorry for the demons. Over and over again. Some of the things he said didn't make any sense. Until, that is, we broke up the concrete."

Emy blinked. "You broke up the foundation? Why?"

"A hunch," Brett said. "We found at least one body buried in the concrete at each site. Strickland owed a lot of money to the New Orleans mafia. In return for debt forgiveness, they buried bodies at his construction sites."

"Jesus."

"I guess over the years, the guilt finally crushed him. He killed himself not too long after his incarceration in Huntsville." He scratched the dog again and it lovingly growled. "But the strange thing was the demons. He never stopped talking about them, describing them, repeating the things they said to him. It was spooky as hell."

"You caught him."

It was a statement, not a question. "I caught him. Was the first big case I broke. Guess it's why I'm your boss too."

"How much time did you spend talking to him?"

"More than was probably healthy," Brett said. "I, um, wanted to understand him. I knew he was psychotic, and I knew what drove him to it, but I wanted to understand how his thoughts put all that together." He shook his head. "Very messy place."

"Yeah," Lee said as he entered the living room. "Lover boy there started having nightmares. Screaming about demons in the night." Lee shook his head. "Drove me crazy for a while."

"Just a while?" Emy asked.

Lee made his way to the couch, picked up the dog, and nestled in beside Brett. He put one arm around his partner and gently kissed him on the cheek. "Oh, he always drives me crazy. But usually in a good way."

Brett blushed. "Anyway, Strickland was...different. It was the first time I really met a bug that was more than a thrill seeker or paid a bounty. But they do exist. I knew that from all the classes and the psychology." He paused for a moment. "Was the first time I really understood just how broken a human being could become."

Lee squeezed Brett's shoulder and he relaxed a bit.

"Our bug could be another Strickland," Emy said.

"Easily," Brett said. "Maybe you've got it right. Maybe he does believe that Gibil or something like the god has possessed him. Or maybe that he *is* Gibil. In human form."

Emy exhaled through her teeth. "So how do we get Dewhurst to believe all this?"

Brett grinned. "Think you'll find him more amenable than you imagine. Word is that he's dealt with more than one psychotic in his career. Wouldn't surprise me if he's up to hunt another one."

"This is crazy. I put all this together last night, but I didn't really think you'd buy it."

Brett paused. "Do you buy it?"

She slowly nodded. "Yes. Guess I was just worried you'd think I was a fool."

Brett laughed. "Emy? You have the technical skills to be a good investigator. More than that, you have good instincts." He placed a hand on her knee. "And I trust you when you think you're right."

She smiled. "Thanks, boss. So we meet Dewhurst when?"

"2 pm. I'm thinking maybe the three of us should meet at the museum. And then you can show us Gibil."

Lee sighed. "You tell her about the cats?"

Emy furrowed her brow. "Cats? This have anything to do with that smashed up car in the parking lot?"

Brett and Lee exchanged a glance. "We don't know. But several dead cats were found in the street this morning. Along with one of our neighbors."

Her mouth dropped open. "One of your neighbors?"

Lee wrinkled his nose. "Redneck that lived down the road. Always called us faggots when we walked the dogs. Gunderson was an asshole, but nobody deserves that."

"Deserves what?" Emy asked.

Brett clasped his hands. "Someone used a garbage can lid to kill the cats. Then they killed him. Smashed his skull to a pulp."

"Jesus."

"Yeah. All that happened this morning. Lee and I woke up to a uni knocking on our door asking us if we heard anything." He shrugged. "Didn't hear a damned thing. They don't even know when it happened."

"So who called 911?"

"Patrolman found him," Brett said. "Then the cops descended on this place like locusts."

Lee snorted. "Cops. Animal control. Coroner. You name it. CSU was here for hours taking pictures and everything else you can imagine."

"Weird," Emy said. "So what's up with the car?"

"They don't know yet," Brett said. "Hopefully Dewhurst can make some calls and find out for us. Because I'm interested. I want to know what the hell is going on."

"Yeah. Can't imagine that makes you two feel safe here."

Lee squeezed Brett's shoulder again. "He carries a pistol at all times. I'm not worried. Besides, we have our own alarm system." He pointed at the dog in her lap.

"But still," she said. "That's really creepy."

"Yeah," Brett said. He turned to Lee. "She and I need to go over the report. You want to stay and be bored by our babbling?"

He shook his head. "No thanks. I'll do some laundry and maybe read." He tapped Brett's knee and stood up, the dog in his arms. "I'll leave you to it."

Brett and Lee kissed and Lee headed downstairs. Emy watched him go and sighed.

"That's my job," Brett said.

She turned to him. "What?"

He narrowed his eyes. "Checking out my man. That's my job."

She giggled. "Sorry. Just wishing I had someone at home waiting for me besides Luna."

"I know what you mean," Brett said. A devilish grin lit his face. "Maybe Bryan can solve that for you."

She rolled her eyes and opened her laptop. "Let's clean up this report, shall we?"

Brett laughed. "I'll put on some music. You prefer 80s pop or disco?"

Chapter 32

P opened his eyes and stared at the ceiling fan. Dust bunnies dangled from the motionless brown blades. When was the last time he'd run the fan? Two months? Three? Before he met Ghere, the house had always been too hot. And now?

He took a deep breath and tried to sit up. His back screamed in pain and he gasped. The top of his spine felt sledgehammered. P winced and pulled the covers from his chest, a moan escaping his lips as his shoulder complained.

"Hit too hard," he whispered to the room. "I hit him too hard."

No you didn't, Ghere's voice said in his mind. *You did it just right.*

P turned himself until his legs dangled over the edge of the bed. He knew it would hurt like hell. Another deep breath, and he slid his ass forward until his feet hit the wooden floor.

He stood with a groan. A ring of fire wrapped his thigh and he cursed. P looked down at his bare legs and several raw and red punctures stared back at him. He could tell the teeth from the claw marks. Suddenly he felt like vomiting.

P stumbled forward, each step an adventure in pain. The burning of his leg wounds was nothing compared to the firestorm in his upper back. Goddamn, how hard had he hit that man?

He remembered the trashcan lid buckling and twisting. With each hit, the metal had seemed to groan. Gouts of blood had flown into the hot, humid air, and with every swing, the squelch of something wet.

P walked to the bathroom in a daze. He needed a shower. Hot water. Anything to relax the locked up muscles in his back and shoulders. He flexed his fingers and stepped into the shower stall.

Cold water hit his body. He screamed in surprise and stepped away from the stream, the frigid water like fire on his skin. Shivering, he reached for the handle and turned it all the way to "H".

He drew back his hand and waited. The stream of water slowed for a second before rushing out again. A cloud of steam rose into the air.

He stepped into the stream and blinked. The water was merely warm instead of scorching hot. P rotated until the water pounded his back and shoulders. He stood still and waited for the heat to do its work.

As carefully as he could, he bent his head to stare at the shower stall's stone floor. Something cracked in his spine. He moaned again, but this time in pleasure. Although the water didn't feel hot on his skin, his muscles started to loosen. A little.

The red marks on his legs burned, but in a good way. He'd have to disinfect them when he was done in the shower. Alcohol, anti-bacterial ointment, and maybe a bandage to make sure they didn't ooze against his pants. But that was for later.

He still couldn't believe what had happened. He'd wrecked the stolen car. He'd blown his surveillance. He'd been attacked by cats, of all things. And on top of that? He'd murdered the guy who saved him from the feline horde.

You did what had to be done.

Yes, he had. After the man's head was little more than a crushed melon, he'd bolted down Inker until he reached the intersection. After that, he'd walked four blocks through the quiet, lonely streets until he felt safe. Or safe enough.

Other cats in the neighborhood yowled into the night, but none had appeared. He'd needed a ride. At that hour of night, most cab companies were shut down or serving only inner city Houston. The bars were all closed and only the after hours places were still open, but those were downtown or in the warehouse district.

He'd considered using his phone to call a cab, but didn't want a digital record. He'd already fucked up so badly, the cops were sure to investigate. They'd have hair samples. Maybe even a stray fingerprint. He'd grinned in the shadows thrown by an acetylene street light.

But they'll have a hell of a time ferreting whose are whose, he'd thought to himself.

He'd continued walking down the street, his eyes examining the mouth of every alley. Cats lived in alleys. He didn't want to meet up with those animals again.

"Why, Ghere? Why do the cats hate you?"

His passenger, the God of Sumer, had cackled in his head. *It's not me they hate. It's you. You are becoming.*

He'd thought about asking what that meant, but didn't. Sometimes Ghere scared him. And at that moment in time, he'd never been more afraid in his life.

After walking more than ten blocks away from Inker, he finally saw what he'd been looking for. A yellow cab slowly made its way down the street. P had waved and the cab had pulled over to the shoulder.

He'd opened the door and slid in. The driver had looked in the rearview mirror, eyes growing wide.

"Where, um, to?" the man asked in broken English.

P had given an address four blocks away from his home.

The driver had nodded, turned on the meter, and driven away from the curb. Middle Eastern music played softly on the radio. P had fought to stay awake. The wreck, the encounter with the cats, and bashing the nosy neighbor's head in, had left him drained.

"You have a cold?" the driver had asked.

P had raised his head to look in the rearview. The driver's eyes were fixed on him. "Why do you say that?" P had asked.

The driver had shrugged. "You are wearing too many clothes," the man had said.

P had laughed at that and hugged himself. The cab had been cool. Much too cool. He'd shivered the entire ride.

After reaching the destination, he'd paid the cabby and walked back out into glorious heat. His body had stopped shivering at once, but the post-adrenal overload had made him feel clammy.

He knew he should have jumped in the shower immediately upon returning to the house, but he just couldn't do it. Instead, he'd stripped off his clothes, put another comforter on the bed, and slid between the sheets. By the time he'd fallen asleep, it had been past 4:30 in the morning.

He raised his arms to the ceiling, the water rushing over his shoulders. P ignored the pain and kept reaching until he was on his toes. Another muscle loosed its iron grip and the corner of his lip twitched.

"Becoming. I am becoming," he said to himself.

And so am I, Ghere responded. *You will need to move faster now. Faster than you like.*

"I know," he said to the empty shower stall.

It had to be soon now. The cops would find the car. They'd find the dead cats. And the dead giant. What else would they find? It might take them days to sort out fingerprints and hair samples and whatever else. Or it might not.

P gritted his teeth. They'd find his fingerprints on record. But they'd have to do something illegal to get at the original reports. He hoped.

"Stop worrying," he said aloud. "You've seen too many damned cop movies."

Ghere rustled in his mind, but remained mute. The sensation of the "other" sliding around his brain made him queasy. The entity, the daemon, God, had access to his thoughts. It plucked them from his mind as easily as a child tearing the petals from a flower. Ghere knew everything he knew, and much much more.

But you must become too, he told his passenger. *You must be made flesh.*

Must be made flesh, Ghere echoed. *And you will be my fire,* it said.

The words gave him a momentary shiver, but he felt the daemon grinning in his mind. It wasn't a threat. It was an honor. Ghere would give him what he'd always dreamed of. Ghere would make it happen. And for that, he would do anything Ghere wanted.

He thought of the arson investigators. Novak, Cullum, and the Aninzo woman. Especially her. Ghere wanted her more than anyone else. P grinned. And he would give her to It.

Chapter 33

For once, Dewhurst beat Tony to the cafe. He had time to slug down two cups of coffee and research Sumerian mythology on his phone, jotting down notes on a small, leather bound notebook.

Upon waking that morning, he'd called Tony, read Aninzo's report another three times, showered, and headed to the cafe. After all the beer he'd consumed the night before, the coffee was a blessing.

He looked at his notes and sipped his third cup.

A possible daemon or nephilim. Gibil, the Sumerian god of fire and light, Its father. A traveling collection of artifacts. Fires in other cities over time. Unexplained blazes followed by a sudden cessation of attacks. All occurred during heatwaves.

Heatwaves. Dewhurst chewed his lip. Aninzo hadn't put any figures in her report, but Dew had already looked up temperatures for the periods of similar attacks. Unseasonably warm. Record heat. Always occurred after the summer solstice.

He tapped his pen on the table. There wasn't a whole lot about the Sumerian gods on the internet. At least not that he could find and almost all of the information was replicated in triplicate. In other words, the reference links he followed from Wikipedia had little to no new information.

So the museum curator was still the best and possibly the only readily available source for information. That made him...wary. Aninzo mentioned a tome in the curator's possession. A diary of sorts. One thing Dew knew for sure—he wanted a look at that book.

"Well, you look busy."

Dew looked up from his notes as Tony pulled out a chair. The metal gliders squealed across the tile floor. He sat down, wiped his brow, and tented his hands on the table. "What's doing?"

The detective smiled, closed his notebook, and pushed it aside. "The usual. Looking to catch bad guys."

Tony grinned. "You and me both. You look for the physical baddies, and I'm busy trying to arrest the imaginary ones."

"Uh-huh," Dew said and sipped his coffee. Tony started to turn his head to look for the waitress when a steaming cup of coffee appeared before him. The tiny waitress disappeared without a word as though she'd never been there.

"How the hell does she do that?" he asked the detective.

Dew shrugged. "She just does."

"So what's up? You said something about having questions?"

"Yes."

Tony studied him for a moment while stirring his coffee. He took a small sip, winced at the heat, and shook his head. "That'll keep for a few minutes." He looked back at Dew. "Well, you going to talk or just sit there?"

"Need a profile."

Tony raised an eyebrow. "A profile?"

"Yeah." Dew took another sip. "It's a strange one."

"Now I'm very interested."

"I'll bet," Dew said. "So what do you know about possession? From a clinical point of view?"

Tony took a breath and scrunched his eyebrows. "Clinical point of view. You mean psychological?"

"Obviously."

"No," Tony said, "not obvious. One of the problems with the word 'possession' is that everyone thinks of it in terms of the movies and the horror books. So you have to be more specific in history."

"Really?"

"Yeah." Tony took another experimental sip of coffee. "The Christian idea of possession is quite a bit different from those of other cultures. I mean they all share *some* common traits."

"Which are?"

"Well," Tony said, "things like a change in the personality of the possessed, speaking in tongues or unknown languages, and knowledge of things the possessed couldn't possibly know." Tony tapped his spoon against the coffee cup. "From a modern point of view, most of it can be explained by psychotic episodes or schizophrenia. I don't even want to know how many people over history were tortured and killed for mental disease under the auspices of religious cleansing."

Dew thought for a moment. "Okay. I get that. So you're saying it's all down to mental problems?"

Tony grinned. "Depends how far out on a limb you want to go."

"Far," Dew said. "As far as you want."

Tony leaned back in his chair. "In Judaism and its offshoots, which includes both Christianity and Islam, the idea of possession is that a so-called 'unclean' spirit targets and takes over a person. That unclean spirit can be thought of as a demon."

"Not a daemon?"

Tony raised an eyebrow. "No. A daemon is something else entirely. Daemons have no defined alignment, if you will. They can be benevolent, malevolent, or simply neutral to human beings. Demons, on the other hand, are always considered evil."

The waitress appeared, refilled Dew's cup, and freshened Tony's. Dew thanked her and blew steam away from the pitch black drink.

"From a psychological point of view, what does that mean for the possessed?"

"How do you mean?"

"I mean," Dew said and leaned forward in his chair, "might the knowledge of possession affect the possessed?"

"Absolutely." Tony sat up in his chair and took another sip. "A person with a damaged mind could easily think they're possessed and even demonstrate some of the traditional phenomenon."

"You sound like you've seen it."

Tony chuckled. "Very little difference between that and someone thinking they're Napoleon Bonaparte. In most cases anyway."

Dew narrowed his eyes. "In most cases?"

"Doesn't matter," Tony said with a dismissive wave.

"Okay, so what about Sumer? Know anything about their idea of possession?"

Tony stared at Dew. His brown eyes seemed to twinkle in the overhead lights. "What are you into, man? Where's all this coming from?"

Without divulging any specific crime details, Dew explained Emy's report. Tony listened with his hands cupped around the mug. When he explained Emy's theory regarding a nephilim of Gibil, Tony's eyes lit up.

"Okay. So some kind of symbol showed up at the fires. And you think it's a calling card for someone who thinks they're possessed?"

Dew nodded. "Does that make any sense at all?"

"Sure," Tony said. "Makes all the sense in the world. You might have an arsonist in the grips of a long-term psychotic episode. And the episode may have gone on for weeks, months, or even years."

"Episodes stop," Dew said.

Tony shook his head. "Not necessarily. Just because an 'episode' sounds like something temporary, it could end up being long-lived or permanent." He glanced down at the table. "Like Trey Leger, for instance."

The words stung Dew. He pushed away the sudden wave of anger and futility that entered his mind. "Okay, given that, what do we do about it? I mean, how do I figure out what this person is going to do?"

"Good question," Tony said. "How much history do you have on Gibil?"

"Not much," Dew admitted. "But I'm going to take care of that later today. First hand."

"If it's not a god that's well-known, then I would start with how your perp did their research. Where did they find out about it, and more importantly, how? If it's not something easily found on a search engine, then you'll have to look at what books are out there, and what the average person has access to."

Dew nodded. "And what if the information isn't readily available?"

"Then the fun begins," Tony said. "You either have someone with a fuck-ton of stamps on their library card, someone who works in academia, or you have to consider the unlikely option."

Dew raised a brow. "Which is?"

Tony's smile disappeared. "That they're really possessed."

Chapter 34

Meeting at the Raven Bar and Grill was a bad idea. After the breakfast she'd had with Brett and Lee, Emy wasn't sure she could eat anything. But Dewhurst had insisted on the location since it was close to the HMNS and had a great chef. She knew the Raven all too well. Whenever she went to shop at Murder By The Book, she ended up at The Raven.

The trio sat at a table, glasses of iced tea wetting stone coasters. The small plate of bread before them was still mostly full. Emy had nibbled a piece of rye, but the detective hadn't touched any. Neither had Brett. She felt a little self-conscious when she realized she was the only one eating. And now they were in the restaurant, her stomach actually craved food.

The hellos had been more than a little awkward, although Dewhurst had held the door open for both of them and his handshake was as firm as ever. The conversation, however, was slow to get started. In a way, Emy thought that was because all three of them were afraid to broach the subject without sounding like fools.

But I'm the fool that got us all together, she thought. She took a deep breath and looked up at Dewhurst. "Thank you for inviting us to lunch, detective." His eyes, gentle and intelligent, flicked to her. "But what did you want to talk to us about?"

Dewhurst's impassive face broke into a thin grin. "The report, naturally."

Brett exchanged a glance with Emy. "What about it in particular?"

The detective stared at the bread for a moment and sighed. He reached out and took a small piece. "Well, for starters, I think it's an excellent piece of research." He buttered the piece of bread and held it between his fingers. "You obviously have a flair for it, Ms. Aninzo."

"Emy. Please."

"Emy. Pardon me." He sheepishly took a bite. His eyes lit with greed as he chewed. After he swallowed, his grin turned into a real smile. "I'd forgotten just how delicious their bread is." He cleared his throat. "Anyway, the separate threads you put together are very provocative. And, at the same time, seem quite unlikely."

Emy's face flushed and she nodded. "I know, detective. Probably a waste of—"

"No, ma'am," he interrupted. "Not a waste at all." He glanced at Brett. "What do you think, Mr. Cullum?"

Brett shrugged. "We don't have any other theories and I think she's on to something. She certainly has me convinced."

The detective leaned back in his chair, but kept his forearms on the table's edge. "I spoke with a friend of mine this morning. He's somewhat of a phenom for psychological profiles and such. Probably because he spends most of his days with lunatics."

Brett laughed. "Sounds like a party animal."

"You have no idea," Dew said. "I explained some crucial pieces of your theory to him." Dew nodded at Emy. "He thinks you're dead on."

"He does?"

"Yes, Ms. Anin— Yes, Emy. He suggested that if the information on Gibil and its possible nephilim is not widely known, we should look for someone with a very well traveled library card, or an avid academic in the study of Sumer."

Brett nodded. "That tracks. But how likely is it for someone to find that information in a library? Hell, she had to go to the exhibit's curator to find it."

"Exactly," Dewhurst said. "Which suggests it's someone in academia rather than a layman."

Emy frowned. "Not sure I agree." Brett and the detective looked at her. That feeling of embarrassment, of impending humiliation, crawled in her stomach. She fought it back and brushed a lock of hair from her eyes. "If it was an academic, why would the fires suddenly start this year? I mean, why not before? Why did they start after the exhibit arrived?"

"Good question," Dewhurst said. "And I find that particular fact a little troubling too."

Brett took a sip of tea and his eyebrows raised. "What if there are more fires? I mean, ones we haven't found?"

"I thought of that," Emy said. "I'd need a lot of help to go through the history to see if there are any others that match the same M.O. But remember, I found the symbol by accident. Our bug is making it more apparent with each fire, but we are looking for it now."

"True," Dewhurst said. "Once seen and all that. But it doesn't matter. The information you pulled on fires in other cities and the crime database doesn't make sense either. Especially not if you consider when the exhibit seems to pop up around them."

"Troubles me too," Brett said. "Let's say our bug is responsible for all those fires going back, I don't know, decades?"

Emy nodded.

"Then our bug would be getting up there in age. And it still doesn't explain the gaps between the fires."

Dewhurst smiled at Emy. "Tell me. Did you research the heatwaves too?"

She blinked. "You mean weather coinciding with the fires? And the exhibits?"

"Exactly that," Dewhurst said.

She bit her lip. "I noticed it, but I didn't really study it."

"Well, I started digging. Amazing the kind of information you can find these days from a cell phone." He took another sip of tea. "The heatwaves all start a month or two before the rash of fires. It's almost like the weather is pushing the perp to start them."

Brett frowned. "Please tell me you're not suggesting the heatwaves are causing the fires?"

Dewhurst shook his head. "Not exactly. I'm afraid I have an even more unorthodox theory."

"What's that?" Emy asked. She was afraid to hear him say it, the same thing that had been flitting through her mind the past few minutes.

"Crazy as it sounds," Dewhurst said, "I think our perp is causing the heatwave."

Brett harrumphed. "Pardon me for saying so, detective, but are you insane?"

"Maybe," Dewhurst said dryly. He glanced at Emy. She didn't like the way he was studying her. It was almost as if he knew she had entertained the same thoughts. The detective broke his stare and waved at the waitress. "Perhaps we should order and then I'll explain my reasoning."

"This should be good," Brett said with a grin.

Emy's stomach fluttered again. She didn't think it would be good. She was afraid to think of it at all.

They ordered. Dew announced he was picking up the check and to go crazy. Emy's stomach had definitely found its second wind. She ordered the grilled salmon special, Brett, the lime chicken, and Dew a steak. Once the waiter left them alone, Dew pulled a battered notebook from his pocket. He flipped to a dog eared page, set it on the table, and scanned the words for a moment before looking up at Emy.

"France. Germany. Seattle. Those are all places that had arson streaks while the exhibit was in town."

"Yeah," Emy said. "Those and the deaths of the investigators were the only links I found."

"Except for the heatwaves," Dew said in a monotone.

"Of course." Emy crinkled a brow. "You found something?"

"Per your report, I had the Marseilles police records looked over by someone in the department that speaks French."

Emy's heart quickened. She didn't know the detective very well, but his eyes glittered with excitement even if his impassive face gave no hint of it. "What did you find?"

Dew glanced at Brett. "You're very lucky to have her, Brett. She'd make an excellent detective."

"I know," Brett said. "But the suspense is killing me. What did you find out?"

"Sorry," Dew said. "The melodramatic runs in the family. In each of the cases, all three that you found, the investigator in charge of the case died. But the notes they left behind had clues, much the same as you found."

"The symbol?"

"Yes, Emy," Dew said with a nod. "The symbol. In Germany, the sigil was found at the site of the fire carved with a knife. It was barely discernible amidst the wreckage, but Van Haufen found it. In Marseille, Detective Charbonneau discovered the sigil when he returned to the site after it was closed." Dew took a sip of iced tea. "And in Seattle, they found the symbol in a tree much as you did."

"Okay," Brett said. "What's the catch?"

A grin slowly spread over the detective's face. "The catch is that the investigators discovered various leads, followed them up, and were murdered as a result."

"By whom?" Emy asked Dewhurst.

"By the perp, I imagine." The detective tore off another piece of rye.

Brett rubbed his clean-shaven chin. "Then why did the fires stop?"

Dew raised a finger. "And that's the question." He popped the piece of bread in his mouth and chewed.

"They never tracked down Til, the man whose apartment they found Van Haufen in." Emy glanced at Brett. "Till must have been the bug."

Dew swallowed and took a sip of tea. "Agreed," he said. "The German man disappeared. His flat was taken by the state and he was never seen again."

"Then what happened to him?" Brett asked.

"I don't know," Dew said. "But I have a couple of theories."

"Do tell," Brett said.

"Maybe Til thought he was possessed. Maybe after he killed the cop, his psychotic episode ended and he realized what he'd done. Maybe he killed himself."

"Okay," Brett said. "What else?"

Dew gave an embarrassed smile. "Maybe his possession ended because he couldn't face what he'd done. Maybe he forced the demon out."

"Wait," Emy said. "Isn't that the same thing?"

"Maybe," Dew said. "Depends on whether or not you think the possession was real or just the product of a damaged mind."

Brett tapped his fork on the plate, his eyes upturned to the ceiling. "Suicide," he mumbled. "No, I don't think so," he said.

"Why not?" Emy asked.

Brett took in a deep breath. "Are we safe in assuming the fires are some kind of, I don't know, religious ritual?"

"I think so," Dew said.

Brett nodded. "Okay. Then if the bug was trying to worship the demon, or whatever you want to call it, wouldn't taking their own life before finishing the job be a profanity?"

"Good question," Dew said. "But what else makes sense?"

Emy shivered. "The impossible." The two men glanced at her. "Maybe the, the whatever, consumed him. Maybe he wasn't strong enough."

"Strong enough to what?" Dew asked. She had expected him to scoff, but instead he looked genuinely interested.

"Strong enough to bring it into the world. Or become it. Or, well, I don't even know how to say it."

Dew picked up his pen and jotted another note. "I'll try and get some medical records for these perps. Maybe they had heart disease or some other malady." He nodded to himself. "That could make sense."

Brett chuckled. "Maybe the fuckers just had a heart attack after they killed the investigators. Died somewhere no one found them."

"That's very possible," Dew said. "Or maybe they burned to dust."

The image of a man turning into a pillar of fire filled her mind. Her father, grinning as the flames consumed her and advanced toward her. Little Emy, burning in her bed while her father screamed in delight. Just before the world exploded and turned black. She shivered again and found Dew looking at her.

"Think of something?" he asked.

"Nothing," she said. "Nothing."

Chapter 35

P sat in front of the computer, eyes scanning the screen, a map of inner city Houston staring back at him. He zoomed in on the city's Third Ward district and took a sip from a cup of steaming tea. Crumbling wood-frame houses, shotgun shacks, decrepit apartment buildings, and shelters filled the northern end.

A muscle in his shoulders cramped and twitched. P groaned, shook off the pain, and returned his gaze to the monitor.

Over two weeks ago, he'd stolen a car, donned a black hoodie, and covered himself in blackface. He'd driven the ward looking for the targets. Ghere had been all too happy to point them out, giggling with glee. P grinned at the memory.

Two apartment buildings, another row of shotgun shacks, and then soul food row. It was so easy. Especially soul food row. There was enough grease and filth there to start something roaring.

In 1912, a fire started in Houston's fifth ward. Due to stiff winds, the shoddy construction of the primarily negro area, and lack of a proper fire department, the blaze spread easily. A church, school, 13 industrial plants, eight stores, and well over 100 homes were destroyed. The damage was extensive. But no one was reportedly killed.

The Third Ward, however, hadn't been affected by such a cleansing event. The screen shimmered. A single lick of fire burst from one of the highlighted portions of the map. It disappeared quickly, but left a burning coal in its wake. The screen shimmered again and a new lick of fire rose south of the first. Then another east. Then west. The ward started to burn. All of it started to burn.

P's penis stiffened. All those people, trapped in their shitty homes, living out their shitty existences, would finally be made productive. No one would miss them, but their deaths would help bring Ghere into being. And help him *become.*

The map on the screen erupted into fire, yellow, orange, red, and finally blue at the base. P's loins shook. His breath hitched as he filled his shorts with semen. The screen exploded with light. He closed his eyes as the orgasm rocked him.

When the convulsions stopped, the map was back, untouched, unblemished, except for the markers he'd placed weeks ago. Perfect. He panted and absently rubbed at his stiff member.

He would have to work fast now. Despite the pain in his back and the itchy ache in his legs from the cat attack, he had to finish preparing. He must succeed.

P slowly stood and another spasm flitted across his shoulder blades. He barely noticed. The elation of the climax was still too recent, too palpable. Ghere whispered in his mind there was more to follow. P couldn't wait.

He walked from his room, unmindful of the wet stain in his gym shorts. The lingering odor of gasoline stung his nostrils as soon as he opened the door to the garage. He clicked on the light switch and stared at his ammunition.

Rows of bottles, jars, and small metal boxes lined the concrete floor. Thick red wax capped the bottles, a fuse sticking out of each. A jelly like substance coated the dozen mason jars. The metal boxes had stamps on their outer shells; stamps of Ghere's sigil.

He wasn't as concerned about leaving evidence anymore. There was little point. Once the conflagration began, it would be too late to stop him. Too late to stop Ghere. Too late to stop them both from *becoming.*

It was a little past four in the afternoon. He had time to take a short nap, shower, treat those wretched cat bites, and assemble more party favors. The transmitters had all been tested. They were ready to be connected to their charges.

P turned off the light and stepped back into the house. He pulled off his gym shorts and threw them on top of the dryer. The shirt was a little more difficult. His shoulder still hurt like hell. It was probably time to take a few more anti-inflammatories. He finally managed to strip off the shirt with a wince and dropped it next to the shorts.

His back prickled with gooseflesh. It was 85° in the house and he was shivering. Another dose of hot water should help. P walked as quickly as he dared to the shower. His leg screamed at him with each step, but he ignored it.

Cullum's face floated across his vision. The man's smiling face, the short sideburns, started to burn. His stylish hair wilted before catching fire. His eyes boiled in their sockets while his skin cracked and blackened. Before long, there was nothing but ashes in his mind.

P stepped into the shower stall, turned the knob all the way to hot, and basked in the stream of water.

Chapter 36

When she'd first seen Gibil's sigil, she'd thought it beautiful. Now it looked ugly and foreboding. Dewhurst was practically bent at the waist, his face hovering over the display case. Brett glanced at Emy, a what-the-fuck look on his face.

It was late in the afternoon at HMNS and most of the patrons had already departed. The museum would close in less than half an hour and here they were, still in the exhibit. Dewhurst finally raised himself.

He looked up at the ceiling for a moment, his lips soundlessly moving. Emy had always thought the man strange, but this was downright creepy. He finally turned to the two of them. "Interesting."

She giggled and her face lit with an amused expression. "You've been staring at the damned thing for nearly five minutes. And that's all you can say?"

A blush of color hit his cheeks. "My apologies, Emy. Sometimes I get lost in thought."

"We could tell," Brett said. "What about the symbol? You agree it's the same."

"Remarkably similar," Dewhurst said. "These are very beautiful." His eyes glanced back at the case. "But that one certainly has a feeling to it."

Brett blinked. "A feeling?"

Dewhurst sighed. "I'm not sure how to say it, Brett."

"I do," Emy said. "It's like you look into it, and it's looking back at you."

"Yes. That exactly."

Brett turned his head back to the display case. He bent at the waist, much as Dewhurst had, and stared at the sigil. Another awkward moment passed. She didn't want to talk while Brett was engaged with the amulet, and she thought Dewhurst felt much the same.

Finally, he stood to his full height and turned with his back to the case. "Sorry. Don't get it."

Dewhurst grinned. "Perhaps that's because you don't buy into my insane theories?"

Brett shook his head. "You're not the only one touched in the head on this case." He jerked a thumb at Emy. "I can't say you've infected her because I think it's the other way around. But you two definitely see this case a little differently than I do."

Dewhurst shrugged. "Leaving out the so-called fantastic, you do agree our perpetrator *thinks* he's possessed?"

"Absolutely," Brett said. "Nothing else really makes sense."

"Good," Dewhurst said. He looked at Emy. "Now. Might you be good enough to get the curator on the phone? I'd like to see this book for myself."

G etting Seamus to escort them down into the HMNS inner offices was easy. Emy simply called the number on his business card and the dwarfish Irishman bounced into the exhibition. After exchanging pleasantries with Brett and Dewhurst, he led them down the back stairs and to his office.

Apparently Seamus didn't take Bryan's hint and clean his workspace. In fact, it was even worse than before. The man had pulled countless volumes from his book shelves, many bookmarked with strips of newspaper and magazines. Corpses of soda cans and candy bar wrappers littered the floor.

When they entered the office, Emy watched Dewhurst's easy smile transform into a look of disgust. The expression lasted only a second or two, but it still made her smile. Brett, on the other hand, was more entranced by the massive stack of books laid around the room.

Seamus backed up to his desk, used his hands to push himself up, and sat on the edge of the heavy furniture. "So glad you called me, lass."

Emy raised an eyebrow. "Why's that?"

His grin widened. "After I left you and Bryan last night, I headed back here." He raised his hands to encompass the room. "I, um, couldn't let go of our conversation. So I started digging." He pointed to the books covering both the floor and the reading table. "As you can see."

Her heart thumped fast in her chest. "Please tell me you weren't here all night?"

A look of horror spread across the Irishman's face. "Of course not. Just most of the night."

Dewhurst cleared his throat and the curator looked at him. "Did you find something beyond Wright's journal?"

Seamus nodded. "Indeed. I. Did." Emy nearly giggled at the man's dramatic phrasing. "Was pretty sure none of these tomes had additional information. And I was right about that. Pity it took me several hours to realize it." He shrugged. "So I made some calls."

Dewhurst shifted uncomfortably. "I'm not sure what Ms. Aninzo told you, Doctor, but any information regarding the case is confidential."

Seamus waved the statement away. "No, no. Wouldn't betray a confidence, detective. Wouldn't dare. No, I wanted to know if Gibil actually had any nephilim."

"And?" Brett asked.

The curator sighed. "Okay. I can tell I'm dragging this out. Sorry. I'm an old man that likes to talk. Long story long, I made a call to a mate of mine who works at the British Museum of Antiquities. He didn't know, of course, but he knew who I should call." Seamus grinned. "I'm damned happy we have good internet here. The long distance bills would have been astronomical."

Dewhurst rolled his eyes, but remained quiet. Seamus ignored him.

"After France, then Germany, then Egypt, I finally tracked down the so-called expert. Took a call to Baghdad, believe it or not."

"Iraq?" Emy asked. "Wow."

The Irishman laughed. "Imagine that. Information on the cradle of civilization found in the cradle of civilization." When he saw the other three didn't find his remarks humorous, he cleared his throat and continued. "I spoke to a Mister Siddiqui. He's apparently *the* expert on Sumer mythos."

Brett stood with his arms crossed, one foot tapping the floor. "And what did Siddiqui have to say?"

Seamus' grin widened. Emy saw bits of chocolate stuck in his flaming red beard.

"Gibil did have a nephilim." Seamus held up a single finger. "And its name is 'Ghere.'"

Emy blinked. "Ghere?"

"Yes, lass."

Dewhurst smiled. "And what can you tell us about this Ghere?"

Seamus nodded to Brett. "Close the door, if you would, Mr. Cullum."

Brett cocked his head and did as he was asked.

"Thank you," Seamus said. He clasped his hands together. "Don't want anyone else hearing this. All hush hush, you know."

Dewhurst's amused smile returned. "And we thank you for that," the detective said.

"Welcome. Now," the Irishman continued, "Ghere was a bad seed. Hated Its father. Hated humans. It's not known why, but it may have something to do with his mother or something else. Regardless, Ghere took great delight in firing buildings, people, livestock, you name it." Seamus leaned forward a little and whispered. "A bit of a bastard, if you ask me."

Brett looked nonplussed. "So why isn't he in the general mythos?"

Seamus shrugged. "Shame, perhaps? The Sumerians had a habit of compounding several things together. Lamashtu, for instance, is a creature of disease, stealer of children, and a whole host of other maladies. Instead of being responsible for a single evil, they found it easier to 'blame' a single entity for multiple sins. Very different from more modern mythologies.

"But Ghere was vanquished, at least according to Dr. Siddiqui."

Emy licked her lips. "How?"

Seamus' smile fell into a thin line. "That was the information Siddiqui didn't have. Pity, really. I'd love to write a monograph on the subject comparing Judeo-Christian exorcism myths with this. But I guess I'll have to—"

"Excuse me," Dewhurst said, "but what information did Dr. Siddiqui actually have regarding Ghere's demise?"

"Oh, right." Seamus scratched his beard. A few crumbs fell to the floor. "He wasn't killed exactly. Gibil's cult finally found him and imprisoned him."

"How?" Brett asked.

Seamus shrugged. "We don't know. According to Siddiqui, there is no known information about how he was imprisoned or in what. Also no information about how he could get out."

Emy loosed a long sigh. "Shit. Back where we started from."

Seamus held up a finger. "Not so fast, lass. If there's a nutter out there who worships Ghere, then he may be trying to free the nephilim from its prison."

"But we've no idea," Brett said, "how our perp would try and do that."

"True," Seamus said. "But I have some ideas."

Emy exchanged a look with Brett. "Like what?"

"First off, he might try and steal the amulet."

Dewhurst sighed. "And why would he do that?"

Seamus grinned. "Ancient history is filled with strange rumors and legends. Apocrypha that has no direct attribution, but seems to run across cultures. For instance, how many stories can you think of where a supernatural being was trapped in a piece of jewelry or something like an urn? Just think of the genie in the proverbial bottle."

Emy groaned. "Aladdin? Really?"

"May have made a blockbuster cartoon," Seamus said, "but the Arabian Nights have been a mainstay of both Western and Eastern cultures since time out of mind. Where do you think those legends originally started?"

"So, what?" Brett asked. "You saying our firebug may try and smash the amulet? Or steal it?"

Seamus shrugged. "That would be the most logical answer. But there's no guarantee he's playing with a full deck. It's possible your, um, *bug*, might have another idea. When Ishtar and Dimuzi bonded, the rain fell from the sky and fertilized the land. As a result, the Kings of Sumer, Akkad, and even Babylon lay with the Priestess of Ishtar every growing season and every picking season. In Sumer, everything is about cycles."

Dewhurst grunted. "So what happened during a drought?"

The curator plucked an errant hair from his beard. "You have to understand something, Detective. Our knowledge of Sumer isn't exactly a full record. There are a lot of missing pieces. More than likely, a lot of what we *should* know burned up in the Library of Alexandria in 48 BCE or was considered apostasy by the Christians or Muslims and destroyed. In other words, I have no idea."

Emy opened her mouth and closed it. The heat. The fires. The nearly radioactive burns on the Hartman bodies. She still had no explanation for those burns or why the fire in the house was normal temperature until it found the father and child in the bedroom. "He's trying to bring it to life."

The three men turned to her. Seamus blinked. "What's that, lass?"

A blush rose to her cheeks. She brushed the locks away from the scarred side of her face without thinking. "What if the fires are some kind of, I don't know, ritual to free Ghere? Does he need bodies? Deaths? Or maybe just a number of acts to bring him back to life?"

Brett turned his gaze back to the curator. "That sound possible, Seamus?"

"Plausible," the old man muttered. "But then again, anything is." He kicked his feet out into space. The heels came back and banged into the desk before he swung them out again and repeated. His eyes bored into the floor.

Emy thought the curator was having an episode of some kind. And then Seamus raised his head and stared at her with glittering eyes and a grim smile. "That could actually be the case. It tracks with other myths, not necessarily Sumerian. But your firebug may have more information than just about Ghere. Maybe he's mixing and matching several different mythologies. But maybe the goal is the same."

"Shit," Brett said. "You saying he's sacrificing buildings and people to Ghere? Giving it strength?"

Seamus raised his hands. "Why not?"

"That's troublesome," Dewhurst said.

Emy turned to him. "You're thinking there's going to be more arsons."

The detective nodded. "Big ones."

After Brett drove her back to her car, she took one last look at the crime scene tape on Inker, the smashed up car in the parking lot, and shuddered. The temperature outside was 106° with a heat index of 114°. It was the hottest day she could remember. So why was she shivering in her car?

Something was wrong. They'd overlooked something. She was sure of it.

The conversation with Seamus had brought up more questions that no one, not even Seamus, could answer. The idea that the information they needed to stop the firebug may have burned up over 2 millennia ago was downright infuriating.

What was the bug thinking? What was the reason? Was he really trying to bring Ghere into being? Did he think he was the reincarnation of Ghere?

Is he Ghere?

She shook away the thought. That was even crazier than the theory she'd come up with the night before. Yet once Brett and Dewhurst had read her report, digested it, and discussed it, the crazy answer seemed the only logical one.

"And that's what's terrifying," she said in the silent car.

Doesn't matter, she thought. She needed to call Bryan and see if he was up for dinner. A slight grin tugged at her mouth. *And maybe he can keep me company tonight.*

She pressed the "Call" button and waited for the beep. She said his name and the phone dialed the number.

"Emy. How are you?"

She grinned. "You already have my name in your phone?"

"Yes. Why wouldn't I?"

Her grin widened. "Wanted to know if you're free tonight. Brett and Lee have invited us to go out. For food."

Pause. "As it happens, I have nothing going on this evening. I, um, was hoping you were available."

"You don't mind eating with Brett and Lee?"

"Of course not," he said. "After all, they did introduce us."

She laughed. "There is that. You want to meet at the restaurant, want me to pick you up? Or—"

"I'll pick you up," he said. "What time?"

"7 pm. We're going to Underbelly."

"Nice. Always wanted to eat there."

"I think Lee knows the chef. This may be a meal not to miss."

"I'll come hungry," he said.

A devilish smile lit her lips. "Maybe you should bring some clothes for tomorrow."

Pause. "Yeah. Um, okay."

"Okay, so see you at 7."

"Looking forward to it."

She said goodbye and snickered. He'd sounded more than a little shocked when she told him to bring clothes. Maybe that was a good thing.

It took her another ten minutes to get back to her apartment. The traffic was light. Thankfully. But that didn't mean she couldn't see overheated cars pushed to the shoulders on the road. A lot of people were having trouble keeping their engines from blowing up, and the weather was only supposed to be warmer tomorrow.

She parked the car in a spot between two large pickup trucks. The first was red and black while the other was a hideous shade of yellow with a confederate flag decal on the back window. Emy wrinkled her nose at it and stepped up on the sidewalk. She took a few steps and stopped.

She was being watched. She knew she was. Emy clutched her purse in her left hand and kept her right at her side near the holster on her hip.

Tentatively, she put one foot in front of the other and headed to the stairs. While she walked, her eyes darted from side to side. No one else was in the parking lot, but the slithering feeling wouldn't go away.

She reached the stairs and took them fast, her steps echoing off the concrete and metal staircase. At least if someone was behind her, she'd hear them.

The door to her apartment was up ahead. Luna was barking. Emy frowned and unsnapped the holster. She turned and faced the stairs. No one there.

Keeping her eyes fixed on the only ingress, she fumbled with her key and finally managed to place it in the lock. A quick turn and she stepped into the apartment.

She immediately closed the door and slid the deadbolt across. Put on the chain for good measure? Hell yes.

Luna's barks faded into a low whine.

She walked to Luna's crate and pulled up the lock. The dog immediately tumbled out and sat in the hallway, tail swishing across the floor, drool gathered in the corner of her cheeks

Emy smiled, knelt, and hugged the dog. Luna growled low in her throat and licked Emy's nose.

"Eeew," she said. The dog opened her mouth in a grin. "Get to your spot."

Luna turned and galloped to her food dish. Emy put her purse on the end-table next to the door and headed into the living room.

Luna sat, her tail still wagging at an impressive velocity. "What's your problem?" she asked the dog.

Luna raised her head, growled again, and ended with something akin to a whine. Emy sighed. "Potty?" The dog jumped up and headed to the door.

She put her keys in her pocket, grabbed the leash, and clipped it to the dog's wide collar. Luna sat patiently, her short snout pointed firmly at the door.

Emy unlocked it, nearly forgot the chain, and opened it. Luna stepped forward onto the landing, turned, and waited. Emy put her key in the door to lock it when Luna loosed a low woof.

"Give me a second, girl."

The key finally turned far enough for the lock to click and she pulled it back out. As soon as the dog knew she was done, Luna tugged on the leash. Not hard, but enough.

With another sigh, she led Luna down the stairs. When they reached the bottom, the dog went a few feet out and sniffed the grass.

That was the routine. Luna sniffed the grass, pretended she'd do her business, and then jerk the leash to go to the pet area. Emy had never figured out why her dog did this, but at least it was an innocuous, if frustrating, habit.

As if on cue, the dog began pulling her toward the pet area. "Heel," she said quietly and Luna slowed her pace. Emy followed. She glanced around the parking lot. She'd never had that feeling before, not quite like that. It was like knowing you were being stalked, but there was no— She bumped into the dog and then she heard the growl.

Luna's tail rose in the air like a flagpole, hackles of short hair standing at attention. Saliva dripped from her jowls and hit the scorching concrete, her head pointed in the direction of the yellow pickup truck.

It was nearly 5:30 in the afternoon, but the sun was still bright enough to make her squint. Luna, on the other hand, didn't seem to have that problem. The dog pulled on the leash the slightest bit.

"What is it, girl?" Emy asked.

Luna barked once and continued growling. Emy shaded her eyes with her free hand and examined the truck again. There was no one inside it. Of course, as high as it sat off the ground, it wasn't as though she could see the floorboards. Hell, if someone was laying down on the seat, she'd have no idea.

She whistled at Luna. The dog stopped growling with a whine, but didn't move. "Come on, girl." Luna didn't break her stare with the truck. Emy walked out in front of the dog and pulled.

Luna walked quickly past her and across her body. "What the hell, dog?" Emy had to turn around to unwrap herself from the leash. Luna was now between her and the parking lot. The dog raised her head and woofed at Emy.

"Potty?" Luna's tail wagged half-heartedly. Emy frowned. "Let's go, girl."

The dog did her business in the green space, but kept her head pointed at the parking lot. When she was finished, Emy bagged the leavings, tossed them in the poop can, and joined Luna's stare.

Nothing had changed. The parking lot was still deserted, the yellow truck was still in its spot, and dammit, she still had that feeling. Obviously the dog did too.

Luna finally broke her stare and looked back at Emy with a pant. "Okay. Good girl."

The dog turned and led Emy back down the sidewalk toward the apartment stairs. As they neared the yellow truck, Luna growled low in her throat, but didn't stop. Emy quickened her pace and Luna took more of the leash.

They reached the stairs and walked up as fast as she dared. At the landing, she pulled out her keys. Luna had turned back to face the stairs, her tail rigid, hackles rising from her short fur. Emy's skin prickled with goosebumps despite the sweat dripping from her locks.

She pushed the key into the door, unlocked it, and stepped in. Luna growled once and followed her inside the apartment.

With the door locked and chained behind her, the icy fear started to depart. She unclipped the leash and Luna went back to her bowl. Emy studied the dog. Luna's fur was back in place, her eyes held their usual glittering excitement, and she panted with a doggy grin. It was like the walk to the dog area had never happened.

Emy sighed, fed and watered the dog, and headed to her bedroom. She stripped off her moist shirt, tossed her sweaty bra onto the floor and eyed the shower. She had a little over an hour before Bryan arrived to pick her up. Between the imagined stalker and the walk to the doggy area, she probably smelled like a gym locker.

Guess I should take a shower, she said to herself. With a sigh, she undressed, and headed into the bathroom.

She soaped up and washed her hair. Once she was clean, she stood under the cool water, eyes closed. Bryan would stay the night. She'd make sure of it. She felt bad for not inviting him home the night before. Especially after telling her how beautiful she was. Emy closed her eyes, and let the water patter down across her back.

Luna. The dog was barking and growling so loud Emy could hear the sound over the water. Her eyes immediately flicked open. She shut off the tap, grabbed a towel, and stepped out of the shower.

She quickly dabbed her body and headed into the bedroom, drops of water still falling from her hair. She looked out the bedroom door. Luna stood in the living room, tail straight, hackles up, growling at the front door.

"Luna?" Emy called. The dog didn't move, but continued growling. Emy called her again, but the dog didn't respond. Cursing, she peered around the bedroom door and made sure the blinds were closed. They were. She stepped into the living room, her feet leaving damp spots on the creme carpet, and moved to within a foot of the dog. "Luna? Hey!"

The dog turned her head and stared at her owner. She loosed a low woof and sat down. Emy patted her head and the dog turned back to the door.

The front door. Luna didn't like something out there. Her skin puckered with goose flesh. She slowly moved forward, Luna bumping into her legs as the dog walked in front of her. With each step she took, the dog took two. By the time she reached the door, Luna had her snout firmly against it. The growl in her throat was quiet, but menacing.

Emy peered out of the eyehole. Nothing there. Just the sight of the apartment across the hall. She sighed and looked down at Luna. The dog was silent, tail swishing back and forth across the floor.

"What the hell is wrong with you?" Emy asked. Luna gave a slobbery grin in response. She scratched the dog behind the ears and Luna cocked her head. Suddenly, she realized she was standing in the entry hall, dripping water on the floor, and naked. A blush rose to her cheeks. "I have to get ready," she told the dog. Luna woofed once and headed back into the living room. Emy peered through the eyehole once more, made sure all was clear, and headed back to the bedroom.

Toweling off, she stared in the mirror. The scars on her body seemed darker than usual. She put it down to the heat of the day and the shower and tried not to obsess.

Luna, she said to herself, trying to refocus. *She's never done that before.*

And the feeling. What about the feeling of being watched? Of being stalked? Did Luna pick up on her emotions, or was the dog actually getting the same vibe? Not for the first time, she wished the damned mutt could speak English instead of woofish.

She finished drying off and headed to the closet. She choose a lacy black bra, blue blouse, a pair of khakis, and black sandals. Once she was dressed, she loitered at the jewelry box, and picked out a pair of lapis lazuli ear rings to go along with her necklace.

By the time she finished getting ready, she only had fifteen minutes to wait before Bryan arrived. She sat on the couch with Luna and scribbled notes for tomorrow's research.

Where else had the exhibit been? Was there a way to track down the owner of the collection? That was a question for Seamus, obviously. What about the other items in the case? Were they all, well, sigils for nephilim rather than the gods themselves? She shivered at the thought.

The knock on the door elicited a low, challenging woof from the dog. Luna leaped off the couch and headed to the door. She sniffed it and her tail started to wag. Smiling, Emy followed her to the entryway. She peered through the eye hole. Bryan, dressed in a black button up, stared back at her. She grinned and opened the door.

"Wow. You look amazing," he said to her.

She blushed and pushed Luna out of the way so Bryan could make his way into the apartment. He reached down and scratched the dog beneath her chin. Luna craned her neck upward and grunted, tail thrashing the floor.

Emy giggled. "You already know her spots."

He opened his mouth to say something, blushed, and smiled sheepishly. "She's a dog. It's not all that difficult." An awkward pause filled the room. He cleared his throat. "Are you, um, ready?"

Emy smiled. "Yes." She walked to the credenza and picked up her purse. She stared at the pistol on the kitchen counter. With a sigh, she picked up the holster and dropped it in her bag. "Okay," she said. "I'm ready."

Bryan blinked at her and looked at Luna. "Don't you usually crate her?"

The dog's ears rose and flattened. Emy scratched Luna's head. "No. She's staying out tonight." Luna sat in the hallway as they left the apartment.

Chapter 37

P stood from his hiding place. The tall hedges were brown from the drought, but they'd still made a great place to hunker down. Through the yellowing leaves, he'd watched the Aninzo woman and her boyfriend come down the stairs and leave.

He glanced at the stairs leading to her apartment. He couldn't go up there again, not without risking discovery. If the neighbors had been home when the goddamned dog started barking, he could have been caught. At the very least, the bitch would have known someone had tried to get in.

P headed through the bushes and back to the parking lot. He walked to the yellow pickup truck and opened the door. Hiding on the floorboards while she took the dog for a shit had been difficult to say the least. His leg hurt like hell and lifting himself off the floor had made him want to scream.

Whatever he'd done to his shoulder wasn't getting better. Maybe he'd torn his rotator cuff or something like that.

Soon, Ghere's voice rasped, *it won't matter.*

P bent down and played with the wires dangling below the dash. A spark jumped across the leads and the engine started with a groan. He put on his seat belt and backed out of the parking lot.

He had to ditch the truck soon. Even as old as it was, the owner was sure to call it in as stolen. P sighed. He'd have to steal another car later in the evening so he could finish his chores.

However long the arson investigator was out of her apartment didn't matter. The dog was a problem he couldn't solve. He'd have to find another way to deal with her. And another place. Ghere wanted to burn her, consume her. And P would make It happy.

Chapter 38

The VPN was slower than molasses. Every search through the crime database took minutes to stream results. And each had been a waste of time.

Dew sipped a glass of water and stared at the screen in frustration. He'd worked through nearly every Houston area arsonist in the system going back twenty five years. The few still in the state were either in prison or in the nut hatch.

The dead ends were piling up and every minute counted. He'd have to do something a little more drastic. Which, of course, was something he did *not* want to do.

He picked up his cell and called Jackson.

"Dew!" Jackson said. "How the hell are you?"

"Doing fine. I need a favor."

Pause. "Well, holy shit. Look at that. The detective coming to the hack for a favor."

Dew sighed. "Well, if it's too much trouble—"

"Just busting your balls, man. What can I do for the pride of the HPD?"

"You can do some searches for me. How far back do the paper's digitized records go?"

"Think we have at least thirty years. Probably forty. They've got interns down in the basement doing that shit all day."

Dew grinned. "Good. I need you to search the paper's 'morgue' for some articles on fires. Anything that involved a kid and a family. Especially if someone died in it."

Jackson grunted. "That's going to be quite the list, man. You're going to be buried in ink."

"I know. But I have a feeling I'll know what I'm looking for when I see it. And, Jackson? This is important."

"Let me guess. The shotgun shacks. And that Hartman thing."

"Right." Dew scratched Frankie behind the ears. The cat immediately began to purr. "And the sooner we get the info, the sooner we can keep this asshole from doing it again."

"You going to give me an exclusive?" Jackson asked.

Dew couldn't help but roll his eyes. Although it was probably for the best, he was a little sad Jackson couldn't see his expression. "You got it. I'll make everything I can available to you."

"Deal," Jackson said. "Jenny's going to kick my ass, but I'll make sure I get it done tonight."

"Thanks, Jackson. I owe you one."

"Yes. Yes you do."

The phone went dead. Dew placed it back on the end-table and stared at his laptop screen. The crime database wouldn't have records of non-prosecuted incidents unless they'd been marked as unsolved. He scrunched his eyebrows. Maybe that was the problem.

Dew brought up the search parameters. He clicked on the "unsolved only" checkbox and entered "fire." He hit return and waited. And waited. And waited.

He put the laptop down and headed to the kitchen. Frankie meowed once and stood next to the recliner, a look of feline disgust on her face. He opened the fridge, saw it was empty of beer, and closed it. Water. He was down to water and nothing else. Dew opened a cabinet above the kitchen island and stared at the liquor bottles. They stared back.

He closed it with a sigh and filled a glass with water. One of these days, he might have the courage to throw those bottles away. Especially the Jim Beam. His mouth watered at the memory of its silky finish and the warmth it would put in his belly.

Dew shook the thoughts away. Damned case was driving him back to old habits. And that wasn't good. If he didn't solve it soon, he might slip.

He walked back to the recliner and put the glass next to his phone. The computer screen was filled with results. Dew glared at it, plopped himself down, and started to read. Frankie jumped back up and sat on the edge near his feet. She curled up and went to sleep. Dew envied her. He sighed as he scrolled through the pages of data.

Chapter 39

They drove back from dinner through quiet, relatively empty streets. When they reached her apartment, Emy saw that the ugly pickup truck was gone. She loosed a sigh of relief. Bryan shot her a glance, but didn't pry. After he parked the car, they headed up the stairs and into the apartment.

Luna waited for them at the door. Her rear-end looked like a propeller had been attached.

"When she wags her tail, she really wags it," Bryan said.

Emy laughed and closed the door. She prepared herself for a scene of carnage as they walked into the living room. Luna's toys lay in the middle of the floor. All of them.

"Dammit, dog," Emy said. Luna ran into the pile of toys and flopped over, feet in the air. Bryan snickered. Emy glared at him and he put a hand to his mouth to stifle a laugh. "She knows better."

"Still," he said, "pretty funny."

"You want something to drink?" Emy asked and headed to the kitchen.

"I'm fine."

She pulled a glass from one of the cabinets, filled it with water and took a sip. In the living room, Bryan had walked into the middle of the toys, squatted, and was rubbing Luna's tummy. Emy shook her head and took another draught of water.

"Good dog," he told Luna.

She opened her mouth and growled.

"You're spoiling her," Emy said. Bryan looked up, his cheeks growing crimson. "You're supposed to be spoiling me."

Bryan blinked at her. "Um. And what, I mean, uh." His voice trailed off.

Emy pulled open a cabinet, chose a bully stick, and threw it into the living room. Luna rolled over, her body making toys squeak, and bolted to the treat. She crunched down on it with her jaws and ran next to the couch.

"That takes care of her," Emy said. "Now you can take care of me." She walked to the bedroom dropping clothes as she went. After a moment, Bryan followed.

Chapter 40

The townhouse was dark. Brett noticed it as soon as they drove down Inker. "Didn't you leave the living room light on?"

Lee shrugged. "I don't remember."

Brett nodded to himself as he pulled around the back of the complex. He touched a button and the gate swung open on the three garages. He pressed another button and the closest garage door slid up.

He pulled the car into the garage and turned off the ignition. As soon as the engine died, he heard the dogs barking, sounding as though they thought the damned world was ending.

Lee moved to open the car door. Brett touched his knee. "Stay here for a minute, okay?"

Lee blinked. "Why?"

"Just call me paranoid, okay?"

"Christ." Lee rolled his eyes. "Come on. So I forgot to leave the living room light on. It doesn't mean—"

"Just humor me," Brett said. He leaned over and kissed Lee on the cheek. "I'll be right back."

Before his husband could respond, Brett opened the car door and stepped into the furnace of the garage. Sweat immediately beaded on his forehead. He walked to the door leading into the townhouse and stopped, right hand on his holster. He slowly pulled out the pistol and kept it raised, the Glock shaking in his hands. Brett closed his eyes for a second, focused on steadying his heartbeat, and cracked open the door.

The downstairs was very dark. Brett took a deep breath, pistol pointed at waist level, and pushed open the door with his left hand.

He stepped through the doorway and listened. The dogs stopped barking and ran down the stairs. Besides the thumping of their paws on the steps, there was no sound save for the air conditioner. He wiped a sheen of sweat from his forehead and closed the door.

The dogs turned the corner and worried his ankles. Brett shushed them and walked to the front door. The deadbolt was still in place. He relaxed a bit.

He turned and looked up the stairs. The portraits of him and Lee still hung in their places. The coatrack stood at the back of the landing. With Lee's cowboy hat hanging atop it, it looked eerily human. Brett reached the wall and hit the light switch.

The stairway light sparked to life, the wooden steps shining beneath it. Brett fought through a shiver and started up the stairs.

Lee was pissed. The car was getting uncomfortably warm. He knew Brett was being paranoid. Even if that murder this morning is what set him off, this was over the top.

He stepped out of the car and closed the garage door. It slid down its tracks and thumped hard to the concrete. He took one last look around the garage and walked to the door leading into the townhouse.

The dogs had stopped barking. Lee frowned. Maybe they'd followed Brett and were away from the door. Or...

Lee put his hand on the door, took a deep breath, and opened it. He yelped as the dogs leaped at him. The two shook with fear, or maybe with glee. He ushered them back inside the house and closed the door behind.

"Brett?" he yelled. "Is everything okay?"

No response.

Lee walked into the foyer. The stairway light was on. He put his hand on the bannister. "Brett?" he called again. When there was no reply, his heart started to pound. A surge of fear-induced adrenaline sizzled in his veins. All the saliva in his mouth dried up. He was afraid to take the stairs. He bit his lip. No, fuck that. I have to know.

He slowly took the steps, each creak of the wood beneath his feet making him wince. The dogs raced past him up the stairs. "Fuck," he whispered. The dogs tore around the corner, their tags jingling. Shaking his head, Lee continued up the stairs a little faster.

When he reached the landing, he looked around the living room. Brett had already turned on the lights in there. Lee looked around the room, found nothing out of place, and headed into the kitchen. Nothing had been moved.

"Brett?" he called again. He heard something, but wasn't sure what it was. The fear returned. He stepped out of the kitchen and walked to the bedroom on shaky knees. The door was closed, the dogs outside it. "Brett?" Lee called again.

The doorknob swiveled. Lee stepped back, his mouth set in an O of surprise.

Brett opened the door, his weapon holstered. "Lee? I told you to—"

Lee stepped forward and put his arms around Brett's neck. "Jesus. Don't ever do that to me again."

"What's wrong?"

Lee pulled back and looked at him. "I thought something had happened! Didn't you hear me calling you?"

Brett shook his head. "I'm sorry. I thought... I thought I heard someone in the bedroom." He pointed behind him. "One of the windows was unlocked so I went outside on the balcony to check and make sure no one was out there."

"I was so damned scared."

Brett wiped a tear away from Lee's eye and hugged him. "Okay. I won't do that again. Ever."

The two men held each other for several moments before checking the rest of the house together.

Chapter 41

God, it was late. Good thing he didn't have any beer in the house or he'd be three sheets to the wind. Dew rubbed his eyes. Staring at the white screen with black text for over three hours had given him a raging migraine. The pain in his head made the left side of his mind tilt and slide. Frankie kept looking up at him with an expression that said "go the hell to sleep." But he couldn't. Not yet.

His searches had, at first, provided more confusion than actual information. "Unsolved" arsons in Houston were a regularity during the 90s and the beginning of the millennium. The last ten years, however, most cases were solved and solved quickly.

But that still left nearly 30 fires to explore, each with its own tome of notes and remarks. And Dew was certain if he spoke with the officers and detectives that worked those cases, he'd find even more information that didn't add up.

House fires, usually started by bad wiring, lightning, negligence, or accidents, had a tendency to attract arson investigation. Especially if said house owners purchased a substantial insurance policy. In those cases, both arson investigators and insurance investigators descended on the scene.

Dew went through pages of information from the police reports as well as the arson reports. Nothing. He was about to close the laptop when an email came in.

Jackson was finally getting back to him. The email had the reporter's typical snark as well as over a dozen attachments. And the "ps" reminded

Dew of his promise. The detective loosed an acidic burp and started opening attachments.

Every article included had a description of the fire, those who were affected, and whether or not the fire was ruled an arson. In two cases, the parents went to prison for insurance fraud and a ton of ancillary charges. Dew started typing notes. Family names, kids' names, etc. He'd work on those first thing tomorrow morning.

The other ten looked to be "clean." Families cleared of all charges. But there was one case that stood out. The Hardy family.

In 1990, the Hardy's rather substantial home burned down in the newly annexed neighborhood of Green Forest. The investigators never determined the actual cause of the fire, only that it started in the nursery. And that's where things became interesting.

The Hardy's nine-month old son, Gregory, burned to death in the blaze. He was presumably asleep in the nursery when the fire started. The smoke alarms in the house failed due to an alarm system malfunction. By the time the Hardys realized the house was burning, the nursery had become a blast furnace along with the adjacent rooms.

The father, Terrence Hardy, suffered 2nd degree burns in getting his family out of the house. The mother, Sharon, was hospitalized for smoke inhalation for several days. Their ten-year old son Donald, on the other hand, escaped injury even though his room was on the second floor next to his baby brother's.

"Wait a second," Dew said aloud. "Next to baby brother?" He read the report again, his forehead creasing in concentration. All three bedrooms were on the second floor. The master, however, was on the house's far west side. The children? Both on the east side, a few scant feet separating the two.

Dew switched to the department search program and entered the Hardy address and the date. The search took only a few seconds to bring up the old case. He was in luck—most of it was digitized.

The arson investigator's notes indicated no evidence of an accelerant, and no immediate discernible cause. However, he postulated the crib or areas surrounding had been the flashpoint. The only electronics in the room consisted of a nightlight and a lamp. The Hardys didn't even have a baby monitor.

According to the investigator's notes, Terrence woke to the smell of smoke and the howls of their infant son. He ran out of the bedroom to get the children. The nursery was engulfed in flame and the east side of the house had already caught fire. He grabbed Donald, handed him to Sharon, and told them to get out.

Terrence ran into the fire, but was unable to get to his infant son. When he finally realized the baby was dead, he escaped down the stairs before the fire spread across the second floor. By the time the HFD arrived, the fire had engulfed the entire second floor.

"Why didn't you wake up your parents?" Dew asked the room. "You slept through all the smoke?" Maybe. Maybe the ten-year old slept like a rock and only awoke when he started to cough. But something felt wrong about that. Very wrong.

Dew frowned at the screen. He went back to the search and entered Donald Hardy's name into the system. He chose a range between 1990 and 1997, when the boy was older than ten but younger than seventeen. He clicked the "search" button and waited. Over a dozen Donald Hardy's had records, most of them marked as "restricted access." That meant that either the court had sealed the records upon adjudication, or the family had petitioned the court to seal them.

"Are you one of these?" he asked the screen. "Are you in there?"

Of the twelve records, only one had "Sec 28.02" marked as the offense. "Arson," Dew said aloud. For details of the offense, he'd have to talk to the D.A. If this was the same Donald Hardy...

Dew shook his head. *Why didn't anyone see this?* The kid. The ten-year old kid. He had to have started the fire. Killed his baby brother and nearly killed his parents. But no one fingered him. Or did they?

He flicked through the other articles with mild disinterest. Instinct told him he'd already found a suspect. If Hardy was still in Houston, he'd be easy to track down. But more importantly, there might be more history in the crime database on the kid. Had he been caught creating another blaze? Or maybe something else sociopathic? If it was before he turned 16, it would be sealed. Dew frowned at the screen and closed the laptop.

Frankie meowed at him. Dew rubbed his eyes again, put the computer back on the end-table, and picked up his cat. She struggled at first and then crawled up on his shoulder, paws firmly clinging to his t-shirt. He was asleep in minutes.

Chapter 42

P yawned and continued screwing together the assembly. Each turn of the screwdriver was slow, methodical, and cautious. The last thing he needed was to set one of the goddamned party favors off and end the transformation before it was complete. He should have finished this hours ago, but he'd been running "errands."

"Errands," he said aloud and finished the upper left corner of the rectangular device. He slotted the next screw and began the process again. While he worked, he felt Ghere's seething anger in the back of his mind. The presence made it difficult for him to concentrate. And it was late. Very late.

If all went well, today would be the last day on Earth for Donald Hardy. After tonight, he and Ghere would become one. Together, they would punish the world, bring back the old fears, the old gods, the old beliefs. They would tear down the new gods of technology and greed. Renew the world's faith in the unseen and the powerful.

Ghere would walk among them, a living flame, meting out justice and punishment in equal degrees. They would fall to their knees in worship and terror. Ghere would take what It wanted, give what It felt was just, and destroy whatever It desired. Ghere would have it all.

P smiled as he finished with the last screw. He carried it to the pile of homemade plastique, attached the leads, and waited for the status light to turn green. It did.

P stood and popped his back with a moan of pleasure. He walked to the garage's interior door and reached for the light, hesitating before turning around to give a final glance at his work.

Dozens and dozens of mason jars filled with nails, steel brads, and ball bearings surrounded the plastique. His bedroom had a similar setup, not to mention the attic. The gas powered water heater would help provide some extra bang when the explosives finally went off. He grinned. His only regret was he wouldn't be around to see the explosion.

He switched off the light and closed the door, shivering as he walked up the stairs. The house was still too cold. He'd have to put another comforter on the bed before he went to sleep. The thermostat claimed it was 89° in the house, but he didn't believe it.

"One last check," he said and sat at his computer workstation. After unlocking the drives and the OS, he brought up the program and ran another test. Every two seconds, a green dot popped up on the map. The program took over two minutes to run and when it was finished, the map was filled with green dots. Every system was ready. All he needed now was to sleep. Tonight he would change the world.

Chapter 43

J ust walking to the parking lot was an experience in hell. Ten in the morning and the temperature was already over 98°. The moment he walked out of the station, the humid sauna heat started him sweating.

Once he started the car, the A/C belched hot, stale air through the vents. Dew rolled down the windows and waited a moment. The stagnant air cleared out of the car and cool air began to flow. He rolled up the windows, wiped his forehead with a hanky, and put the car in gear.

The drive was going to be long. The Houston city limits covered over 672 square miles. And that didn't even begin to touch the so-called "Greater Houston Area" which encompassed places as far north as The Woodlands and as far west as Katy. Fortunately, he wasn't going that far north or that far west. Instead, he was headed toward a crumbling neighborhood in the northwest.

After the Hardy home had burned down, the family moved a little further north and to a more upscale neighborhood: Champion Forest. Using insurance funds and a local downturn in the housing market, Terrence Hardy purchased and renovated an old McMansion. The family lived there through their son's teenage years and stayed when he left for college. In 2006, both parents died in a car accident. Less than six months later, Donald, their only surviving child, moved into the house.

Dew headed to I-45 and finally managed to skirt the construction and make it onto the road. He made it to the Shepherd curve before traffic came to a standstill. Dew cranked up the air conditioner and prayed the car wouldn't overheat.

He passed by cars with their hoods up, boiling clouds of steam rushing from overtaxed engines. His fingers tightened on the wheel. Stop and go. For a mile. The police radio occasionally belched in the silent car. The frustration of the traffic jam slowly disappeared as he went over the facts.

Don Hardy had been living in Austin when his parents died. He had a degree in computer science with a minor in electrical engineering and worked for a tech company in the state's capitol. Once his parents were out of the picture, he'd quit his job, and returned to live in his childhood home.

From the information Dew had gathered earlier that morning, it was clear Don hadn't worked a day since his inheritance cleared probate, other than for occasional contract computer work (usually remote) or volunteering for various organizations around the greater metro area. He'd been a school bus driver. He'd been a cross walker. He'd volunteered at homeless shelters and even at local libraries. He knew every inch of the city.

None of it made sense. It was like the man had been trying to find his place in the world and constantly failed to find his calling. Probably had to do with the fat stacks of cash his parents had left him in their will.

After procuring Hardy's social security number, he'd compared it to the sealed record. Sure enough, the Donald Hardy in Champion Forest was the same Donald that had been arrested at some point during his teenage years. For arson.

Those facts, however, weren't enough to get a search warrant. And this little fishing expedition wasn't going to get him much in the way of evidence. He was sure of that. But he was certain that if he met the man, he'd feel that crawling sensation; the same prickly feeling that shook his bones when he'd found a perp. If that was the case, he'd fight like hell to get that warrant.

If Hardy wasn't home, Dew would take a look around. Maybe hang out for a while, see if his suspect returned. Was a long shot, but every minute they didn't have a lead was another minute for the bug to set up his next target.

Dew exited FM 1960 and headed west. He passed half-empty strip malls, payday loan boutiques, and pawn shops. At one time, the area had been stuffed with money and a popular destination for white flight. No longer. Most of the older families that moved to the area in the 70s and 80s had moved further north or west.

He drove down the dozen or so lights until he reached Champion Forest Drive. A right at the light, and he was on his way. He turned into the neighborhood and wound past the older houses. No one was outside in the punishing heat except for a few lawn services that hadn't finished their rounds. With water restrictions in place, the normally verdant green lawns and trees were yellowed and wilted.

Dew took a left and drove into a cul-de-sac. Several giant houses loomed ahead, Victorian knock-offs complete with the occasional turret and balconies. Except for the sprawling two-story Roman pillared monstrosity in the center. Dew swung the car in front of the house.

This was the Hardy domicile. Dew checked in on the radio and gave his coordinates. Standard procedure. If something happened, HQ would know his last position.

He stepped out into the heat, locked the car, and headed up the long concrete sidewalk to the front door. The grass here was so dry it might as well have been sand. He knew if he touched it with a shoe, he'd hear the crunch of baked flora. The house shined as though freshly polished. Donald Hardy had obviously taken its upkeep very seriously.

The door appeared old, but in good condition. The grain was perfectly stained with beautiful ornamental glass inset in the top half. Dew wondered if it had been replaced in the last few years.

Double-paned, Dew thought with a grin. He reached out and pressed the door bell. He heard the distant sound of bells chiming and waited. And waited.

The sun was high in the sky, but he was beneath the facade overhang and protected by the shadows. At least there was that.

Another moment passed. Dew sighed and pressed the door bell again. He did his best not to press his nose against the door and peer inside. Instead, he focused on the tiny view afforded him by the ornamental glass. There wasn't much to see.

He saw a staircase off to the right, several paintings, and a few sculptures. The art hung from the walls while the figurines sat upon attached stands. There was no furniture in sight. His view of the house ended in a pair of textured double doors.

Steps inside the house. Dew raised a brow and took a step away from the door. He pulled his badge and held it in his left hand, his right staying near his holster.

A figure appeared from the right. A lined and flushed face stared out at him. Even through the glass, Dew could see he'd been asleep.

Several locks clicked and the door swung open silently on well-oiled hinges. The man was a little shorter than Dew with a scalp unblemished by hair or any marks at all. The arm holding the door was hairless as well, but scarred in places. A pair of brilliant green eyes stared out beneath a prominent brow. The man yawned displaying white teeth.

"Yes?" The voice was higher pitched than he'd expected.

Dew produced a toothy smile. "Mr. Hardy?"

The man nodded.

"My name is Detective Dewhurst. I'm with the Houston Police Department."

The man's expression of disinterest didn't change.

"I'd like to ask you a few questions, if I may."

Hardy blinked at him like a reptile. "What about?"

Dew manufactured a blush. "Sorry to say, sir, but there was a problem in digitizing some files from the early 2ks. Your parents' case was among the number we have to reconstruct."

"That was nearly ten years ago, Detective."

Dew nodded. "I know, sir. I'm sorry to show up on your doorstep like this. I just happened to be in the neighborhood, so to speak, and thought I'd take a chance you'd be willing to talk about it." Dew wiped sweat from his forehead. "One last time."

Hardy pursed his lips and narrowed his eyes. "You look a little uncomfortable, Detective."

"Is it that obvious?"

Hardy finally smiled. "Give me a moment to put something on. I'll be right back."

The door closed. Dew shifted his feet. Hardy didn't look at all like he'd imagined. From the pictures Dew had pulled, Donald Hardy should have been heavyset like both his parents and hairy as hell. Instead, the man bordered on gaunt and he was completely hairless. *What about the scars?*

Were those burns on his skin? Age old burns, maybe from the house fire? No, Dew thought. The boy hadn't even been treated for injuries at the scene. Those were from something else, but they sure as hell looked like burns.

Hardy hadn't opened the door all the way either. He'd held it open just far enough to show his face and one arm. So the question was, what did the rest of him look like? Scarred as well?

Dew's back jittered with electricity. The feeling was stronger. This had to be the perp. Simply had to be.

The thump thump thump of feet on the stairs grabbed his attention. He didn't see Hardy until the man bounced down the last few steps and headed to the door, one hand still rubbing sleep from his eyes. The lock on the door clicked and this time, the door opened wide.

Dew blinked. Hardy stood at the threshold in a long-sleeved white shirt buttoned all the way to the neck. He wore a pair of stylishly faded blue jeans, but from the way they fit, Dew was certain he wore something beneath them. Same with the shirt. Heavy woolen socks covered his feet.

What the hell is wrong with you? Dew wondered.

Hardy smiled, but there was absolutely nothing friendly in it. "Come in, Detective."

"Thank you, Mr. Hardy." The words tumbled out with forced levity. Dew walked across the threshold, thumbs inside his front pockets. If he needed to pull his weapon, he could do so without too much struggle. Mindful that Hardy would be behind him, Dew managed a slight turn while entering the foyer, keeping Hardy somewhat in front of him.

But Hardy didn't even look at him as he shut the door. Dew felt stupid for being so paranoid, but Hardy was the perp. He goddamned well knew it.

Hardy closed the door with a nearly silent thump and swiveled the locks. He finally turned and raised his eyebrows. "Would you like some coffee, Detective? I'll need one if we're going to talk."

Dew shook his head. "No, thank you. But please go ahead."

The man nodded. "If you'll follow me."

He turned and headed to the closed double doors. When Hardy reached them, he held down one of the handles and pushed.

The double doors swung silently open, Hardy stepping through them without a backward glance. Dew was glad for that because his jaw damned near dropped open.

With the exception of a leather recliner, a reading table next to it, and an ancient looking lamp, the room was empty. There was no TV. There were no rugs over the immaculate wooden floor. The walls were bare, the wood paneling deadening the sound of their footsteps.

"Spacious," Dew said.

Hardy didn't turn, but headed through the area to another entryway. "I prefer to live simply." The man opened the mahogany door and stepped inside the kitchen. Dew followed.

The kitchen had an actual table, but only a single chair. The expensive looking wooden cabinets hanging above the sink and counters were spotless. The fridge, a hulking thing made of brushed metal, reflected the sunlight coming through the windows. Dew glanced around the room and noticed that as long as the shades were up during the day, there would never be a need for lights. Whoever designed the house craved sunlight.

The house was hot. Not just warm, hot. The temperature outside had him sweating within seconds, and while the house was certainly cooler, it was anything but comfortable. If he didn't know better, he'd think it was damned near 85° in here. Maybe hotter.

Hardy opened one of the cabinets and pulled out two glasses. Both looked to be expensive crystal. From the brief view he was afforded, Dew was certain the deep cabinet was full of the same glassware.

Lifting one of the glasses to the filtered tap, Hardy touched a button. 10 oz of clear water flowed into it. He turned and handed it to Dew. "You look like you need some of this."

Dew smiled. "Thank you, sir." Dew raised the glass and took a sip. The water was the best he'd ever tasted. "Wow. What kind of water is this?"

Hardy blushed. "I have it imported."

"Really?"

"Really." Hardy pulled a large coffee press from one of the lower cabinets. The marble countertops reflected the bright steel and unblemished glass. "Afraid mine will take a while longer."

He put five scoops of coarse grounds into the press, filled a kettle, and started the stove. A bead of sweat rolled down Dew's cheek. He didn't understand how Hardy could possibly be comfortable in this house wearing such heavy clothes.

"Take a seat, Detective. I'll stand." Dew thanked him and sat in the ornate chair at the table. Hardy stayed in the main kitchen area, but they could see one another though the bar. "So tell me. What do you need to know?"

Dew took another slug of water and carefully placed the cold glass on a lacquered wooden coaster. He pulled a battered notebook from inside his back pocket, opened it to a dogeared page, and quickly scanned the words. Or at least, that's what he wanted Hardy to think he was doing.

"According to what little records we actually have, your parents died in February 2006." Dew looked up at Hardy. "Is that right?"

He watched the man's eyes for any hint of guilt or apprehension, but he needn't have bothered. Hardy's eyes were flat as stone. "That is correct, Detective."

Dew nodded and looked back at the page. He pretended to scribble something. "To the best of your recollection, what happened?" He scrawled something unintelligible on the page and looked back at Hardy.

The man cocked his head slightly and chewed his lip. "I was in Austin. I got a call on the night of the 21st from the family lawyer. My parents' car rear-ended a tow truck going eighty on the freeway. They were killed instantly, or so I was told."

Dew blinked. Hardy didn't. "Did the police ever contact you with a reason for the accident? Alcohol? Drugs? Manufacturing defect?"

Hardy nodded, but his expression didn't change. "There was an investigation. Autopsy revealed no drugs, no alcohol, no nothing in their systems. They theorized, but never proved, there was a mechanical failure. But that's only because a witness claimed there was smoke coming from the tires like the driver was trying to stop the car."

Driver. Not dad. Not my father. The driver.

Dew fought to keep his expression friendly and bored. "Isn't that a little odd?"

"Yeah," Hardy said.

He waited a beat for the man to continue, but Hardy refused to say anything else without a prompt. "What do you think it was?"

A low-pitched wine crescendoed into a scream of steam. Hardy held up an index finger and pulled the kettle off the stove. He poured the boiling water into the coffee press and put the kettle on a dead burner. Dew watched the man's hands move below the bar. Hardy swiveled his head and smiled at Dew. "Sorry."

"It's quite all right, Mr. Hardy."

Hardy finished stirring the grounds in the press, and leaned back to face Dew. "What were you asking?"

"What do you think caused the crash?"

"Oh. Right." Hardy raised his eyes to the ceiling as if lost in thought. Dew watched him impassively. "Guess it's possible it was some sort of mechanical failure. I mean, we've moved a long way from the cars of old where everything was gears and cranks and tied together and welded. This is the computer age." He shook his head. "And computers fail more often than anyone would have you believe."

Dew raised his brows. "What do you mean?"

"You taken your car in for a tune-up lately?"

Dew shook his head. "No, sir," he lied, "I have not."

"Well, they hook your car up to a computer. That computer talks to the one in your car. It controls fuel mixture, rate of combustion, and etc. On some of the newer cars, the car's computer can be hacked to do all sorts of crazy things."

"How do you know all that?" Dew asked.

Hardy grinned. "I'm a bit of a nerd. I research all kinds of technology."

Dew scribbled another illegible note. "That makes sense." He looked up at Hardy. "I'm sorry to be presumptuous, but are you currently employed?"

The corner of Hardy's mouth twitched before blossoming into a toothy smile. "Why do you ask?"

Dew shrugged. "Just curious. Sounds like you know your science."

Hardy brushed an invisible piece of lint from his shirt. "I've been fortunate to go to great schools and my independence allows me to study whatever I like."

"And work wherever you like?"

"That too. Work is just a distraction. I spend a lot of time volunteering."

"Oh, really?"

"Yes." Hardy opened a cabinet and pulled out a large black mug. Dew heard him push down on the coffee press and pour the coffee. "Houston Zoo. Local libraries. Things like that."

"How often you do that?"

"When I'm bored," he said. "I very much enjoy it, don't get me wrong. But my home is a long way away from the museum district. It's much easier to volunteer for things up here."

"Of course." Dew closed the notebook and took a long draught from the glass of water. He was sweating freely now. The room seemed to be growing hotter. "So what are you up to these days?"

Hardy brought the steaming mug to his lips and took a long sip. Dew wondered how the hell the man could drink coffee that had just been boiling a few moments before.

"A little of this, a little of that, Detective. I'm working on my own projects at the moment."

"Ah," Dew said. He drained his glass and set it back on the coaster. "Wish I had time for that."

"Everyone should," Hardy said. "Unfortunately, not everyone is as lucky as me."

Dew smiled and slapped his notebook shut. "Unfortunately," he echoed. Dew pushed back the chair and stood. Hardy remained drinking his coffee, hands cupped around the mug.

"Well, thank you for the information." Dew tapped the notebook with his free hand. "I know it doesn't seem like much, but it's helpful. You don't happen to have any documents from the investigators, do you?"

Hardy slowly shook his head. "I don't think so, Detective. I tend to throw away such things as soon as they're no longer important."

"Not much of a sentimentalist?"

"No. Not at all," Hardy said.

"Okay." Dew flashed a smile. He hoped it didn't look predatory. "Well, thank you for your time. I can see myself out."

Hardy rounded the bar into the dining area and stood a few feet away. "Please allow me, Detective." The man walked in front of Dewhurst and led him through the spartan living room and back into the foyer.

"How long did your parents live here?" Dew asked as they neared the front door.

"About sixteen years," Hardy said. "We moved here after the fire."

"The fire?" Dew asked. "Your house burned down?"

Something gleamed in Hardy's eyes. Dew dared not stare at the man intently. He didn't want to give a tell. "Yes. My childhood home burned down in 1990. We moved here afterwards."

"Wow," Dew said. He dropped his gaze to the floor as if in thought and slowly raised his stare. "Everybody make it out okay?"

"No," Hardy said in a dead tone. "My brother died."

"My condolences."

Hardy's mouth twitched, but remained a flat line. "I barely knew him. He was an infant. Was much worse for my parents." He opened the door wide and seemed to inhale the heat coming through the doorway. "Was nice meeting you, Detective. Please let me know if there's anything else I can help you with."

Dewhurst pulled a business card from his pocket and handed it over. "I'd appreciate that." He offered his hand. Hardy stared at it and blinked. A moment of awkward silence separated them. At last, on the verge of pulling back his hand, Hardy shot out a hand and gripped Dew's firmly. The man's flesh felt electric and impossibly warm as if fire burned in his veins. "Goodbye, Detective."

"Goodbye," Dew said. He released his hand and walked out into the sun-blasted yard.

Chapter 44

The morning was hectic. She and Bryan showered together which turned out to be a big mistake and made them both more than a little late for work. They still managed to have breakfast, but Emy ended up at work well after nine.

She walked into the office still smelling Bryan on her skin. It was a great way to start the day. Too bad it didn't stay that way.

By the time she reached her desk, her phone had chirped three times. She checked it while making coffee and frowned. She had an email from Brett, one from Dewhurst, and yet another from the HPD translational unit.

The email from Brett was frantic. Novak wanted to see them both for a full status report at 1030, and Brett had included a link in the email to an article at The Post. After reading it, she knew why Novak wanted a meeting.

Sighing, she logged into her computer. Her messenger client started and immediately popped up a dialog.

Brett: "You're late!"

Emy: "Sigh. Sorry."

Brett: "Novak is on the warpath. Meeting at 1030"

Emy: "Got your email. Read the article. Good to know we're being accused of dragging our feet because the fire happened in a black neighborhood to a black historical site."

Brett: "Novak's going to try and cover his ass. Just be ready to feel some heat."

Emy: "Are we okay?"

Brett: "I'm more worried about what our bug is going to do next. And I'm pretty sure someone was in my house last night."

Emy stared at the screen, brows furrowed. Luna's barking and growling. The unease she felt in the parking lot. The feeling of being watched.

Emy: "Did your dogs freak out last night?"

Brett: "How did you know?"

"Shit," Emy whispered.

Emy: "We need to have lunch after Novak gets done with us."

Brett: "Yeah. I think we do."

She closed the messenger app, synced her laptop with the latest arson reports, and downed her coffee. The thirty minutes before the meeting went fast and she only had time for 2 cups of black magic before she marched through the cubes and to a conference room. Novak was waiting.

The portly man sat at the head of the table facing the door. A leather notebook lay on the desk as well as a too expensive pen. Dark circles beneath his eyes and his expression told her just how much shit she and Brett were about to take.

"Ms. Aninzo," Novak said in a low monotone.

"Mr. Novak," she said. Emy sat down in a chair near the projector. Without looking at him, she opened the laptop and cabled it to the device.

Brett appeared in the doorway, water bottle in his left hand, laptop in his right. "Sorry. Had a call to make."

"Close the door," Novak said.

Brett didn't blink an eye. He closed the door and sat across from Emy. The room fell silent except for the low whir of the A/C. Brett opened his laptop and glanced at Emy while looking uncomfortable and resigned.

Finally, Novak broke the silence. His face flushed, he opened his mouth and spoke in a low, furious tone. "You both have read the paper?" He didn't wait for a response. "Both the police commissioner and the head of the HFD have been dealing with calls from the City Council for the past several days. They claim we've shown no progress, have no suspects, and haven't investigated this properly because of where it was and what it was. In other words," he said, his angry eyes glancing from Emy to Brett and back again, "my department isn't doing its job because these are hate crimes against blacks."

Brett shook his head. "So the fact the Hartman family was white and burned by the same bug doesn't give us the benefit of the doubt?"

Novak leaned forward, his index finger pointed at Brett. "You haven't proved that." He pointed at Emy. "And her theory doesn't hold water. At least not to the rest of the department."

Emy fought hard not to roll her eyes. If Novak knew everything they knew, and wasn't such a pompous ass, she'd bother filling him in. But now was not the time. Hell, there may never be a time.

"Bullshit," Brett whispered.

"Excuse me?" Novak asked, his normally pale cheeks now a furnace of fury. "What did you say, Mr. Cullum?"

Brett sighed and locked eyes with his boss. "Tom? That's bullshit and you know it. We've been busting our asses trying to find this guy or at least some kind of link to him. We've—"

Novak held up a hand. "It doesn't matter what you've done." Brett stopped talking and tented his hands on the table. "What you've done," Novak said, "doesn't mean shit. Until we prove the shotgun shacks weren't burned in the commission of a hate crime, we're going to be seen as dragging our goddamned feet!"

"Sir?" Emy asked. Novak's nuclear gaze swiveled to her. "What do you suggest we do?"

"Find. The. Bug." Each word elicited a spit of saliva that flew onto the table. "That's all you can do. And I suggest you do it soon. While we still have our fucking jobs."

"We're doing our best," Brett said. "We have been—"

"How many hours you log this weekend, Mr. Cullum?"

Brett blinked. "Excuse me?"

A malicious grin lit Novak's face. "You say you're doing everything you can. Are you? How many hours did you log?"

Brett sighed and Novak's face grew a touch more crimson. "Tom? Emy and I both have logged a lot of overtime already. We're investigating other arsons around the world that have matched this bug's signature. And there's no telling how many other arsons in Houston had this mark that no one noticed."

"You didn't answer my question."

"I think," Brett tapped his fingers on the table, "that we are doing everything we know how to do."

Novak leaned back in his chair. "Then maybe I should give it to another team? You're out of ideas?"

Brett shook his head. "No, sir. We are following up leads. It's what you pay us to do."

"Correct," Novak said. "Paid. To. Do. Civil servants serve. And you better hope you find this guy soon or you'll both be out of this department on your ass."

The room went quiet. Emy didn't dare make eye contact with Novak.

Instead, she let her eyes bore into the table. After a moment, she heard Brett close his laptop.

"Get to it," Novak said.

"Yes, sir," Brett whispered. He stood from the table. Emy closed her laptop and followed suit. The pair left the room, Brett slamming the door behind him.

B rett walked to his cube. Emy followed. Instead of his usual jaunty step, he practically stomped on the carpet. Emy wondered if he was imagining Novak's face beneath his shoes.

When they reached his cube, Brett put down his things and faced the wall. He clenched and unclenched his fists several times before finally turning around, a grim smile lighting his face.

"What. A. Fucking. Asshole." Emy tried to hide a smirk, but couldn't. Brett's eyes narrowed and then he giggled. "I sincerely hope no one heard that."

Emy smiled. "I think you're mistaken that he's liked. Or that anyone gives a shit."

Brett rolled his eyes. "Okay. Fair enough." He looked at his watch. "It's nearly eleven. Feel like an early lunch?"

She nodded. "Then maybe you can tell me why you let me walk into Novak's lair with no backup."

"Yeah." Brett's smile grew. "You're not going to believe the phone call I just had."

Chapter 45

The cop made his way down the walk. P's expression faded from a light smile into a deep sneer. His mind felt like a playground filled with 3 year-olds, screaming, chortling, and throwing tantrums.

He's on to you, Ghere said in his mind. The voice had a hint of humor beneath Its deadly serious tone.

"Yes," P said. He continued watching from the door until the detective reached his car and drove off. The sneer melted into a thin line. He rubbed his arms trying to warm them. The shirt wasn't heavy enough to dispel the cool air in the house. He was on the verge of opening the windows to let the heat in. The glorious heat.

P turned and walked back through the bare living room and into the kitchen. Instead of holding the press by the handle, he wrapped his hand around it while he dumped the grounds into the sink.

The flesh on his hand warmed immediately and slowly began to burn. The sensation quickly passed. His face didn't change expression when the nerve endings started their screaming. Now they were dead or just past caring.

Transformation. It was coming. Soon. P was ready for that. He tipped the mug to his lips and quickly drank the last of the scalding liquid. His tongue and gums sizzled, the flesh turning into the raw red of first degree burns. He barely noticed.

P placed the empty mug back on the counter and leaned over it, his scaly palms turning cold against the heavy marble. He shuddered with the sudden temperature change and ground his teeth.

"Fucking cop," he hissed.

And what are you going to do about it? Ghere's voice asked.

P walked out of the kitchen and headed upstairs. He'd done his best to limit exposure to the frigid first floor. Each trip from the second floor had become more and more unpleasant as the change began to take hold. If not for the violation of his security and privacy, he would have opened the windows long ago.

His parents, when they built the house, had ensured the A/C units were capable of dropping the temperature to as cold as they wanted. What they hadn't done, however, was ensure the furnace was capable of doing the opposite. When he was younger, that was just fine. When he'd taken possession of the house from his late parents, it had been fine too. But now?

Since Ghere had taken Its place in his mind, his body, the air was always too cold.

But not for much longer.

He reached the second floor landing, hung a left, and headed to his study. His paradise. The place where he felt most at home and always had.

When he was a teenager, it had been his room. The room. But once he left for college, his parents dismantled it. All his possessions, his posters, knick-knacks, books, and trophies were boxed and stored. The clothes he'd left in the house were given to Salvation Army or maybe Purple Heart. There was probably a homeless kid out there wearing one of his ancient t-shirts right now.

P forced the thought away, shivering and shuddering from the cool air. He produced a key from his pocket and unlocked the deadbolt.

He swung open the door and immediately the shivers departed. Hot, stifling air hit him in the face. P smiled, walked across the threshold, and locked the door behind him.

The large, rectangular room faced the west so he could enjoy the sunset and the room could warm. His study was the hottest room in the house and always had been, but that didn't stop him from flicking a switch and turning on the three space heaters. Their grates glowed red and the air immediately turned hot.

P groaned with satisfaction and walked to his desk. Four widescreen monitors on swing arms stared at him with dead screens. He sat down in the chair and moved his fingers across the touchpad. The screens flashed to life.

He typed in a username/password and sat back as he waited for the drives to decrypt. The shivers and chills had been difficult to block while the cop had been in the house. He wasn't sure he'd hidden his discomfort, but the look on the man's face when he saw the woolen socks covering P's toes told him the cop suspected everything.

Had he covered the scars on his arms quickly enough? Probably not. The cop probably saw them when he opened the door before he clothed himself. He stared at himself in the monitors' reflection, studying his eyes. He could almost see the flicker of flame in the pupils. Almost.

The detective might have suspicions. Might even come back with a search warrant. P grinned. It wouldn't matter. P would soon depart his house for the very last time, the last of his possessions either abandoned or safely in his warehouse. "Let them come," he said aloud.

Ghere cackled in his mind. P had already pushed up the timeline. He was ready. He'd have time to deal with the arson investigators, maybe even the cop. Especially once the distraction began. Ten hours from now, it would all start. And soon after that? He would become something altogether new and divine.

Chapter 46

I t didn't matter what you wore, it didn't matter how often you showered; two minutes in the heat and your clothes turned into a damp mess, your hair into a frizz, and your deodorant into skunk. Emy sipped her iced tea and wrinkled her nose. The entire restaurant stank of sweat. It was early and the eatery was hardly packed.

Most of the patrons wore business casual, although a few dressed in shorts and T-shirts. The difference between the better dressed crowd and the more casual patrons was the number of sweat stains blossoming down the backs of their shirts and beneath their arm pits. The frosty A/C was refreshing, but only dried the sweat. Once again Emy was thankful her deodorant was still working.

Brett rubbed his hands together. During the short drive to the restaurant, he'd babbled in a rapid fire string of words. The upshot was that HPD had found fingerprints on the smashed up car in the parking lot across from Brett's apartment. The fingerprints also matched those on the garbage can lid used to murder Brett's neighbor.

Emy tried to get a word in, but Brett was too busy talking for her to get much more than a "uh-huh" wedged into the conversation. When he shut off the car, he was still talking a mile a minute. He turned off the ignition and stared at her. Smile manic, eyes glittering with energy, he bounced his eyebrows up and down. "Ready to eat?"

She nodded. "Before we melt in the car? Yes."

And that short walk from the parking lot into the restaurant was why she felt like she needed a shower and a fresh change of clothes. Brett seemed oblivious. When the iced tea arrived, he immediately ordered for the two of them and engaged his phone as it exploded with vibrations.

She heard him put the phone down with a sigh and stared at him. "What was that all about?"

"More Novak fallout."

"I'm afraid to ask."

"You should be," Brett said. He tented his hands around his glass of tea. "His ulcer is acting up. Said something about going home early and he expects a report from us this evening. Progress report."

"Progress," Emy echoed. "You tell him about the perp near your place?"

Brett's expression melted into a thin line. "No. He wouldn't give a shit."

"True," Emy said. "So they have the fingerprints. Now what?"

His smile returned and he waved a finger in the air. "We should have the results later this afternoon."

"This afternoon? That's bullshit," Emy said. "They have to want to get this guy."

"Sure," Brett said. "But they're overloaded." He nodded to the shaded window. "Three more shootings last night. And that's not including the brawl."

"Brawl?" Emy asked. She hadn't seen any of the news. There hadn't been time.

He took another sip of his tea. "Yeah. After the Astros game. In the parking garage. The heat has everyone going insane. Between the rash of murders, our firebug, and various other incidents, the crime lab is backed up to hell and gone. And everyone's putting a rush on everything. And it's only going to get hotter."

Mention of the heat made another bead of sweat roll down her back. "You call Dewhurst yet?"

He shook his head. "Haven't had time. As soon as we get some food, I'll give him a shout."

Emy stared down at the silverware on the table. The metal fork's tines were slightly bent, the blade covered with water spots. "Timing," she said aloud.

"What?"

She looked up to see Brett's eyes studying her intently. A slight blush rose to her cheeks. "I was just thinking about the timing."

"What do you mean?"

"You think someone was in your house."

Brett nodded. "Someone was. I didn't tell Lee just how sure I was." His fingers tapped the glass of iced tea. "After he fell asleep last night, I made sure my pistol was on the nightstand."

Emy shivered. "Luna went bonkers yesterday. She was barking at the door while I showered. And then when I took her out to do her business, she snarled at a pickup truck in the lot. I didn't see anyone in there, but she sure seemed to think someone was in it. And she didn't like them."

Brett's mouth opened slightly and then closed with a click of teeth. "We've been in the news. On TV. The papers." He shook his head. "Would be pretty easy for someone to find our addresses."

"Not to mention," Emy said, "the fact our bug is some kind of computer whiz."

"Shit. I don't like this."

"Nor do I." Emy ran her fingers through her hair. She knew her scar was uncovered, but she didn't care. It somehow seemed very unimportant. "I don't like carrying a pistol, but now I'm wishing I'd put more time in at the range."

A grim smile lit Brett's face. "That makes two of us."

Chapter 47

Captain Spillane was less than impressed. He stared at the printed form reading Dew's summary with suspicious eyes and a grim line of disbelief. Dew sat in the chair across the desk, his hands perfectly still as he watched his boss look over the warrant. It was easy to tell this was going to be a bit of a fight. He wished he had a cigarette or a cigar in his hand so he could calm himself. It might have helped him feel less anxious. Might. His fingers wanted to thrum on the chair's armrest, twiddle, do anything besides stay still. Even his feet wanted to move and kick.

Hardy was the guy. Dew was sure of it. After leaving the man's house, he'd driven back to the station as quickly as he dared to write up the search warrant, document his suspicions, and request a juvenile record release as well. Dew had done his best to put the circumstantial evidence together without mentioning demons, amulets, or supernatural circumstance. He almost wished he'd included those too. Maybe then Spillane would simply burst a blood vessel instead of studying the papers like an interesting turd.

Finally, Spillane laid the sheets of paper back upon the desk. He stared at the oak table for a moment before tenting his hands in front of him and raising his eyes to Dew's. "This is pretty flimsy," he said.

Dew shrugged. "We have no fiber, no prints, nothing to go on here. But this guy fits the profile. And if we get unrestricted access to the juvenile records, I bet there's something else there we can use."

Spillane frowned. "Dew? This Hardy guy has money, doesn't he?"

The flicker of hope he'd had while writing the report suddenly went dark. He sighed and put his hands in his lap. "Sir? I've done my best here. We have means and opportunity."

"True," the captain said. "But what you don't have is motive. You don't have anything here that speaks to that. Why would this guy drive down from the 'burbs to torch houses and landmarks?"

He tried not to roll his eyes. The last thing he needed was to piss off the captain. "He's an arsonist, sir," Dew said. "Their motives are to set fires, burn buildings, and commit destruction. And a serial arsonist?" Dew shook his head. "Their motives might include murder." Spillane rolled his eyes and Dew felt a murderous rage burn in his stomach.

"Dew," Spillane said, "you're a damned good detective. Hell, you'd have my job if you'd wanted it. And if you played nice with others."

Dew said nothing, afraid to even nod.

"But," he continued, "this goes into the 'hunch' category. The Mayor and city council want a quick resolution to this case, but dragging in someone who gives money to their campaigns, volunteers at libraries and museums, is not someone they're going to like for the crime. Even if I could get a judge to sign off on this, the fallout's going to be ugly."

"I understand that," Dew said. Keeping his voice calm and less than insubordinate was becoming a real chore. "That's why it's a search warrant. Not an arrest warrant."

Spillane sighed again and flicked his eyes to the office window. Out there, traffic was starting to build. Soon the roads would be clogged with angry commuters, frying in the heat, and wondering how long it would be before their engines overheated. "Search," he mumbled. Dew waited until the captain switched his eyes back to him. "I'll try and get Judge Hines to look at it. Maybe he'll be generous."

The flicker returned. Hines was usually a sure bet on a warrant, even one as thin as this. "Thank you, Captain. If we could get it by this afternoon, I think we can stave off another fire and possibly save some lives."

Spillane's face flushed. "I get it, Dew. Don't push me."

"My apologies," Dew drawled. "That's not what I meant."

"Of course it is," the captain said. "You've got a lot of pressure coming down. Some of it from me. So I get it."

"Thank you, sir."

The captain dismissed him by picking up the phone and dialing. Dew stood and left the office, pulling the door closed behind him. He pulled his cellphone out and checked the time. 1330. In another three and a half hours, the roads would be nearly impassable with traffic and Judge Hines and most of the DA's office would be heading into it. He sure as hell hoped Spillane was able to get Hines to listen.

He headed back to his cubicle, removed his sport coat, and sat in front of the computer. The darkened screen seemed to accuse him. Or maybe a void daring him to stare at it. What was it Nietzsche had said? "When you look into the abyss, the abyss also looks into you?" Something like that.

Hardy was his guy. He knew it. He knew it in his bones, in his gut, through every single instinct he'd ever had as a cop. Dew glared at the screen. If he wasn't a cop, he'd drive back over to Hardy's and put two in the man's head. He was that sure Hardy was the bug.

But he'd wait for the search warrant. Camp out here until something broke. Besides, he couldn't very well leave. The second Hines signed the warrant, he wanted to have it in hand and leading a fleet of cop cars into the fucker's driveway. Dew grunted. The house had been so hot, so goddamned uncomfortable, and that asshole had worn enough clothes for a trip to Alaska in the fall. What is wrong with you, Hardy? That was a good question.

Arsonist. Psychopath. Someone with a hole in their heart, in their soul, who could burn people alive without feeling any guilt. Someone who would do anything to feed their need regardless of the damage it caused. The night a man and his child burned to death in their house by his hand, Hardy probably went home and slept the sleep of the just. The sleep of the innocent. Because in his mind, he was.

Dew shook away the thoughts. That wasn't constructive. Leave the fucking psychoanalysis to someone like Tony. None of that was going to help him catch the fucker. No, the only way they'd catch him was to either find a garage and house filled with evidence, or the stupid bastard burning himself alive on accident. "Fat chance," he said to the darkened monitor. People like Hardy didn't make mistakes. "Unless he escalates."

Little by little, people like Hardy ramp up their violence, their damage, to enhance the thrill. Like a junkie whose constant usage requires more and more product to get high, arsonists and serial killers ultimately upped their game for the same reason. The more they escalated, the better the chance for a major screwup. Physical evidence. Maybe a fucking parking ticket like the one that gave up Son of Sam. "We couldn't get that lucky," he said.

Escalation. The word kept bouncing around in his mind. The bug had started with uninhabited structures. Then he'd torched a house and killed a father and daughter. What was next? Something larger? Something with a higher body count, or more danger involved?

The greater Houston area had more than 4 million miserable assholes in it. Area? Nearly 1,700 square miles. And maybe today, maybe tonight, or maybe tomorrow, their bug was going to light something else on fire and likely kill. Dew hit the space bar on the keyboard and the monitor sprang to life. It asked for his password. He'd watch his email and he'd wait. As soon as that search warrant hit his account, he'd have four cops at the house waiting to bust this asshole.

Chapter 48

The parking garage was hotter than hell. Sweat stains had spread across his normally well-creased, spotless white dress shirt. An acidic burp rose from his tortured stomach, the sound barely audible in the parking garage's din. Novak wiped a sheen of sweat from his forehead and flung the droplets to the pavement.

He walked to his reserved spot on the first floor where his car, a leased Lexus in cherry condition, sat waiting for him. Novak rounded to the driver door. The car sensed his key proximity and unlocked, the click of the buttons lost in the wake of a loud car starting up down the row.

"Goddamned kids," he muttered. Novak opened the car door, threw his brown leather satchel into the passenger seat, and heaved himself in. Even in the shade of the parking lot, the car's interior was broiling. He'd already been sweating, but now it poured off him.

As the car's engine growled to life, he put the air conditioner on maximum, and set the internal temp to 70°. The car's roar diminished slightly as the belts kicked in and hot, stale air rushed through the vents. Novak cursed, closed his eyes, and waited until the air cleared. He really should have kept the driver door open while the car flushed out the crap. Finally, a wave of arctic air rushed through the vents and slammed into his sweating body. Novak grinned.

He put the car in gear and pulled out of his space. It was early. Not many city employees were leaving this early in the day. Good thing, too. He'd have no problem getting home and beating traffic. The only question was whether he could keep his bowels in check long enough to reach the shitter at home.

Before the meeting with that faggot Brett and that ugly, eyesore of a woman Aninzo, he'd had a call from the Mayor's office. What about? About how all the black groups were enraged that no progress had been made on the case. One of the few remaining items of black history in Houston had been destroyed. Never mind if it was a reminder of the squalor that the black population suffered after reconstruction. That wasn't important. What was important was that some cracker had destroyed history. Black history.

Getting screamed at by Madame Mayor, *Her Honor*, was hardly the best thing for his career, let alone his stomach. He was damned close to having a political career, which is what he'd always wanted, and now his inept investigators were going to ruin it.

Novak belched again and his rectum puckered in response. His guts roiled and sloshed with acid and undigested food. He'd already destroyed one of the men's room toilets and now he hoped he made it home to destroy his own. Shitting in his suit pants? Not really on his bucket list.

He pulled out of the garage and into traffic. As expected, there were very few cars in his way. The car's thermometer read 103°. He clicked on the radio and a Hall and Oates tune filled the cabin. Novak sang along. If he kept his mind on something other than the political shit storm whirling at the office, he might actually make it home without ruining the upholstery.

He signaled and changed lanes. The light ahead turned red and he heaved a sigh. Never failed. Whenever he was in a hurry, he always caught the damned light. His stomach gurgled again. Novak went from muted whispering to full blown song. He didn't have a voice for it, and the dissonance bordered on painful to his own ears, but it was another way to try and forget about his stomach.

He slowed the car and came to a full stop, his voice still crooning in an off-key barrage of syllables. A car pulled up next to him. He stopped singing in mid-wail and slid his eyes over. The driver was looking at him. He could tell that much from his peripheral vision, but nothing more than that. Novak's face flushed with embarrassment and his stomach turned over.

Novak gritted his teeth. The pressure in his bowels threatened to explode. He closed his eyes and choked off the sensation. His body responded by sending his sphincter into raging contractions. Novak writhed in his seat as he fought to control his body. A car horn honked behind him and he opened his eyes. The light was green.

He groaned and slowly darted out into traffic. The car next to him had already sped through the light. Novak glanced in the rearview and saw a red faced hipster growling at him. Novak wanted to apologize. At the same time, he wanted to take a shit on the guy's hood.

The next few blocks were much the same. Every time he thought he had his body under control, waves of pain and pressure wrapped his gut like a vice. Drivers passed him in disgust. His slow starts from the line were infuriating even to him, but he didn't dare put an ounce more G-force against his bowels than absolutely necessary.

The cabin was cool now, the heat having evaporated beneath the barrage of the A/C. But that didn't mean he'd stopped sweating. Between the pressure in his bowels and his fear of shitting himself, water oozed from his pores and down his back.

"Just another ten minutes," he said to the radio. Hall and Oates had given way to Styx. He mumbled along with the half-forgotten words doing his best to focus on the music and not the discomfort.

He turned left off Main and headed to his apartment near the BBVA Compass Stadium. "Not long now," he said to himself. He nudged the car into the complex and to his reserved space.

When he finished his subpar parking job, he turned off the ignition and sat in the car. Heat immediately replaced the frigid air trapped in the cabin. If he stayed in the car much longer, he'd risk having a BM right there in his seat. But if he moved, it might happen anyway. A bead of sweat rolled off his forehead and dripped onto his shirt.

"Fuck," Novak growled. He carefully leaned over and picked up his satchel. He made a quick glance through the car windows, ensuring no one would see him if the unfortunate happened. When he was certain no one was looking, he gritted his teeth and swung open the driver door.

The last of the cold air escaped through the door as if it had never been there. The sun, high in a cloudless sky, immediately punished him with searing heat. Not for the first time, he cursed the building designers for not putting in a goddamned covered parking area. He would gladly have paid for it, now more than ever.

He scooted out of the car seat, his buttocks pinched together. A bolt of pain made him shake from anus to shoulder. Novak grunted and duck walked to the door. Fortunately, he didn't have any stairs to climb, but even with the elevator it was going to be close.

He pressed the button and waited. Dogs in the complex started barking and snarling. He thought he even heard a cat yowling in the distance. Great, he thought, the animals are going crazy now. The heat was doing in everyone and everything.

He frowned at the elevator's art-deco doors, his body rigid and quivering with strain. When the elevator finally dinged, he let out a frustrated sigh and walked in.

Right as the doors were about to close, a hand slipped in between the doors, and they reopened slowly. A shorter man dressed in a Texans hoodie and distressed blue jeans walked in. Novak bit his lip as he fought the urge to yell at the guy. The man stepped to the back of the elevator and stood silently a few steps away.

Novak cleared his throat and focused on the doors. They were still open. He stabbed his index finger for the 3 button and practically punched the "Close Door" button. The elevator dinged again and the doors slid closed.

The car jerked a little as it ascended. The stuffy air was nauseating. The guy next to him smelled like something that crawled out of a house fire. And how the hell could he stand wearing those heavy clothes in this goddamned miserable heat?

When the car dinged again, Novak walked out as rapidly as he dared. He was halfway down the hall when he realized the hoodie wearing stranger hadn't pressed a button for a floor. He turned slightly to see if the man had left the elevator, but he couldn't see him. His gut roiled again. It was coming. The dreaded hershey squirts from his youth were back and this was going to be an epic bout of liquid waste.

He pulled the keys from his pocket, unlocked the door, and walked. As soon as the door was closed and locked, he dropped the satchel and practically ran to the toilet, shedding clothes as he went.

His ass was barely over the porcelain when his bowels exploded. Novak sat down, wincing with the discomfort and the sensation of soupy shit splattering against his bare buttocks. Tears of pain mixed with relief rolled down his sweaty cheeks. Or maybe it was the eye-watering stench.

He nearly laughed out loud. Jesus, that was close. Another minute or two and he would have defecated in the damned elevator! Then maybe that hoodie guy could have used the hood as a mask. This time an actual laugh escaped his mouth.

Once the terrible bout of gastric distress passed, he could barely feel his legs. Too long on the damned porcelain altar. Novak slowly raised himself, wincing at the wetness of his ass. Yup, toilet paper wasn't going to do all the work. He'd need a damned shower. "Or a bidet," he said with a laugh.

He wiped as best he could, kicked off his shoes, and the rest of his clothes. He entered the shower stall and turned the faucet. Ice cold water streamed out. He shivered and yet his hand lingered over the temperature controls, but only for a few seconds. The cold felt good. The cold was what he needed. He exhaled a long sigh and slowly twisted the handle to warm the water.

Slowly rotating beneath the waterfall spray, Novak let the powerful jets scrub the sweat and grime from his face. He tilted his head and let the water drain in, hoping his copious earwax would melt. Maybe then he could hear that little faggot better. Novak smirked.

The water warmed quickly, no longer refreshing, but bordering on painful. Novak found the faucet by touch and swiveled it a few centimeters toward cold. The water temperature dipped slightly. There. That was better.

Novak turned around, the water pounding into his upper back and drizzling down the crack of his ass. The heat felt good, but it was still a little too warm. He put his hand to the faucet and swiveled it another few centimeters to cold. The water's temperature changed just the slightest bit, but it was enough to be comfortable again.

He rubbed soap on a loofa and began scrubbing his neck and back, luxuriating beneath the hot water. After a few scrubs, his eyebrows drew together. Was it getting hotter again? Jesus, what the hell was going on with the water?

He turned the faucet again toward cold, as far as it could go without turning off the shower itself. A brief spurt of cold water shot from the shower head. The momentary temperature change was enough to make him shiver with pleasure before the heat returned again. Only now, it was even hotter. His skin began to burn.

Moaning in pain, he reached for the metal handle once more. A scream escaped his mouth and he stared down at his already blistering palm. The metal had been so hot to the touch, it had flash-fried his hand. A column of steam rose from the drain as if from a kettle and scorched his legs, his balls. Novak screamed again and scrabbled for the shower door. His fingers touched the handle and immediately fused to the molten hot metal.

His skin began to boil. He exhaled another scream and tried to breathe. The air scorched his lungs and he backpedaled to the burning hot ceramic tiles. He reached out and punched the shower stall glass. The flimsy door smashed outward, a massive fog bank of steam rushing through the hole. Novak fell out of the shower stall and onto the floor.

The relatively cool air puckered his unburned flesh with goosebumps, but it didn't last. The heat returned to his back and legs as though someone had set him on fire. Throat burning from either his screaming or the scorched air, Novak tried to lift himself from the hot ceramic tile and his eyes caught sight of a pair of shoes standing at the bathroom entrance.

The hoodie wearing man's indecipherable silhouette lurked like a shadow in the door frame. Novak was in too much pain to find it odd. Instead, he raised a plaintive hand to the figure. "Help," he wheezed through damaged lungs and a burned trachea.

The man slowly lifted the hood revealing dark, sunburned skin and a hairless head. He could have been twenty or sixty years old for all Novak knew. But his ageless appearance is not what finally snapped Novak's mind from hope into a whirlpool of terror. It was the man's burning crimson eyes. Flames seemed to dance across them as if the inside of his skull was on fire.

"No help," the man said. He raised his hands in supplication. "Become," he said, his voice a deep choral growl. The man's eyes suddenly became bright orange, a color so deep it was fire itself.

The ceramic tile beneath Novak's body turned to hot coals. He writhed and screamed as the bathroom wallpaper caught fire, the room filling with indescribable heat. The air around him burst into flame, his dermis catching fire as well. In the last seconds of his life, Novak smelled his own flesh roasting and the stench of burned meat.

Chapter 49

They were finishing up lunch when Brett's cellphone rang. A few minutes later, the check was paid and they were in his car racing toward mid-town. By the time they arrived, a crowd of cops, fire department personnel, reporters, and gawkers filled the parking lot in front of the apartment building.

When Emy stepped out of the car, the crushing heat slammed into her like a sledgehammer. She didn't know if it was just the sight of the burned out apartment on the luxury apartment complex' upper floor, her mind imagining the incredible heat of the fire, or if the sun had decided to cremate the planet, but it was already hotter than it had been an hour ago.

The thermostat in Brett's car claimed it was 105°, but the heat index had to be at least 115°. Emy made sure her badge was visible and followed Brett to the nearest fire truck. While Brett asked questions, she made her way through the crowd and to the police barricade. She flashed her badge and walked inside the perimeter, her eyes locked on the burned out shell of the apartment.

The rest of the upper floor was intact, as though the fire had only consumed a single apartment in the large building. Novak's apartment to be precise.

"Emy?"

She heard Brett's voice, but didn't turn. "Yeah, boss?"

He stepped beside her, rubbed an arm across his sweaty forehead, and pointed at the apartment. "Look familiar?"

"Yeah," Emy said. "Like a firebomb detonated in there. I can see that from here."

"So can I," Brett said. "Our friends in the HFD say it was so hot, the water just turned to steam."

"Shit," Emy said. "When can we go in?"

"Soon," Brett said. "Fire went out pretty fast."

"Any other damage?"

"No. Just the one apartment. Just Novak."

She dropped her eyes to the pavement. "They find him?"

Brett sucked in a long breath of air. "They found *someone*. Nothing left but bone and teeth."

"Jesus," Emy said. Streams of sweat ran down her back beneath the light blouse. Hell, even her pant legs were getting soaked with it. "How long until we know for sure?"

Brett shrugged. "CSU will go in soon. Once they, well, do a little sifting, we should be able to get in there and take a look around. I don't think I'm going to have to press to get a rush on the ID."

"No shit," Emy mumbled. God, this was bad. She'd hated the asshole since she'd met him, but not even a misogynistic, homophobic piece of shit like him deserved to be cremated in his own fucking home. "How fast did it happen?"

"They're still interviewing witnesses," he said. "But I think it had to happen damned fast."

"Like at the Hartman house."

"Right," Brett said. "Just like at the Hartman house. Burned up and went out a little too easily."

"Goddammit," Emy said. "We still don't have any idea about the accelerant used in that one. And this?" She shook her head. "This looks even more bizarre. How come the rest of the building didn't get scorched?"

"Divine combustion?" Brett said and chuckled. The sound died quickly in his throat when he saw the expression on her face. "That was supposed to be funny," he said.

She wiped another sheen of sweat from her forehead. "Sorry," she said. "Guess our little discussion yesterday has me wondering."

Brett nodded to himself. "You're not the only one." He jerked a thumb back to his car. "Let's get some water. We're going to die out here if we don't stay hydrated."

He left her side and walked away. She barely noticed. Even from this far away, she could see a mark on the far wall inside the burned out bathroom.

She couldn't tell if it was the bug's signature, but she knew it was. She knew it in her gut.

Emy turned and faced the crowd of onlookers. Sweaty faces, damp clothes, the furtive eyes of gawking spectators stared back at her. She paused over each of the faces, looking for something akin to pleasure, to need. A bald man with dark sunglasses stared at her from the back of the crowd. A chill went down her spine. She blinked, and he was gone.

She flicked her eyes across the faces looking for the man again. She didn't find him. Sunstroke. Had to be sunstroke. No one could simply disappear. Not like that. Maybe she'd hallucinated him in the first place. "Like a mirage," she said aloud.

Emy took a moment to scan the area once again before finally giving up. If the arsonist was in the crowd, she wouldn't find him. The only question that mattered now was where he was.

Chapter 50

Anger. Relief. And it was cold. The stolen car's thermostat was set to 88°, as high as it would go, and the damned thing was still blowing cold air. P's hoodie, smelling like smoke and charcoaled beef patties, lay in the trunk in a cedar box. If he was stopped by a K-9 unit, or anyone looking for the tell-tale scent of burned wood and flesh, the cedar would be enough to throw them off. The car's plate, switched at a big box store parking lot, wouldn't come up as a theft for another few hours. Especially since its owner was on vacation.

He was white. He could drive nearly anywhere in the city without fear of a cop tailing him, much less pulling him over, so long as he kept his speed at the legal limit. And P was careful. Speeding was not something you did when you were trying to hide in plain sight.

P pulled into the three city-block sized warehouse park, swiped his card, and drove inside. Just to make sure no one was tailing him, he drove past his building several times before finally being sure he was clear of any surveillance. Apart from the facility's cameras, that was. But he'd already handled that.

Just as he'd stolen unprotected WIFI for the Hartman house, he'd found the building's WiFi access point and cracked it weeks ago. Planting a worm in the system to target the camera software hadn't been difficult either. A single email to a manufactured email address and boom, the cameras stopped recording live images. If someone went looking through the records, all they'd find were scenes where the camera glitched out and took stills.

Any possible half-images of the scene would be put down to software or hardware malfunctions. Besides, he doubted anyone would begin trolling through the data before it no longer mattered.

He pulled his phone and opened the warehouse door with a tap on the screen. He couldn't hear the sound over the car's roaring heater and engine, but he saw the reinforced steel door rise into the overhang. Before he left the complex each visit, he sprayed down the gears with lubricant to keep them as silent as possible.

Being cautious, being meticulous, foreseeing complications before they ever arose were the ways he'd stayed away from law enforcement. Not to mention out of prison or on death row.

P drove the stolen car into the garage and immediately closed the door. He stayed inside the heated vehicle until the garage was once again in complete darkness. P braced himself, afraid the garage would feel like a freezer, and opened the car door.

Glorious heat flooded across his skin driving away goose flesh and his fear. P stood and raised his arms above his head, stretching away the creaks and kinks from the stress of the drive. When he'd first rented the warehouse, he'd been glad of its A/C to keep his precious "secret" belongings from being spoiled by the ebb and flow of Houston's hot summers and the occasional cold winter. The warehouse, weather-proofed and well insulated, maintained any temperature he set. Year-round. But now, that was hardly a concern.

P opened the trunk and removed the disconnected computer equipment. Moving around in the stifling hot air calmed him. Killing that fat shit Novak had left him thrumming with energy. Standing in the heat, watching the fire department extinguish the flames, and hiding amidst the crowd of excited, ghoulish onlookers had done little to evaporate the excitement. Instead, it had only increased it. Until, that was, she showed up.

He'd watched her from the crowd, she and her supervisor, the Cullum man he'd been unable to burn two nights ago. The night of the cat attack. P shivered at the thought and looked down at his arms. The scratches looked more like cauterized burns now than caused by claws. But at least they no longer bled. If he wasn't on the verge of his becoming, he might have worried about getting rabies. What a joke.

He'd tried again last night, but no luck. Cullum and his husband had arrived home at just the wrong time. He hadn't had an opportunity to set up, much less ambush. Oh, well. He'd get the fucker tonight.

When Aninzo and Cullum arrived at the scene, he'd carefully melted into the crowd, not at the front, not at the back, but right in the middle. He wasn't as tall as some of those around him, but he did nothing to find a sightline. The sightline, Ghere had told him, would reveal itself. As always, God had been right.

As the onlookers shifted themselves to get a better view of the burned out apartment, the sightline to the two arson investigators opened up like a flower. He saw her. Her hair, jet-black with moisture, fell across her face like a rope and did little to hide her scars. Oh, they were beautiful, glowing in the reflection from the sun-scorched concrete. Ghere's marks, Its kiss, Its loving caress, painted her face and body like a sacred tattoo. And she didn't appreciate the glory of It.

Aninzo had probably wandered through her childhood, her adolescence, shit, her whole life, thinking of those touches as a blight, ugly, a reason for others to find her hideous. Pathetic. If she had any inkling of how lucky she was to have been kissed by Ghere, she wouldn't try to hide them.

It didn't matter. She would soon know Ghere's glory. She would soon become one with the flames. P smiled. Just as her boss would. Just as the entire city would.

When she'd looked at him, saw him standing in the crowd, it had been difficult not to smile at her, not to give her a sign that he saw her too. Saw her everything, her very soul crying to be consumed in fire. Crying for Ghere to finish what It had started so long ago. In the end, she would become fire like everything else.

He set the computer equipment upon the long shelf to be with its brethren. P whistled as he opened the computer case and stuck a mason jar filled with gasoline inside. After pulling the homemade fuse through an empty peripheral slot, he carefully screwed the base back together. He repeated the process for the remaining computer. Neither of them would ever be used again. For that, he had a laptop. When it was time to leave the warehouse, it would all go up in a fireball. The very start of the night's fun.

P grinned as he checked the connections, the cell-phone detonator, and packed his satchel. Double and triple checking his to-do list, he made sure every precaution had been taken, and every item he needed was carefully, lovingly placed in the satchel. Wire cutters. Four cheap burner phones, four bricks of homemade C-4, a putty knife, a long loop of homemade det cord, an easily concealable Gerber automatic knife, and a Glock. The pistol was more of a last resort since he wasn't exactly a great shot, but it paid to be cautious. It always did.

The only tricky part of the plan would be the amulet, and it was a must. Ghere couldn't be reborn without it. The entity had made that very clear. Ad nauseam, in fact. His little bag of goodies would help, but ultimately, it would be the flames that would make it possible.

"Fire fire everywhere," he said aloud. "And not a drop of water shall touch it."

P's smile flashed his white teeth, glowing against the contrast of burned, chapped lips. Strips of flesh had already fallen from his legs and chest. He was a snake shedding its skin revealing raw, tough, red flesh beneath his normally pale dermis. When he finished his transformation, he'd be God. And God would be him.

He checked the satchel once more, touching every item in the leather bag as if to assure himself it was real.

You are prepared, Ghere said in his mind. *We are prepared.*

P chuckled. "And tonight, we become."

Become, Ghere purred. *We will become.*

Chapter 51

An hour in the hot sun was more than anyone could take in this heat. Emy thought she was literally going to melt. She and Brett had gone through all the bottled water in his car. Two bottles a piece. Normally she'd have to pee after consuming that much liquid, but the sun seemed to draw it out of her skin before it had the chance to reach her bladder.

HFD had given them the all clear to search the burned out hulk of an apartment. Although the blaze was out and every piece of charred wood and steel had been doused with water, residual heat still added to the miserable temperature inside the apartment.

Forensics had taken their photos, marked the placement of the nearly melted body, the twisted remains of the shower stall, and any other materials that survived the fire. And that wasn't much.

Upon walking into the apartment, Brett and Emy had traded an uneasy glance. The rest of the apartment was stained with smoke and the stench of burned flesh, but no fire damage. No. Fire. Damage.

Emy shook her head as they walked into the master bedroom. The walls were still there, still up, still holding the room together. But once inside the master bath, all that changed. The wall next to the shower stall was simply gone. This was what they'd seen from the parking lot. Well, them and everyone else.

The fire had consumed the master bath like a dragon breathing on ice. The ceramic tiles that had once covered the shower stall walls had nearly vaporized. The toilet had shattered from the heat. Or maybe that occurred when the porcelain went from an extremely high temperature to the assault of cold water. Most anything shattered or twisted from rapid temperature change. The aluminum that made up the shower stall frame had completely melted into puddles.

But it was the wall. The fucking wall. The wall separating the bathroom from the outside world had simply vanished as if annihilated by the heat. The remaining shards of brick that had made up the facade had separated into their constituent layers. The steel supports hadn't faired much better than the aluminum stall frame. And the concrete? It had come apart like a sedimentary rock in a strong spray of water.

She and Brett stared at the wreckage for several moments before either spoke. The world had gone silent as though the very apartment had disappeared from reality and into a lifeless void. "Well," Brett said. She started and stared at him. "This is about as impossible as it gets."

"No shit," Emy breathed. "A fuel air-bomb does this kind of damage. I can't think of anything else."

"Glad we agree on that." Brett walked into the bathroom, his boots crunching on the brittle remains of the ceramic tile. He pointed at the remaining wall. The glyph was there. Large. Slightly darker than the rest of the burned wall. "Getting bolder?"

The bug was getting bolder, all right. He'd just fucking killed the Arson Department head and done it in such a way that there was no chance any physical evidence remained. Emy stared down at the yellow outline on the floor. Novak's remains had been there just a few minutes ago before being carried out in a body bag. She bet the complete skeleton, still covered in the charred remains of fat, blood, muscle, and fried tissue, couldn't possibly have weighed more than thirty pounds all told. Before he'd gone home, before he'd been fried like a piece of hamburger that dropped into a charcoal furnace, he'd weighed close to 300 lbs.

"I mean, how the hell could this even happen?" Brett asked. "You're more up on your chem than I am, but I can't think of any accelerant that could do this."

Emy shook her head. "No." She studied the glyph. "No accelerant. At least nothing that could possibly be—" Emy choked back a shiver. If you finish that sentence, she said to herself, Brett's going to think you've lost your fucking mind.

"What?" he asked. "Possibly be what?"

"Nothing," she said. "Sorry. Just doesn't make sense."

He touched the holster on his hip. "I'm going to call our department liaison. See if we can get some cops to watch us."

"You think that's necessary?" Emy asked.

"Yeah, I do. Someone was in my fucking house," Brett said. "Someone could have killed my dogs, my husband. Me." He locked eyes with her. "You live alone, Emy."

"No," she said, "I have Luna. She—" Brett chuckled. "What?"

"Luna can't hold a Glock," Brett said. "And no offense, but she's vulnerable too."

Emy blinked. "Fuck. Yeah. You're right."

Brett dropped his eyes to the outline. "I should feel something," he said. "Anger. Grief. Something."

"Then why don't you?" Emy asked.

He shrugged. "Maybe because all this?" he said, gesturing to the flamed out room. "Maybe all this is just too much of a mind fuck. Or maybe I just hated the useless bastard that much."

That'll come later, she thought. Maybe grief, but more than likely guilt. And the guilt would only be for not feeling grief. Emy sighed. "There won't be any fingerprints."

"No," Brett agreed. "Our bug doesn't leave those. And any physical evidence he left in here would have been destroyed. Our only shot," he jerked a thumb to the hallway behind them, "is that the bastard left something when he entered or exited the apartment. Somehow I doubt he did that either."

"Me too," Emy said. "Have to get HPD to rush through anything they find."

"That won't be a problem," Brett said. "Murder of a city employee? Someone in the HFD? They're going to be screaming for blood too. When Dewhurst hears about this, I'm sure he'll be all over them too."

"Think we should call him?" Emy asked.

Brett nodded. "You do that while I finish talking to the HFD. Make sure we have all our bases covered."

"Aye, aye, boss," Emy said.

He wiped beads of sweat from his forehead with his sleeve. The fabric was already dark with moisture. She wondered just how many times he'd repeated that routine. She glanced at the sleeve of her own shirt and wondered the same about her.

Emy and Brett carefully walked back into the hallway across the plastic sheeting forensics had left in their wake. She hoped like hell they'd find something, but she knew they wouldn't. Where are you now, Bug? The thought flashed across her mind like a prayer.

Chapter 52

He found Brett and Emy waiting for him in the apartment complex parking lot. The only remaining HFD personnel were cleaning up the mess and moving away rubble. Houston City Maintenance was helping, but it would take time. Two uniformed cops kept watch over the yellow-taped perimeter while HFD and city maintenance did their thing.

As soon as Emy called him, Dew had vacated his cube, hit the parking lot, and drove like a bat out of hell to the site. "The site." That was the cold, nondescript, emotionless word used to describe a crime scene. Dew supposed it was used to keep law enforcement, as well as victims, from experiencing an emotional response, but he knew damned well there was no such thing. You could attempt to defang something unpleasant by giving it a cutesy or bland name, but a crime had victims. And victims never forgot. And most cops didn't either.

Dew opened the car door and stepped into the punishing heat. He grabbed the plastic bag sitting on the passenger seat and met the two arson investigators, bag offered in supplication. "I grabbed a couple of these from the station. Figured you'd need them."

Brett took the bag from him, opened it, and grinned. He pulled out two sports drink bottles and handed one to Emy. She took hers, spun off the top, and downed it one continuous gulp. Brett laughed and did the same. When they both finished, he put the empties back into the bag. "And you brought us two extras?"

"Well, like I said, I figured you'd need them." Dew turned from the two investigators and stared at the burned out room on the second floor. "Wow. That's, um, impressive."

"That's one word that comes to mind," Emy said. "Another is 'impossible.'"

"Really?" Dew squinted in the harsh sunlight.

"She's right," Brett said. "Unless you know of a way to create a 1500° fireball in a 100x75 foot space that doesn't affect anything else in the vicinity."

Dew whistled. "That hot?"

"At least," Emy said. "The fire started there, fried Novak into charcoal, and didn't so much as scald anything outside the bathroom."

The detective shook his head. "That does sound impossible."

"It is," Brett said. "And yeah, it was our bug."

"Really?" He flicked his eyes away from the building and glanced at each of the investigators. "He leave a mark?"

"Left more than just a mark, Dew." Emy pulled a bandanna from her pocket and rubbed it across her forehead. Both she and Brett were drenched in sweat. Dew didn't know how they could stand it. "He left a goddamned big drawing in there."

Dew raised an eyebrow. "How big?"

"Big," Brett said. "I figure the diameter was at least 3 feet. But that's not half as strange as what it was made with."

"Oh, I can't wait to hear this," Dew said. "Hit me."

Emy and Brett traded a glance. She gestured to him to continue. Brett swiped his forehead. "It was a flash image."

"Flash image? I don't understand."

Emy rolled her eyes at Brett. "You know when an extremely bright light hits an object? If something is in front of it, that 'something' can leave a shadow," Emy said.

Dew blinked. "Okay. I can't figure out which of us has heatstroke. What are you saying?"

"We don't know," Brett said. "I mean, we do, but we don't. What I'm saying is that it appears an object, the glyph, blocked part of the flash and left its outline in the wall."

"Christ," Dew said. "How the hell did the perp drag something that big in there to leave a shadow?"

"No." Emy shook her head. "That's not the half of it, Dew. Along with the heat, what could cause a flash that bright? It's the kind of thing you find in a nuclear blast, a thermite blast, or maybe a volcano going off. Any accelerant we can think of wouldn't create that shadow without destroying the rest of the damned apartment, much less the building."

Dew fought the urge to wipe his own forehead. Sweat dripped down his face like a faucet. "So where does all this leave us?"

Brett shrugged. "No where. Just as confused as we were before. But," he said and jerked a thumb at the building, "he's escalating. Obviously."

Dew studied the two investigators. They had just lost their boss, inspected the place where he died, and they both seemed somewhat in control. When Emy had called, her voice had been calm, but he'd still detected a tremor underlying the words. But here, at the site and talking about the case, there didn't seem to be any grief. No uneasiness. Professionalism at its best? Shock?

"I'm going to talk to the department about setting up a uni or two to watch your homes," Dew said. "May take some time to get you a 24/7 detail."

Brett chuckled, but there was no mirth in the sound and his eyes hardened. "Novak is dead, Dew. I'm the de facto head of Arson. For now, at least." He pointed at Emy. "Pretty sure the two of us are going to spend our time digging through whatever forensic evidence there is and find this asshole."

Emy nodded. "That said, I would like someone to make sure my building doesn't burn."

"And this asshole stays away from my husband," Brett added. "Pretty sure we're going to be hunkered down with our files."

Dew opened his mouth to reply when his cellphone rang. He held up a finger and answered it. It was the captain. The search warrant had been granted and patrol cars were already heading to the Hardy house. Dew thanked the captain and hung up. He couldn't help but grin.

"What is it?" Emy asked.

"Suspect," Dew said. "Went and visited him this morning. I found a connection." Dew nodded as much to himself as the two investigators. "I'm damned sure he's our bug."

"No shit?" Brett said. "So when do you—"

"Right now," Dew said. He turned and walked back to his car. "I'll make the call to set you up with some protection. And I'll let you know what we find in his house."

"You better!" Emy yelled.

Dew waved at the two of them and slid into his car. The moment he turned the ignition and the cold air began to blow on his skin, he shivered in delight. "Okay, Hardy," he said to no one as he pulled out of the complex, "let's find out just who the fuck you are."

Chapter 53

He didn't want to leave the warehouse. Even as the sun slowly died in the sky, and his transformation was nearly at hand, he didn't want to leave. The air was so hot, so wonderful in his lungs and on his skin. No matter how high he'd turned up the vehicle's thermostat, it couldn't come close to matching the silky, heavy, scorching embrace of the warehouse's natural heat. He'd have to wear the hoodie just to survive the car ride.

Hoodie, sweaters, long-sleeved shirts. They all itched against his deteriorating skin. The more he *became*, the more his dermis flaked off in long strips like snake skin. Unlike a shed skin, however, the strips and patches practically disintegrated into powder. He'd had to use the vacuum several times a day in his home, ensure every part of his clothing covered the damaged skin to leave no trace, no physical evidence, nothing a forensics team could possibly use. But none of that would matter soon. When he *became*, there would be nothing physical left.

He sat on the ripped and taped up bean bag chair, legs crossed beneath him, hands resting on his knees. The satchel lay within reach on the warped and half-rotted end-table. The urge to lift his arm, slide it over, and caress the tough, soft, well-worn leather, was pathological. He knew it. Just another shred of being human he would leave behind.

P closed his eyes, allowing the afterimage of the light to slowly fade. Once the world disappeared from his consciousness, an orange glow appeared at the edges of the darkness. The eldritch light seemed alive, pulsing and moving like liquid, dark red flecks floating atop rivers of orange.

A crimson diamond ripped through the black background, bisecting the darkness. The shape blinked at him.

I am the flame. I am the fire. You are the vessel, Ghere purred in his mind. *And we shall be reborn.*

"Reborn," P said aloud. He whispered the word again and again, his smile growing with each repetition. The darkness behind his eyes exploded into bright orange and yellow flames, a blaze that licked at his very soul.

P floated in the flames, the fire bathing him, holding him. With his eyes still shut, he felt the caress on his skin, his remaining body hair wilting before burning away in puffs of smoke. Every cell of his dermis prickled in a mixture of pleasure and pain. He would never be cold again. He would never be alone again. He would become one with Ghere, and together they would bring humankind a new world. A new God. A world without darkness, a world of orange and red light. The world they deserved.

His phone emitted a series of chirps. The images and sensations departed leaving him cold and shivering. He opened his eyes and glanced at the burner phone laying on the table. He picked it up, flipped it open, and stared at the screen. P sneered at it before snapping the phone in half and throwing it to the floor.

They were at the house. His house. The house where his new self had been born. That detective. Dewhurst. He'd known. There were probably a dozen cops in his home at this very moment. "Not for long, though," he said aloud.

P pulled a different phone from his pocket, unlocked it with a code, and brought up his custom app. He selected "House" from the menu, grinned, and pressed the button. Within the next hour, maybe sooner, his home would disappear. The moment one of the cops entered the garage and took a look around, it would all be gone. He wished he was there to watch it, to have Ghere bless the cops with his burning touch. Oh, well. He'd see plenty of that this evening.

Everything was in place. It had taken more than two weeks of work, most of it done in the dead of night, to prepare for the final becoming. He was ready. Ghere was ready. The city of Houston didn't know what was coming, but all the cops in the world wouldn't be able to stop it.

P sighed and stood from the bean bag chair. He rubbed his arms, oblivious to the long strips of powdery skin flaking beneath his hoodie. He was cold. Sunset would happen in another hour. It was time to get into position. And maybe put on his parka.

Chapter 54

B y the time Dew arrived at the Hardy house, two detectives and half a dozen unis were already outside, sweating in the intense heat. Three lab geeks had already put down plastic and begun scouring the house for evidence.

When he reached the doorstep, one of the unis, Mahoney by his name-plate, nodded at him. "You Dewhurst?"

"Yeah," Dew said. "House cleared?"

The cop nodded. "It's a big house, Lieutenant. But I think we checked every nook and cranny. Just gave forensics the all clear."

"Good."

"Guess traffic was a bitch?"

Dew grunted. Rivulets of sweat were already beginning to make their way down from his forehead to his cheeks. "You can say that."

"Well, if you think it's hot out here," Mahoney said, "wait until you go inside."

"Great," Dew said. "You check the thermostat?"

Mahoney nodded. "Set to 88°. This Hardy guy must be insane."

"He is," Dew said. He nodded to the officer and walked across the threshold into the foyer. One of the forensics geeks stood at the garage door precipice. "Have you opened it yet?"

The geek, an overweight woman in her forties named Valerie Jones, shook her head. "Not yet, Detective. We decided to check the kitchen first, since that's where most household cleaners are kept."

Dew rolled his eyes and put his hands on his hips. "If he's creating accelerants, I doubt he's mixing them in the damned kitchen, Val."

"You'd be surprised," Val said. She jerked a thumb at the stairs. "They're checking the bathtub. If he's been mixing chemicals, he probably used the tub to do it."

"Anarchist Cookbook?"

"Wouldn't surprise me," Val said. She put her hand on the garage door knob. "Care to join me, Detective?"

"Let's take a look," Dew said.

"Lieutenant?" Mahoney said from the open door. "Captain Spillane on the radio. Wants an update."

Dew cursed under his breath. He turned and headed out of the house. "Guess you're going in by yourself," he called over his shoulder.

"Lucky me," Val said.

He waved a hand and walked to his car. He picked up the radio. "Lieutenant Dewhurst for Captain Spillane, over."

A tinny voice said "Patching you through."

Dew impatiently tapped a foot and looked back at the house. He needed to be in there. If Hardy had left any evidence, he'd find it along with the help from the forensics team. Hell, maybe even the unis would find something. It was a large house and searching it would take a lot of time. Time he didn't think they had.

"Dewhurst?"

"Here, sir." The radio crackled and his superior's voice broke up for a second. "Say again, sir?"

"What's your status?"

"No one home," Dew said. "The forensics team just entered the garage and they're checking the upstairs—"

The world erupted in a shockwave of bright flame and shattered windows. The force knocked Dew into the car door hard enough to break one of his ribs and smash his face into the window. The plexiglass spiderwebbed from the impact and rivulets of blood flowed down his face. Dew's ears rang loud enough to make his brain feel as though it were melting. He crumpled to the concrete street, turning like a twisted rag doll, his face pointed toward the Hardy house. Or rather, what was left of it.

The garage had vaporized leaving only the concrete supports in place. The house's upper floor no longer had a roof or much of anything apart from twisted steel and aluminum. The concrete pillars holding up the facade had fractured enough to weaken and crumble, their charge folding to the floor in a crash of stone on stone. Chips of lumber, concrete, metal, and glass fell all around him, the base of what might have been a statue crashing down into the hood of his car. Even with his ears ringing, he heard the muffled crunch. Dew held an arm up above his head, just in case another piece of debris decided to land on top of him, and crawled into the car. The windshield cracked as a hailstorm of construction debris rained down.

The radio might have been squawking with frenzied questions, but it was impossible to know. He couldn't hear much of anything at all. He pulled the transmitter back into his hands, and thumbed the receiver. "Dispatch! Officers down!" He screamed the Hardy house address. "Need first responders. Fucking send everybody!"

The insect whine of what might have been a response hit the periphery of his hearing, but it was completely unintelligible. Dew stumbled from the car, blood obscuring the vision in his left eye. Three unis were down on the concrete. He walked on unsteady feet toward the closest and choked down his gorge. Blood covered the man's uniform, a piece of rebar sticking out from the middle of his chest. A pool of blood slowly spread out from beneath his lifeless body. Dew's vision wavered making the world tilt to one side. He shook his head to clear it and nearly lost his balance. Pain pounded through his skull like a vise tightening and releasing over and over again.

A few more steps and he reached the other uni. The man was on his side, but he was breathing at least. Dew rolled him over. One of the uni's eyes was nothing but pupil, the other filled with crimson liquid. Head injury. Pretty goddamned severe too. He might live. If the EMTs arrived soon.

Dew took another step toward the third but stopped. A concrete block had smashed in his face. His body twitched twice and went still. Dew sat near the wounded, but still breathing, officer, and held the man's hand. Despite the ringing in his ears, he thought he heard the sounds of sirens.

Rest. He had to rest until they got here. He watched the frame of the house collapse into itself. Anyone that had been inside was gone along with any evidence of what Hardy was up to next. Dew's eyes hardened against the pain. He was going to find this fucker. He was going to find him and put a bullet between his eyes the first chance he got.

Chapter 55

HFD was gone. The cops were gone. The site had been cordoned off with crime scene tape, neighbors interviewed, and the cleanup finished. In other words, it was time to begin culling the information they'd gathered and look for evidence. But that was bullshit. Technically, they still didn't have confirmation the remains belonged to Novak, although both Emy and Brett had already agreed on that subject.

Brett had already called in a few favors and the body would be at the morgue as soon as possible. Since the badly burned body had no remaining flesh on its fingers, identification would require a dental cast and comparison to any dental records on file. Considering it was already the evening hours, that would be impossible until morning.

Novak, twice divorced, still had his latest ex-wife listed under next of kin. HPD would no doubt call her and inform her of his possible demise, beg for medical information, and require a faxed signature. That could take a day or two in itself.

If the body wasn't Novak's, it would raise even more questions. But considering there'd been one body in the apartment, the surveillance cameras caught him entering the complex fifteen minutes before the fire, and the remains appeared to be his height and body type, everyone assumed it was him. The rest was just formalities and legalities.

HPD had already contacted them both regarding Dew's request for police stakeouts at both of their homes, but Emy wasn't sure she wanted to go back to her apartment, apart from picking up some clean clothes and to take a shower. Brett had dropped her off at her car and the drive home had been relatively fast.

She walked up the stairs to the apartment, hit the landing, and headed for the door. From inside her apartment, she heard Luna growling. "Just me," she said as she inserted the key. The growl cut off, replaced by a plaintive whimper. Smiling, she turned the key and opened the door. The moon colored dog backed away from the door, tail wagging like a propeller. Emy slipped inside, shut the door, and fastened the heavy chain after swiveling the dead bolt.

Luna sat, expectantly waiting with her snout in the air. Emy bent down and kissed the dog just above her nose. "Good doggie," she said. Luna's tail swished across the floor like a duster. Sighing, Emy headed to the small laundry room, unbuttoning her shirt as she went.

Spending hours in the furnace of a parking lot bathed in the punishing rays of the sun had left every centimeter of her clothes drenched with sweat. The sports drinks Dew had brought them had probably saved both she and Brett from complete sunstroke, but she still felt headachy and shaky. Or maybe that was the result of imagining the head of her department laid out on the floor like a carcass that had spent too much time on the spit, and watching his remains being carried out on a stretcher.

Novak. Prick. Asshole. Ignorant political creature that knew absolutely nothing about modern arson investigation. A man that had made his way to the top by trampling everyone in his way. She'd felt nothing at the crime scene when she saw his body. Nothing but the general fuzz of shock. Brett hadn't seemed as though he'd fared much better. But as she peeled off her soaked shirt, jeans, panties, and socks, she shivered. And not from the air conditioning on her skin.

She'd never have to be nervous around him again. Never have to suffer the stares he gave her when he thought she wasn't looking. Never see the look of distaste on his face when he caught sight of her scars. And never was a long fucking time.

He'd been an asshole, but no one deserved to die like that. And the fact he was gone didn't make her happy, didn't fill her with some sense of karmic justice. Instead, she found herself leaning against the stacked washer and dryer with tears sliding down from the corners of her eyes. She defiantly wiped them away, let out a quiet sob, and tossed the soaked clothes into the washer.

She stood there, completely naked, as the washer cycle started. Her eyes darted to the holster sitting atop the washing machine. Taking it off was the first thing she'd done upon entering the laundry room. Until a few days ago, she'd never kept a pistol around her at her own home. Until now, she'd never felt the need. She wondered if, when this was over, she could ditch the new habit.

Luna appeared in the doorway, a squeaky toy gently held between her teeth, tail wagging in slow, tentative strokes. A sad smile breaking across her face, Emy approached the dog, knelt on one knee and hugged her. The dog nudged her throat with a cold, wet nose. After they shared the tableau for a moment, Emy kissed her again on the snout, and headed for the shower. Luna followed.

While she washed the stink of stale sweat from her skin and shampooed her long, black hair, she did her best to chase away images of Novak's face. She needed to focus on the bug. This was an escalation. A huge escalation.

As far as they knew, the bug had never started a fire in daylight. And this attack was very targeted. It was difficult to argue that Novak had been a random victim. No. Their bug watched TV, surfed the local news, or listened to the radio. Had probably heard Novak at one of the many press conferences. A quick internet search would no doubt have led their bug to his address. Or hell, the bug may have even followed him home from work.

They had the security camera files. The techs back at the forensics lab would no doubt be culling through them now, looking for likely suspects. Novak's gated apartment complex would have video of every person entering through the main entrance. All the cars' license plates, faces of their drivers, not to mention the makes and models of the vehicles themselves, would all have been captured. If their bug used the main entrance, they had him on tape. They simply had him.

Dew had mentioned he had a suspect. That meant he had an address, physical description, as well as photos from a driver's license, passport, or some other form of ID. All they had to do was locate him on the surveillance videos, and it would all be a done deal. Dew could arrest his man and Brett could close the case. One more bug locked up and ultimately headed for prison. "Or lethal injection," she said as the water sprayed across her back.

An innocent man and his daughter had burned to death. A civil servant had too. The city AG would push for the death penalty. Emy only wished they could cremate the son of a bitch alive. It was what he deserved.

Emy frowned as she let the cool water soak her hair to wash out the conditioner. Did she really think they'd catch this bug alive? That he'd allow himself to be caught at all? And while the fires at both the shotgun shacks and the Hartman house had used accelerants to start them, the bug hadn't used gasoline or a similar chemical to start the flames in Novak's apartment. No. The Novak fire, as she started to think of it, was different. More, what, targeted? Intense? Directed? The words were close to describing it, but not quite what she wanted. "Controlled," she mumbled.

Yeah. Controlled. How did you set fire to just a bathroom with heat that intense? How come the fire hadn't spread through the apartment and to the entire building? Although Novak lived in a swank complex, any fire of that magnitude would have easily burned through all the construction materials and their flame retardant countermeasures. That kind of heat should have spread through the apartment and adjoining units like a hungry plague, devouring everything in its path. Instead? One room burned with a heat she'd never before seen and nothing else had been touched except by smoke. It made no goddamned sense.

How did the bug do it? A goddamned nuclear flamethrower? But why did the fire go out so easily? Almost as if it had accomplished its mission and fizzled out. "Controlled." She thought of Pyro from the X-Men, how he couldn't start a fire, but could control it, master it, make it do his bidding. But that was in comic books, for Christ's sake, not in the fucking real world. That was impossible. Wasn't it?

The amulet. The fires that always occurred during heatwaves. Dead arson investigators. Mysterious disappearances of suspects. And everything unsolved over the past half century. Probably even longer than that. "Don't forget the symbol," she said to no one.

Ghere, a nephilim of the Sumerian god Gibil. His sigil adorned the sites around the world, the very same one she'd found at the shotgun shacks, the Hartman fire, and in Novak's apartment. In the first two instances, the sigil had been hidden, or at least difficult to find. This last, however, was there for anyone to see. It was almost as if the bug was ready to be caught. Or ready for the public to know who he was.

And what did that mean? The books all said that escalation usually preceded a spree of some sort. Escalation was usually a sign of the bug preparing to self-destruct or that some part of them wanted to get caught. She didn't think the latter was likely. Their bug was too, well, too committed for that. Self-destruction made much more sense. One last glorious fire before going out in a hail of bullets. Death by cop. Or more likely, death by his own fire.

She shivered beneath the warm water's caress. Their bug was different. He worshiped a deity. Each fire seemed like some sort of offering and each fire was larger, more precise, more targeted than the last. "More controlled." And that was the worry.

When a bug escalated, they got careless. They left more and more physical evidence in their haste to bring their life's work to conclusion. But their bug hadn't left anything, no physical evidence apart from the tiny computer they'd found at the Hartman's. Dew had said it was virtually untraceable. She doubted "virtually" entered into the equation. If the bug had left it behind, he'd been sure it couldn't be traced.

They'd have to go through the evidence gathered from the Novak fire to be certain, but she knew they wouldn't find anything. Their bug knew how to program computers, how to build surveillance equipment, and how to spoof internet protocols. And the Novak fire? The heat would have burned away everything. And even if they found his fingerprints at the scene, he'd no doubt already left his old life behind. At that point, it would all be in the hands of Dewhurst and HPD to find him through traditional detective work. BOLOs, person of interest pleas in press conferences, and bank/credit account surveillance would be the only tools left. And if he didn't want to be found, she doubted he would. Not until the next attack.

Emy finished rinsing her hair, turned the faucet to cool the water, and simply stood there. Her skin thanked her for the temperature change, although she shivered anyway. She felt dehydrated and bordering on nauseous. "You're drinking water for the rest of the night," she said. Emy turned around once more to cool herself, and turned off the shower.

While toweling off, she noticed Luna sitting at the threshold of the bathroom door. The dog faced the bedroom, her hackles slightly raised, and her tail straight-out along the floor. "Everything okay, girl?"

The dog's tail swished a single time across the carpet. Emy had seen her do this before, the same night that a burglar had looted the apartment below her.

Emy threw her wet hair into a tight ponytail and picked up the holster sitting on the bathroom counter. She quickly dressed, water from her damp hair immediately turning the collar of her blue t-shirt dark. She thought about putting on a pair of shorts, but chose jeans instead. Although the denim would be that much warmer in the scorching air, they were much more practical. Especially if she ended up crawling around cabinets at the station for files or found herself in the midst of yet another fire site.

After strapping the holster to her belt and putting on a pair of tennis shoes, she was ready. Luna still sat at the threshold, but the hackles on her fur had finally laid down. The dog was more relaxed now. Emy patted her holster as if to ensure the Glock was really there and ready.

"Okay, Luna," she said. The dog's tail rapidly cut across the carpet. "Ready to go?"

At the word "go," the dog sprang up and turned, her jowls unable to hide a doggy grin. She opened her mouth and loosed a happy growl.

"Good girl," Emy said.

The dog followed her into the kitchen. Emy poured dog food into a plastic container, grabbed a few treats, a bone, two dog toys, and stuffed them into her backpack. She even included a pair of poop bags. As she shouldered the backpack, she picked up her phone from the kitchen counter. The display showed two calls, two voicemails. Frowning, she unlocked it.

Brett had called. She listened to the message and her frown deepened.

"Emy, call me back ASAP." Brett's voice sounded out of breath and panicked. "You need to get out of your apartment as fast as you can. Call me from the road."

The message ended. Brett didn't leave any details, probably so he wouldn't panic her, but how could she not panic after hearing that? Emy chose the second message. It was from a number she didn't recognize.

Sirens wailed in the background along with the sounds of shouting people. "Ms. Aninzo," Dew's voice drawled. The detective sounded exhausted and his speech slurred the slightest bit. "A man named Donald Hardy is the bug. I've sent my notes and findings to Mr. Cullum. I'll be back at the station as quickly as I can." In the background, she heard someone telling Dew to get off the phone. The sound of a door slamming shut rattled her eardrums. "Hardy is dangerous, possibly armed, and is now responsible for the deaths of four police officers and three forensics technicians. Be very careful."

The message ended. "Jesus," Emy said. Luna looked up at her, the dog's tail vertical and still, hackles raised. "Okay, girl. We're leaving."

Luna followed her to the entryway. After she leashed the animal and checked the peephole, she unlocked the door, and stepped into the scorching, humid Houston night. Luna led her down the stairs and into the parking lot. The dog stopped at the landing directly in front of her. Emy watched as the mutt's snout nosed the air, sniffing and snorting. Finally, Luna tentatively stepped forward in the direction of her car.

Emy kept one hand on the leash, the other on her holster. "Escalation," she muttered. She didn't know how Hardy had done it, but he'd killed a lot of people this time. And by the sounds of it, all of them cops or police personnel. He could be out here. She was certain he'd been here before. And he'd been in Brett's house. There was no question about it now. The bug had been stalking them.

Novak's death was just the latest proof of that. And if he was killing cops now, no one was safe. Least of all anyone tied to the investigation. Bryan's face flitted across her mind. "Oh, shit." She hurried her steps to the car, Luna picking up speed to stay ahead of her. Before unlocking the vehicle, she checked the backseat. Empty. She glared at the trunk before leading Luna to it. The dog sniffed the trunk, paused, and looked up at her. "Good girl," she said.

She loaded Luna in the backseat and tossed her backpack in the passenger side. As soon as she sat in the car, she locked the doors and pulled her holster from her belt laying it next to the backpack. She wasn't giving anyone a chance to get her. If they tried to get in, they'd have to break a car window. With her pistol within reach, she'd be able to at least get a shot off before they had a chance to do much more than grab at her. And the 90lbs of protective dog in the backseat wouldn't hurt either.

Before putting the car in gear, she called Bryan's cell phone. The phone rang as she pulled out of the apartment complex parking lot, her eyes swiveling from side to side looking for someone watching her. The parking lot was empty of people, as was the sidewalk outside, but it didn't make her feel any better. Luna growled low in her throat once. Emy stopped at the precipice to the street, her eyes fixed on the alley in front of her. She squinted into the new night, wishing there was a streetlamp. For a moment, she was certain she saw the shadow of a man deep in the alley's bowels.

"Emy?" Bryan said over the car speakers.

She jerked at the sound of his voice. "Bryan. Thank Christ. Where are you?"

"At the Menil," he said. "We got a new—"

"You watched the news at all?"

He paused. "No. I've been setting up a new exhibit."

Emy swallowed hard. "Bryan? The bug killed my boss. And he's killed some cops."

"Jesus," Bryan wheezed.

"Yeah, so—"

"Are you okay?" he asked.

She nodded to herself. "I'm fine. I'm leaving my apartment and heading for the Forensics Institute."

"Good," he said.

"I think he's targeting people involved in the investigation," she said. "That means you're in the crosshairs too."

"What?"

"Look. I want you to get in your car and meet me at the Institute. Do not go home. Understand?"

"Wait," Bryan said. "I don't understand. Why should I—"

"Just do it. Please? For me?"

He paused for a moment. "Won't I be safer here? I mean, we have security—"

"Please! Just do it!"

Another pause. She could almost see Bryan frowning. "Okay," he said. "I'll pack up and meet you there."

A surge of relief spread through her. "Thank you. Call me when you get there and I'll buzz you in."

"Will do." He cleared his throat. "Are you okay?"

"I'm—" She shook her head. "I'll be better when I know you're safe," she said. "Get moving. I'm on my way there now."

"Will do," he said. "Drive safe."

"You too." The call disconnected.

As she drove to the institute, she called Brett. Instead of hello, his first words were "Where the fuck are you?"

"Heading to the institute," she said. "What's the situation?"

"The cops went to the bug's house. It exploded. Dewhurst was hurt, but he's alive."

"Fuck me," she said. "He left me a message."

"Well, I talked to him," Brett said. "The guy's name is Donald Hardy. Wealthy. Well-educated. And he's a goddamned ghost. Slight build, about 5'10, and hairless."

Emy cocked an eyebrow. "Hairless?"

"That's what Dewhurst said. Was there a uni outside your apartment?"

"No," Emy said. "I didn't see one."

"Fuck," Brett hissed. "Lee said there's one outside our house."

"He's not with you?"

Brett sighed. "No. He's not. Long story. Look, get here ASAP."

"Luna and I will be there soon."

"Thank Christ," Brett said with a laugh. "You're bringing your security blanket with you. Good plan."

Emy smiled despite the unease shaking her core. "Give me ten minutes and I'll be there."

"Be careful, Emy."

"I am," she said. Brett ended the call.

The next light turned red, bringing her to a halt. She glanced at the car next to her and saw a teenage girl. She relaxed and checked the rearview. There was a car behind her, but it was impossible to make out the driver with the headlights blinding her. Paranoia. Their bug finally had a name and she had a physical description. And now she'd expect to see him everywhere she looked. She only hoped he wasn't actually following her.

Chapter 56

A janitor's job was to sweep up after people, keep a building clean and tidy. That meant dealing with men that couldn't aim their dicks when they were peeing, wiped shit on the toilet seats, and women who stuffed the garbage with bloody maxi-pads. He'd long ago gotten used to the stench, the awful messes, and the general disregard for sanitary conditions that most humans had, at least when it was a public building. David Brown was more and more convinced that public buildings were the genesis of all disease outbreaks.

The office park, more of a strip-mall with a tin roof, substandard electrical systems, and air conditioning that always seemed on the fritz, was his second home. The building's tenants included an independent insurance company, a vape store, a bail bondsman, and a computer startup that never seemed to have anyone in it. His job? Clean the toilets, vacuum the floors, replace burned out light bulbs, and do his best to keep the offices looking clean and tidy.

It was a lot better than working at the courthouse where the accused, the tax payers, and the cops seemed to take great delight in making as much of a mess as possible. Fuck that job. The moment he'd had a chance to clean a "private" building, he'd jumped at it. And now he had a night shift to himself, good pay, and a good relationship with the building owner. Hell, the guy even shared some weed with him now and then.

He'd already finished the insurance office. The bail bonds company never really closed, so he wouldn't get in there until after midnight. Besides, he could duck into the unused geek nest, have a toke, a smoke, and wipe the dust away. Maybe then he'd go to the vape store at the end of the building and clean them as well.

He used the master key and opened the offices of SiliconGlenn, LLC. The logo, a hideous gray, metallic valley with the letters S and G wrapped around one another in an almost indecipherable squiggle, stared at him from the front desk credenza. He locked the door behind him and walked past the unopened mail that had piled up by the mail slot. The white plastic bin had overflowed with direct mail catalogs, credit card offers, and nondescript envelopes that were probably from the insurance company just four doors down.

David sighed and lifted the heavy bin to the credenza. He carefully emptied it, stacking up the mail as best he could, making a mental note to put the empty bin back in its place after he swept the floor. Not that anyone ever seemed to be here.

Three computer desks sat unused beyond the credenza. Each had a single-unit computer, one of those i-things, but he'd never seen them powered on, let alone someone working at them. Weren't those computer folks supposed to work all hours of the night?

David pulled his broom from the wheeled garbage bin, sighed, and began sweeping the foyer. He hummed to himself until he heard a sound coming from the main office area. He stopped in mid-sweep, head cocked like a dog listening to something humans couldn't hear. The sound came again, a chirruping beep, like a computer starting up or maybe one of those power alert systems.

Carrying the broom in one hand, he walked to the workstations. A red light blinked beneath the nearest desk. "What the hell?" He knelt down and looked at the underside of the desk. Wires connected several small bundles taped to the surface. A cell-phone, plugged into a charger and to a power strip, blinked with a red light. It chirped again. David Brown heard a solenoid click and then, he heard nothing at all.

The offices of SiliconGlenn exploded in a fireball that lit up the night sky. The shockwave shattered the sheetrock walls separating the offices from one another, ripped off the roof, and annihilated the three employees working at the bail bond company. Across the city, other small offices detonated in the same fashion. The "becoming" was at hand.

Chapter 57

Emy reached the Forensics Institute in fifteen minutes. Traffic was relatively sparse, but it seemed as though she caught every red light on her journey. She passed the occasional abandoned car, its hood up in the air with clouds of white steam rising from the radiator. As long as the heat continued, cars would keep dying in the throes of rush hour traffic. She was sure the wrecker companies were doing a booming business.

She held her card to the parking garage attendant, he waved her in, and she found a spot next to Brett. Instead of turning off the ignition, she grabbed her pack, stepped into the garage's heat, and opened the rear driver-side door. Luna climbed out of the backseat and sat at attention. Once she was sure she had everything, she turned off the ignition, set the alarm, and breathed deep. The parking garage was enclosed enough that the super-heated air seemed to scorch her lungs. Luna, who rarely panted, was already drooling from her jowls. Emy smirked at the dog. "Let's go."

With Luna by her side, she entered the building and headed to the elevator. Two security guards stared at her, the dog, and then back to her. She produced her badge and they confirmed her identity. After that, she was home free to head to her cube.

Luna paused every few steps to grab a quick sniff. Emy didn't notice. She led the dog through the maze of cubes to Brett's. Her boss had a headset on and was speaking fast.

"Arnold? I'm doing what I can here. I don't have a lot of personnel!" He swiveled in his chair and held a hand in the air. "Yeah, I know. Believe me.

How many units are out now?" Brett's eyes widened. "Shit. How many more available?" Brett listened and shook his head. "We're fucked. Call in what you can, man. I'll do the same. Bye."

He pulled off the headset and sighed. Luna crept forward and put her head on his knee. Brett smiled at her and rubbed her chin.

"What's going on?" Emy asked.

"Let me guess. You didn't listen to the radio on your way here."

She shook her head. "No, I didn't."

Brett raised Luna's chin and smiled at the dog as he scratched behind her ears. Luna was in doggy heaven. "Well, grab your shit and let's head to the war room."

"War room?"

"Yeah," Brett said. He loosed another sigh and rose from his chair after patting Luna on the head. "The conference room. I have some things set up in there for us."

"Um, okay."

She followed Brett back through the cube maze and to the conference room. The large projector displayed feeds from three local news stations. Two pitchers of ice water, runners of condensation gathered around their surfaces like silver streams, sat on a tray along with two glasses.

After closing the door, Emy let Luna off the leash. The dog looked up at her expectantly before taking a slow walk around the table and lying down in a corner.

Brett laughed. "My Papillon's would be tearing through this place like three year olds on meth. Not her, though."

Emy placed her pack on the table and looked up at the screen. Her mouth dropped open. The three feeds showed fires at three different sites. The news tickers across the bottom all reported explosions around the city. So far the body count was unknown because the fire department didn't have enough trucks to battle the blazes. Over a dozen fires now.

"Holy shit," Emy said. "How the fuck is he doing this?"

"You're assuming it's the bug."

"Who else?" Emy asked.

"How he's doing it?" Her boss growled and took a seat. "That is a very good question," Brett said. "Arnold says each blaze started with either incendiary or explosive devices. It's a fucking firestorm out there."

Emy slowly sat in the chair closest to Luna. "Boss? What do we do?"

He shook his head. "I don't know." He tented his hands on the table, eyes fixed on the screen. "I just don't fucking know."

"There has to be more to this," Emy said. "I mean why now? Why's he doing this now?"

"I don't know," Brett said. "Maybe because Dewhurst found him out?"

"No," Emy said. "This took preparation. Twelve different fires so far? He had to plan this out in advance. Way in advance."

"Maybe," Brett said. "Fucker has been one step ahead of us the entire time. Now he's so far in front, I don't know that we'll catch him."

Emy tapped a finger on the table. The bug was starting his end game, whatever that was. Hardy had to have a plan. If he wanted to blow something up, he could have managed larger buildings, more public ones, where the body count would be catastrophic. By the looks of the locations listed on the tv screens, he had mainly targeted strip malls and the occasional small office building. The sun was down. Most of the locations would be vacant of people, save for maybe janitorial staff or the occasional dedicated wage-slave. So why? Why those targets?

She opened her laptop and pulled up a map of Houston. She connected to the city's emergency database and pulled up the addresses of the buildings. For each one, she laid a red virtual pin on the map. She felt Brett eyeing her while she did this, certain he was going to ask a question. But she continued placing the pins. As she did, her stomach sank. "Fuck me," she said.

"What?"

She connected her laptop to the projector. The feeds from the television screens disappeared, replaced by the map she'd laid out. Brett stared at it. "Those sites form a cluster." He raised a finger and pointed toward the lower quadrant. "Except those."

"No," Emy said. She pulled up the virtual marker and began connecting the dots. With each connection, Brett's frown increased. Before she'd even finished drawing the lines, he was clucking his tongue.

Brett pounded a fist on the table. "You have to be fucking kidding me."

The map was now covered with lines. East Houston, the least wealthy portion of town, had the most dots, but they formed two lines meeting and then swaying outward. The other sites, north, south, and west, formed a crude 3/4 circle completed by one eastern dot.

"The sigil," Brett breathed.

"Apart from that section in midtown, the fires are everywhere. But that one's a blank."

"So far, you mean," Brett said. "Man, this shitbag is pulling out all the stops."

"Got that right," she said. "The only question is how many more fires are there going to be? Is that circle going to tighten up, look more like the outer ring, or is it done now that he's left his mark?"

"Fuck, fuck, fuck!" Brett took one last look at the map before turning his attention back to Emy. "Every single HFD firetruck is out there. We have first responders, both public and private, heading to every site. There's not going to be anyone left to stop the blazes if this continues."

"Fire chief calling in for help from Montgomery and Fort Bend?" The two counties were the largest outside of Harris, where Houston was.

Brett nodded. "They're sending everything they can. Even Galveston county is sending help. But they're going to take at least another thirty minutes to arrive. In the meantime, we're screwed."

She pulled out her phone and put it on the table. No messages. She frowned. "Bryan is supposed to come here. I hope that's okay."

"It's fine. Lee skedaddled and took the dogs to a friend's house. I think Dew was right. We're in the firing line on this one." He paused for a moment and loosed a husky chuckle. "Pardon the pun."

Emy pulled up the image of the sigil from Novak's apartment. She zoomed in on the map and quickly put down a series of blue dots. After a few minutes, the shape on the map became more distinct. "I think those are our likely targets," she said and shivered. One of the areas she'd marked contained three section 8 apartment buildings. Section 8 housing was for low income residents and families, those that lived hand-to-mouth well below the city's median income.

"What's the Mayor saying?" Emy asked.

"She hasn't held a press conference yet," Brett said. "I think she's most likely freaking the fuck out like the rest of us."

Emy tried to push away another shiver as her phone dinged with a message. Brett's phone chirped a second later. They looked at the message and then at one another.

"National Guard? Are they serious?" Emy asked.

"Any port in a storm," Brett said. "You know damned well we're going to have looters too."

Emy sighed. The message had been from the emergency system used by civil servants in law enforcement. "Guess we'll have our own marching orders soon."

"Arnold wants us to stay put for now." Arnold, the HFD Fire Chief, no doubt had his hands full. "Although we might get drafted to help out as first responders."

Emy nodded. She checked the time and frowned. Bryan should have reached the Institute by now. She looked through her address book, found his number, and touched it to call. The phone rang three times before going to voice mail. Her frown deepened. "He's not answering. He sent the call to voicemail."

"Maybe he's driving," Brett said. "I'll bet traffic is a zoo right now."

"Not from midtown," she said. "That area is fire free."

"Where was he?"

"The Menil," Emy said. "He was working on some new exhibit. I don't think—" She stopped in mid-sentence and looked back up at the map.

"You don't think what?" Brett asked.

Cold phantom hands squeezed at her soul. "Shit," she breathed.

"What?"

She slowly raised a hand and pointed at the sigil. "With the exception of the far west dot, all of them are away from mid-town."

"So?" Brett said.

Emy gulped. "Where's the HMNS?"

Brett blinked at her and looked back at the map. "Oh, fuck," Brett said. "You don't think he'd—"

"Yes," Emy said in a dead voice. "I think he's going to try and get the amulet."

Her phone buzzed again. She lifted it, but already knew the text wasn't from Bryan. It was from Bryan's phone, but she knew it wasn't him.

"Museum. Now. If you want him to live."

She froze for a moment, eyes glued to the screen.

"What is it?" Brett asked.

"He's got Bryan."

Chapter 58

The Houston Museum of Natural Science was closed. Had been for hours. With the exception of the janitorial staff, a few personnel still working in the basement, and the security guards, the large building was a tomb.

P had hacked the security system months ago so he could keep watch on the comings and goings after it closed. He knew everyone's routine. He knew which guards would be on duty, which of them had had a former career in law enforcement (two), and the ones that were fat, slovenly, and likely to cave when threatened. Which was the rest of them.

Even the academics in the basement were accounted for. The curator for the Mesopotamian exhibit was one of the few still in the building, locked in his office as usual. The guy never seemed to sleep. "You'll sleep forever after tonight," P said to himself.

He had parked the stolen van in a handicapped space inside the parking garage using a stolen keycard. Using a cellular internet connection, he monitored the security cams from the laptop. He'd already spoofed the security station so their monitors showed the same 5 seconds of empty footage over and over again. The guards would have no clue he was in the building until it was too late. P grinned.

He turned slightly and glanced behind him. Bryan, the bitch's fuck buddy, lay unconscious in the van's bed. Capturing him had been easy. P had simply waited until the first city fires started and then headed to the Menil where he knew the curator would be. He'd parked the van next to the man's car and kept his eyes on the Menil's staff exit. He didn't have to wait long.

Bryan walked out of the museum in a bit of a hurry, his valise slapping the side of his leg. He made a beeline for his car, digging into his pants pockets for his keys. He didn't even notice P crouching at the rear of his vehicle. When Bryan slipped the key into the lock, P pounced on him, hitting him in the back of the head with a blackjack. The curator fell to the concrete with a thump. Smiling, P had dragged the man across the concrete and to the van's rear door.

As soon as he put the unconscious man inside, he followed suit and closed the doors. Zip tying both his hands and feet had taken seconds, as did placing the gag. Just to make sure he stayed out, P had doused the rag with chloroform. Failing that, he always had the taser. Turning in his seat and hitting the guy with electric shocks would be easy even if he was driving. Planning ahead had once again paid off.

The canisters of fuel lining the van's sides made for a nice channel to keep Bryan's body from rolling across the floor as P took the turns necessary to reach the HMNS. The last thing he needed was to have the asshole hit the van's wall and start bleeding all over the place. He was in a stolen vehicle, and the fake plates would help get him past a cop, but if someone noticed blood spilling out of the van's rear doors, it might be a bit of a problem.

The *becoming* was happening. Every minute or two, he picked another burner cell from his bag and sent a text. Somewhere in Houston, another building blew up. The cops, the fire department, first responders, everyone would be rushing to his distractions, doing their best to contain the damage and save buildings and people caught in the blazes. It was perfect.

P made one last check of the cams to ensure everyone was where they were supposed to be, grabbed his two backpacks, and left the van. He walked to the staff entrance from the parking garage and into the museum. The sensors on the security guard console had already been turned off. A keycard swipe later, he was inside the hallway leading to the main desk.

A security guard, alerted by the closing door and P's footfalls, appeared in the hallway. The fat man's uniform barely held his bulk, the buttons down the front straining to keep his gut from falling out. P smiled at him and raised his hand as if in greeting. The security guard's mouth fell open in surprise just before a silenced 9mm round struck him in the forehead. He crumpled to the floor. P walked past him without even looking down.

He turned the corner just as the other security guard was raising himself from his chair. Before he managed to do more than get his legs underneath him, P fired again and put him down for good. He grinned. No alarms. No alerts. And no one left to impede his progress. For now, at least.

P put down his packs and dragged both bodies behind the main desk credenza. Cramming them beneath the opening wasn't too difficult, although he couldn't do much about the smudges of blood left in the hallway. Fortunately, the sub-sonic round had done little more than penetrate the guard's cranium and bounce around until his brains probably looked like porridge. The blood smear was faint and you couldn't even see it unless you walked into the employee entrance hallway. He felt Ghere smile in his mind.

He glanced up at the balcony separating the open lobby from the second floor exhibit hall. Up there, his prize waited. His salvation. His becoming. He only had a few more things to take care of to make sure he wasn't interrupted, and then he could become.

Bryan's phone chirped in his pocket. P pulled it out, saw who the call was from, and sent it to voicemail. He then brought up the text message app, typed in a message, and lay it on the counter. He silenced the museum phones, making sure they wouldn't make a sound if someone called. The last thing he needed was a curious janitor hearing the security phone ring and ring and ring without anyone picking it up. Once that was done, he opened one of the backpacks and hurriedly affixed a small block of homemade C-4 beneath the desk. He plugged in the cellphone detonator, armed it, and stepped back to admire his work.

The two security guard corpses were crammed so far beneath the desk that they effectively hid the bomb. Even if someone discovered them, the chances of them finding the relatively small brick were pretty slim. Besides, this wasn't going to take long.

He read the message on the phone once more, making sure it was how he wanted it, and clicked send. He tapped his watch and started the timer app. He had fifteen minutes, maybe twenty, before that Aninzo bitch showed up. P picked up two more packages from the pack, headed to the front entrance, and carefully placed one at each door with adhesive. When he tapped the arming buttons, red lasers created a nearly invisible line before each door. When someone opened the doors to step through, they'd be flattened by the homemade claymore. Ghere laughed in his mind.

Blood and fire. That's what it would take to become. He only wished he could watch it all unfold, be there when whomever Aninzo called showed up to stop him. With the fires and explosions rattling the city, all the first responders on the payroll, and some from neighboring counties, would be too busy to assist. P thought it likely only Aninzo and Cullum would show up. Which was exactly how he wanted it.

The explosion at his home more than likely killed that detective. Dewhurst. P smirked. The bastard had been blown to bits by that bomb. Oh, how he wished he could have seen the house shatter, debris flying in the air, hopefully with a body part or two for good measure. Blood and fire. That was all he needed.

He ran back to the security desk, zipped up the remaining backpack, and brought up the security console. Sure enough, the lazy guards had left it unlocked. He cycled the security system to lock the basement office doors. He couldn't do anything about the emergency exits, but it wouldn't matter. As long as no one could get upstairs to interrupt him, they were free to file out of the building two by two. It wouldn't save them. Nothing would save them. The becoming was at hand.

Ghere gibbered in his mind, ancient greasy syllables echoing in his skull. They had a sing-song cadence and quieted the butterflies in his stomach. He wasn't worried, just excited. Ghere's constant babble kept him from shivering out of his skin. The quiet, calming sound focused his mind.

P headed to the stairs leading to the second floor. He'd skirt through the gem exhibit and make his way to the amulet. The moment he took it from the glass case, there would be little anyone could do to stop him. But first, he needed to wait for his prey to step into the trap.

Chapter 59

H e'd fought the EMTs. He'd fought the doctors. He'd pulled every single excuse from his bag of tricks, but they still wanted to keep him for observation. Until, that was, his phone had exploded with text messages and automated phone calls. All personnel were to report in for instructions. And the chief didn't give a rat's ass if you were off-duty.

Dewhurst stood from the ER table, put on his shirt, and attached his holster to his belt. One of his doctors saw him leaving and moved to stop him. The look on Dew's face had been all that was needed to make the man get out of his way.

He still couldn't quite see straight. They'd said he had a bad concussion. No, shit. He didn't need a fucking medical degree to know that. The shock-wave from the explosion had been enough to slam him into the car. His brain? Yeah, that slammed against the inside of his skull. It was enough to give you double vision, one hell of a headache, and possible brain damage. Fortunately, the double vision had faded. Mostly.

Dew had no car. His own was still at the Hardy site, covered in dents, debris, and spiderwebbed, shattered glass. The first thing he needed was a ride. And since the alert had just gone out, he'd have to hurry to find a uni still at the hospital. Ben Taub wasn't too far away from the station. All he needed was five minutes in a patrol car and he'd be there.

He walked through the hallway and through the ER's wide automated doors. The humid, heat saturated air hit him like a hammer. Dew winced as another bolt of pain flashed across his skull. His vision wavered for a moment, but he instantly saw what he was looking for.

A patrol car. A uni was hurrying toward it, one hand held against his billy club to keep it from slapping his leg.

"Hey!" Dew yelled. "Officer!"

The man slowed his pace, and turned to face Dew. "What?"

Fighting the nausea creeping into his stomach, Dew pulled his badge from his coat. "I need a ride to the station."

The cop waited until Dew came close enough for him to read the badge. "Be my guest, Detective."

The cop unlocked the doors and Dew got into the passenger seat. After he belted in, the officer drove the patrol car out of the parking lot and onto Main. Dew leaned back in the seat as a wave of exhaustion rolled over him. The radio squawked again and again as other patrol cars called in for instructions or gave their location. "Any idea what's going on?"

The cop hissed. "More fires than you'd believe, sir."

Suddenly Dew didn't feel tired anymore. His eyes snapped open and he willed away the double vision. "Where?"

"All over the place. East Houston is one big fire. Last count was 15." The officer grunted. "They only had 12 until a few minutes ago."

"Goddammit!" Dew yelled and winced from another bolt of pain.

"Sir?"

"Just keep driving," Dew said.

The bug. Hardy. He'd boobytrapped his house. He'd probably spent days or even weeks prepping these other fires. What did he use? Household chemicals? Over the counter accelerants? It didn't matter. After Dew put a bullet between his eyes, he could figure out how the insane fucker had done it.

How many were dead now? How many had died in the manufactured furnaces that used to be houses, offices, or large buildings? How many first responders would perish due to heat or smoke inhalation? Dew clenched his fists.

The ringing in his ears had subsided since the house had first blown up, but the annoying whine and whistle was still there, just muted. So when his phone rang, he wasn't sure if it was just his imagination. Dew put his hand on his pocket and felt the phone's vibration. "Shit," he mumbled. He pulled out the phone and stared at the screen, glaring at it to keep his eyes focused. The screen said "E Aninzo."

Dew accepted the call, cranked up the volume, and put the phone to his ear. "Ms. Aninzo?"

Despite his diminished hearing, the sounds of a fast moving car filled the background. "Detective. We have a serious problem. Our bug is at the museum."

"Museum?" Dew asked. What museum? Did she mean— Aninzo kept talking, but Dew lost the words. "Emy! Slow down," he said. "Start again."

Her monstrous sigh filled his ears. "Hardy has my friend Bryan. They're at the museum. We think he's going after Gibil's amulet."

"Gibil's amulet?" Dew felt stupid. His thoughts couldn't quite connect to one another. He shook his head, hard, and another flash of pain wiped away the confusion. "Where are you?" he asked.

"On our way to the museum. We tried calling the switchboard, but no one is answering."

Dew gritted his teeth. "Get there. Wait outside. Do not go in, understand?"

"But, he's got Bryan!" she yelled.

The desperation in her voice made him feel like a callous asshole for what he was about to say. "Emy. Listen to me. Bryan is either already dead, or he's not. But if you don't wait for me, Hardy's going to kill you both. Is that understood?"

Emy sobbed through the line and went silent. She loosed a shuddering breath, no doubt on the verge of tears, and simply said "Understood."

"Good," Dew said. "Park out front. We'll meet you there as quickly as we can."

"Hurry," Emy said and the line disconnected.

Dew stared at his phone for a moment. If Hardy was at the museum, and if he'd had time to prepare, just getting inside was going to be a problem. "Officer?" he said.

"Sir?"

"We're not going to the station."

The officer swung his head to glance briefly at Dew. "Sir, we've been ordered to—"

"I don't give a fuck what we were ordered to do!" Dew shouted. "I know where the perp is. Head to the Museum of Natural Science."

The officer kept his eyes on the road. "I'm not getting fired for this, sir."

"No," Dew chuckled. "You're going to be a goddamned hero. Put on the lights. Only use the siren if you have to. You have a vest in the trunk?"

"Yes, sir. And a spare shotgun."

"Good. Now. Get there. Fast."

Chapter 60

The air was warmer than ever. In all her years in Houston, the night had never been so hot. It was as if the summer sun was hiding behind the rising moon, using it as a shield while it burned away the Earth.

Brett had parked his car in the tow-away zone in front of the museum. Upon arrival, he'd flipped on the hazards, unbuckled, and pulled his Glock. Emy had done the same before letting Luna out of the backseat. The dog's tail had wagged, but she'd already begun to pant in the heat.

"Should have left the dog," Brett said.

Emy said nothing. When they'd packed up at the conference room, grabbing a few supplies before stuffing them into her backpack, Luna had looked at her with an expectant doggy grin. She couldn't leave her in the office and she sure as shit wasn't taking the time to drop her back off at the house. So now the dog was along for the ride. For better or worse.

They stood before the museum's main entrance, the wan moonlight combining with the red glare of distant fires to sparkle on the bronze bust of the sun standing just meters away from the HMNS entrance. With her pistol hanging at her side, she felt more and more as though reality had somehow disappeared leaving the three of them staring into an abyss of a building.

The museum was darker than she'd ever seen it. The warm, inviting lights that usually shined down from the lobby's high ceiling were off, or at least dimmed. Through the windows she could see the ticket vending cubicles as well as the information and security desks. She expected the rest of the cubes to be empty, but not the security desk. No one was there.

Brett took a few steps toward the entrance, his weapon shaking slightly in his hands. "I don't see anyone," he said in a low voice.

"Me neither," Emy said. She followed him up the steps until they were a mere meter from the glass doors. From their vantage point, they both saw the lights on the second floor. The exhibit hall was brightly lit as if waiting for excited children and curious adults. "He's up there," Emy said.

Brett nodded. "Goddammit, Dewhurst. Get here already."

A minute passed. Then another. The sounds of distant sirens filled the night air. If there were any patrol cars, ambulances, or firetrucks that weren't already on their way to the fire sites, they would be soon. And here they were, attempting their own rescue and prevent their own blaze. Hardy. The bug.

"You think the entire building is empty?"

Emy shook her head. "No. He's no doubt got the security guards tied up."

"Or he killed them," Brett said in a monotone.

"Or that." Emy wished Bryan were here. No, that wasn't right. She wished she hadn't told him to leave the Menil and join her at the institute. Then he might have been safe. Instead, he was either trapped inside the museum with that lunatic or dead. She wiped a nervous tear from her eye. "Try calling the switchboard again," she said.

Brett pulled out his phone and did just that. Emy shut out the sound of her own breathing and Luna's panting to try and hear any phones ringing. Nothing. The museum was an island of solitude, somehow disconnected from normalcy and expectation.

Luna growled low in her throat. Emy glanced at the dog and followed her gaze. The dog's tail was straight up in the air, hackles raised on her back, jowls lifted exposing her sharp, powerful canines. Luna's snout pointed at the path leading to the parking garage. Emy unclipped the leash and put it in her pocket. "What is it, girl?" The dog growled again and took a few steps down the path. "No, Luna. Stay." The dog turned and looked at her, whined twice, and turned back to the path.

Brett blinked. "I somehow get the feeling she knows something we don't."

Emy glanced upward to the top of the parking garage and lowered her eyes. "You think he has the garage wired?"

"Possible," Brett said. He thought for a moment. "Hey, there's an employee entrance connected to the garage, isn't there?"

"Yeah," Emy said. "It's how Seamus took us to the garage when we invited him to dinner."

A smile tugged at the corners of Brett's mouth. "Maybe that's how Hardy got in." He glanced back at the museum entrance and nodded to it. "Do you think that asshole could see us if we went through there?"

Emy nodded. "Yeah. I do."

"So he could pick us off. Or just drop a pack of explosives in front of us."

"Right," Emy said. Luna looked back at her as if to ask what the problem was. "I think maybe Luna has the right idea."

Brett pulled out his phone, typed on the keypad, and sent a message. A few seconds later, the phone beeped. "Okay, I told Dew to meet us in the parking garage."

"He'll love that," Emy said. "Luna?" The dog looked at her with a doggy grin. "Let's go."

The dog immediately sprang forward, loping more than running, to the parking garage side door. Once she reached it, she sat on her haunches. Emy pushed on the door, but nothing happened. She swiveled the door knob, but it didn't move. "Locked."

"Get your dog and stand back."

Emy walked a meter away and clapped her hands. Luna left the door and stood beside her master. "What are you going to—"

Brett raised his booted foot and kicked the doorknob straight on. Something in the mechanism cracked. He tried to push the door again, but nothing happened. "Okay. Fuck this. We're going up the ramp."

The three of them ran around the building and to the parking lot's vehicle entrance. The large, chainlink gate was up, which didn't make sense. She was fairly sure that was unusual this late at night. Upon reaching the automated gate, she looked up and froze. "Brett?"

He stopped too. "What?"

Emy raised a hand and pointed. A black security camera with a blinking red light on its side pointed directly at them. "You think he's watching us?"

"Shit," Brett said and sighed. "To be honest, I think he's been watching us this whole time."

"Dammit. Whole fucking garage could be a booby trap," Emy said.

"Could be," Brett said. He studied the sides of the gates as well as the walls. The ingress and egress ramps separated a few meters from the parking gate, forming a fork. "All roads lead to Rome," he said.

"What?"

"Nothing," Brett said. "I don't see anything that looks like a bomb."

"Neither do I." Luna whined again and walked a few steps up the ramp. Emy exhaled a shuddering breath. "Okay, girl. Let's go."

That phrase was one Luna knew well. It either meant a walk, a potty break, a ride in the car, or playtime. Emy didn't know which one the dog thought they were going to do, but it didn't matter. Luna loped up the ramp, her nose staying a few centimeters above the concrete, sniffing like a bellows.

Emy and Brett followed, the pair of them sweating freely now. The garage air was so stifling, they might as well have been trapped in a wet sauna. As soon as they reached the top of the ramp, the handicapped parking spots came into view. A white van sat in the nearest spot. The engine was still ticking, cooling down.

Luna approached the vehicle slowly, her nose alternately rising to sniff the air and lowering to the concrete. Her tail wagged twice. She turned and stared at Emy.

"What is it?"

The dog woofed once and touched the door with her snout.

Emy approached the van when her phone chirped, the loud noise stopping her in her tracks. She pulled out the phone and stared at the screen. Another text from Bryan's phone, although she knew damned well he hadn't sent it.

"I wouldn't do that if I were you," the text said.

"Don't move," she said aloud. Brett stared at her but said nothing. "I think he has the van rigged."

"Oh, good," Brett said. "He say that in the text?"

"I'd say that was the gist, yes."

"Great." He searched the wall and found what he was looking for. "There's the employee entrance."

"Where?" Emy said and turned. Brett pointed at it. She followed his gaze and found it. A second later, the glowing red light on the card reader by the door went dark. Her phone chirped again. She stared at the words and a shiver ran down her back. "He's leading us in."

"I'm not getting a good feeling about this," Brett said.

She glanced at him. "If you want to stay—"

"No," he said. "You're not going in there alone. But we should wait for Dew."

A second later, her phone lit up with another message. "Come. Now."

She wiped a sheen of sweat from her forehead. "I can't wait for him," she said and walked to the security door. Luna left her station by the van and followed her master.

"Well, fuck," Brett said. "Guess it's time to meet the bug."

Emy pulled on the handle and the door opened. Luna sniffed the air, growled, and stepped into the darkened hallway. Brett and Emy followed.

Chapter 61

The radio had squawked and raged the entire way to the museum. There were so many emergency personnel on every channel that it was damned near impossible to communicate. Dispatch was overwhelmed with instructions, 911 was completely out of service due to the volume of calls, and there was no one left to send in any case. The National Guard was being dispatched because of reports of looting. Police and news station choppers buzzed through the night, their searchlights constantly swinging back and forth over the city.

Midtown had no fires, so of course it was the part of town receiving the least notice from anyone. When the looting started down here, it was going to be impossible to stop. Before long, there might be tanks in the goddamned streets.

Dew pulled the spare shotgun from the trunk, threw the kevlar vest to the patrolman, loaded his pockets with spare shells, checked his pistol mag, and slammed down the trunk. The officer held his shotgun in both hands and looked at Dew expectantly.

He'd tried to call in their position three times, but the radio chatter made that impossible. There would be no backup for this little mission. No backup and no EMTs when the shit went down. They were on their own. Dew checked his ragtag collection of supplies once more, racked the slide on the short barreled pump-action shotgun, and pointed at the museum entrance.

Emy had sent him a text telling him they had gone in through the garage. As he stared at the entrance, he thought he understood why. Even from here he could see a camera trained on the doors, its red light blinking like a cyclops with dust in its eye. He ground his teeth and started walking, the officer close behind him.

The patrolman had obviously never learned how to step quiet. His footfalls echoed softly as they approached the corner where the museum's outer wall and the parking garage met. Not that it mattered. Hardy knew they were there. The only question was whether or not he'd be at the entrance to greet them. Dew frowned and lifted his gaze to the top of the parking garage, eyes searching for a silhouette. He saw nothing, but felt as though they were being watched. Probably the damned camera, he thought.

"You have a plan, sir?"

Dew swung his eyes back to the entrance. His head still hurt and the cuts on his face itched. Every bone in his body ached and his skin felt too hot. Considering the temperature, that was hardly a surprise. "Through the front door," he said softly. The officer changed his grip on the shotgun and nodded. "If you see someone, challenge them. If they don't answer, shoot at them, but don't shoot them."

"At them?" the officer said. "You kidding?"

"There are two Arson investigators in there, officer." Dew gestured to the doors. "Friends of mine, you might say. And I don't want them getting shot."

"Oh. But what about the perp?"

Dew shrugged. "He's pale, about five-ten and batshit crazy. Will probably be wearing something heavy and warm."

"What?"

Dew chuckled. "I know it doesn't make sense. Just keep it in mind."

"Yes, sir," the patrolman said.

Dewhurst squinted, willing his eyes to quit blurring and focus. "Let's go," he said and started up the steps to the landing. When they were a meter from the doors, Dew stopped. He carefully studied the lobby, looking for anything out of the ordinary. The security desk was empty. No janitorial staff, no curators, and, so far, no bodies. He'd half expected to see Emy's and Brett's corpses lying in a pool of fire on the marble floor. Instead, the lobby was dimly lit and completely empty of any human presence. But the second floor wasn't.

Although he couldn't make out any details, much less see the exhibit hall itself, the ambient light from the balcony glowed and flickered. "You know the museum layout?"

"Yes, sir," the officer said. "The stairs are inside the first floor exhibit hall. And the elevator is in the same place."

Dew chuckled. "You have children, officer?"

"Yes, sir," he said. "I've seen every inch of this place at least a dozen times."

"Good," Dew said. He tried the door handle. As expected, it was locked. "So much for the easy way in." He raised the shotgun and slammed it into the glass. The strong pane spiderwebbed with cracks, but didn't shatter. "Shit." He felt a wave of vertigo and nearly vomited. He stumbled backward and caught himself before falling down the steps.

The officer put a hand on his arm to steady him. "You okay, sir?"

"Sorry," Dew said. "Bit of a concussion."

"Dammit, I knew you looked a little too pale."

"Don't worry about it," Dew said. He stepped forward to try again and the officer held out an arm.

"Let me handle it, sir."

"Thank you," Dew said.

The officer nodded to him and walked to the door. He reared back his arm, and smashed the glass with the butt. There was time enough for Dew to hear the crunch of glass and then the world filled with light.

Chapter 62

Luna found the blood smear in the employee entrance hallway. She sniffed at it, whined, and walked by as though she'd already forgotten about it. Emy didn't forget. Brett didn't either.

They followed the dog into the main lobby and toward the entrance to the main exhibit hall. Emy called to the dog and brought her back to heel by her side.

"The dinosaurs are up front," she said. "But so are the stairs to the upper floor."

"I remember," Brett said. "There's also another set of stairs if you walk past the T-Rex."

"Right," Emy said. She glanced down at the dog and frowned. Emy shook her head and pulled out the leash. She quickly attached it to Luna's collar and held it out to Brett. "Take her."

Brett cocked an eyebrow. "Why? She's not—"

"I'm going up the staircase that leads into the exhibit. Past the gems. You take the back."

Brett sighed and took the leash. "You know he's going to be expecting this."

"Of course he is," Emy said. "But he can't take us both at the same time."

"True," her boss said. Brett scratched Luna behind the ears. "But why aren't you taking her?"

"It'll take you longer to get up those other stairs. And he won't have a line of sight on you. When you reach the top, or if you hear gunfire, let her off the leash. She'll find me."

"You are out of your mind," Brett said.

"If Luna catches sight of him attacking me, she'll rip his nuts off," Emy said. "Besides, I'm a better shot than you are."

"That's not saying much," Brett said. "Last time we went to the range, you were lucky to hit the ring."

"And you were lucky to hit the paper," she shot back. The two glared at one another for a moment and Emy grinned. "You do remember which end fires the bullets?"

A ghost of a smile touched his lips. "Yeah. I do."

She patted the dog's wide head. "You be good for Brett," she said. Luna licked her hand. Emy walked past Brett and into the main exhibit hall. The T-Rex skeleton seemed to growl at the sky in defiance of extinction. The sight made her shudder. She turned left and headed to the stairs. When she glanced over her shoulder, Brett and Luna were making their way through, his eyes cast upward looking for threats.

Emy faced the staircase. One flight, a landing, and another flight. Concrete and metal steps. Noisy, if she didn't step lightly. Nerves tingling with fear and adrenaline, she made her way up the stairs, curling her body before she reached the landing, pistol raised to the second floor. No one was there. She knew where Hardy was. He was with the amulet. She relaxed slightly. He wanted her to come there. To witness. To witness what? How he created the fires? Or was there something else?

She fingered the lapis necklace. The stones seemed cooler than the air conditioned museum. Damned near cold. She shivered again and continued walking up the steps. When she reached the second floor landing, she cleared the area behind her as well as in front of her.

The gem exhibit, a permanent fixture, was lit up in blues and greens, the displays made to enhance the natural colors of the gems and geodes inside. She drew in a breath and entered the room, suddenly wishing she'd paid more attention in her law enforcement drills. How to clear a home, how to approach a suspect, how to keep from panicking when facing an armed assailant. Her teeth clicked together and she held her jaw tight, breathing through her nose as quietly as she could.

Each step through the darkened exhibit hall was torture. Hardy could be hiding in any of the shadows, behind the display cases, or simply waiting for her at the gem hall exit. If he had a firearm, he could shoot her long before she saw him. She willed her eyes to adjust, but the shadows were simply too thick. The glare from the ancient history exhibit made it even more difficult to see.

When she was little more than two meters from the Gem Exhibit entrance and the short hallway to the ancient exhibit, the air split with a distant boom and the tinkle of shattered glass. Emy yelped and ran to the wall, pistol held in the air. Her heart hammered in her chest so loud, she wasn't sure she'd be able to hear Hardy if he was right next to her.

She paused for a moment, her eyes flicking between the far wall shrouded in darkness and the ambient light streaming in from the exit. Somewhere below, she heard a scream of pain and then nothing. He booby-trapped the building, she thought. Just like he had the van.

The van. Bryan was in the van. She was sure of it. The way Luna had made a bee-line for it meant he was in there. If he was still alive, he was safe for now. And if he wasn't—

Emy bit her lip, anger burning in her stomach. She couldn't think about that right now. She couldn't let fear of his death give Hardy an edge. The only way to save Bryan was to kill this asshole and get the bomb-squad to the van. Or make him tell me how to defuse it, she thought.

Her pocket buzzed and the phone chirped loud enough to make her heart stop. Grinding her teeth, Emy reached into her pocket with her free hand and brought out the phone. New message from Bryan's phone.

"I see you."

A surge of adrenaline rocked through her body, along with shivers strong enough to make her shake. She raised her head and looked at the corner of the room. A surveillance camera pointed directly at her, a red light blinking on its side.

The phone beeped again.

"Put the gun down. Come into the light."

Emy sagged. He had her. She raised the pistol into the air, and slowly lay it on the floor. She stood to her full height, willing herself to take deep breaths against the panic threatening to rip away all rational thought. When she felt she had herself under as much control as she could muster, Emy stepped away from the wall and to the exhibit exit.

The overheads were muted, but still seemed a thousand times brighter than the dim twilight inside the gem hall. The large colorful poster at the ancient exhibit entrance no longer looked like she remembered. The picture of a ziggurat had been marred by Ghere's sigil, the symbol stretching from the temple's base to its top. The English words on the poster were blacked out, replaced in crimson with what looked like cuneiform script. Emy blinked at the strange symbols. They seemed to glow from the paper. Even

Ghere's sigil pulsed with a strange energy, the entwining lines slowly wavering across one another as if in copulation.

Emy looked up, searching for more cameras. She spotted another at the entrance. Hardy had the place wired. He'd probably hacked into the security system and had every single camera in the museum under his control. She smirked. If he was watching all the cams, it meant he would be distracted. She still had a chance. Especially if Brett and Luna had managed to come in without being spotted. And if he had been watching her the whole time, they might be able to get the drop on him.

Hands at her sides, Emy walked through the arched entrance and past the Code of Hammurabi replica tablet. The glass cases filled with spot-lit cuneiform tablets created a channel through the hall, a wide aisle winding through the five large exhibit rooms. He wasn't in the first room, nor the second. She passed beneath the replica of Ishtar's Gate and into the hall of the gods. And there he was.

Hardy stood by the large horizontal case containing the amulets Seamus had shown them days earlier. Wearing a heavy hoodie and a pair of jeans, the man might as well have been dressed for winter rather than the record-breaking heatwave outside.

The hood covered his face in shadows making it impossible for her to make out any features. A computer tablet lay atop the glass case. Hardy wasn't staring at it, however. His face was pointed directly at her. The long-barreled suppressed pistol in his right hand tapped against his thigh.

Emy stopped and stared at him. Waiting. The more time she burned, the more of a chance Brett had to flank him. Or Dewhurst, if the detective showed up. "Now what?" she said.

Hardy chuckled. "Turn to your right. Ghere wants to see your face."

Ghere. Was Hardy referring to the imaginary voices in his head, himself, or the nephilim? Emy didn't move. "Why do you need to see my scars?"

He waved the pistol at her. "Because Ghere has unfinished business with you."

The words rattled around her brain looking for some logical mooring. "What?"

An echoing boom reached her ears. It had been on the first floor. Hardy cocked his head to one side. "I hope that was Detective Dewhurst," he said.

She felt close to tears. Dew? "You boobytrapped the entrances?"

Still hidden within the hood, she couldn't see his face, but his words were condescending enough. "Why wouldn't I? Couldn't have my little meeting with you interrupted."

With his free hand, Hardy removed the hood. Emy choked back a curse.

The man's face was a horror show. Long strips of dead skin jutted out from beneath his eyes and chin. His nose was little more than a nub, the soft pliable cartilage seeming to have burned off. 2nd and 3rd degree burns oozed fluid, drying in long dark yellow pus stains against his raw, red skin.

"What's happening to you?"

He ignored the remark. "Turn for Ghere." His words came out in a dry, forced croak. She still didn't move. With a sigh, he raised the pistol and pointed it directly at her face. "Turn. Or I'll end this now."

Shuddering with tension, Emy turned in a half circle, the ancient raised purple and red scars glowing beneath the spots. She held the position for a moment, listening to his excited breaths. He moaned, but not in pain. It was the sound of exaltation. She turned her head slightly to glance at him. His free hand stroked his inner thigh.

"So beautiful." Hardy's body twitched several times as if in a seizure before he regained his composure. "Ghere missed you," he said.

She turned her body to face him once more. "Missed?"

Hardy nodded, his blistered lips curling in a perverse grin. "Philippines," Hardy hissed. "Your father."

Father. The nightmare that had haunted her for decades flashed in her mind. Her father at the doorway, his body turning into a pillar of flame as a pair of impossibly red and orange eyes stared at her through the smoke. A phantom hand of fire reaching out from the smoke and caressing her face, the skin melting in the heat with a wave of brain-freezing pain. And then the world had gone dark, punctuated with the sounds of screaming and the crackle of fire consuming everything.

"My father died in the house fire."

Hardy's grin turned into a sneer. "Your father was the house fire, you stupid woman. Ghere found him in the cargo ship transporting this." He gestured to the amulet. "He was becoming. But he lost his nerve." Hardy laughed. "What a fucking coward."

The world seemed to tilt. Her father? A bug? "No, he—"

"So young," Hardy said, his eyes seeming to glow. "You didn't understand what you saw. Or what was happening. And you escaped."

"I—" Emy shook her head. "No, that's not what happened."

Hardy's eyes began to glow orange alternating with flashes of deep red. "That is what happened." The voice that came out of Hardy's mouth was no longer his. It was deeper, choral, and other worldly. A plume of smoke rose from his clothes, the tang of burning cotton and denim filling her nose. "But you won't escape again."

A flickering orange teardrop of flame rose from his shoulder, its base the darkest blue she'd ever seen. Smoke rose from his shoes, his pants. The hoodie was disintegrating before her eyes, as was his flesh. The remains of his dermis flowed like wax from his skull, revealing a charred mass of bone. Hardy grinned as his cheeks disappeared in strips of burning flesh and his lips fell to the floor.

The amulet in his free hand glowed white hot, its center a scarlet diamond eye staring at her with malevolent glee. Emy tried to scream, but began coughing instead. More and more smoke billowed out from the burning figure standing before her. Or what used to be human.

The incredible heat warped his bones, reforming his legs into those of a quadruped. His arms lengthened, thinning, the fingers forming into flaming claws. Hardy's skull crunched as it transformed into a diamond shape, a wide piece of bone jutting over his burning eyes.

The fabric burned off in a final cloud of flame and smoke revealing a naked thing made of fire. The pistol fell through its fingers to the floor, the plastic and composite portions melting around the metal barrel. A round in the magazine exploded and a chunk of steel flew past her face into the wall behind her, shattering one of the display cases.

Emy took a step backward, her body shaking with fear. The Hardy-thing raised its head to the ceiling and roared. She continued stepping backward, tripped over a piece of a ruined display case, and fell to the floor, her hands screaming with pain from glass shards crunching into her flesh.

The Hardy-thing lowered its head and moved toward her, its eyes glowing through the thick cloud of black smoke. The wall of the exhibit caught fire and the heat singed the hair on her arms. It continued moving toward her, the amulet held before it like a weapon.

Chapter 63

When he was a few steps from the second floor landing, Brett paused to clear the balcony. It would be all too easy for Hardy to snipe him and Luna from between the slats of the railing. He needn't have bothered. There was no one there and he was fairly certain Luna would have alerted him regardless. The dog scrambled up the last two steps, straining the leash and practically pulling him.

Brett nearly lost his balance, righted himself, and gently tugged on the lead. Luna immediately stopped pulling but turned to look at him with indignation. He could almost hear the dog saying "Hurry the fuck up!" He knew how she felt.

On the other side of the museum, Emy was making her way through the gem hall and to the exhibit. He and Luna would have to take a few extra turns to meet her. And Hardy. Don't forget Hardy.

He cleared the last steps and walked on the landing. A quick check of the hall, and he felt a little more safe. Not much, but a little. Luna's tail had become a flagpole, her hair standing up in hackles. She sniffed the floor, snorted softly, and began walking. Brett followed, the leash held loosely in his hands.

A distant boom echoed through the building and he stopped, a surge of adrenaline shortening his breath and rattling his nerves. Luna growled low in her throat, her snout dropping closer to the floor, a runner of saliva hanging from her jowls. The dog turned her head to glance at him once more before starting forward. Brett followed.

The booming sound came from downstairs and from the other side of the museum. At least he thought that's where it was. Did Hardy boobytrap the museum? Brett shivered and checked the hallway walls for anything out of the ordinary. From what they knew of the man, it was possible he'd rigged up several computer controlled devices. How small, how deadly, was anyone's guess.

As Luna slowly padded down the hall, her well-trimmed nails clicking softly on the tile, Brett cocked his ear to listen. He thought he heard the beep of a phone somewhere ahead and to the right. Brett and his charge would enter through the exhibit exit. The sign affixed to the bronze tripod at the end of the hall thanked visitors and implored them to visit the gift shop at the end of their museum tour. Brett knew that because he'd seen the sign for himself when he and Emy had come to look at Ghere's sigil. Or was at Gibil's? Shit, not even Seamus had seemed completely sure of that.

The dog sniffed the air, snorted, and quickened her pace. Brett clutched the Glock that much harder, his fingers aching from the strain. The pair reached the exhibit's exit. "Stay," he whispered to Luna. The dog looked at him, blinked, and turned back to regard the open doorway. Brett hoped she understood. He crouched and walked to the precipice. Chest tight with tension, he slowly peered around the corner, pistol held high. The room was empty. At least of human beings. The display cases were lit up with their usual spots and ambient lamps.

From somewhere in the exhibit, he heard a voice. Had to have been in one of the adjoining rooms. If he remembered, Ghere's amulet was a mere three rooms away. He checked to make sure there weren't any traps on the threshold, stood, and walked into the room, Luna padding along behind him.

She stayed by his side, every muscle in her body tensed. He knew how she felt. He put his other hand on the weapon, readying it to fire if he so much as saw a scrap of the man known as Hardy. They walked into the next room.

It too was empty, but the voice was louder. A tenor pitch, but there was something wrong with it. It kept getting deeper, more hoarse, more strained. He tried to catch snatches of the conversation, but the words were just gibberish. Silently cursing, he continued through the room until he was in an aisle of display cases. Through the open doorway, he saw a man holding a pistol, the barrel pointed at something he couldn't see. He didn't have to see. The fucker had his weapon pointed at Emy.

Luna growled again, but the sound was nearly inaudible in the air conditioning's din. Brett crouched and moved forward. He stopped in mid-step, nearly losing his balance. The man had flipped off his hood showing a tapestry of 2nd and 3rd degree burns. The flesh seemed to be crawling away from his skull. Tendrils of black smoke rose from his shoulders, his legs, his feet.

He heard the man-thing say "But you won't escape again." The voice dunked him into a previously unknown well of freezing fear that covered every bit of his flesh, making his bones ache, and his feet shake. And then the thing was no longer even man-like.

It held something aloft, howled at the ceiling in triumph, and stepped forward. Brett's eyes caught sight of Emy cowering in the middle of the floor, blood dripping from her hands.

Hardy had become something made of fire, waves of furnace heat emanating from him. Brett's face and skin prickled with their intensity, but still the spike of freezing cold remained in his gut.

Luna howled in rage. He dropped the leash in surprise and the dog ran forward. The creature turned around in surprise. The dog sat in the middle of the aisle, teeth bared in a snarl. The sound of crackling flame and scorched air did little to quell the rattle of Luna's clicking teeth and the terrible roar loosed from her mouth.

The creature took a step backward from the dog and pointed its hand at her. The dog moved faster than he'd thought possible, her front paws raised slightly, before her rear legs pistoned. She leaped through the air and connected with the thing's arm.

T he explosion knocked him down, but didn't knock him out. He wished it had done the latter to the patrolman, whose scream of pain only lasted a few seconds before going silent. Dew's ears, already punished from the house explosion, rang so loud he thought his skull would split. He stared into the glowing, starless night, and realized what had happened. He raised himself off his ass, the vice holding his brain tightening several turns, the headache making his vision waver like heat haze. The sight of the museum entrance quickly banished the distraction.

The glass doors no longer existed. The right edge of the doorway burned with a tiny, guttering flame, but a cloud of smoke lingered, making it impossible to see inside the museum. He turned his head and saw what was left of the patrolman.

The officer lay in a busted heap, arms folded at an impossible angle. His legs were missing just above the knee and glass shards jutted from his chest.

A piece of collar bone peeked through his shredded uniform. For years to come, Dew would remember his screaming, terrified expression with broken cheekbones staring up into the sky.

Dew shook himself and nearly fell. The unforgiving concrete lip pressed against his knees. He waited for the dark spots in his vision to clear, and stood. Something wet dribbled down his chest. He looked down to see blood streaks on his white shirt. He didn't feel it, but he thought some glass might have ripped into him and bounced off. He got lucky. Really lucky. If the officer hadn't told him to back up, he'd be dead too.

He stumbled forward onto the main landing, retrieved his dropped shotgun, and scanned for any telltale trap signs. The side where the mine or claymore or whatever the fuck it was that had gone off, was clear. A red laser light glowed on the other side, flicking in and out of existence as dust and smoke wafted into the building. As carefully as he could, he crossed through the furthest fractured part of the entrance, and crept in.

The exhibit was on the second floor. That's where the bastard would be. And if Emy and Brett were still alive, that's where they would be. He hadn't been able to keep the officer from dying, but maybe he could at least save them. Regardless, he was finding this asshole and putting him down.

Walking as fast as he could while checking for traps, he made his way into the main exhibit hall and approached the stairs. Dew fingered the shotgun and walked up, the weapon pointed upward to clear the corners. Nothing. No sign of traps, no sign of anyone.

The ringing in his ears made it nearly impossible to hear anything outside of his own skull, but at least his brain was less fuzzy. Dew increased his pace, sure that Hardy was in the exhibit, along with Emy. If he wanted her that bad, he'd have provided her safe passage into the hall. "Fuck it," Dew breathed. He reached the landing and walked as fast as he dared into the gem hall.

Eyes darting and checking the shadows, he saw a Glock in the middle of the aisle. Dew nodded to himself. Hardy made Emy drop her weapon. That meant she was defenseless as well as cornered. Dew picked up the weapon, put it in his belt, and continued walking.

Even with his damaged hearing, he heard voices. It sounded like Hardy, but not like him at all. The voice was, well, changed. Transformed. When the voice rose in volume, he moved as fast as he could into the exhibit, snaking through the first room, and through the second. Another room and he'd have a sightline to the exhibit case where the amulet was stored. And that's when he heard the crackle of flames.

The walking pillar of flame was less than five feet away. Emy's throat locked in a silent scream, terror freezing her to the floor. The thing growled, the amulet glowing white hot in its hands. A swirl of darkness rose from the burning sigil, like a miniature tornado. A pair of diamond shaped eyes opened in the center as the floating whirlpool grew.

A new voice entered her head, its low rumble shaking her core. "I will be whole," it said in her mind.

Emy took a breath of super-heated air, trying to scream. Her lungs burned, chest filled with fire. The only rational thought in her mind repeated itself over and over. I'm going to die!

The creature pointed the amulet at her, the eyes within the otherworldly darkness glowing brighter and a crimson smile appearing. She felt as though the demonic face were peering into her soul. Her skull filled with the sounds of pained screams, howls of fear, and the crackle and spit of burning flesh.

Something smashed into the creature's arm and the amulet flew from its hand. Emy's shocked eyes saw Luna, a streak of burning white, blur past her and strike the wall. The dog's hair had caught fire and she howled with pain. Emy scrambled toward the dog, her fear suddenly forgotten. As she moved, she heard the sound of someone yelling and the explosions of pistol shots.

Emy reached the dog and rolled her frantic, panicked form over the floor to snuff out the flames. Luna's whines were barely audible over the sound of gunfire and the hungry growl of fire. She put herself over the dog, one hand hitting the floor and striking something metal. She peered at the amulet in stupid fascination. The darkness that had welled out of it had disappeared. The metal felt cold, as though it had never been in the fire creature's hands.

She picked it up and turned around. Hardy was still on fire, but holes had appeared in his body of flames. Hardy jerked again and again as bullets punched gaping wounds through his otherworldly form. Emy rose to her haunches, her nose filled with the scent of smoke and burnt dog hair. She held out the amulet toward the Hardy-thing.

The gunfire suddenly stopped and for a moment, the rest of the universe disappeared leaving her alone with the pillar of flame, its hands raised to its melting face. Her neck felt as though it was on fire, the necklace burning her skin. The amulet was no longer just cold, but freezing. Emy felt a surge of energy and a single word echoed in her mind. "Jump." She did.

Just as the creature had brandished the amulet toward her, she held it out like a weapon and leaped. The creature leaned backward in surprise.

Emy felt her hair starting to burn, her clothes, everything. The pain enveloped her until it was no longer even a sensation. And then she struck the Hardy-thing with the amulet. The world exploded in a flash of blue and Emy went blind.

———

Dew stood at the room's threshold, eyes wide, staring in disbelief. He had emptied his weapon into the fire creature, each shot punching a hole through its orange and red body. The moment he'd seen it, his brain had ceased all thought and reflexes kicked in.

He'd seen the dog fly into the thing and bounce out of sight. That's when he'd fired as many rounds as he could, as fast as he could. But while reaching for an extra mag, he saw tendrils of blue light snake out from the area where the dog had disappeared. Then Emy came into view, her body clothed in ethereal light, so blue it was nearly black. She leaped into the air toward the thing, something held out in her hand.

The creature tried to back away, but it was too slow. She smashed into it and the room flashed with a collage of dark color. The world went white, an afterimage obscuring his vision, but quickly departing. Emy's body lay on the floor in a crumpled heap, still clutching the amulet. Hardy, naked, smoke rising from his remaining flesh, fell to his knees. The man's eyes flickered with fiery light.

Dew slammed the fresh magazine home and stepped forward, the pistol pointed at Hardy's head. The man was crying, but he had no eyelids, and certainly no moisture left in his body. Dew saw exposed, charred bone through the remains of his skin and wondered how the man was still alive.

"It promised," Hardy said, his voice shaking with fear and pain.

Dew remembered the Hartman corpses in the morgue, the blown up officers outside the house, and the dead patrolman below. "So did I," he said. Dew squeezed the trigger and the top of Hardy's skull disappeared in a spray of streaming blood and charred brain.

Hardy's body wavered for a moment before his muscles relaxed and the corpse fell backward, eyes staring at the ceiling. Dew kept the pistol aimed at the body, waiting for it to twitch, move, anything. It didn't.

"Detective!" a voice shouted from the other side of the room.

"Brett?"

"Don't shoot! We're clear!"

Dew ran into the room as Brett did from the other end. "Check on Emy," Dew said. He stood over the corpse, his weapon still pointed at its head.

After what he'd seen, he wasn't taking any chances. Brett moved to the side and knelt down next to Emy. Dew chanced a quick glance and saw a small pool of blood next to her head. "She alive?"

"Yeah," Brett said. "We need a fucking ambulance."

Dew kicked the corpse. It didn't move. He heard a whine from behind him and turned. Luna lay in the corner, her fur mostly burned off, blisters from second degree burns already rising on her back, head, and legs, one of which had snapped partway between the dewclaw and elbow. He took one last look at the corpse, debating on whether he should shoot it one more time. The whine came again. He snarled in frustration and turned. "You got Emy?"

"Can't move her."

"Bullshit," Dew said as he scooped up the dog. She yelped in pain and then went silent. "We can't wait for an ambulance. There isn't going to be one. Pick her up and let's get to the elevator. We'll get her to the hospital."

With Luna's head near his shoulder, he smelled the stench of burned dog hair mixed with the coppery hint of blood. The dog's pained eyes stared at him. She licked his cheek and went limp in his arms. He couldn't help but grin. Brett had Emy over his shoulder in a fireman's carry. The two headed to the elevator as fast as they dared leaving the smoking corpse behind.

EPILOGUE

Rain pattered against the windows, a staccato beat welcome to her ears. Emy opened her eyes. With the overheads off, the wan ambient light from the window barely dispelled the gloom. The nurses had come in a few hours ago to change her dressings, but she'd barely been awake for it. White gauze covered her left arm and hand, the skin damaged by intense heat.

She'd done her best to keep from abusing the morphine button, but it was tough. Her hand and arm alternated between numb and on-fire. Worst of all, her skin itched as though ants were crawling all over it.

A crack of thunder rattled the windows and she smiled. Never a dull moment in Houston weather. She had snatches of memory of being carried out of the Museum, a rush of rain quickly soaking her clothes and her hair. She remembered being in the back of a patrol car, the siren whirring like a banshee, slumped against Brett's shoulder. Luna, her snout and head criss-crossed with burns and blisters, peered at her from the front seat and disappeared. At least that's what she remembered.

The thought of the dog brought a surge of panic, making her breathe in ragged sips of air. Her heart monitor raised in volume with a thrash metal beat. "Hey," a voice said from the shadows.

Emy's heart stopped in mid-beat as a form rose from the corner. She tried to sit up and a tidal wave of pain rushed up her left arm. Emy hissed.

The form held up its hands. "It's okay, Emy. It's Brett." She stared in disbelief as her eyes adjusted to the gloom. Brett walked to her side and put a hand on the railing. "You need me to call the nurse?"

She waited until the pain subsided to speak. "No. Just surprised me."

Brett's face lit with a sad grin. "Sorry about that. Heard you struggling."

"Struggling. That's one way to put it." She put her hand on his. "How long have I been here? Every time I wake up, it's raining and dark."

He winced. "Three days."

"Three days? Where is my dog?"

He squeezed her hand. "Luna's fine. She's with a vet. They're treating her burns and a broken leg. She'll be okay."

A tear slid down Emy's cheek. "Really?"

"Really. I promise."

Emy squeezed hard. "I haven't heard from a doctor," she said.

"That's because you've been crashed out since you got here," he said. "If you can stay awake, I'm sure they'll bring him to you."

She nodded her head toward her immobilized left arm. "How bad is it?"

Brett shrugged. "Bad. But not fatal. As I understand it, they were worried about nerve damage, but the fact you're experiencing pain is a good sign you'll recover."

"Jesus," Emy said. "It's like—" She stopped and wiped another tear away. "Like being in the house fire all over again."

Brett frowned. "I'm sorry, Emy. So sorry we didn't kill the fucker before that happened."

The rain intensified, filling the uncomfortable silence that had fallen in the room. She glanced out the window at the dark sky, forks of lightning crossing the bruised and swollen clouds in the distance. From her high floor, she could see the storm hovering over downtown like a death shroud.

"It's been raining since we left the museum," Brett said, as if hearing an unspoken question.

"Flooding?"

Brett nodded. "The usual spots, but so far, the ground seems to be soaking it up as fast as it comes. Which makes no sense to anyone. The weather folks are stumped as to where this thing came from. It's like the heatwave broke and the sky exploded with teary happiness."

Emy chuckled and winced. It hurt to laugh. It felt good too. "That was a little too poetic, Brett."

"I have my Byron moments," he said with a grin.

Byron. Poets. Artists. Shit. "Christ, where is Bryan? Did you find him?"

"He's—"

"Is he okay?"

Brett paused, took a breath, and stroked her hair. "He's fine, Emy. They let him out of the hospital yesterday. I'm sure he'll be here later."

"What happened?"

"The van was boobytrapped. Dew finally got the bomb-squad there to defuse everything, although it was touch and go for a while. By the time we got him out of there, his concussion was the least of his problems. He spent a long time in a hot van. Very dehydrated. They kept him for observation and pumped him full of fluids, but he'll be fine too."

Emy's lips quivered. "Nearly lost everything."

"Nearly," Brett said. He leaned down and kissed her forehead. "But you didn't. Lee and I are going to take care of you and Luna once you get out of here. At least until you can take care of yourselves."

"Thank you," she said.

Looking into his eyes made her want to smile, and at the same time it made her want to cry. His eyes misted a bit and he ended up wiping at them. "You're very welcome."

"You filling out a lot of paperwork?"

He laughed. "Like you wouldn't believe. I'm going to have to hire another investigator just to get through the fires from Monday night."

"How many?"

He sighed. "Hardy set up 27 sites. All 27 blew up with a variety of home-made explosives and accelerants. He really did a number on East Houston. We lost two HFD personnel and four cops. Better than we expected, actually."

"Jesus."

"Dewhurst tells me it looks as though Hardy leased a number of offices and apartments around the city with fake names and a spiral of dummy companies. Fucker must have spent nearly every dime of his wealth to make this happen."

"Make what happen? Kill a lot of people? Or—" The image of the fiery figure walking toward her, the eyes from the amulet, the incredible heat, roared back into her mind. She shuddered with the memory and her arm ached with pain. "What happened?"

Brett blinked. "With Hardy?" She nodded. "What do you remember?"

How the hell was she supposed to answer that question? The images and sounds all muddied together into a tapestry of fragments. "I remember seeing fire. Like he was made of fire."

Her boss nodded. "What else?"

The dog shooting through the air and knocking the amulet from the thing's hands. And then—

She tried to sit up again and nearly blacked out from the pain.

"Shit, stop that," Brett said. "Let me adjust the bed for you. We do have that technology." The top half of the bed slowly rose until she could see Brett face-to- face. "There. Better?"

"Yes. Thank you." She saw the stubble on his chin, his red-rimmed eyes and rumpled clothes. "How long have you been here?"

Brett blushed. "Since you were admitted. Except for a couple of trips home to grab a shower and make an appearance at the office." He chuckled. "I didn't want you to wake up and be greeted with three days of B.O."

Emy grinned. "I appreciate that."

"You want to talk any more about what happened?"

She took in a shuddering breath and slowly exhaled. Her lungs still felt fragile, as though she'd scorched them. "I saw the amulet on the floor. It—" She licked her lips. "It felt cold in my hands. I thought it would burn, and it did, but not from heat. It was so goddamned cold."

Brett cocked an eyebrow. "Cold?"

"Frozen," she said. "I've never touched anything that cold before. And—" She stopped again, debating on whether to say it.

"Emy," Brett said. "Just say it. Believe me. It won't sound any crazier than what I think I saw."

"Okay," she said and swallowed hard. "I heard a voice tell me to attack the thing with the amulet."

Brett's expression didn't change. He merely nodded and squeezed her hand again. "Anything after that?"

She shook her head. "Just fragments of you and Dew driving us to the hospital."

"You don't remember the flash?"

"What flash?"

He told her about the bright blue light that filled the air as well as the way the fire simply disappeared, somehow snuffed out of existence as though it had never been there. When she asked what had happened to Hardy, he tried to wave away the question, but she wouldn't let it go. "He's dead, Emy. Dew shot him. And that's all you need to know."

Emy shivered. "He's gone."

"He's gone. For good."

"What about the amulet?"

Brett's face paled and he stared down at the bed. "It's missing," he said. "By the time museum personnel and CSU arrived at the scene, it was gone. Along with the other artifacts in that case."

"Holy shit," Emy said. "Didn't the security cameras capture anything?"

"They would have," Brett said, "if our good friend Hardy hadn't hacked them. He managed to turn off the fire suppression systems too." He shook his head. "So much effort put into starting a goddamned fire. Guy was a genius, really. He just happened to be as insane as he was intelligent."

She yawned loudly, unable to stifle it, and exhaled foul breath. "Shit. Sorry."

"Wow. I'll see if we can't get you a toothbrush," Brett said with a laugh. "They might even let you walk around today."

She glanced at the IVs hooked up to her arm. "With all this shit?"

He nodded. "It's all part of the deal."

"Good to know."

Silence fell over the room again, broken only by the soft patter of the rain, thunder, and the shuffle of personnel and patients through the hallway beyond her room. She could still hear the voice that had told her to jump at the fiery thing. It had sounded like her father's, but not just his. His was only a single voice in a choir of thousands. She wondered what that meant.

"Anything else missing from the museum?"

"Not that we know of," Brett said. "I imagine Seamus will let us know if anything else got up and walked away."

The words made her shiver. The amulets. The sigils of ancient, all but forgotten gods, spirited away by someone? Or some thing? She touched her neck, looking for the comfort of her necklace. "Wait. Where's my necklace?"

He opened his mouth, stopped, and squeezed her hand again. "I have the chain, Emy. But the charms?" He shook his head. "They all came off. I guess the heat melted the clasps. But I have them," he said. "They'll be ready for you when you're out of here."

Something in his voice made her think he was lying. She locked eyes with him, boring her stare into his. A flush of color rose on his cheeks. With a sigh, he walked back to his chair, and removed something from his valise. What he brought back was nearly unrecognizable.

The four strings of golden metal were warped, the necklace no longer holding its shape when splayed. Emy felt like crying again. This had been the last gift her mother had ever given her. Given at the time of her death. An inherited heirloom passed down several generations, brought by their first Caucasian ancestor. It was the last tie holding her to her past.

"Where are the charms?"

Brett fished in the pocket of his jeans. He brought out the stones and held them in his palm. Emy shivered. The lapis lazuli charms, once shining bright blue stones mottled with light and brass streaks, were a dead white.

All color had been drained from them. Even the threads of impurities seemed to have disappeared.

Another wave of fatigue washed over her. Seeing the last token of her mother destroyed was simply too much. "I think I need to go back to sleep," she said.

Brett stroked her forehead and patted her hand. "I think that's a good idea. Gives me a chance to get some coffee."

"Leave the necklace and the stones," she said.

He hesitated for a moment and finally lay them on the table beside her. The dull rocks tinged as they gently tumbled on the metal. He spread the necklace around them as carefully as he could. "I'll see if I can get the doctor in here before you completely crash."

"Thank you, Brett."

"Hurry up and get better," he said. "Lee wants to make you and Luna a hell of a dinner."

She chuckled as he disappeared out the door. Emy reached out and picked up one of the rocks. It felt too light, as though most of its mass had somehow been burned away along with its color. She stared at it, remembering how it had looked in her hands just a few days ago. Bright. Shining. Filled with history and light. And now it was as interesting as a chunk of drywall. She wiped another tear from her cheek and moved to drop the stone. Her eyes blinked at it and she brought it back to her face. She'd seen a hint of blue, almost like a wan glow at its center. She willed the glow to return, but it didn't.

Emy closed her eyes. She needed time. Not just for her damaged skin to heal, but for the memories to fade so they wouldn't turn into more nightmares. The one thing she didn't tell Brett she remembered was the Hardy-thing claiming her father had been possessed by Ghere. Did the necklace stop him from killing her back then? Or did her father somehow defeat the thing inside his body to keep her safe? It was impossible to know. But somehow she knew she'd been saved that day by the part of him that was still human. Still him.

The forensics teams would test Hardy's corpse. They would find nothing to explain what happened to him, or how he'd stayed alive. She knew that much. She also knew they'd never find out what accelerant he'd used to create the impossible heat. Although she'd never admit it, she believed that whatever had possessed Hardy had also created the fires. Ghere, struggling to escape the amulet. Emy shuddered, wondering where it would appear next.

ACKNOWLEDGMENTS

This novel wasn't written so much as birthed and it was one damned long pregnancy. I first began writing Ghere's Inferno four years ago after witnessing a house fire. While on the way home from a bar, two friends and I drove past a burning house. No cops. No fire trucks. No one outside watching. No one knew.

The three of us jumped out of the SUV, shouted like hell for people to wake up, and eventually were dumb enough to try and get them out. The idea that a family might be trapped inside the blaze while asleep terrified the hell out of me. What's more, a dog was trapped inside the gate.

While my friends tried to bang on the side of the house, I tore apart the metal and wood gate and retrieved the dog, all the while coughing from the smoke and chemicals filling the air with the heat of the spreading blaze curling the hair on my arms.

To make a long story short, the dog survived, no one was home, and we all made it out alive. I was sick for two days and it took another three to recover my voice. All in all, it was a pretty damned harrowing experience.

All that aside, this project suffered two false starts, each of which resulted in the digital file being chucked into the virtual bin, or what Stephen King once called "data heaven." With some better ideas in mind, I made a third attempt. It stuck.

Alas, it was derailed again by other projects, including my work on The Rider and again when I began The Black. When I hit a wall while writing the third book in the Derelict Saga, I reread the draft for <u>Ghere's Inferno</u> and decided it was not only worth saving, but I wanted to finish it. So I did.

And finally, it's out in the world. Four years of trying, of my editor demanding I finish it, and of friends and colleagues asking about it, and it's finally finished. I hope its extended stay in the womb helped the story rather than hurt it.

Regardless, I have to thank a number of folks who both made this book possible and constantly reminded me it was a tale that deserved to be read.

Shout-outs to my beta readers for all their hard work, careful attention to detail, and suggestions to make the story better:

- Arioch Morningstar
- Tom Cooley
- David Sobkowiak
- James Monroig
- Vivian Sheibel
- Ron and Lori Williams
- Robert Stikmanz
- Robert Noble
- Scott Senate

I'm also greatly indebted to my editor Sue Baiman for her constant badgering, her enthusiasm for the story, and her faithful belief in my writing. This novel would not be in the world without her.

Paul E Cooley
December 5th, 2017
Spring, Texas.

ABOUT THE AUTHOR

A writer and Parsec Award winning podcaster from Houston, Texas, Paul E Cooley produces free psychological thriller, suspense, science-fiction, historical urban fantasy, horror stories, essays, and reviews available from Shadowpublications.com and iTunes.

His best-selling novel, The Black, was released in 2014 and won the 2015 Parsec Award for best novel. In addition to contributing his voice to a number of audio productions, he has also collaborated with NYT Bestselling Author Scott Sigler on The Rider.

He is a co-host on the renowned Dead Robots' Society writing podcast and enjoys interacting with readers and other writers.

facebook.com/paulelardcooley

twitter.com/paul_e_cooley

amazon.com/Paul-E-Cooley

www.ingramcontent.com/pod-product-compliance
Lightning Source LLC
Chambersburg PA
CBHW060522180626
46817CB00002B/458